ONE of the Carben dwarfs' hats was floating on the surface, along with a short dwarfish bow and quiver of arrows. Another of the creatures was flattened against the smooth wall across the way from Brian. Before the crouched figure was a long, lithe shadow, solid gray, with great gray talons extended in front of it, reaching out to grasp and drag its victims into the troubled river.

"Stop!" commanded Brian, surprising even himself. He recognized the trembling Carben dwarf as the leader who had spoken to them in the upper levels of the delving, and threatened to hold them as slaves.

Books by
NIEL HANCOCK

THE CIRCLE OF LIGHT SERIES

THE WILDERNESS OF FOUR SERIES

Published by
WARNER BOOKS

The Wilderness of Four—2

THE PLAINS
OF THE SEA

by Niel Hancock

WARNER BOOKS

A Warner Communications Company

For my good friend and fellow gypsy, Flobird,
wherever she is in the Meadows of Windameir.

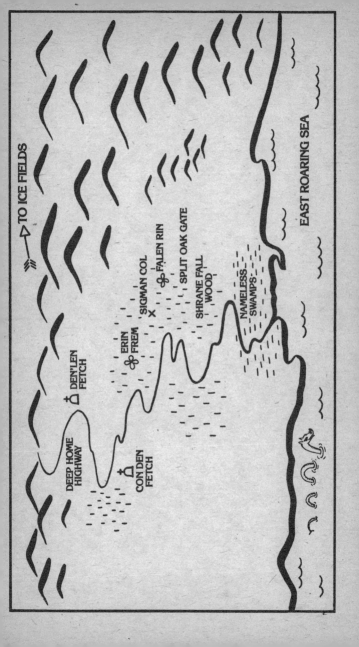

The Prelude

IN the deep silence of the snowy passes of the great Wilderness of Four, there moved abroad the beginnings of the hordes of the Dark One, the sister of the Lady Lorini of Windameir. Throughout the vast regions of the Lower Meadows her shadow began to be felt, blocking out the light and life of those places, and striking an icy splinter of fear into the hearts of those who yet dwelled on Atlanton.

And as the Darkness began, so began the call to arms for all those who felt the Flame of Windameir in their hearts. From the deep delvings of Den'Lin Fetch came the dwarfish Guardian of the Light called Brian Brandigore.

These tales take place in the years shortly after the Golden Age, and are ancient stories that occur many lifetimes before the beginning of Circle of Light.

IN SEARCH
OF DEEP HOME

Den'Lin Fetch

IN the darkness the dwarf sat, legs crossed, ears tuned to the noise the stone made as it sang its ancient song, of depths that ran forever beneath the sun, and of the beings who dwelled there.

The dwarf, Brian, was deeper than any of his kindred had ever dared go, and he had not heeded their warnings when the older dwarfs had cautioned him not to pry too deeply into the forgotten vaults and tombs of the earth's secrets. It was not wise, they said, to go beyond good common sense, and to make an enemy of the friendly earth.

And far below where any spanner should be going were the prisons of the beasts, which had been chained by dwarfwrought chains ages before, those chains fashioned by the most ancient of dwarfish clans, of a mountain's breath and the sea's song.

It was those forefathers of Brian who excited him most, and he had read and reread all the lore books and histories of those times, and never tired of having them told to him by any of his elders who could remember the stories, or how they went.

Brian, although no longer a spanner, as the young dwarfs were known, was ill fitted for the established social order of his clan, and did not fit well into the thriving community that was safely located beneath a tall range of mountains, where an underground river bubbled and chuckled one to sleep, and wakened one again, with its cheerful tales and songs. This river began its long trip to the sea, it was said, not far from the spot where Brian sat in the darkness listening.

Brian knew that was not true, but not much was written of this sea, or the river's beginnings, and not many members of the dwarfish clans that he knew of had ever ventured aboveground long enough to make the journey, and the news they had of it was all secondhand, or third, passed down from one source or another, which meant that the stories were always colored to make them more exciting, or sometimes there was an occasional lore master who would be visiting their little community, traveling to or from one of the many such settlements that existed in that particular range of mountains.

Brian's home was called Den'Lin Fetch, and it was the most remote of any of the dwarfish settlements, before one reached the bleak Easterlands, and the ice fields that lay there. At one time, Brian knew, the first of the dwarfish Elders had dwelled in that terrible wasteland, the Elder whose name every dwarf after him bore.

Brian's own name was Brandigore, but for high ritual days, of which there were many, his full name was Brian Brandigore Roundhat of Deep Home. Those ritual days brought all the community to the Grand Dome for celebration, and the band would gather, and all the brightwares would be put on display, from the pots and pans and ax heads to the gaily colored cloaks and hats and shoes, all stitched and sewn and fashioned by the skilled hands of the hearty dwarf clan.

His own mother was one of the most artful of seamstresses, and she had made Brian and his father the most elegant of cloaks, and the most colorful of hats, and his vest was such as few dwarfs ever owned, short of Roundhat himself, and he was known to be the most well-dressed dwarf Elder of all.

Brian thought of all these things as he listened for an answer to his persistent tapping, done with the small chisel and hammer he carried, as was the dwarfish habit when belowground, and that had been given to him long before, by Chinby, the blind lore master.

Nothing came back in reply but the dull echo of the clink of the hammer, and he was beginning to lose patience with his quest.

This was the fourth time he'd thought he'd found the door to the river, where its roots lay, and where the legends said the tunnels to Deep Home began.

In the last of the days of that first settlement, those who dwelled there were driven out by the Darkness that had begun to grow forth again, as it did from time to time, and the beasts had been freed from their prison by the terrible Fallen King, and those that survived that terrible war sought to escape by delving tunnels ever deeper into the mountain, until they hit the heart of this river, and by fashioning small

13

rafts for themselves from barrels and casks cut in half, managed to elude the beasts and find safety beyond the wastelands of the snow and ice, which had driven them belowground long before.

Those first dwarfs had then sealed up the ancient shafts, to prevent anyone from following.

No one but a few of the older dwarfs knew of the whereabouts of those tunnels, and they had either vanished into the lands beyond the mysterious sea or gone to the Tombs, their secrets safe forever.

But Brian searched on, driven by some hidden need within himself, some fire that constantly burned in his heart and drove him relentlessly. The others laughed at his foolish quest, and good-naturedly suggested he take up his father's trade, which was smithing, and forget all the fancy business of ancient Deep Home, and Roundhat.

Those things were no good to anyone now, except as tales around the supper fire, or stories to put young spanners to sleep, according to those who constantly tried to interest Brian in other pursuits.

A slight humming echo began to attract his attention, and he concentrated his thoughts on the sound, feeling it with every fiber of his being, seeking out the source, testing it with the complete sureness that his innate dwarf senses gave his kind in the dark confines of the underground world they inhabited, and had dwelled in for so long.

Before Roundhat, Brian knew that there was a time when Deep Home had been a community aboveground, long, long before anyone had written of the histories of dwarfdom, and that time was lost far back in the past, a mere haze of thought, a rumor of belief that was very seldom ever thought of or discussed, even by the old lore masters, whose job it was to instruct young spanners in the bright heritage that was theirs.

Brian had taken to a blind lore teacher in his early years, who had come to Den'Lin Fetch from beyond the Easterland borders, and he had told him something of life among the outer folk, and the beasts that inhabited the bleak snow fields and icy wilderness, and that there had been a time when the lands were green and fertile, and grew many forests, and fields of wildflowers that ran for miles in all directions without interruption.

The young dwarf had been intrigued with the tales of life

14

overground, and spent long afternoons, when others were hard at their anvils, or sewing, or potting, or mending, listening to the yarns of a bygone past.

There was no book these tales were written in, and almost no one, save the blind dwarf, had even known of anything that had been in those lost days, or the nature of who dwelled there, or what they had done, or what the weather had been like.

And no one knew what had become of them, or why they had disappeared.

The old dwarf hinted that it was the race that came before the ancient clans, and that the dwarfish forefathers had long ago dwelled overground, and gone about much as the other kinds who carried on their lives in that particular manner.

He found that thought very mysterious, and wondered at the possibility of ever being able to live in such a strange fashion. He had been overground on many occasions, and found the experience a little frightening, but after talking to the blind dwarf, he'd begun to wonder if there weren't more to it all than what he'd seen.

When he had asked his father about the old stories of life overground, he had simply snorted in his gruff manner, and replied that if they lived overground, they weren't dwarfish, and certainly could claim no dwarfish blood.

No self-respecting member of the earthlings would ever be caught trying to fashion a life beyond the warmth and security of a delving.

There would have been no stone work, nor metalcraft, nor any of the other beautiful things that decorated and made each delving a living thing, a breathing part of the earth.

Brian knew these things, and was truly a dwarf at heart, and that meant more than simply being small and nimble. It was a way of life, a philosophy as well, a belief that was as deep-seated in dwarfhood as any outside physical attribute, yet he was still intrigued by these tales the blind dwarf told, and he had decided that once he'd found the river's heart, and knew how to get to the old lands, where Roundhat had lived in Deep Home, he would explore those lands overground as well, to see if he could find any clue as to what would lure any sort of being into dwelling in the open that way, exposed to all the whims of nature, and driven to and fro by the seasons, forced to scour everywhere for food and water, while the dwarf clans had found it a simple thing to grow the staple food for their dwarfcake, and water was merely a matter of walking to the stream to get it, although the dwarfish builders had found clever plans to construct their delvings in such a way that the water was diverted through cuts and channels to exactly where it was needed, and each dwarf halfing, as they called their dwellings, had its own stream or river burbling through, and the chores of washing up the dinner plates and tea things was no more a job than stepping to the stone basin. It made sleeping especially pleasant, listening to the soft murmur of the stream through the dim rushlit silence, or hearing it, even during the work time, when the bright stones they had found were uncovered, lighting the delvings as brightly as if the sun had found its way into the depths of the shafts.

And too, there were places where the sun holes were, in some of the tall domed vaults that the dwarfs had wrought from the living stone.

One of these places was the door that went overground, and it was in such a place that Brian had made his journeys into the world above the delvings, although he had never gone there alone.

Always he was with his father, or one of the other dwarfs, or with the harvest crew who went regularly to reap the fields they had sown, or to gather new fuel for the rush lamps, or to gather more wood for ax shafts, or the thousand other chores that forced the dwarfish clan to be out overground for short periods of time.

Most of the dwarfs Brian knew looked with distaste at those periods of time, and for the most part it was always drawn lots that made up the work parties who had to go, for no one enjoyed the task, and most of the dwarfs looked at the world overground as a thing to be borne, for the food, and other things it afforded them, but to be avoided whenever possible.

Brian, until he had met the blind dwarf, had felt the same, and rarely went beyond the delvings, except when he was assigned to a work crew, or with his father, but after speaking with the old dwarf, and hearing all the tales he had spun, a new interest was awakened, especially in the lands overground where Roundhat had dwelled, in the original Deep Home.

Roundhat was the nickname lovingly given to the austere and stiff-necked dwarf whose real name was beyond pro-

16

nouncing, even among the scholars, and so it was eventually dropped from the lore books, and the lore masters, with the exception of a few, gave up trying to show their students just how to roll the tongue, and hold the lips, in order to pronounce it correctly.

It was said, and Brian believed it, that Roundhat had been given the name by the one who had found him, abandoned near the terrible borders that ran along the ice fields of the Easterlands, and that that person was the last who had ever spoken it properly, which was why the ancient dwarf had taken up calling himself Roundhat, which was easy to say, and easier to remember, and the dwarf was such an outgoing, energetic character that all those who lived in the olden times had flocked to him as a natural leader when the Troubles began.

No one spoke of that much, except the lore masters, and everyone seemed to want to forget it, if they could, but every season it reared its ugly head, and crept in upon the minds of the dwarfish clans, no matter where their delvings were.

Brian had been frightened witless as a spanner when his father had been brought home senseless by a party of grim-faced dwarfs, their bright cloaks blood-spattered and muddy.

His father had been lucky, and lived, but there were others that day that had been slain by the beasts, who had waited in ambush for one of the work parties to come overground.

In later days, the dwarfs had taken to using many doors to the outside, carefully blocking and concealing them from intruders, and as time went on, the number of entrances grew as the beasts multiplied and could watch more than one or two openings at once.

When it reached the point of losing six sturdy dwarfs on a wood-gathering outing one autumn, the dwarfish clans banded together and formed a mutual defense league, and began to fashion themselves weapons of various kinds that would help them protect themselves from the growing menace.

Roundhat, who had dealt with the most terrible of the old beasts, had devised means that would enable the small, stocky dwarfs to be more than a match for even the giant monsters that had begun to stalk the lands that had become the snow fields of the East, and those were the weapons the dwarfs had fashioned from the instructions and drawings in the ancient lore books.

Brian was as handy with those weapons as any, and had

been the best archer of his age group, and was always asked to go on the overground outings because of his fearlessness, and the deadly way he could wield his stout dwarf bow.

But those were far from his thoughts as he sat glued to the ancient stone steps that ended at the blank face of the dark granite wall.

His rush lamp had burned out long before, and it had been hours since he had moved from the spot, feeling his way across the smoothness of the stone inch by inch, testing it carefully with the fine chisel and small hammer, which had been given to him by the old blind dwarf of his spannerhood.

After receiving the gift, Brian had thanked the old dwarf, but been told that he must hold them for a time that was to come, when they would be needed by all dwarfdom, when the day of the beast had come full circle and was upon the world again.

"But they are only tools," objected Brian. "What use would they be against one of the beasts you speak of?"

"Not against a beast," corrected the old dwarf. "But they will open a door that will swallow them. It will help you to find their old prison."

The small hammer now rang softly in his hand, and the finely wrought chisel, which had several minute scenes engraved on both sides of it, answered the hammer, as Brian chipped away, exploring a weakness in the stone that might tell him of the whereabouts of the doorway to the heart of the river, where the shafts to the old delvings of Deep Home lay.

A Prophecy of Change

ON those days that the overground chores were done, the dwarfish settlement gathered in the Central Halfing, with its lofty dome that reared upward into the living stone, its ornate carvings moving in the shadows cast by the rush lamp glow and the bright inner suns of the stones that contained the light, which the dwarfs called the elfmoons, after the strange clans that lived overside and sometimes came to the same forests as the dwarfs, to gather food, or fuel, or wood for building.

The elfish clans were once numbered a good many, Brian knew, but a strange darkness had moved into those lands the elves had dwelled in for so long, and now they were sadly depleted in number, and divided among themselves.

Brian had learned early never really to trust any elf dealings, and the blind dwarf, Chinby, had told him stories of the wily creatures, and their clever ways, and their ability to trick and confuse those who had commerce with them, and the dwarfish clans had been abused more than once by high-handed elves, who wanted to trade one thing or another for the wonderful dwarfwrought ore they mined.

His father told him of dealings even more recent than ancient history, and ended by saying that the elfish band had shorted the dwarfs by giving them bolts of the elf cloth that had been cut in half in such a way as to make them look like the full measure.

Those affairs with the elf clans did not endear them to the dwarfs, and although Brian felt no animosity toward the overground creatures, he did not feel especially drawn to them either, and although the community of Den'Lin Fetch had been dealt with unfairly by that last band of elfin kind, they were not hostile toward them, but rather aloof, and would prefer simply to cut off their friendship, so that when a chance meeting would occur in the wood, or field, or by the river, the dwarfs would simply ignore the elves, and hurry on about their business.

This had puzzled the elves at first, but then they began the teasing, and now it was very unpleasant to meet the wily creatures, for their wits were quick, and their tongues sharp, and some of the things they said stung the dwarfs to the quick.

A dwarf, by nature, was a slow fellow thinking on his feet, and he liked to mull over the endless possibilities of any event or occurrence, and to turn it about in all its lights, and to ponder on the many twists and turns each instant might have.

The elf, on the other hand, was almost insistent on having a quick reply to any question, and of a most impatient nature, except when it was something to do with one of their little puzzles they were forever spinning for themselves, and in that case, they would remain immobile for hours, clear blue eyes dark with thought.

All of elfkind had those startling blue eyes that changed colors as they spoke, and you could tell almost by looking at them if they were angry, or teasing.

Brian felt they must be serious over some things, although he could not understand the silliness of the riddles, which would turn their eyes such dark blue.

He once heard one of the elves talking to a friend, and it was gibberish to Brian, whose mind did not run along those avenues of thought.

He snorted to himself, thinking of it again.

Whatever would a silly creature be doing, wondering how many leaf falls would occur between a single mountain breath?

But that was the nature of their games, and it was no wonder the dwarfkind were not obliged to spend much time with the idle elf clans, for they had much work to do, and many shafts to sink, and halfings to finish.

He knew the elf clans were clever with their hands as well, though, and whenever they did their work, between silly games with each other, it was of a most beautiful nature.

The cloth they spun was of a lightness that felt almost like sheer air, and the colors were more beautiful than the full rainbows reflected through a clear stretch of water.

His mother made him a vest of such beauty that he was content sometimes simply to stare down at it, and the cloth seemed to change hues in every light, whether rush lamp or elfmoon.

He had to give them their handiwork, and he was glad that the last dealings with them had given the dwarfs enough of the wonderful cloth to sew many cloaks, and vests, and trousers.

One of the things a dwarf liked best among all things was to have a bright colored cloak and vest, to match his cap.

It was a poor dwarf indeed who had no one to sew his clothes, and who had to go about in ordinary colored garments. Those were the ones, Brian usually found, that ended up being lore masters, or smithys, whose work was of such a nature they were usually covered with grime from the slag of the fires or the soot of the ashes, or spattered with ink from their pens.

His own clothes were among the most beautiful, and his mother was much sought after by the Elders of the settlement, to do their sewing as well.

The other thing the dwarf loved was food, especially baking. That was their pride and joy, and the truth of the matter was that the way to a dwarf's heart was through his stomach.

The great ovens they had built into their halfings were always fired, and oftentimes the back part of that same oven was used from the other side by a smith to heat his ores, or by the potter to fire his wares.

Brian remembered that as a tiny spanner, he would sit and watch his mother at her baking, churning and kneading the dough into the various shapes that pleased him so, and then, after what seemed hours of suspense, out they would come, nut-brown and piping hot, to cool on the long counter.

His mother was still at her baking after all the time between, and he still loved the dwarfcakes that were shaped in the fashion of a sturdy dwarf hammer, or ax head, and the years of his spannerhood flooded back each time he sat down to the table to eat, although of late, they had lost some of their old charm and appeal.

It wasn't that he was unhappy, exactly, but more restless than he had ever been, and even though he talked to his friends of these odd feelings, he had an idea that they simply listened to be polite.

"I don't know what it is, Jeral. I feel all fluttery inside when I think about finding the door to the old shafts, where they say the heart of the river is."

Jeral, a gruff-spoken smithy, looked away into his fire.

"A lot of mulhash, that lot of tales they've been putting into your chutes," he grumbled. "You'd be a sight better off by far if you'd take up your oldster's craft."

Jaran, Jeral's brother, was even more verbal and to the point.

"That's a waste of time, Brian. You've spent your entire spannerhood listening to old blind dwarfs that have never amounted to anything, and can't work, so all they have time to do is sit around making up yarns for fools like you to listen to."

Although Brian argued for hours with his two friends, he had begun to believe they were right, for his life had taken a turn for the definite worse since he was full-grown, and still gave no indication of what he was going to settle into doing.

There were the comments, although never made directly to him, but spoken loud enough for him to overhear.

"It's a shame about that poor thing. He's old enough to be in his own halfing now, and be out finding a decent young one to do his baking and sewing, but all he ever thinks of are those stories that blind old fool told him."

It hurt the worse, for they were accurate, in that Brian was interested in the stories, and did put much belief into them, and to the tools he had been given.

"He'll find out one day when it's too late what he missed, and how silly he's been all this time. No one will have him, then."

Brian had met one lane he liked, and found her to be funny, and at the same time, full of a sense of history that matched his own, and she had not felt that the blind dwarf had been such a fool as all the rest made him out to be.

And though the other dwarfs had complained of the old dwarf who spun such tales, they nevertheless cared for him, and made sure he was fed and clothed, and had a proper bed. No matter what else could ever be said of dwarfdom, they could not be accused of not taking care of their own. There was no such thing as a forgotten dwarf who ever perished from hunger, or cold, or any of the other forms of murder that various kinds used upon themselves to do each other in.

The lane's name was Senja, and she lived in the delving of their next neighbors, back away from the borders, where Den'Lin Fetch was located.

She knew how to bake as well as his own lanin, and could sew wonderful things with her clever needles, and the cloth she fashioned with her skill was enough to have a dozen courters at her halfing after her hand, and although Brian never admitted it to her, he was jealous of that fact, and had found it difficult to tell her of his true feelings, so he had stopped going to visit her, for fear he would feel the deep pain he experienced whenever he saw her out in the delvings with another, or on the various occasions when they would be overground, at their chores, or even on the times when the entire delvings would go overside on a feast day, to roam through the forest or fields, calling on the Great Lan to provide them with food for the new season, and the woods with new trees.

22

Senja was not shy, as were so many of the lanes, and was something of a legend in her delving of Con Den Fetch, and was even heard speaking out her mind in the great gatherings of Council.

What was more astonishing to her elders was the fact that the things she said made sense, and much of what she suggested was backed by great logic, which sometimes baffled even her, and caused the older dwarfs to mutter to themselves that here was a lane who would never find a proper mate, for she not only was pleasing to the eye, but had a good head on her shoulders as well.

Jeral and Jaran both chided Brian for his affection for Senja, and promised him he would be hers before another season was out.

"He'll look fine and fat in a new coat she will sew for him," teased Jeral.

"And everyone will comment on how many new buttons she has had to sew on, because of her baking," echoed Jaran.

Brian responded by sulking, and pretended to be unaffected, but something inside him wished for exactly that kind of life, staid and settled, and with a clear-cut purpose that would be easy to follow, and pleasant to carry on.

He watched his father go about his daily life as cheerfully as a dwarf could ever be said to go about anything, and his lanin followed her own line of thought, and did the things that were expected of her, and seemed content with her lot.

It was not that dwarfs were actually grumpy or ill humored, but some said there was something left over from the days they spent overground, when they dwelled among the far Easterlands, where their lot was such a hard one that the seriousness of it all never quite softened, even though dwarfdom, as a rule, had passed into a time of relative ease and prosperity by the time of Brian's birth, and most of the old horror of the ancient beasts who had driven Roundhat from Deep Home, and many others to follow, had passed into seldom repeated tales, or rare incidents of unpleasantness overground, when one of the work parties would chance into an ambush by a roving pack of the raiders from the wild Easterlands.

Brian, who had never been threatened in such a way, often wondered how he would behave, and what he would do, were he ever forced to fight for his life and actually use the deft skill he had with his bow and darts by shooting one of them

23

at a living thing, even though it might be one of the horrors that had been described to him as the monsters from beyond the borders.

He could hardly believe his ears, from the telling of the awful creatures that were described to him, and he thought to himself that surely the things that were told to him had been exaggerated out of all proportion by those who had wished to make a good tale better, or by young spanners trying to impress their lanes.

Jeral had only heard the same stories that Brian had, but Jaran, who was a season older, had actually had a meeting with one of the beast packs, and the work party he had been with had barely escaped with their lives, and only then because a second group, from Con Den Fetch, had heard the battle and joined in to help drive off the invaders.

Jaran would raise his thick eyebrows in an arch, and clear his throat loudly, but that's as far as he would go in describing that battle.

He still carried a nasty bite scar across his left arm that ran from his wrist to just above his elbow.

Jeral said it was from a single snap of a jaw, and that that was how large those beasts had been.

"If it had been a degree or two higher up, my brother would have come home with a lot less to say about the whole affair."

This remark amused Jeral, but left Jaran grim.

"It is one thing, little brother, to laugh at your own expense, but rude manners to laugh at others. The fact I might have lost my skoggin to some lump of a snarl from across the line is no small thing to me, and I'm glad I still have the use of it, and my good flipper as well. It might suit you well to be so lucky when you cross tracks with some of that lot."

"You'd miss me, Jaran, you know you would. If it weren't for me to keep at you, who would get you to laugh once in a while?"

Brian, never ceasing to be amazed at the chaff Jaran put up with, asked in a more subdued voice, "Were they really that big?"

"Big enough, my friend. I could have used your bowhand that day, fair enough. That's the one thing that seems to even up our match."

"And the hardshirts," added Jeral. "They've stopped more than one or two fatal bites, I'd wager."

"Enough to know that going out overground is foolish

24

without one, and foolish without an armed party to do nothing but keep watch, and patrol."

This brought up a subject that Brian had been hearing more and more about at the meetings in the Council Halfing, which was the arming of large companies to do nothing but patrol the woods and fields overground, where the dwarfs of Den'Lin Fetch went to fill their larders and gather their materials.

"Do you think it will come to that, Jaran?"

"It has already come to it, if you ask me. I'm not for all that time wasted away from my work when it's my lot to do the duty, but I'm also not for being fallen upon again by that pack of snarls that almost did for us, either."

"They'll be using you more, for sure," said Jeral to Brian. "Seeing as how you can't seem to find more to do with your time than tap around down in the kellers for those old shafts."

"Those old shafts might be a handy thing to know about if things overground are getting as bad as you make them sound."

"Knowing how to string a dart would be a lot handier," mumbled Jaran. "And being able to lend a hand at the anvil probably wouldn't be too far off center."

He began pumping the bellows into action with powerful sweeps of the scarred left arm, his sleeves rolled high over his elbows.

Brian leapt to help his friend, as did Jeral.

"What is this thing you're forging?" he asked at last, watching as the red-hot ore cooled on the anvil and began to be shaped into form by the quick tappings of the expertly handled hammer.

"The old books gave me one good thing, Brian, and that was a picture of what one of Roundhat's heartseekers looked like."

And saying, he held up the still blazing shaft for the two friends to see, and as they watched, he plunged it into the bucket of water he kept beside his forge.

The exploding steam hissed and roared, and Brian watched in amazement as the finished product came out of the white cloud of mist.

"A heartseeker," he echoed, looking at the terrible curved blade, glowing dully in the faint light of the elfmoons.

"A heartseeker," repeated Jaran. "And more to follow, to arm the bands we must now keep overground."

Brian's thoughts were troubled as he sought rest, much later, after he had left his friends, and tossed and turned on his sleeping bunk.

Jaran's conviction that the patrols would begin soon vaguely disturbed him, although it was not that he was afraid, for he already went upon those duties, to help guard work parties.

It was more in the sudden knowledge that there was something that was changing in his life, and that it would never be the same for him again.

When he had seen the cruel shaft of the heartseeker, he had known within himself then that the time was upon him that the old blind dwarf spoke of, and it would not be far behind a time when the halfing of his spanner days would be left far behind, and all those pleasant things that went with it.

His thoughts touched once, sadly, on Senja, then the hammer and chisel that hung by his bunk.

There would be a day to come when they would find the ancient doors of the beasts' prison, and perhaps the shafts into the most fabled of all dwarfish works, the delvings of Deep Home.

With that thought, he slept, and dreamed, of things that awakened an awe within him, and opened his secret heart onto the truth of it all.

A Friend of Chinby's

IN the daily routine of Brian was the getting-up ritual of putting out the rush lamp and uncovering the elfmoon in his room, then going about the task of dressing, which was never much of a problem, because all his clothes gave him great pleasure, and the routine was so set by such a long time at doing it that the dwarf seldom thought about the affair, and went on planning in his head the chores that were his for the day, or the ore he was working, or the cloth she was making into a suit of bright color for herself, or husband, or child.

There were the Falthing Tithes then, held in the Council Halfing, and all the dwarfs went to offer up a portion of their day's work in exchange for the welfare and safety of the delving.

Afterward, Brian would eat with his parents, or sometimes he would go to the Commons, a kitchen run by the community for those of the delving who had no mate to cook for them, and it was there all the spanners gathered as they grew older, and it was there that the great Dipping Time was held every twelfth day.

Dipping Time was a formal ritual to the dwarfish clans of all natures, no matter where they dwelled, and went back in ancient history all the way to Roundhat, who, it was supposed, started the affair which now had become as much a part of the dwarfish tradition as their life underground.

It was a gathering of all the delving into the main room of the Council Halfing, and the community split into dwarf and lanin, and lane, and spanner, each in a separate corner, and then the music began, played by the stately dwarf reed pipes, and lute, and the flow of stout bodies would begin, to and fro across the polished stone floor, hands sometimes joined, or sometimes held over their heads, or by their sides, back and forth to the music, changing partners as they glided among the notes of the songs, and finally, afterward, there were the tables of food and drink, where the dwarf clan would gather to feast, and exchange recipes, or other bits of news they might not have heard in the course of the days between.

All dwarfs loved to eat, and Brian was no exception, and he eagerly looked forward to Dipping Time, for it was the one point in his life that still gave him some amusement, and helped him to overcome the dullness that had started to creep into all the things he had known for so long.

Jaran and Jeral traced his trouble to the old blind dwarf, who had filled his head with such tales that he no longer kept his head belowground, as any dwarf should who had any common sense at all, and they let him know it constantly.

"You should give all that up, Brian. You're not a lore master. Leave that to others who can't do anything else."

"Jaran isn't just blowing through his hat, Brian. You have all the brains you need to do whatever you want, but you shouldn't waste yourself daydreaming about all those old stories. They make good tales to put small ones to bed with, but you're a grown dwarf now, and should be giving some serious thought to your craft."

"And it wouldn't hurt if you were to seek out a lane to settle in with," teased Jaran. "Senja is probably waiting for you to make the proposal."

Brian, blushing fiercely, denied that he was interested in Senja, or settling into a good solid dwarf routine.

"I don't have any heart to go into my father's craft, nor take Senja into a halfing of my own," he blurted. "The problem is, I don't know exactly what I'm feeling, or what direction to take."

"That will pass, Brian. I think everyone goes through that when they're trying to decide."

"Did you, Jeral?"

"Of course. So did my thick-necked brother here, although he would never, never admit it."

"I always knew what I was going to follow," corrected Jaran. "You may mark that."

Brian smiled slightly, as close to a dwarf laugh as most of his kind ever came.

"I believe that. You never seem in doubt about any issue. I wish I were the same."

"You are," insisted Jeral. "You'll find that this will all pass, Brian. It's just a part of gaining your age."

"Then I wish I would get on with it," mumbled Brian. "I've been here in this frame of mind long enough."

"There's a little patience for you. Wait and see, that's what's needed now. Fill up your time with a good solid routine, and look to your craft, and you'll find you'll soon be over all this nonsense."

"I'd like to believe that, Jaran. I hate this restlessness."

The older dwarf laid the tongs he had been working with on the edge of the forge.

"Just find a good routine, Brian. Take up a craft. I'm not one to notice such things, but there is talk around the Council Halfing that you might not be such a catch for any of the lanes who have gained their age lately. I know your father and lanin are upset about it, because they have talked to me about you."

28

Brian blustered, and blew himself up a bit, for it angered him to be the topic of so many conversations that he hadn't known about, and embarrassed him that his own father would be talking to Jaran about his decision as to what to do with his life.

"We've teased you, and tried to help you see the pointless path you're on, Brian. It will lead you nowhere. We all agree you have too much to offer to waste it doting about old tales, and ancient history. The lore masters do it because they have nothing better to do."

Such were the conversations he had almost daily, unless he was overground with one of the work parties, and he began to like that time most of all, for it gave him time to think, and no one could fault him for being lazy in his duty to the delving, for all knew that the parties that went above the tunnels felt easier when he was with them.

Still, it wasn't satisfying either, and although it did fill up a certain amount of time for him, Brian anguished over his lot, and wondered what his life would be like when he was a graybeard.

The rest of his time he still spent in the kellers of the delving of Den'Lin Fetch, tapping away with the finely wrought chisel and hammer that had been given him long before.

That was the main purpose that kept him going recently, for the urge had grown stronger within him to spend more and more time in the dark silence of the kellers, and he had spent so long on some occasions, it caused his father to chide him gently about wasting so much of his workday lying around the bottom of the halfing levels, tinkering with a set of tools that weren't worth the ore that was in them.

"Look at that," pointed out his father. "What sort of work could you do with that hammer? It's barely big enough to tap a stone fly to death, much less drive any sort of *real* chisel. And whoever saw a tool with those pictures like that? I doubt you could pry open a chestnut with something that small."

Brian had tried defending his beliefs at first, but tired of it after never seeming to make any headway.

And in the last days of the most recent attack of restlessness, he had simply given up saying anything at all, and tried as best he could merely to do his work as he was called on to do so, and the rest of his day, when he wasn't sleeping,

29

was spent in the kellers, probing for the doorway to the old shafts.

This routine was broken one late afternoon while he was overground with a group that had gone in search of a new wood supply for ax handles.

Brian was lounging under a tall oak, keeping a wary eye out for a sign of the beast packs that might threaten their safety, when a slight sound above him caused him to look upward, toward the very top of the tree.

His bow had automatically come up, strung with one of the small shafts that the dwarf arrowsmith had made.

At first, Brian had seen nothing except the golden rays of the sun glinting through the leaves, blinding him to the darker green shadows.

He made out the faint outlines of the leaves against the sun, but nothing more, yet the sound came again, and his keen dwarfish hearing, developed by life underearth, where vision was oftentimes only the ability to perceive things through one's ears, led him to scan an area directly overhead, near the thick trunk of the tree.

Something there moved again, and he knew it wasn't a noise that belonged to a tree blown by wind, or small forest animals, but before he could begin the slow dwarfish thinking of what it could be, if it were none of the others, he was brought up short by a most unusual voice that greeted him by name.

"Greetings, earthling, Brian Brandigore. You spend good time trying to find me today."

The voice was not shrill, but close to it, and its range was high above the gruff-talking dwarfs'.

"Come out of that tree, whoever you are! Knowing my name won't stop a dart from my bow."

"Oh, I'm no enemy to you or your kindred, Brian. In fact, I've come a great way to help you defend yourselves against the Troubles that are coming."

"If you're no enemy, then come down where I may see you."

"I can't do that, Brian. You have friends who are with you today who would have no qualms about driving one of those nasty darts through my thick hide. I'll stay in my tree, thank you. And it would probably help if you wouldn't stand down there looking like you were talking to someone."

"Who are you, that my kin would find it necessary to stick you with a dart?"

"Not anyone you've known before, Brian, although I'm familiar with your name."

"How come you to know that?"

"You know a good friend of mine, a dwarf by the name of Chinby, the blind one."

Brian's brow knitted in great confusion.

"Chinby is my friend, but how came you to know of him? You're no dwarf, whatever else you may be."

"I'm no dwarf by a long shot, Brian," laughed the voice, almost tinkling in its lightness and humor.

The laughter disappeared when a group of the other party of woodsmen came into sight and began the walk toward the tree Brian stood under.

"Look away, Brian. We will have no time to talk now. Meet me tonight in your old keller, below the third landing."

Brian's confusion multiplied.

"How do you know my delving, or where my keller is?"

His hand tightened on his bow, and a cold hand of suspicion crept over his heart.

"I know where your delving is, and your keller, because I've seen you there," replied the voice. "But it is no matter. If you want to find out more, meet me there tonight, after you sup."

"How will you get there?" asked Brian. "There's no way any but a dwarf of Den'Lin Fetch can come there after the outer doors are closed and bolted."

"I'm not coming by the outer doors, Brian."

"Then how?"

"You carry the keys to my doorway upon you," replied the voice. "And the reason they seem so silly to all your kinsmen is that they're elfish tools, hammer and chisel, that Chinby gave to you."

"The doorway to the old shafts!" breathed Brian. "But how could you know where those lie? You're no dwarf!"

"I know where they lie, because I have found the other end of the shafts. I found it quite by accident, a long time ago, with Chinby. Our family had known the ancient dwarfish folk that lived there. It's a long story, Brian, and I have no time. Tonight! I'll tell you all tonight. Speak to no one about this!"

Brian started to protest, but his instinct told him the stranger was no longer there in the shadow.

There was no other place for the odd voice to have come from, yet the tree above him now was empty of everything except the leaves and wind.

"We've finished, Brian," called the leader of the woodsmen, a thick dwarf named Clamor. "Let's get home to our soup."

As the rest of the wood-gathering party filed past, Brian studied the tree still more closely, and all the other trees surrounding it, searching for clues as to how the stranger would have been able to reach the oak without being seen, but it was impossible, and he decided that dangerous or not, he would meet this strange being tonight, to find out about the ancient doorway to the lower levels, and to see what kind of creature was able to move about in daylight without being detected.

The word elf had come up, and he felt that this stranger was one of that clan, but he wasn't sure what it meant, or if it meant anything at all.

He was preoccupied on the short walk back to the aboveground door that led to the delving, and Clamor had to call out to him more than once to hurry along or get left overside for the night.

That was nothing new to Brian, but to some, it was a terrifying thought, to be locked out of the security of Den'Lin Fetch, at the mercy of everything in the wilderness that was all the country above the delving.

He hurried on, and helped them close the great stone door that blocked the passageway to the open air, and followed slowly behind, going back over the mystifying conversation he'd had.

This elf, for that is what Brian decided the stranger must be, had known Chinby, the blind dwarf, who had told him all the stories of Roundhat, and Deep Home, and all the other histories of the heroes of dwarfdom, and all the stories of the old delvings, and dwarfish warriors and their lanes, and this Chinby was a friend of an elf, who belonged to a race that was not to be trusted, and who, according to all the older dwarfs in Den'Lin Fetch, were a shifty lot, and had no good sense about anything, and as like as not, would be gone right at the moment you needed them the most.

They conceded the fact that that drifting bunch spun exceptionally fine cloth for sewing dwarfish clothing, but other than that, they were worthless, and to be avoided at all costs.

There were some that even went so far as to say that the elves were a dangerous lot, and treacherous as well, and that any that had dealings with them would be rewarded by only trouble and grief, if not something worse.

All these things ran through Brian's head, but when he stopped to really think about what he felt toward the stranger, there was no fear there, but a great curiosity, for the very thing that he had been searching for was promised to him for the asking, and all the other answers that he had been seeking for so long were most likely held by this dwarf friend, for that's what he must be, or his family have been, because he was sure Chinby was not one who would have friends of the wrong sort. Brian was positive of that much, no matter what the others all said of the blind dwarf.

Chinby had lost his sight in a great battle with a huge pack of beasts that had attacked his delving, and he was a hero himself, although over the seasons the others forgot, and the further away the danger was, the more the hero Chinby slipped their mind.

Not that they were cruel, or that Chinby minded being neglected, for he didn't, but as time wore on, the only ones who sought out the old dwarf slowly stopped, all except Brian, who never tired of the stories and tales.

And if this stranger was a friend of Chinby's, then he must be a friend indeed.

Having come to his decision, Brian hurried on after the others, and helped them stack the wood in front of the halfings where it was needed, then went to his own to bolt down his supper in such a hurry that his father remarked on it, and his lanin told him he wasn't eating enough for a full-grown dwarf, and that he would lose his strength if that was all he was eating.

Usually Brian took time to placate his parents, but his curiosity was burning his mind with a thousand questions, and he could hardly contain himself long enough to make hasty excuses about going down to the kellers to search for one of the rare stones there, to polish for a present to Senja.

Hurrying away toward the stairway that led to the lower levels, he found his heart racing wildly, and he knew he was on the verge of an event that was going to change his life forever, and that there would be no going back to the old ways.

33

The hammer and chisel were locked tightly in one strong hand, and his eyes burned brightly as he raced swiftly through the lower depths that descended into the kellers, far below Den'Lin Fetch, into the darkness that held the secrets of the dwarfs of old, and which now promised to deliver some answers in the form of an elf, who was coming to call through the most ancient of dwarfish doorways.

Shanon

IN the dark silence, Shanon the elf sat waiting, his piercing blue eyes lidded, his thoughts turned in.

He had spent many days watching the young Brian Brandigore, trying to form some impression of the dwarf, to see his inner being, as well as what was presented to the world outside.

Chinby, his good friend, had lived among all the known dwarf delvings that still existed in the Lower Reaches, and it was Chinby's judgment of dwarf nature that he trusted, and relied on, for being an elf, it was all beyond him, as to what made one of the stocky, morose creatures any different than the next, or what great sorrow must have befallen their race to cause their features to be forever set in a sour-humored scowl.

Chinby told him the lore of the dwarfish clans, all the way back to the most ancient of all dwarfs, or at least it was the oldest one anybody knew or read of, and of Roundhat's exploits, and his dream of a delving that would girdle the bottom of the world from one side to the other, and of joining all the dwarfish folk together once more into one great clan.

Shanon listened with interest to the fate that had befallen the ancient clans of dwarfdom, for it was much the same story with his own kindred. First a small split, then a larger one, until finally there were open wounds that lay festering between the fletch of waterfolk elves and those of the wood.

In the olden days, the competition between the two was good-natured, and consisted of a lot of high-humored joking, and many farfetched claims and counterclaims.

Then had come the time of the Ancient Troubles, and the split grew more than friendly overtures could patch, and after a time the waterfolk of elfdom and the woodland folk parted ways entirely, and had not been seen sharing settlements since.

Shanon, a waterfolk himself, lived with a great sadness that troubled his normal good nature, and that was the sorrow of seeing his own kind divided into hostile camps. He knew of the older, more happy days of elfdom, when the two folk mingled easily with each other, and of the glorious settlements they fashioned when they had worked together to do so.

Those settlements, danes as they were called by the elfin clans, were truly a wonder to behold, built as they were close by the water, with towering woods behind, and the beauty that those danes possessed was hard for even an elf as articulate as Shanon to describe.

He, of course, had never seen the danes of the two races of elves in their full splendor, and only saw the long-deserted dwelling place of Erin Frey, which was once the seat of both water and wood folk, in the days before the divisions, but that look, even in all the ruin it had fallen into, tugged at his heart with such a sorrow that it was all he could do to pull himself away.

That look also kept him from returning to the ruined dane of Erin Frey for a long span of time, for it was too painful to look on all the fallen beauty of it, yet at long, long last, that place of such sadness was where he met the blind dwarf Chinby, sitting next to one of the singing fountains, long silent, and running his old, knobby dwarf hands over the delicate carvings on the wall that bordered the empty pool.

"Welcome, sir elf. Perhaps you can tell me more of the beauty of this strange carving? What was its meaning? And where have the folk gone who dwelled here?"

Shanon had been so taken aback by the presence of a dwarf in Erin Frey that he remained speechless. It took him another moment to realize that the old dwarf was blind.

"Have I offended some holy spot, sir elf? If so, I am sorry. It is difficult for me to see with my hands. Forgive me."

Recovering himself, Shanon quickly reassured the dwarf.

"It is no holy spot in the sense of the word you mean, stranger, yet it is holy to those of us who come here to see the beauty of a bygone day."

It suddenly struck Shanon that the dwarf had known he was an elf, yet he could not see.

"How is it you knew I was an elf, old one?"

"Nothing but an elf walks that way," explained Chinby. "It is a skill I have had to develop since my eyes gave out on me."

"I might have been anyone, trying to sneak closer to you."

"That is different, too, good elf. A person who is trying to conceal his footstep signals louder than anyone. It is the sound of deceit or trickery. No, I knew it was not some other heavy foot, trying to creep close to me without my knowing."

"How are you called, old one? My name is Shanon."

"Chinby is my name. Come closer, Shanon, so I may see you with these old hands."

A sharp feeling of distrust kept Shanon rooted to the spot a moment, every elfin sense on the alert, but he could detect nothing hostile in the hunched old dwarf, and so stepped forward.

"You hold back, Shanon. Is it all the things that have been spread about elf and dwarf never being able to exist side by side?"

Shanon laughed quickly, to hide his embarrassment.

"I guess that's so, Chinby."

"There was a time our two clans were one, you know."

Shanon shook his head to signal that he didn't, then remembered the dwarf couldn't see.

"No, I've never heard that tale."

"Not likely to, if things in your neck of the woods are as bad as they are in mine. To hear the stories now, you'd think the two folk, elf and dwarf, were blood enemies, and not to be trusted, depending on whichever side of the wall you're on. First it was the elf folk did this and that, then the dwarf clans went out and did such and such, and now nobody remembers what happened, and it makes no difference anyway, for it was all long ago, and should be forgotten. Those times were hard, and I suppose it's understandable, with the pressures they were all under, but it drove apart a good friendship that

36

is going to have to be renewed before all the business of the Troubles is finally laid to rest."

Shanon, finding it hard to overcome his own prejudice against dwarf folk, was having a difficult time accepting Chinby's version of the story.

"My being a dwarf is getting in the way of your believing me, eh, Shanon?"

The elf blustered, but was too long in denying it.

"That's the shame of it. Here we sit, you and I, two perfect and total strangers until a few moments ago, and right away the wedge is driven between us, simply because I come from dwarfdom, and you're an elf." Chinby laughed, although there was a trace of sorrow woven through it. "More's the pity, I say, for it will be a long road, going in opposite directions."

"I said nothing of leaving, Chinby. And what you say is true. All I've heard my entire life is what dullards and sneaks dwarfs are, and that they are to be avoided at all cost, and that smart elves go a long way around to avoid dealing with a dwarf, or their ilk."

"Now reverse that, and you'll have what we hear in our dwarf delvings. But as I said, the two races were one once, even before the so-called sires of our two kinds went about their heroic business and set up their first delving or dane."

"How could that be?" asked an incredulous Shanon, still finding it hard to accept some of the things the old dwarf was saying.

"It was simple, my good Shanon. There were no dwarfs, or elves, or beasts, or anything of the sort. We were all from the same home, and all belonged to the same family."

Shanon's eyes narrowed.

"That couldn't be."

"But it is so, my friend, whether you believe me or not. There was a long period of prosperity, and all was grand, in those days. Then we got a little off the path, and first one brother, then another, thought he wasn't getting his rightful share of the family holdings. In the end, the family was split up among all the kinds there are, and each went his own way." Chinby gave what could have been mistaken for a gruff laugh. "And here we are, all this time later, arguing over nothing, and sitting amid the ruins of one of your danes. Perhaps tomorrow we'll go, and I'll treat you to the ruins of some of my kindred. They lie not far from here. A delving that was more beautiful than any."

Shanon had grown quiet.

"I think I'd like that."

And the two, the blind dwarf Chinby and the elf Shanon, had gone to the ancient delving that Brian dreamed of, where Roundhat had founded the new Deep Home, all those ages past; and then just as had Erin Frey disappeared into ruin, so had Deep Home, falling now into dusty oblivion.

The dwarf held up a hand as they entered the outer door.

"Tell me, Shanon, are you afraid?"

"A little," replied the elf truthfully.

"Then you won't be harmed. Your honesty is good. There are guardians here that will not allow any to pass whose hearts hold the least deceits. Now is the time to speak honestly with me, if you haven't."

"I don't have need to fear your guardians, Chinby, except I might wonder what I'm doing here at all."

"You're doing here what may prove to be the longest chore of your life, Shanon, and the most frustrating and heart-breaking, and that's trying to bring the two clans back together again. There is a time coming when we shall have a need to stand united, or we shall all perish away, and every other goodness and truth as well."

"That's a bit high-flown for me, Chinby. I'm not very good at causes. Give me a simple task like building a net or spinning a bolt of cloth, and I'll like it better."

"That's how we shall look on it then, simply that. Now come, we have a long walk ahead of us."

The two had wound around shallow tunnels that were total blackness, but Chinby led the elf surely, never once halting or hesitating, and on they went, ever downward, until Shanon began to find it hard to breathe.

Just when the elf, who was never far beyond the open air of the forest, and the sunlight, began to feel he could stand the confines of the close shaft no longer, he sensed a sudden change and smell to the dank, musty air, and his spirits soared, when reaching out with his arms, and feeling all about him, he could no longer touch the walls and roof of the smothering shaft they had been walking in for so long he had lost all track of time.

There had been strange sounds there, too, other than their own muffled footsteps in the thick darkness, but the dwarf had mumbled a few words, or grunted, it seemed, and the noises had disappeared.

Chinby motioned him to stand nearer with a tug on his cloak sleeve, and with a flash of brilliance that dazzled Shanon and hurt his eyes, the great chamber they were in leapt alive with a flood of muted light from the elfmoon Chinby had uncovered. Its shimmering flame, deep within the stone, lit the eyes of other elfmoons all around the huge chamber, and from one to another the light went, on and on, until the most distant corner and tunnel of the immense dwarfish dwelling was afire with the soft golden white light.

There amid the splendor of the ancient delving, Chinby gave Shanon his lore lessons in dwarfdom, and it was there that the dwarf instructed the elf in the forging of the tools, hammer and chisel, that would open the prison door of old that contained the beasts. They were also to reopen the tunnels to the dwarf hall of Roundhat, which was where they were. Chinby was exacting in his measurements and directions as to how the tools were to be fashioned.

"It is all written, Shanon, to the hairbreadth and weight, and the exact size they must be. And these scenes that I have described to you must be engraved on the chisel."

"I'm no smithy," complained Shanon. "I can get you fifty smiths that could do this job better than I, and with less trouble, Chinby."

"They are not you, my friend. This must be done by an elf who bears no grudge against dwarfdom, and whose heart is without deceit. Your other smiths might make me a finer set of tools, yet they would be worthless, for these must be forged by an honest hand, and a heart not bent on keeping the two races apart."

Reluctantly, Shanon had gone on practicing at the insistence of the old dwarf, and they had spent countless days belowground, in the very depths of the forges of Deep Home that the dwarf Roundhat had delved, after they had been driven from the wilderness of snow and ice to the far Easterlands.

At last Shanon threw up his arms helplessly.

"I can't do it any better than this, Chinby. And I can't stand another hour down this hole you call a delving. It's all very nice, but I miss the wood and river!"

Chinby wagged his old head, clucking to himself.

"I'm sorry, Shanon, you must make allowances for my

thick head. I've quite forgotten you're not a dwarf, and must go topside every once in a while."

Shanon, not knowing whether to be flattered at the old dwarf's words, or angry, laughed.

"Well, there's a roundabout compliment, I suppose, being mistaken for a dwarf. But I'm not sure I'm *not* a dwarf, after all this time underneath this pile of rock you call a delving."

Chinby had agreed that they indeed needed a rest from their labor, and took him to a remote glen, close by the river, just as it went underground.

There was a deep pool, and hidden falls, and it was one of the more secret places of dwarfdom, being one of their doors aboveground, and so a thing to be guarded closely, and not many knew of the whereabouts of all the doors to any dwarfish delving.

Chinby told Shanon that he was the first elf to ever hold that sacred trust.

"But there's no one there any longer," argued Shanon, although he was touched by the faith that had been placed in him.

"But there will be again, one day, and you are making it possible for that day to come."

"You speak many riddles, Chinby. I hardly see how you or I can possibly make any difference to any of this. What's done is done, and that's an end of it. Erin Frey is past, and so is your Deep Home. We may as well face that."

The old dwarf shook his head slowly.

"I can see how you would think that way, friend, but it will come to pass as I say, if we do our task as well as we're able. I have a young spanner picked out in the delving of Den'Lin Fetch who will be with you, once I'm gone, and you two will finish the rest of this, along with the others who are coming over the Roaring. Myself, too, if I'm still able to creep about a bit."

"You mean the Sea of Roaring? No one lives on the other side of there, everyone knows that!"

"According to what you've been told, Shanon, but there again you must listen carefully to what one is saying to you. Try to hear more than what he's saying, and listen to his heart."

"What others would be coming here? I've never thought of anyone actually being on that side of the Roaring."

"Lots of folk are there, including some of our relatives, who left long ago to seek more peaceful lands to carry on their lives. But now they shall be reunited, and the Roaring will have been made solid again."

"Who is this dwarf you're speaking of? And where is Den'Lin Fetch?"

"The dwarf is a spanner by the name of Brandigore, and the delving of Den'Lin Fetch lies at the end of this river. There are shafts here that run all the way. When you go, that's the way you shall travel, for it is the safest, and also the most concealed from the other dwarfs who dwell there. None of them believe in the old things any longer, so they never suspect there is a doorway there among them, in the bottom of their kellers."

"Whatever would I want to do that for? Why don't you go?"

"I am going, as soon as you've finished forging the tools. I will spend some time there soon, for no one pays me any mind, and I can give him the tools, and prepare him a little for what is to come. When it is time, I will send you word."

And with that, Chinby closed the discussion of Den'Lin Fetch and the dwarf Brandigore, and went on to give him the names in dwarfish of all the flowers and trees in the beautiful glen by the river, and told him the tales of the most ancient stones, who lived far below sight of the sun, and who married the daughters of the mountains.

Chinby stayed with Shanon for a time after that, until the small hammer and chisel were finished to his satisfaction, then he led him back to the doorway to the outside, where they had first entered.

In parting, the old dwarf held out a knobby hand to the elf.

"You are a remarkable fellow, Shanon. More than an elf, yet, and I think you'll find that someday these little tools of ours will be well repaid."

"Will I see you again, Chinby? You speak as though you are leaving for good."

"I've got places yet to go that a fellow like you wouldn't find very interesting. No, stay here awhile, with your river and wood, until I send you word to come to me."

And that was the last time Shanon had seen the old dwarf for so long that he almost forgot all about the signal that would one day come to announce it was the time for the rest of the plan they had agreed on, long before, in the secret glade by the river.

The signal had arrived in the guise of a river elf, who

stopped Shanon near the cool banks of a small backwater, where he had been counting lilies, and handed him a roll of tattered elfin cloth.

Bewildered, Shanon unrolled the parcel, and there in a cramped, formal hand was the single word Chinby, printed carefully, as a blind dwarf would, feeling each letter as it ran onto the cloth.

He searched for anything further, but found nothing.

Shanon asked the river elf where he came by the parcel, but the fellow was elusive, and said a friend had given it to him to deliver, since he was coming so far upwater and knew Shanon by sight.

And so, hardly knowing why, Shanon the elf set out on the long journey to reach the hidden shafts of the ancient dwarf delving, to seek out the one Chinby had told him of, who dwelled in Den'Lin Fetch.

It was with great misgivings that he left the bright sunlight of the afternoon and wound his way downward into the dwarfish shafts, but he had not gone far before he found the first of the carefully printed scrolls, all in high elfish, from his long-absent friend, Chinby.

Elf and Dwarf

AS accustomed as he was to the darkness, and as keen as his senses were, Shanon was still startled momentarily by the sudden appearance of Brian.

The deep silence of the heart of the earth was disturbing to the elf, and he'd thought, as he waited, of what terrible misfortunes and ill winds had caused the dwarfish legions to take up such a life. Chinby had given him the histories of the oldest of dwarfkind, and the promise that there would come a day when the dwellers of the earth would be free once more to take up their old homes in the lands they had been driven from, although they had lived so long in their present delvings, it was a common fact that few of the dwarfish clans would ever choose to return.

Chinby also told him of the farthest reaches of the Easterland wastes, where it was said a terrible army was being mustered by the Fallen One, of creatures that were half animal and half mountain argyle, and that there would come a day when those hordes would be unleashed upon the world that the dwarf and elfin clans now shared, however reluctantly.

Chinby would say no more, and Shanon began to suspect that the blind dwarf knew more than he was willing to share.

"There will be others to tell you what you need to know, and a new clan will come forth to combat the threat."

"What new clan, Chinby? You mean more than elves and dwarfs?"

"There are beings from all kinds who will be there, and all of them will be from the Great Lan Himself," replied Chinby.

"Is that the same as Arlen Zephus?"

"He is One," answered the dwarf.

"But what has all this to do with the dwarf you told me of?"

"There will be the time of the great beasts, first, and they must be dealt with."

"Can you tell me no more? I know it gives you great pleasure to keep me guessing, but I'm a simple elf, and have no great patience with your puzzles."

Shanon was shocked to hear the old creature laugh. It sounded strained and ill-fitting, yet it was a laugh, all the same.

"You'll have all your answers, and then some, my good elf."

"I hope so."

He had gotten nothing further from Chinby, and all his questions still gnawed at his mind.

"Greetings, elf."

"My own to you, Brian."

"What brings you into the kellers of dwarf delvings?"

"Chinby!"

It was Brian's turn to be surprised.

"Chinby?" he echoed, bewildered.

"Chinby said he would warn you of elf doings, so that you wouldn't be confused when the time came for us to meet."

Brian remained silent, sizing up the sharp-featured elf.

"You hold the tools I forged, Brian."

And Shanon described the scenes engraved on the small

chisel, and said that his own mark, an *s*, was wrought in the upper corner.

Brian knew that well, and that it would have been impossible for anyone to know that but himself. He fell into another long silence, thinking about the many talks he had had with Chinby, trying to remember any clue as to the meaning of all these strange events, or if the old dwarf had ever said anything that would have prepared him for this meeting.

Shanon, although impatient, was polite enough, and knew enough about dwarfs that he didn't interrupt Brian's musings.

There had been many talks about elves and their doings. Of that, Brian was sure, and Chinby had related more than one experience that had left the dwarf clans with much to find fault with in their dealings with elves. However, like all things, there were good and bad sides to every question, and Brian felt that that must also be so in the case of elves.

And there were the deep wood dwarf clans, out of his own knowledge, that he knew to live overground, and they were spoken of as darkly as any other undesirable subject that was ever discussed at table. Of course, it could be said they weren't *really* dwarfs, by the mere fact they kept their halfings, if they could be referred to as that, in the deeper parts of the forest, half above, half below ground, and their digs seldom went much beyond a few feet down.

There were other names that more likely fitted those strange clans, and Chinby sometimes referred to them as the lost cousins, the Carbens.

Brian didn't know whether those clans were of a sort that didn't respect the way of things, or if they had gone bad from having their delvings overground, and Chinby never spoke ill of them, only that they had abandoned their old way of life and returned to the open air.

Shanon went over in his own mind the things he had learned from the blind dwarf as he waited for the next move from Brian. One thing for certain, when dealing with these difficult creatures in their own territory, they were agonizingly slow to decide on a question, and not overly given to great displays of emotions.

The waiting dragged on, until Shanon was almost on the verge of calling the dwarf's name, when Brian abruptly cleared his throat and spoke.

"So you've known Chinby? And he is the one who told you to seek me out?"

"And that we are to make a journey together," added Shanon.

"A journey?" repeated Brian. "Wherever would we be going together?"

"He only said that we would find that out in good time. I think he mentioned some others, crossing the sea to find us."

The dwarf shook his head in the darkness.

"My friends have been trying to tell me all along that this is foolishness, and that I have wasted my life ever dabbing around in these things that Chinby talked of. Maybe they're right. I don't think a journey is what I need at the moment, and no offense to you, my good elf. I can barely stand it overground long enough to go with the work parties, so I can hardly imagine myself staying so long as to make a journey to the sea."

"Nevertheless, that is what Chinby said. Perhaps I have come to the wrong dwarf."

Brian, his pride stung slightly, grumbled.

"You've come to the right dwarf, no mistake. But what I'm wondering is, do I have any further proof that the elf that's here in my keller is one to be trusted?"

"You have my story, and the tools that I forged, just as Chinby instructed me. I have no idea why I'm here, either, except that it seems to be the only thing worthwhile doing. I found no pleasure in the other elf affairs that are going on, or any of the crafts that the others are learning. I've always been quite the one for long strolls through the wood, and trips to distant danes, to see what the other clans are doing, yet they all seem the same, and I'm not sure where I fit in. Chinby seemed quite certain that I was the elf for this job, just as he was firm that the dwarf who would be able to undertake it was you."

"You sound like myself, elf. We could be brothers, were it not for the fact of our differences."

"Are there really any? Except for the lore that we've made up, to give ourselves a history."

Brian studied the elf curiously.

"You seem a strange lot, to be sitting here at the bottom of a dwarf dig, talking about all these things, as though they had nothing to do with you."

45

Shanon laughed, a light tinkling sound that echoed for a long while.

"I guess we're a pair, the two of us. All my kindred are busy doing whatever it is that makes an elf what he is, and all your folk are doing the same, and here the two of us sit, jabbering like magpies in some dark hole, as if we had good sense."

"I'd say you're not far off, on that count. Perhaps it would be best to forget this whole business, and go on about our lives, as we should be doing. I'm not so far gone in age that I can't take up my father's craft. And I'm sure you could do the same."

The elf sat thoughtfully silent for a while before replying, thinking of the dwarf's words.

"You might be right, Brian. I don't know that Chinby ever had anything else to look forward to, for he has no sight, and lore master is all he was ever able to do. You and I could be useful to our own danes and delvings, if we chose."

"And I have a lane I'm courting," confided Brian in a sudden burst of candor, his ears burning.

"Perhaps we should leave this for a bit," suggested Shanon, for the longer he remained in the dark keller of the dwarfish delving, the stronger was the pull of the outside air and sunlight. It was very subtle at first, but after a long enough while, it began as quietly as a thirst, and went on growing.

"It wouldn't hurt to wait and see," agreed Brian.

Beginning to like the idea more and more, Shanon thought of the fact that he would soon be outside, and away from these dim kellers, and he became almost light-headed.

"It was all probably a mistake. Chinby may have had some wrong information. We probably won't have to do anything more than just try to fit in with our own kindred and see how things will work out."

Brian, a little bit slower to decide what it was he was feeling, did finally agree, and said as much.

"I think we might be a bit hasty in our decision to go off on a chore as tricky as this one sounds, with no more real information than we have. It's fair to say that our facts are a bit thin, when you come down to examining them."

"No facts at all," concluded Shanon. "For the life of me, I can't fathom what made me pick up and come all the way here when Chinby sent me that note. There wasn't really anything to it, except his name. And the other notes he left

46

were simply fables to me, as far as I could make out. Good stories, but hardly the sort of thing to base a journey on."

"Do you still have those?" asked Brian.

"I've kept them safe," explained Shanon. "I was never really sure of them, or what they could possibly be leading up to. I have meant to ask you if you could make anything of them."

Shanon fumbled through the small pack he carried. "We'll have to find some light. I can't see what I'm looking for."

"Here," replied Brian, handing the elf one of the small stones from his pocket. "These are named after your kin. We call them elfmoons."

"Chinby told me. I saw them in the old delvings."

Brian was immediately alert.

"Which old delvings?"

"Why, the ones where I forged these tools. Chinby took me there."

"Did he say anything else?"

"Only that they were very old, and had great meaning for those of his race."

"Let me see those scrolls," said Brian, his heart suddenly racing.

In the light of the small elfmoons that Brian had placed on the floor between them, he began to study the carefully folded and rolled scrolls. As the dwarf held one of the parchments close to the stone, Shanon let out a small cry.

"Hold that up a bit. There! Like that! See? That didn't show up before."

"What?"

"Here!" said the elf, pointing to a line of runes that bordered the entire outside edge of the paper. "There wasn't anything on that sheet before, except that elfish script in the middle."

"I can't read that, but all the outside print is dwarfish, of a very old order. Some of the words are words that Chinby taught me. I don't think most dwarfs use any of them anymore."

Shanon struck a fist to his palm.

"Chinby is a very clever dwarf, right enough. He made it so that I would be able to read exactly what I needed to know, and he's left you some instructions as well, or I'll eat my hat."

Brian scowled, studying the dwarf runes.

His eyes suddenly widened.

"It's the way to one of Roundhat's old settlements! It's not

47

Deep Home of old, but almost as good. It's where they came after they left there."

He turned in awe to the elf.

"You were there."

"That's where Chinby took me to forge those tools you have."

Brian's brow knitted.

"He never told me he knew where those delvings were. I just thought he'd read about them somewhere, in some of the old lore books."

"Chinby seems to be a dwarf who gets around much better than you would suspect of a blind dwarf."

"Are these all the scrolls you found?"

"They were all in the tunnels to that dig," replied Shanon. "It took a long time for him to show me how to spot the right shaft to choose."

Brian was astonished.

"You mean he showed you how to reach the inner delvings?"

"It was hard, for he had to describe to me what it all looked like, and how to feel the shaft walls for the marks, and to smell the right smell. Like he said, you can smell the shafts that lead to a dead end. They all stink of dirt."

"You have no idea of what Chinby has done," shot Brian. "He's taught you the secret order of a delving. You could find your way around Den'Lin Fetch if you wanted, without too much trouble."

"I could find my way out, at least," replied the elf.

"That's a secret that's never been given to any outside dwarfdom," complained Brian. "I don't know what to think about Chinby now. If he is so easy with his tongue as to give away our most sacred workings, then who else has he seen fit to talk to?"

Brian wrung his hands, head bowed.

"I shall have to report this to the Council right away. They should know we're all in danger."

"From who? Me?" Shanon laughed easily. "I don't think your Chinby did any such blathering as you're talking of. He had to give me the secret, so I could come to fetch you. Otherwise, I'd have been stuck somewhere overground, as you call it, and would have been lucky to have ever found your delving at all, much less you."

"It's just not done," insisted the dwarf. "I may be a lot of things that they have accused me of, but I'm not one to turn

48

on my own, or let any danger befall dwarfdom, if I'm able to prevent it."

"The only danger to dwarfdom I can see here is that there's a bit too much thickheadedness to be had down these holes. Maybe the long time out of the sun has dimmed your reason to the point you don't make good sense."

"I'm a dwarf!" bellowed Brian. "That's something you wouldn't understand."

"I don't, and no mistake," replied the elf. "And from talking to Chinby, I had gotten the idea that maybe there was something more to dwarfs than all this followha of shafts and digs, and slow-witted creatures who hid out in holes in the ground. He was forever telling me of the grand things the dwarfish clans had done, or were doing, and how practical they were, and what good sense they had. I may be wrong, but I was suffering under the impression that most of dwarfdom had enough brains to see what was what, and to not fly off the handle at the least provocation."

Shanon had worked himself up into something of a snit, for after the discovery of the dwarf runes on the scrolls that Chinby had given him, he began to suspect that there was more to the blind dwarf than met the eye. His instructions had been plainly outlined on how he was to reach Brian, and Den'Lin Fetch, and the nature of that delving, but evidently Chinby had included instructions for Brian on those same scrolls, in dwarfish runes which didn't show up, except by the soft glow of the elfmoon, and which would not have been evident to anyone but a dwarf, and beyond that, to a dwarf in a delving, where the light would be the proper sort to illuminate the strange-looking runes.

"What does your dwarfish scribbling say there?" asked Shanon. "Or do you think you'll risk the loss of your precious delving at my hand?"

"You make light of my concern, and that doesn't sit well, friend elf. If the case were reversed, and it was one of your danes that was exposed to me, we might see another tune."

"We might, indeed," agreed Shanon. "I fault nothing of your concern, Brian. I simply mean to say that I am no cause for your alarm. Chinby had a point in mind when he chose me for this errand, although I grow to like it less and less, and in order for me to carry it out, he had to give me certain directions so that I could find you."

Calming himself somewhat, Brian went back to studying the scrolls.

"Nothing much in this one. A list of names, dwarfish by the sound of them, but I can't make any sense out of it. I've never heard of any of them before."

"Who are they?"

"The names are just names. Here's Gim, Marin, Clarin, Dram, Leim, Ramkin, Aurel, and Glin. I don't think I've ever heard of any of them. They're certainly not any of the names out of the lore books I know of. And there's something else here about the sea."

Here Brian's eyes met Shanon's.

"What does it say?" asked the elf quietly.

"It says that there will be a host of others awaiting us, on the shore of the Roaring Sea, and that there will be a great gathering of the dwarfish clans, to strike out against the beasts."

"What else?"

"The way to reach there," went on Brian. "It has all the directions to the shafts that lead to the old Deep Home Highway, the river that runs all the way from the far Easterlands to the Roaring."

"Anything else? Mine were all instructions on how to reach you, and how to find you, and what to say, so that I would know it was you."

As Brian scanned the two remaining scrolls, his frown deepened.

"It says here we are to leave on the first day of the Golden Leaf."

"Which is your day for what?"

"Which is the day for tomorrow. The trees begin to bare."

"Tomorrow?"

"That's what it says on the parchment. And here's something from Chinby, printed in his own hand."

"What does he say?"

"Good luck, and that he'll be with us again at the Roaring."

"If we decide to go," corrected the elf.

"I'm going," said Brian, a note of determination suddenly in his voice.

"What's changed your mind so quickly? We had almost agreed to let well enough alone a moment ago."

"Senja is there."

"So?"

50

"She is going to be there, so I'm going to be there. I can't let her cross the Roaring alone."

"There's no reason I should go," went on Shanon. "And that's the first I heard about *crossing* the sea."

"No reason at all you should go."

The elf studied Brian a moment, looking deeply into the square features and the straightforward glance of the stocky dwarf.

"That's just the ticket then. No reason at all that I should. What elf ever had a more binding cause than that?" His laughter tinkled through the gloom a moment, then echoed back, as if there were a hundred elves present. "Besides, I've always wanted to see the sea."

"Is that an elf's reasoning? You may find more than you bargain for."

"The best of all elf reasons! It's a long way from a hole in the ground," concluded Shanon.

Senja

CHINBY had been a frequent visitor to Con Den Fetch, and went about as often there as he had in Brian's delving.

The Elders of both settlements felt the same way about the old dwarf, that blind and helpless as he was, it didn't hurt to let him have his small comforts, or to let him spin his farfetched yarns as he wished. And Senja, like Brian, had been captured at an early age by Chinby's tales of bygone glories, and the strange things he spoke of, weaving elaborate tapestries of lore and myth together in such a way that it fairly dazzled the mind's eye and ear.

The spanners in Con Den Fetch constantly hounded the old dwarf for more of his amusing tales, and often Chinby would be followed about the delving by a dozen or more young ones, both spanner and lane alike, fascinated by the intrigue and mystery in the stories the old lore master told, and it was seldom that one could find him all alone.

Senja always chose her moments when Chinby was free of his loud following, to talk and listen to the lore master. The others loved the diversion of his tales, and loved to watch as he played all the parts of a story, but inside, she knew that they merely toyed with his affections because they were young and bored, and because their elders told them not to pay heed to any of the tall yarns that Chinby was telling.

He was treated as one who was harmless, yet beyond reason, and many of the followers that went about with him through the daily rounds of delving life openly made fun of him, knowing the old dwarf couldn't see the faces they made, or their looks of pity and amusement.

Senja had gained a reputation as defender of Chinby, and had she not been the lane of a prominent family, she would have suffered greatly by her actions. Her loud voice, when she was angry, was often heard berating the others who teased or heckled Chinby, and although Chinby often reassured her, and told her it was no matter, Senja would never let a single incident pass unnoticed, if she were within hearing or seeing of it.

Senja's father had spoken to her time and again about the views of his friends on her outbursts, and the taking to her heart the cause of the old lore master.

"He's perfectly well able to take care of himself," he insisted.

"There's no excuse for bad manners," shot back the young dwarf lane, her eyes afire with anger at those who would tease and insult an old blind lore master.

Con Den Fetch, being farther away from the borders, and in a generally safer area than many of the other delvings, had grown lax in the long, peaceful years, and because the dangers in the immediate woods and fields were not so great, the stories of heroes and great feats by their ancient dwarfish forefathers began to lose their appeal.

There were other delvings that took more kindly to Chinby, but he singled that settlement out, along with Den'Lin Fetch, and chose to spend most of his time between the two.

Brian never knew where his friend and teacher went when he was away, nor did he ever venture to ask, for as kindly and quiet-spoken as Chinby was, the young dwarf sensed a hardness underneath, a core that was deep set and immovable, a character developed by hardship, and danger, and great trials. He was sure the old dwarf would have told him, had he ventured the question, but something in Chinby's bearing made Brian feel that it would be better to remain silent.

There was also a fear that Chinby would tell him all, and Brian, torn by indecision and feeling the restlessness that had been with him for the past seasons, did not know if he was ready to hear what Chinby would have to say.

There was a vague yet distinct undercurrent within all the settlements, although it was perhaps weakest in Con Den Fetch, that was hard to explain or put a finger to, and the dwarfs of the various settlements would have been hard put to try to get it into words.

Brian, more sensitive to it than most, only knew it as a dim ache somewhere near the pit of his stomach, and that it grew stronger at times, when he listened to the tales of Chinby. He might have called it fear, but it was only the very hazy shadow of fear, for there was nothing really material about it, other than the most roundabout clues, such as dealing with the threat of beast raiders attacking a work party when overground.

Still, Chinby had struck a raw nerve deep inside him, and Brian wasn't sure he was ready to have it explained to him, lest he be made aware of the lurking shadow that hovered near the borders of his senses.

Senja, like Brian, was a believer in Chinby's tales, and knew, as secretly as all true beliefs are known, that the odd-sounding names and far-off stories of war, or the other ancient dwarf heroes, were all history, and had happened exactly as the blind dwarf said. She could not explain how she knew, or why, other than the vaguest notion that she had been there to see the sights Chinby described, and had known, or perhaps even been, some of the characters he told of.

Members of her family laughed openly at her odd ideas, and teased her endlessly about the things she said, until at last, she no longer spoke to anyone but Chinby of the beliefs she held in her heart. He was the only one she had to confide in, and she longed to see him after he would be absent for great lengths of time; then he would abruptly appear out of nowhere, astounding everyone with his ability to avoid all detection in going and coming.

Chinby told her he came by the old Deep Home Highway that ran from the far Easterlands all the way to the Roaring, and she believed him. He told her that he would show her his door one day, when the time was right, and that that time was coming soon, and he would have much to tell her of various events, and that she would be called upon to do many things that might possibly be frightening to her, but would be necessary, to complete a most important task, one that would carry the entire fate of dwarfdom on its successful completion.

Senja was an unusual lane, in that she was often better at the spanner games than the spanners themselves, and she turned many heads with her rather straightforward behavior, especially among the lanins of the delving, for they all chided her, and told her she would never be able to make a proper halfing, because no spanner would take such a mate. This never troubled Senja, for she never found anything interesting in the lifestyles of her mother or the other lanins, and always preferred the more active role reserved for the spanners and dwarfs.

That had been one of the reasons Brian had been so attracted to her upon one of his first visits to Con Den Fetch, when he had gone with his father to visit a distant cousin who made his home in that delving.

She had been present at a ritual day ceremony, and twice Brian had danced with her during the long afternoon feast celebration, and she had completely baffled him with her quick replies and not at all shy glance. She questioned him about everything that went on in Den'Lin Fetch, and his trips overground, and all the hundred other things that made up his day.

Senja had even asked him about the old tales she said she had heard, and wondered what he thought of them, or if there was any truth to them at all. He had answered her cautiously, not knowing whether she was baiting him or if her reasons were of a more serious nature.

"I have heard that there was once a colony, long ago, in Deep Home. Roundhat himself was the Elder, and they say it was the most glorious of all times for our kindred. Have you heard that story?"

Brian weakly admitted that he had.

"You don't seem to have much to say of it? Are you not interested in such goings-on?"

"Oh yes, they tell me that it was indeed a grand time. I have heard that their feast days often lasted a week at a time, and that it's said Roundhat once danced an entire day to the band, and danced with every single lane and lanin in Deep Home."

"I have heard that," agreed Senja. "And it is said that there is an underground highway from Deep Home that stretches all the way to the Sea of Roaring."

Brian was somewhat shocked to find another soul so interested in the ancient history and lore of Roundhat, and the ancient legends and tales of dwarfdom. That she was a lane mattered little to him, for outside of Chinby, there were no others that he could speak freely to of the deeper thoughts that troubled him, or the restlessness that made it impossible for him to settle into the normal routine of a responsible dwarf.

He feared to say too much, yet he longed desperately to speak to someone of his thoughts who wouldn't tease him or upbraid him for his outlandish ideas.

He showed her the small hammer and chisel that never left his side.

"These are the keys to that highway," he confided, his heart pounding heavily in his throat.

He waited for her to laugh, ready to retreat into a more neutral line of idle chatter, such as he knew the other lanes were partial to, of sewing or mending, or any of the other things that occupied their rather limited lives.

"Let me see! Let's walk out to the tables, and stop all this bobbing up and down!"

He had been slightly surprised to find a lane who didn't make an issue of the feast days and the dancing, but didn't object, and followed Senja to one of the many long tables laden with food and drink, and there he handed her the two small tools that Chinby had entrusted to him.

A slight smile came over her features, and he at once thought that she was going to make fun of the tiny hammer and chisel, but she handed them back, evidently satisfied.

"I have heard that these were in existence. It was said that they were carried by one among us, and given to a certain dwarf for safekeeping, and that one day they would be called upon to do great deeds."

Not wanting to mention Chinby by name, and not knowing whether to trust this brash lane or not, Brian put the precious tools away.

"They may prove to be handy one day," he conceded,

55

"although I hear from my friends that they are too small to be of much use to a dwarf in his work."

"It depends on what his work is," corrected Senja. "If it is cutting and shaping stone, they would hardly survive."

She smiled oddly at Brian before going on.

"But if they were to be used to find a hidden doorway, or the highway to the sea, then they are the only tools that would be of use."

Brian, thoroughly confused, and wishing desperately for Chinby, fell into an embarrassed silence, unable to tell if he had said too much already, or if he should quietly excuse himself and go. And that did not suit him either, for he was already infatuated with the outspoken lane, and found her company very pleasing, even with the discomfort she was creating with her open smiles and oddly knowing talk, as if she had some mysterious way of reading his mind.

Neither of them had mentioned Chinby by name, and Brian felt as though he would be breaking a trust to do so, for he grew tired of having to defend the old dwarf to his other friends, or family, and he had known Senja only a short while, and did not feel like having to go into long explanations to an almost complete stranger, no matter how much he was drawn to her, for Chinby was hard to explain, and he wasn't even sure himself why he felt as he did.

Senja seemed to feel many things in common, but as any good dwarf would, they took their time in forming their opinions, and wanted time to mull over these new thoughts and ideas, and to ponder the many sides of the questions that were aroused within them.

Brian's father had stayed on two days after the feast day, and he had seen Senja two more times, although they had no opportunity to talk further, or exchange more than polite greetings.

They returned to Den'Lin Fetch the following morning, and Brian went through the odd sensation of missing the young, outspoken lane, almost from the moment they were beyond the outer gates of the delving.

Senja, having listened to the endless stories of Chinby, knew all about the dwarf who carried the small elfish-wrought tools that were to find the path to the old settlements of dwarfdom, and that were to play a major role in the battle to open the way to rid the delvings, and all the other settlements as well, of the beast hordes that sometimes raided the dwarfish lands.

Chinby had told Senja of the terrible wars that were being waged, and had been waged, and the lane listened, stricken with the gory histories. They all seemed so remote to her, safe in Con Den Fetch, and it was hard for her to conceive of such terrible affairs, yet she believed her friend, and did not doubt that the truth of the matter was exactly as he stated it.

Con Den Fetch was a very provincial settlement, and had not many visitors from the other delvings, with the rare exception of travelers from Den'Lin Fetch, and the dwarfs there were very set in their ways, and dearly loved the creature comforts, which were many, and very seldom did any of the dwarfs there ever venture beyond their own front gates.

One of the rare times that had happened, the harvest party had run into a band of their kinsmen from Den'Lin Fetch, under heavy attack from a huge pack of the beasts.

They had helped their cousins to drive off the invaders, and gone home to report the dreadful state of affairs beyond their own delving borders, and it was resolved in council that they would venture no farther than necessary to gather crops and supplies, and that they would halt the journeys that might take them into danger of running across any of the beast packs that somehow always seemed to be hunting near the borders.

Den'Lin Fetch was constantly on the path of the raiders, and the delving of Senja's kin decided that it would be wisest to let that strange settlement take care of its own.

The feeling was, that if the dwarfs of Den'Lin Fetch were willing to run the risk of living so close to the Easterland borders, then they should be the only ones responsible for dealing with the consequences of their actions. Their cousins in Con Den Fetch could not be expected to always be on hand to bail out any of those dwarfs from a settlement that insisted on living in such a wild place, and risking such great dangers.

Senja had always secretly wanted to live in that delving, and had hoped, from time to time, to be able to get permission from her father to visit their many kinsmen that lived there. He was a stern figure, who always wanted spanners, but had gotten only Senja, and he was in no way in agreement with her desire to visit the outpost delving of Den'Lin Fetch.

"You'll never set foot in the likes of such a horrible place," he said angrily upon hearing her impassioned plea to be allowed to visit.

She did not mention Brian, or her wish to see him again, but only stated that she had always heard it was a beautiful delving, and that it would be interesting to see.

"But what's horrible about it, Father? I hear it has wonderful stone work, and they say the river runs right through the center of the Council Halfing. It's supposed to be one of the most beautiful in all dwarfdom."

"Nonsense, Senja! It's a mere crude shelter, compared to our own home. I don't know who's been filling you full of such mulhash stories, but I'd wager it was that old blind fool you insist on bringing to dinner."

"He's no fool, Father. He's one of the old heroes. You should be ashamed of yourself!"

"Hero or no, he eats my food, then fills your ears with enough misinformation to land you in a spot of trouble if you listened or paid heed. His stories are amusing enough, but they're merely that. I don't mind listening to him over dinner, and I admit he does spin a yarn well."

"They're not yarns, they're the histories! Our histories!"

Senja's father had a way of agreeing with her whenever she became angry. He never knew what to do when that happened, and was afraid to scold her, for fear she might break down and cry, as her mother often did. When that happened, he was always helpless to explain himself or try to defend what he said, and it always ended up with Senja's lanin getting her own way.

He was determined, however, no matter how angry she got, or how hard she cried, not to give in to let Senja visit the delving of Den'Lin Fetch. There were no good prospects for a match there, and he was totally unwilling ever to think of his only lane going there to live, which she would surely have to do, were she to meet a spanner from that settlement.

"Father, all I want to do is see it! Brian and his father have visited Con Den Fetch on two occasions now, so I don't see that it's so dangerous. They always come and go, with no one but the two of them."

"They're foolish, is what they are. If they had a lick of sense about them, they'd travel in a group. It's not safe outside our gates. There's no end to the beast packs there on the border, and it's utter nonsense, those two traveling alone."

"I think they're brave, is what I think!" exploded Senja. "At

58

least they're not afraid to stick their noses out beyond their own front doors!"

"That's enough, dear," soothed Senja's lanin, who always intervened whenever things got too hot for her husband to handle.

She didn't really profess to understand the young lane, but she sensed that it was no good for the two of them to fight, so she treated Senja as one might treat a somewhat fearsome object, hoping to mollify her and keep her satisfied enough to calm down, and not go into the raging fits she would sometimes launch into.

And her lanin noted that the biggest part of the problem had begun after the first visits of the old blind dwarf they called Chinby. Senja's lanin was sure they could trace the cause of all their troubles to that one, unfortunate source.

Reading Between the Lines

SENJA looked over the small, carefully printed note once more, her brow furrowed in deep thought.

"Be at our ancient door to the Deep Home Highway tonight after supper," it read, and was signed with Chinby's name.

She had not dreamed that there would come a time so soon that she would be asked to do anything more than simply listen to his yarns, or defend him to her friends, and she was clearly not expecting anything of this nature. It was one thing to sit and talk, and dream of the old bygone glories of dwarfdom, but another thing entirely when it came to the actual going about of trying to recapture the wonderful times that were no more than ancient lore to her.

Doing and talking were two different things, she decided, and she wasn't fully sure that it would be the best thing for her to disappear suddenly, to go away with Chinby, and leave no word of explanations for her father and mother. She disagreed with their views, and knew that the delving of Con Den Fetch lived in an atmosphere of strict isolation as much as possible, and that there was more to the business than simply being a good seamstress, or potter, or halfing wife.

She knew those things, yet she wasn't sure what exactly it was that was missing, or how to go about filling up the emptiness she felt.

That had all changed when Chinby came and she began to listen to his magical tales of the old delvings of their forefathers, and of all the grand schemes and plans, and as long as the blind dwarf was around to answer her questions and reassure her, Senja was willing to let herself believe that there was a destiny that dwarfkind was to fulfill, and that it would need her assistance in doing so.

When he was gone, her resolve wavered, and she was faced with the unpleasant task of trying to decide on her own what was the best thing to do, or what direction to move in.

Chinby had always been direct, and not at all stern with her, which was one of the reasons that she liked the old dwarf so well, because he was such a contrast to her father, and left some of the decisions up to her, rather than telling her what she had to do or not do.

Now the moment had come when Chinby was saying it was time to take action, and she was hesitating, partially from fear, and partially from rebelling at having anyone make her choices for her.

It had all sounded wonderful and romantic when Chinby spoke of the movement that was afoot that would help reunite all dwarfdom, even those strange beings who were the deep wood dwarfs, the Carbens, who lived only half belowground. Chinby spoke of the wonders of the races of Deep Home, and of the unions there were then, of dwarfdom and all other kinds.

That had been unsettling at first, to think of having anything to do with the likes of elves, or animal clans, or any of the others. The old dwarf spoke of the high race of men, who were taller than elves, and fair to look upon, and of beings who were much like mankind, but much older, and much more powerful.

"Who are they, Chinby? Where do they come from?"

"They're Elders, of a sort," replied the old dwarf elusively.

"Are they friendly?"

"They are one with all kinds, Senja. They have been since the Beginning, and are all things."

"But how could that be? You say they are mankind?"

"They are, but more. You shall see for yourself one day."

"I have heard from you that mankind has done some evil things."

"As have we all, my dear, at one time or another."

"The dwarfs have never done those things you said that men have done."

"We must not overlook the dwarf Carben, who amassed his following and took by force the delvings of the Western clans."

"But those are the ones who live overground now. They're not really dwarfs."

"Yet they were, at one time. And I think if we look closely enough, we'll find they still are yet."

"No one of our clans would ever have anything to do with them, after their treachery."

"I have been among them," said Chinby softly. "I think they have lived long in the sorrow of what Carben created, with all his fancy talk, and brave promises of a delving that would unite all dwarfs, for all time."

Senja gasped, looking at her friend with a new interest. She had known he had been among many delvings of dwarfdom, but it had never occurred to her that this old, fragile-looking blind dwarf would have been able to find, much less visit, the settlements of the overground half-dwarfs that dwelled in the innermost regions of the vast forest lands that bordered the Dark Hills and led on to the rocky coasts of the East Roaring.

"Carben has gone to the Tombs many years since, and I think his clan has been slowly dwindling away, little by little. Some of those dwarfs there have returned to their homes of old, although it's not an easy thing to do. They have found much difficulty in these later years. There is much unrest among them."

"There should be unrest," snapped Senja. "After what they've done, they should be left there, to rot!"

"Hardly, daughter. I think we shall find strong allies among those clans of Carben when we travel through on our journey. I'm sure there will be many there that will gladly join ranks, to help us along with our little errand."

"What errand is that, Chinby? What journey?"

"The journey I have been telling you of all along, Senja. You have not been hearing all I have to say to you."

"I've listened, Chinby. But what journey?"

"There is coming a time when we will be moving to the Roaring, to meet those from across the water. They are coming to seek our aid, and we shall have to stand together if we are to continue on as we have."

Senja shook her head, a puzzled frown crossing her broad brow.

"Sometimes I don't know what to make of you, old one. I begin to think perhaps you are old, and forget the things you speak of. Everyone says I should take your stories for simple tales to amuse a youngster."

"And how do you take me?" asked the old dwarf, a thin smile on his lips.

"I don't know."

"That's honestly said. I can continue on with that. And I think that as time goes on, you'll find the truth of what I speak says everything much better than long explanations on my part, which would only confuse you. It is not time for me to tell you everything, but there will be a day when you will have all your answers."

That day had come for Senja on the morning she received the brief message from her friend, who had been absent six months or more. She had had no word until the parcel arrived, and had begun to think that the blind dwarf lore master had finally disappeared from her life, as her father told her he would.

"It's no good you going on about this, Senja. Sooner or later this precious Chinby of yours will take a powder for parts unknown, probably with half our goods with him, and that will be the end of that."

She had argued, but with each passing day that Chinby was gone, her resolve slipped, until at last she was no longer sure. And not an hour had passed that she had not agonized over his disappearance, and at last she had grown angry at him for deserting her.

When her friends came by her halfing to torment her about the blind dwarf's disappearance, she pretended she knew nothing of what they were talking about.

"So your old fool finally left you dangling, did he? After all those promises, too. What a shame."

"I think Senja had in mind to take him home to keep for a lap pet, from the way she doted over him."

"Too old for that," chided another. "He probably wasn't blind at all, anyhow. How else could he have known all the things he knows, and been to all the places he goes? I think it's just a trick to get sympathy and handouts."

"You're probably right," agreed Senja viciously, although she kept her voice under control. "You're probably all right, and I have no idea where he's gotten to, and I don't care. I have other, more important things to do than worry about the whereabouts of some blind old fool like that."

This had startled her friends somewhat, and they hated to lose any fun they had with teasing her about Chinby.

"You've changed your tune quick enough. I thought you liked him."

"It was a mistake. My father was right. We're all better off with him gone. I wouldn't be a bit surprised if we never caught sight of him again."

Feeling her slip beyond their grasp, they tried one last play.

"I wouldn't be so sure of that," said one lightly. "There's word out that he's been seen at the outer gates, not more than half an hour ago."

Senja's heart leapt into her throat, but she remembered in time that Chinby never came to Con Den Fetch by a road he would be seen on. He always managed to unsettle everyone by just appearing, and Senja knew from the tone of his note that the old Deep Home Highway ran directly beneath the kellers of Con Den Fetch, and that Chinby was familiar with that path, and used it in his travels.

Of all the times he had visited their delving, he had never once been spotted by the guards who were left to secure the outer gates that led overground, and no one had ever seen the old dwarf aboveground traveling his rounds, which took him to all portions of the known delvings, and beyond.

"Good news for you, Senja. Now you can listen to him again, and tell us all his yarns about all those things he talks of."

She had caught herself, and did not reply, but nodded her head sagely.

"Then we shall see what he has to offer this time. I have grown bored, and could use more amusement."

"It didn't sound that way when you told us that you were

both going to the Roaring Sea, on a journey that would last for a long time, to find our other cousins who live across the water!"

"As if anyone *did* live there! I've never heard anything more unbelievable in my life."

"All that live across that sea are animals, and not very nice ones, at that."

Senja let her friends go on, hoping they would tire of baiting her, and leave.

She always came back down to the fact that she truly wanted to believe Chinby more than anything in the world, and wanted what he said to be true.

Glancing from one to the other of the familiar faces, she felt a total stranger in a hostile land, and suddenly she knew that she was indeed very lonely, although she was among others known to her for as long as she had lived.

That was a sad thing for her to come to grips with, and it made her feel even worse when she returned to her halfing to help her lanin prepare the midday meal for her father. The kind old face was the same that Senja had seen from almost the very moment she had been born, but again, she felt the separation, and the cold finger of loneliness that touched her very heart, and she shuddered, despite the heat of the kitchen, where they were baking the dwarfcakes her father loved so well.

"Do you think Father would mind very much if I were to marry? And move to another delving?"

Her mother, snow-white hair rolled tightly into a bun behind her head, clucked noisily.

"There'll be plenty of time for that later, Senja. You're much too young to be thinking of starting your own halfing yet. And I haven't seen a suitable dwarf among the lot who have come calling on you."

"There's always Brian Brandigore," said Senja gently, testing the reaction that would bring.

The old lanin shrieked, and threw her hands in the air.

"You'll give me a bad heart, talking like that! Why, he lives on the border, in that uncivilized hole they call a delving! And no manners to speak of at all."

"I thought you liked him."

"Oh, I like him, right enough, he and that father of his, too. But I like them in Den'Lin Fetch, bless their souls, and out of our hair."

64

She clucked her tongue again, wagging a finger at Senja.

"Don't you let your father hear you talking like this. He has enough troubles on his mind, trying to find that finger of ore in that lower shaft."

"He told me he liked Brian," went on Senja, taking out some of her anger at her friends on her lanin.

"Liking is one thing, but matching with one from Den'Lin Fetch is nothing but sheer nonsense! Why, we haven't had a match from that delving since your Great-Aunt Eula ran away with that smithy there, more's the pity for us, because now we have to treat their children just as if nothing had ever happened. I guess that's the only reason we have anything to do with those from Den'Lin Fetch at all."

"It sounds like an exciting life," offered Senja.

Her mother clutched her heart with one hand, and ran the other across her forehead, mopping it with her apron.

"You'll be the death of me yet, Senja. I'll swear, I don't know what goes through your head sometimes." She stamped her foot down hard, and snorted. "Exciting, indeed! I guess if you call living with barbarians exciting, it is, well enough. And they have to send guard patrols out with them every time they go overground for wood or food. I can't imagine for the life of me why they go on doing it. I'd just pick up and move back to where it was safe and I didn't have to always have to think of one of those beast packs breathing down my neck."

"We have those beast packs outside Con Den Fetch, too, Mother. They're everywhere now."

"Not as bad, you snippity thing! We may have a few strays here, but I'll wager you they come from Den'Lin Fetch. I wouldn't be a bit surprised if they didn't follow along after that young Brandigore and his father when they first began to visit us."

Senja's reply was lost in the noise of the arrival of her father.

"What's for the table, dear?" he called in his best-mannered voice, noticing that his wife and daughter had that look on their faces of two people having what he would call "a serious chat."

"You sit," ordered Senja's mother, and she began to bustle about the table, making a great deal more noise than was necessary, and laying out the plates for the meal.

"What would you think, Father, if I were to say I might be matched to Brian?"

Senja could not resist delighting in watching her father begin to fidget, turning red from his collar slowly upward, until the coloring reached his nose.

"Mulhash, is what I'd say, if you were asking me seriously, which I take it you're not. I don't think my own flesh and blood would be dense enough to ever even consider a match such as that."

He pounded a fist down onto the table, setting all the plates to dancing in the air, and causing her mother's eyelids to flutter rapidly, and her hands to dart to the sideboard for support.

"I told her not to bother you with such nonsense," chided her mother, "but she seems determined to put us both in an early grave."

"No such thing, Mother," replied Senja, laying one of the fresh-baked dwarfcakes before her father, ignoring his icy stare.

"Surely you're not serious!" he bellowed at last, pounding the table again, causing the still steaming dwarfcake to flip over twice in midair before landing back on his plate.

"I'm as serious as can be," insisted Senja. "And tonight I'm going to meet Chinby at our usual meeting place, and go with him to the Roaring Sea. Brian is to meet me there."

A slow look of bewilderment crept across her father's face, then it was replaced with an almost smile.

"You're at your jokes again! She's at her old jokes again, Mother! See? Look at that smile."

Senja, having satisfied her own conscience by telling her mother and father the truth as to her intentions, felt the guilt begin to leave her, and she decided then and there that that was exactly the course of action she was going to follow. She had told them the truth, and it was up to them to believe her or not, but she had spoken her mind, and now was relieved of the burden that had troubled her when she got the message from Chinby, which was how she was to tell her parents of her plans, and yet still be able to carry them through without them attempting to stop her.

Senja hurried through the meal, barely eating anything, which upset her mother, but she was anxious to see to the things she would be needing to take with her. Chinby had left all up to her, it seemed, from the telling of her parents, who

66

had to be told something, for they were, after all, the ones who had raised her, to the matter of what to take along on a journey that was beyond her wildest imagination.

Somewhere in the time from meeting her friends to the telling of her parents, she had decided that she would, no matter what the risk, go with Chinby if he showed up at their meeting place in the kellers of Con Den Fetch.

And the idea of Brian Brandigore somehow fascinated her, although she could not say exactly why, or why she had suddenly made the statement that she was going to be his marriage partner.

Chinby had never so much as openly said it, but along with the rest of his sometimes rambling tales, one had to be able to read between the lines.

Down to the River

BRIAN Brandigore became a baffling mystery to the delving of Den'Lin Fetch, and every halfing was alive with the talk of his disappearance. It was even rumored that the young dwarf had gone off in company with an elf, which was in itself enough of a disgrace to his family, but it was said that this particular elf had all the knowledge of the secret ways of Den'Lin Fetch, and that it would be necessary for the delving to redo all its outer gates, and block up the lower kellers in case that information ever fell into the wrong hands.

The delving was up in arms, and at the Council Halfing, it was decided that work would begin immediately to seal off the lower levels where Brian was in the habit of spending long hours of his time, and his father volunteered to do the work himself.

The old dwarf was heartbroken beyond consoling, although everyone hastened to reassure him that it wasn't his fault, and that the young spanner had fallen under the thrall of Chinby, the blind lore master, and there was where the guilt should be laid.

Brian's lanin spent hours crying into her needlework, and would not go out on ritual days, for fear of having to face her neighbors.

It was a most unpleasant time for the elder Brandigores, and not long after Brian had gone, word had come to them that Senja, of Con Den Fetch, had vanished also, another innocent victim, supposedly, of Chinby.

Brian, not knowing how to break the word of his departure to his family or friends, had talked the matter over at length with Shanon, and finally arrived at the conclusion that if they were simply to go, it would be easier in the long run than to try to explain their errand, or where it was they were off to.

"I should leave word," insisted Brian for the tenth time, struggling with his conscience.

"Of course," agreed Shanon. "But the elfish code always says that any message we leave should never tell the direction we're bound. Bad luck!"

"You don't think I should tell them we're going to the sea?"

"I wouldn't," argued the elf. "Too much risk of being followed. And what would we be able to tell anyone if they were to start questioning us?"

"I could tell them I was going after Senja!"

"A wonderful romance, Brian. But think of what her father would say if he thought she was running away with one of you borderland dwarfs? That might cause more hard feelings than any other story you could tell."

"Besides, how would they ever find us, Shanon? There's no danger of anyone coming after us once we're in the old shafts to the river. You're the only one, except for Chinby, that knows about those tunnels."

"It's a long way to the Roaring, according to what Chinby said. I don't know if we'll be able to keep to the river all the way. And I don't have any great desire to stay underground as long as it might take us to finish this journey."

"But how else will we get there, if we don't follow the river? I don't have any idea how you'd go about getting all the way from here to the sea across ground."

"Nor do I, but I have an idea that we might find some clues in Erin Frey, if we were to look. I think I remember seeing some old charts in a book room there once. It didn't mean anything at the time, because I never thought I'd be needing anything of that nature."

"Where is Erin Frey?"

"Not far from where Chinby took me to make those tools. That delving wasn't a great distance from Erin Frey."

Brian hesitated.

"I don't know. I hate just to vanish without a single word."

"You can leave a note. Just don't spell it out as to exactly what you'll be doing."

"I don't have any idea of what I'll be doing," corrected Brian. "I wish I did."

"Going after Senja," added Shanon. "That's a good enough reason for you. And I'm going along to see the Sea of Roaring, and to get some fresh air aboveground for a while."

"I should tell my father," went on Brian. "He'll never forgive me if I don't."

"He'll never forgive you if you do, my friend. You'll only hurt him more, going off on a half-mulled notion like this. I'm sure he had ideas of you following with his craft, and settling down in Den'Lin Fetch, with a nice homegrown lane."

"How did you tell your father you were going?" asked Brian suddenly. "I'm sure he was curious as to your leaving."

"My father was dead long before," said Shanon softly.

Brian looked more closely at his new friend.

"I'm sorry for that, Shanon."

"Don't be. My father was hardly ever at home when I was growing up. He was always up one river or down another, and we heard from him whenever he got close enough to our dane to stop."

"What happened to him?"

"I don't know exactly. He was gone for a long time, and my mother never told me more than odd news of him. She said he'd gone off with a company of wood elves, up in the high country along the Last Lands, and was never heard from again. I don't know whether it was true, or something my mother made up to tell me."

Brian had a difficult time imagining so loose a family with a father always away, and a settlement so unorganized as to allow all such carrying-on. It was difficult for him to think of a day without his father shuffling in to eat his hurried breakfast, on his way to his forge, or the daily routine of his lanin spinning her yarn to make the wonderful cloaks and vests. He concluded his thoughts with the idea that there must be more to an elf than he thought, and that not everyone was the same.

It still plagued him to think he would have to leave Den'Lin Fetch without a word, until he at last decided to write a farewell note and leave it at one of the meeting trees overground where the wood parties assembled when they went to collect wood or food.

Shanon agreed that it would be all right, provided he didn't give out too much specific information.

"Just let them know you're safe, and will be gone for a space of time. That should suffice."

After much phrasing and rephrasing, Brian at last decided on a brief message.

Dear Father and Mother,
Please do not worry, as I have gone on an errand for a friend of mine. It would not be wise to say too much at this point, since I do not know exactly how long I am to be gone, or how far I shall travel. Be of good cheer, and I will see you next when I am able.

Your obedient
Brian

Shanon thought it was somewhat overdrawn, but an elfnote and a dwarfnote were obviously two different things entirely, and rather than hurt Brian's feelings, he said nothing, and even agreed to take the message himself, so that Brian wouldn't run the risk of being spotted and questioned.

It was already past time for the dwarf to be back at his halfing, and he was sure that his mother was beginning to wonder by now why he had not had his late-night tea and cake, as was his habit when returning from one of his long sojourns in the kellers of the delving.

After Shanon was gone on his errand, Brian had a brief while to think of what it was he was embarking upon, and there in the gloom of the elfmoon, half shaded by his cloak, second thoughts began to occur.

He thought at once of following the elf out to the meeting tree, and getting the note back, but then he remembered Senja, and that she would be at the sea with Chinby, according to the message that he had had through Shanon.

The thought occurred to him then that he only had Shanon's

word that those messages had been from Chinby, and had it not been for the fact that they had been in high dwarfish, he would have been more suspicious than he was. The elf said he understood none of the dwarf runes, and Brian believed him, or told himself that he did.

He realized that he was looking for any excuse to delay going, or perhaps even put it off altogether, if it could be done without too much loss of face.

The thought of leaving Den'Lin Fetch, perhaps forever, began to frighten him, for the reality of the trip was upon him, and it was not one of a dwarf's traits to do things on the spur of the moment, without a long and thorough preparation.

Remembering a dozen things that he needed, Brian began the list again in his head, and finding he had nothing at all with him but the two small tools, he was on the verge of trying to sneak back to his halfing to gather up some other items to take with him on this journey, when Shanon returned, startling him.

"Where are you off to, Brian? I've delivered your note. There's nothing more for us to do now but get a start."

"I've got to pick up some things from my halfing, Shanon. I can't just set off without even so much as a decent knapsack, and a bow, or a change of vests."

Shanon shook his head vigorously.

"If you go back now, you'll never leave, Brian. It's now, or we forget the trip, and Senja, and Chinby, and the sea. That's perfectly all right by me, although I don't doubt but that there will be a disappointed lane at the Roaring if you don't show up."

"Why all the sudden interest in my going? A few hours ago you were ready to drop the whole affair."

"Elves are good at changing their minds, Brian. I think we ought to go now, just for the sheer thrill of a trip. And I know where you can get plenty of supplies for a journey, if you don't mind elfish goods. At least you won't have to explain anything to anyone there, and we can get a good start, without a lot of hubbub."

"I don't mind explaining myself to my own kin, but how am I to explain a dwarf outfitted as an elf?"

"You'll be welcomed by the elves, done up as such."

"I'm more worried about what I would say if I come on some of my own folk."

"They'll say what handsome equipment you have, and how

71

delightful a vest," teased Shanon, "and probably want to know where they can get one, as well."

"I don't know where my senses have gone," blustered Brian. "But I guess I must be as loony as they have accused me of being. All right! Let's get on with it. I've waited all this time until now not knowing what it was that was going to become of me, and now I've found out. Disappeared with an elf! I can hear it all now, and all the yammering it's going to cause, as well. There won't be any use in my ever bothering coming back here, after this."

"All the better," said Shanon cheerfully. "There must be a hundred places a lot more interesting, and not half so gloomy."

"Den'Lin Fetch is still my home, thank you. I haven't said anything against your settlement, or your family."

"No offense, Brian. I guess elves are just a more wandering lot. We change homes two or three times a year, just to keep from falling into a rut. I guess you dwarfs are a bit more stay-at-home."

"I guess we are," huffed Brian.

Shanon looked steadily into Brian's clear gaze, and his own blue eyes had turned a darker shade, flickering dimly in the shadowed light.

"This is the start of something that well may see neither one of us ever getting back here. But I think you'll make a good companion, Brian. Chinby spoke highly of you, and said that of all the dwarfs still left near the borders, you were the most likely one to ever replace Roundhat."

The elf extended a fine-boned hand.

"We'll shake hands to this alliance. The first of its kind in a long while, according to Chinby. It has been many a turning since elf and dwarf have banded together."

"Humph," snorted Brian. "I wouldn't call you and me a band! And I certainly wouldn't want to think that anyone else in Den'Lin Fetch would be caught dead thinking about what we're thinking about. Jeral and Jaran would hoot me out of the delving if I were to tell them what we're planning."

He snorted aloud again.

"Going to the sea, and hanging about with that old blind fool? You've lost what little brain you ever had," said Brian, imitating his friend Jeral.

"That's exactly why we're not going to tell anyone about our plan. It's too easy for us to be talked out of going, and I egin to wonder at my own reasons for allowing myself to be aught up in all this dwarfish to-do."

Shanon had taken his forest cap off, and twirled it around a inger.

"Still, I guess it's that, or spend the rest of my life wondering what it was I had the opportunity to see, and didn't."

He pulled the hat firmly back onto his head, covering the ong blond hair.

"Those are strange reasons, Shanon, for going. But I guess hat's the difference between us."

"You mean because you have a home and family, and I lon't?"

"Well, it seems that way, on the surface of it. You didn't lave to say your good-bye to anyone, and it doesn't sound as f there would be anything to hold you back."

Brian thought he might have struck a raw nerve, for the elf rowned a moment, but then his face cleared, and he laughed ightly.

"It does seem that way, doesn't it? And it was certainly asier for me, when it comes to it, to say my farewells. Yet an lf is just as fond of home as any dwarf, Brian. Those things lon't change, no matter who you are."

"You don't make it sound like that."

"I don't, because if I thought too long on it, I'd probably go ack, instead of going on with what I should be doing."

Brian, in no mood to be thinking too much about anything oo long, agreed.

"We should either make a start, or go on about our sepa-ate business, Shanon. I feel that this has been coming a long ime, and that Chinby knew what he was talking about vhen he told me all those old stories. It's true that he did aint a somewhat dim view of the elfish clans, but now that I ook back on those stories, I think it was me that put my own udgment on elfish behavior. You have shed much light on he subject, and I am indebted to you for it."

"As I am to you, Brian. It's as well we go on. You'll get to ee the old doorway you've been looking for all this time, too. Ind the odd thing, you weren't far from discovering it on our own. Those tools Chinby gave you would have opened it vith no trouble, but I wonder what you would have made of it f you had chanced across it."

"I'd have followed the river to Deep Home," answered rian, without hesitation.

"I guess you would have, at that. Still, it would have been a lonely find. Just like I discovered Erin Frey. It was too saddening at first, to sit and see all the beauty of it, and yet it was empty."

"Do you know what happened to them?"

Shanon shook his head.

"The Troubles, I suppose. There's a lot of elf lore that has to do with those times, but what it all comes to is that no one knows for certain exactly what happened, except that a huge number of elves crossed the Roaring, trying to find lands that were safe to dwell in."

"I guess it's the same as any lore. That's the way I found my own. Chinby said that some of my ancient kin had crossed the sea, but I hardly knew the meaning of it, until a short while ago. Now it looks as if we're going to discover some of this lore for ourselves, if we make it as far as we're speaking of going."

"We'll make it, Brian. Never let yourself doubt that. Between the two of us, we should be able to manage anything."

"Not a single lick of good sense to be had between us," huffed Brian. "Otherwise, we'd have forgotten this plan as soon as it had ever been mentioned."

The elf studied his new friend steadily.

"Not to amount to more than I could put in my hat. And that's the beauty of it. I feel as though I'm finally doing something worthwhile, and it seems to be the most outrageous nonsense when you try to look at it through the eyes of a normal elf or dwarf."

Brian had risen, stretching himself.

"I'm going to fall asleep soon if I don't look to my feet. I'm anxious to see these shafts that you use as a back way to a dwarf keller. Show me how you've been coming among us without our spotting you."

Shanon laughed.

"It's no mean feat, being able to get into a dwarf delving. I've seen some tight-kept secrets, but dwarf doings are among the most closely guarded I've ever come across."

"Evidently not close enough," blustered Brian.

"I only found these things because I had a teacher who was dwarfish," comforted Shanon. "Without him to teach me, I never would have dreamed of half these things that he showed me."

And saying, Shanon reached out a hand and touched the

74

solid stone beside Brian, tapping lightly with his fingers. It was a short tattoo, two long taps and a short, and right before them the entire face of the rock began to slide noiselessly back, revealing a new damp smell, of wet stone, and the river, and there was a small, faraway sound of rushing water.

Brian's eyes widened, and his heart was racing wildly.

"I've been looking for this ever since Chinby gave me the tools and told me of the old shafts. I never dreamed I'd be shown how to reach it by an elf."

"The key is unimportant, when you find it works the lock. However we open the door is a good way, so long as we reach the other side."

The dwarf had stepped through the opening of the outlined doorway, and once beyond the old keller wall, he realized that the tunnel he was now in led even farther downward, toward the very core of the earth.

The smell was of very old mountain roots, and musty tunnels that had not been used in a great while, with the odd exception of a wandering elf, who had gone to and fro on the most ancient of dwarfish highways, the river from Deep Home, which led on through the deepest heart of the hills and forests, on to the coast, so far away it seemed impossible ever to be able to reach it.

Brian turned to ask the elf a question, and found, to his surprise, that where the opening had been, there was nothing but a slate-gray wall once more, as if it had never been disturbed.

"We're on our way," said Shanon. "The first doorstep is done with, and there's nothing for it now but to go on."

The elf stepped out quickly toward the noise of the rushing water, and Brian, pausing now and again to study the ancient tunnel he found himself in, hurried along behind.

At the sudden rounding of a tall cross-shaft, the smell and noise of the water grew greater, and Brian almost pitched headlong into the swift-running current that cut through the smooth stone. One moment there had been solid floor, then there was the river.

"Our transport," shouted Shanon over the noise of the river, pointing at two keg halves bobbing merrily on the flow of the current.

Brian sighed, and remembered all the tales Chinby had told of the old days, and the escapes made in barrels just such

75

as these. It was as if all the ancient histories of dwarfdom had come alive off the pages of the lore books, and burst into flame in the pounding of his racing heart.

An odd ripple of sadness passed over him, but quickly faded, as the old Brian of Den'Lin Fetch disappeared, to be replaced by a new Brian, on his way to the very roots of all that was dwarfish, in Deep Home.

And beside him, far within his own thoughts, was the elf, Shanon, who was to be his close companion for the rest of his long and very eventful life.

ANCIENT DANES
OF ELFDOM

Mathiny

AS he had promised, Shanon planned to lead Brian into the old elfish dane of Erin Frey, to equip them with the necessities for a trip such as they were embarking upon.

The elf had not taken into account the swift flow of the river, and the two of them had had to struggle slowly along, straining and sweating, by pulling on the laid rope lines that ran along the smooth walls, bolted every so often, for the help of those going upriver. At times, they were able to paddle the small, sturdy boats, when the waterway widened into a low tunnel and the current ran slower.

They passed through many grottoes that seemed to stretch on for miles, lit by elfmoons that had been placed there in the long-forgotten past, casting eerie shadows on the face of the deep black water and the worn smoothness of the moss-covered tunnels.

It was in one such vast underground cave that Brian began to notice the odd ripples that had started to follow along behind his keg boat, staying just out of reach, speeding up when he sped up, and slowing down when he slacked off on his oar strokes.

He called out softly to Shanon.

"I think there's something in here with us!" he hissed, his heart pounding.

It was not a pleasant thought to be trapped down in the underground river with an unknown assailant.

Shanon's tinkling laughter echoed wildly about the chamber.

"I should hope we're being followed," he barked, getting his breath. "Those are the dwarfish watchdogs. It wouldn't do to let just anyone in here, going back and forth between the delvings that were laid out on the river. You should have read your lore a little more carefully. That's a fine thing, to have to be schooled in your own doings by an elf."

Brian blustered loudly.

"No one ever got around to telling me all these things. It seems Chinby spent more time in your instruction than he did mine. All I knew was that there were shafts, and the river. All the rest has been news to me."

"Chinby gave me warning about the watchers. He said they have been here for as long as the river, and the ancient dwarf lords made friends with them. I'm a water elf myself, so it's no unusual thing for me to get to know how to talk to them, and let them know I mean them no harm."

"Did Chinby say any more than that? Or was he his usual tight-mouthed self?"

"Only that he knew there was a band of raiders that found Deep Home once, and planned to plunder all the treasure there. They found the river, and knowing something of dwarfs, they knew there would be more delvings along the water. They loaded all the booty they could carry on rafts, and set off down this way."

Shanon paused, looking over his shoulder at the bubbles that followed along after them almost lazily.

"And that was an end of the raiders. There was never any sign of them, or their rafts of booty, although Chinby seemed to think it all returned to its rightful place, in Deep Home. He said that story has been repeated over again, endlessly, since the old delvings have fallen empty."

"I don't know why someone hasn't found them, and resettled. I think it would be a great honor to dwell in the house of my forefathers."

"I don't know," said the elf slowly. "I visit Erin Frey often enough, but it is too sad to think of trying to live there. All the elves I know of think the same. There's something a little forbidding about it."

"How do you mean?"

"It's hard to explain, Brian. I guess as close as I can come is to say that when Erin Frey was deserted, elfdom was at its peak. All the Elders of the water and wood folk dwelled together in harmony, and there was a beauty there that was partly because the elves were at peace. But then the time came when wood elf and water elf split apart and went their separate ways. It is that way still, only worse. I don't think

79

anyone will be able to stay in Erin Frey until the two clans are as one again."

"Sounds exactly like a dwarf tale to me," mumbled Brian, having to row harder to keep up with the deft elf, who was handy with boats, and who propelled himself easily along. "Chinby spoke of the deep wood dwarfs, who left the earth delvings, and the others, who did not wish to be too near the borders, and the beasts that have begun coming out of the ice fields. With one thing and another, it's been pretty much as you've described your elves, all divided among ourselves, and everyone out to see to it that no one is getting anything more than their share."

Shanon laughed bitterly.

"The thing of it is, no one ended up with anything. The wood elves thought they'd get more for themselves by becoming a separate clan, but come to find out, they only ended up with what they had to begin with. Same with my kin. Turns out the wood elf is exceptionally good at fashioning shelter, and fancy furniture, and decorations, and the water elf is more at home with cloth and spinning, and boats. One without the other is like only half a partnership."

"Exactly," agreed Brian, keeping a wary eye out on their faithful followers. "I can see how it has hurt even Den'Lin Fetch. Senja's parents won't let her have anything to do with anyone of my delving, because we've lived apart so long now that it doesn't seem right that one could find a mate, or friend, from another delving. It just isn't done, is what they said. We've gotten so used to being separated that it only seems natural now."

Shanon rested for a moment, shipping his oar across his lap, and letting his raft slow gently down.

"We're getting close to an exit now, where we can reach Erin Frey, and the supplies I spoke of. I think we should arm ourselves, and see to whatever else we might find a use for on this little outing."

"It'll feel awkward, not having my own dwarf bow," complained Brian. "But I guess it'll be better than nothing at all, these elf weapons you speak of."

"Only of the very best make! These were weapons forged by your own forefathers, long ago, Brian. The elves of Erin Frey decorated them, and turned them into things of fine art, but the workmanship is dwarfish, through and through."

"We'll see," snorted the dwarf.

As the two friends let their boats drift slowly into the eddy that washed noisily at the foot of a landing pier, Brian noticed that the bubbles of their pursuers had vanished.

"Where have our friends gotten to? Don't they want to make sure we leave?"

"I don't think they go by what we're doing, as much as they know what we're thinking. I believe they're able to tell when someone is here to rob or plunder these old delvings. Don't ask me how, I just think they know things. That's what you feel when you look back and see those bubbles trailing along behind you."

"What did you think when you saw them first?" asked Brian, feeling somewhat embarrassed that he had acted so frightened.

He seemed to waver between having to impress Shanon, and on the other hand, telling him of all the uncertain feelings and fears that he felt, especially since deciding to undertake this strange journey that Chinby had arranged for them to take.

Arrange was not the right word, thought Brian angrily. If the journey had all been arranged, there would have been no need for all this skulking around, trying to round up equipment and supplies for the trip, or trying to decide what route to take, or how to tell those left behind what you were doing, or where you were going.

"And Chinby's a dwarf!" exclaimed Brian aloud. "You'd think a lot more preparation would have gone into all this, by listening to our blind friend. Here I am, half starved, no prospects, off with an elf on a journey to the sea, which is bad enough in itself, and I haven't had the chance to explain to anyone where I was going, or what I was to be doing. The worst of it is that I don't know myself exactly what it is I'm supposed to be doing, other than meeting Senja and Chinby at the Sea of Roaring."

"What's wrong with that plan?" asked the elf, carefully dragging the keg boat up onto the landing, and flipping it upside down.

"Nothing's wrong with it," snapped Brian. "As far as it goes, it's perfect!"

"We'll have our hands full just getting that far," went on the elf. "Chinby said there might be things that stood in our way."

"Like what? You mean dangers?"

"That's why he wanted us to use the old highway. Not much to arouse anyone's suspicion, traveling down here. You can't get interested in something you can't see."

"I wonder what dangers he was talking about?" continued Brian. "Other than the watchers?"

"Those would be danger enough, if our motives were to rob any of these old delvings."

"What else did Chinby say about the things we would have to watch out for?"

"Dwarfs, for one thing," exclaimed the elf. "Deep wood dwarfs, or dwarfs of the old clan of Carben."

"Carben? He's been long in the Tombs by now."

"But he had a whole clan that followed him."

"Why would we have anything to fear from dwarfs? I'm a dwarf, and you're traveling with me, so that as much as makes you a dwarf, too."

"An honor, I'm sure," shot Shannon. "Just as long as I don't have to prove myself by staying too long underground."

They had tied the keg boats up securely side by side, and were preparing to go upward into the higher landings, beyond which, Shanon said, was the gate to the outside.

"It's not far to Erin Frey from the outer door, and we should be able to gather all the things we'll need, or at least almost all the things we'll need, by dark, if it's not already dark out now."

Shanon blinked in the half-bright lights of the elfmoons.

"That's the most awful part of staying too long away from the open air. You begin to forget whether it's day or night."

"Not after you get enough practice at it," explained the dwarf. "You know, after a while, exactly as if you were living outside."

"Maybe you do, if you're a dwarf," said Shanon. "But I prefer to get my facts the straight and easy way, by just looking with my own two eyes."

"It's not hard," went on Brian. "If you hang about long enough, a sixth sense sort of lets you know what's going on outside. Chinby is a perfect example of how well one can adapt."

"Chinby is an exceptional fellow," agreed the elf. "I've never had the pleasure before of knowing so unusual a chap."

"You won't be likely to find another like him."

"Let's get on to Erin Frey, then, quickly. I don't like the idea of being too long away from our friend. I have an idea all of this will begin to make sense as soon as we're able to find Chinby again, and your friend, Senja."

"That will be for starters," said Brian, feeling foolish as he followed along after the tall, lithe form of the handsome elf.

Shanon led them upward, in a roundabout, rambling way, pausing now and then to sniff out the air in the tunnel as the old blind dwarf had taught him.

Brian was amused at the effort that Shanon put into his guiding chore, and chided him about it.

"You sound like a hound," teased the dwarf. "It shouldn't be so difficult to sniff out the upper air from that stagnant smell coming from the kellers."

"An elf isn't used to any of these," complained Shanon. "I would never have thought any of these smells existed, until I had the dubious fortune of running into your friend Chinby."

"He's your friend, too," reminded Brian.

"I forget that when I'm here like this," shot the elf. "You wouldn't think a friend would be responsible for creating something so unpleasant as this crawling around in the bottom of a musty old dwarfshaft."

"I don't find it all that unpleasant," argued the dwarf. "I've spent much worse times aboveground. And I've spent plenty of times wishing I were safely back down a familiar tunnel."

"No doubt," conceded Shanon. "And I don't doubt that these old shafts weren't once really beautiful, as a dwarfish mind might see it. That's not the point I'm trying to make. What I'm saying is, an elf is a funny fellow, and if you keep him out of the fresh air too long, he begins to turn into a regular beast of a fellow that's hardly fit to keep company with."

"That sounds like a good enough excuse for what's happened to all dwarfdom," mused Brian. "I can remember when all conversations didn't run to the serious streak that's in all of us."

"It would be news to me to find out a dwarf had a light side."

"Oh, we do, indeed," said Brian. "We've always maintained our good sense of humor."

"I've never heard laughter from any but Chinby," said the elf. "And I think the only reason he does any laughing is because he's old, and a hero, and no one can say anything to him about it."

"A laugh is a serious matter," mumbled Brian. "You act as

though it were just a lighthearted thing to do, under any given circumstance. That's not the dwarfish way. We learn early on that to laugh is the highest form of self-expression, and that to waste that precious gift on all and sundry is a great ruin against ourselves. So we become guarded, and careful that we don't hurt others or ourselves in our beliefs, which come from the very beginnings of the roots of all kinds. I've thought about perhaps three or four good laughs in my time, and it's only been recently that I can see that there will be others. But it's not a thing to be taken lightly, or jumped into, without some sort of knowledge and understanding about the whole affair."

At this long and drawn-out discussion of the fine art of laughing, the elf burst out guffawing, in his tingly, elfin way.

"You make it all sound too grim, Brian. Too much living out of the sun, that's what's done it. You need more time aboveground."

"That only makes it worse," said Brian. "If you take one of our kind out of the element he knows and understands best, he'll only withdraw further. A dwarf becomes very depressed when he's beyond his own delvings."

"What are you and Chinby, and Senja, going to be like once we reach the Sea of Roaring? I don't think there's any way you can find much dirt to get under there."

"Chinby said the entire coast is riddled with old delvings," explained Brian. "And I'm not at all sure what our errand will be there, but I hope to have it over and done with, and be back in Den'Lin Fetch before too long a time slips by."

"Chinby talked as if we might be crossing the Roaring," offered the elf cautiously. "And if that's the case, I don't know if we'll be back this way for quite a long time. Perhaps never!"

Brian, hating to have any door closed for good before he got an opportunity to weigh all the possibilities, shook his head.

"Why would anyone of us want to make a sea crossing? Not only would it be dangerous, but I'm not really sure there is anything on the other side half so good as what we already have here."

"He also spoke of those who were coming from across the Roaring."

"Old tales," shot Brian. "Old tales meant to put a spanner to sleep."

"Well, that may be, but I'm taking along a few things from Erin Frey toward that end, just in case."

The two friends had reached an upper landing shaft that rose gently toward the surface, and the air gradually grew lighter, laced with outside smells of flowers blossoming and the thick, pungent scent of rain in the forest.

"We're almost there," called Shañon, going on ahead of Brian, who had stopped to examine an intricate stone-carved relief, all done in the finest of inlay work, and hand-polished until the deep gray walls looked alive with all the dazzling colors of the elfmoons, reflecting off the reds, and blues, and greens.

Directly ahead, Shanon knew the opening lay, concealed from the outside world by a great boulder that was drawn up in such a way as to make it appear that the stone was solid from one side of the tunnel mouth to the other, and when looked on from aboveground, it only seemed more piles of the great boulders, all stacked together in a heap.

There was no visible clue, except to another dwarf, or to an elf that had been trained in what to look for, and Shanon was anxious to get on with his newly appointed task, which seemed primarily the job of keeping the dwarf with him from falling into harm's way.

At the very entryway, where the shaft opened out aboveground, Shanon paused, waiting for his friend to catch up to him.

He was on the point of calling out when he saw the first signs of danger, and by then it was too late to warn Brian. Every sense tingled within Shanon, and he quickly turned one way, then another, trying to discover what had set off all his warning devices. There was something that was different about the way the huge boulder lay, closing up the doorway.

He was trying to figure what exactly it was that was different, but getting nowhere, when a voice, directly at his ear, startled him, and turned him into a cold rage.

"It's a long time since we've seen an elf in these digs," started the voice.

"It's been a long time since one has had the foresight to try to find a suitable place to live."

"Should we kill it?" asked another voice, deeper still, and unsure of itself.

"Oh no," replied the first voice. "This is an excellent

opportunity to find out some things we've been needing to know about Erin Frey. And here's a live, first-rate guide."

Shanon, whirling all about, could find no one to address his speech to, so he simply mumbled in the direction of the voice.

"Who are you? Come out, so that we may talk eye to eye!"

"I have no face to show you," said the first voice. "You wouldn't know me in any disguise. Your friend may know me better."

Brian, hearing the conversation, came to join Shanon.

And out of the semi-gloom where the elfmoon did not reach, near the entryway to the outside, there stepped a figure that was not quite dwarfish, nor elfish, nor anything in between. Its hair was long and dark, and the features square as a dwarf's, but it was somewhat taller than the normal dweller of the delvings.

"Who are you?" shouted Shanon again. "How have you come here?"

"I was finding my tongue to ask you the same thing," said the stranger.

Brian felt a sudden urge to lie to this odd creature, not to tell him his real name, nor the real name of the elf with him. It was an eerie sort of feeling, and he couldn't put his finger to it, but it seemed to him that the stranger before them had no good in mind for them.

Even as Brian was thinking all this to himself, which did not take long, another dozen of the half-dwarfish figures loomed out of the entryway, blocking off the tunnel completely.

"What use have you for the outside, unless you're going over to the elves' old dane? We've been trying to find a way in there for a long time, but we need a guide. And look what we have now!"

Shanon, blood boiling at the audacity of the stranger, snapped angrily.

"If you have it in mind to defile any of the holy places of that dane, you'll pay dearly. There is quick justice for any who break those codes."

"Only if there is enough power to back up idle threats. I don't seem to see that you two will be in much of a condition to do anything about where we go, or what we do."

The leader of the odd band pulled back his lips into more of a snarl than a smile.

"You look like you've never seen a deep wood dwarf before."

The apparent leader, who was called Mathiny, strutted back and forth now, relishing the wordplay between them.

Shanon looked backward at Brian, and nodded, very imperceptibly.

"We have more reinforcements on the way up from the river. We hope you'll join us?"

Mathiny neighed a short bark of almost laughter.

"You'll all be joining us, it seems," he gloated. "We have need just now of some strong backs, as well as a guide to take us to our new settlement. And we have to have a hundred new trees chopped. You'll be sure to be getting enough exercise now, by staying with us."

As the half-dwarf finished speaking, Shanon leapt nimbly around the two guards who had been trying to position themselves behind him, and grabbing Brian by the cloak, jerked him along behind him, running hard for the lower landings, where they had the keg boats tied, and where the watchers swam in unending, silent circles.

The Carben Clan

AS Brian and Shanon ran, they could hear the noisy cries and shouts of their pursuers.

"Don't kill them," called Mathiny, the leader. "We need them alive."

"They'll go well with the others," shouted another, "except the blind one won't be any good for our uses."

A cold stab of fear plunged into Brian's heart, and he thought his knees would surely give way beneath him, but they didn't, and he ran on, trying to keep pace with the swift elf, who hardly seemed to be straining at all, and who was breathing easily, in spite of the pace.

Brian tried to call out to his friend, to see if he'd heard the terrible news, which he was certain meant that Senja and

Chinby had been taken by these half-breed dwarfs, who were a part of the family of Carben, who had moved his clan overground long before, and now lived in half-dwarfish fashion in the deeper woods and wilder places of the lands above earth.

The elf moved swiftly, and only glanced over his shoulder from time to time to see that his friend was still with him. Finding that Brian's legs were not made for speed, he slowed his pace, and began to follow different shafts now and again, which were not the tunnels they had taken on their way up from the river, rising to the higher levels.

Brian, winded, but still in control of his senses, began to think that Shanon had lost his way, and that the two of them would end up hopelessly trapped in a dead-end tunnel. He had no idea where they were, not having noticed his surroundings on the way out, except to admire the different dwarf craftywork in stone and inlay, and he was regretting now that he had ever trusted an elf to be able to move about belowground without making mistakes.

No one but a dwarf, he angrily chided himself, would ever be able to go about the intricate tunnels and layers of a dwarfish delving without error, and even an elf of the very brightest kind, schooled by a respected lore master, would never be able to find his way about under pressure, and would eventually wind them up in an enemy's grasp, along with Senja and Chinby.

A bitter regret filled him for a moment, as he thought of the end he had come to, just as the delving of Den'Lin Fetch said he would, in trouble, and tied up with unsavory companions. All the grandness of the plans of the old blind dwarf were forgotten, and his heart was black with a dark anger, at the elf, Shanon, for leading him wrong, and causing them to be captured, and at himself, for ever agreeing to go along on such a fool's errand.

What he had forgotten was that they weren't captured yet, and that Shanon, with his true elfish sense of cunning and cleverness, had been steadily leading them down to the river, doubling back from the strange tunnels into those they had come from on their trip out.

Panting, and still running hard, Brian saw that they were but one level above the river, and although he could barely hear anything over the crash of his pounding blood in his ears, it seemed as though they had eluded their pursuers.

"They've been sidetracked a moment upstairs," whispered Shanon in a pinched voice. "It won't take them long to get back on the scent, but that's all we'll need to get the rafts and be gone. If they try to follow us on the river, we've got the watchers to help rid us of them."

"They have Senja and Chinby," gasped Brian, trying to catch his breath. "We've got to help them!"

A stricken look crossed the elf's fair features.

"A stroke of ill luck! They must have been waiting out here somewhere, and run into those half-cousins of yours."

"They're no kin of mine," barked Brian.

"They're dwarfish, right enough, whatever you say, and more like the sort I've dealt with before."

"They're an old clan that moved aboveground a long time ago," explained Brian. "They have no ties with our delvings any longer. Carben was an evil sort, and it seems his kin have turned out the same."

"Whoever they are, they mean us no good," went on Shanon. "If they have our friends, I don't know what can be done, except to return to your delving for help."

"Or to Con Den Fetch. It might be closer to reach there."

"Then we should find out where these half-cousins of yours are camped, and how many of them there are."

"How are we to do that? I think we're lucky to have escaped at all, much less be scouting around to find out how many they are."

"You underestimate the powers of an elf, Brian. You fellows are good sturdy sorts at huffing around down here in these basements you call delvings, but an elf is a chap who can move about without disturbing the countryside around him, and go and come as he pleases, with no one knowing the difference if he doesn't wish them to."

Brian remembered his first meeting with the secretive elf, and knew he spoke the truth.

"What shall we do, then?"

One of the dwarf's best qualities was to embrace a policy which worked better than something which didn't. This included tools, methods of delvings, and politics, as well as new ideas that might lead to the success of a doubtful venture.

All dwarfs did not have the foresight and open-mindedness of Brian Brandigore, and it was those qualities that marked him as different from his fellows, and propelled him into the strange journey he had undertaken, foolish enough in itself, if viewed in the eyes of his friends Jeral and Jaran, but extremely ill conceived, since he was in the company of an elf, that shifty breed of beings who were always known for their deceit and treachery.

"We'll go on to the boats, and you can wait there," said Shanon. "I don't think any of that lot will find you, but if they do, just stay on your raft. The watchers should take care of the rest."

"Wouldn't it be just as well to go on there and wait, and let that happen? If they are as fierce toward any enemies as you say, then that might be our best plan."

"It might, but then we wouldn't know any more than we already do of the whereabouts of Senja and Chinby. If these fellows have them, it would be well to know where they're being held, if we're going to help them escape."

Brian nodded, blushing.

"I forgot that."

"I'm more used to this than you, my friend," laughed the elf, catching the other's red face. "You are but a baby at these games. I've had to plan at this sort of affair for longer than I care to remember."

He laughed easily again.

"It may be why all your kind thinks of the elf as a slippery fellow, and difficult to pin down."

"I'm finding out that I shall have to rethink all my thoughts about what I've been told as a spanner," said Brian earnestly. "It's obvious that I've gotten wrong information more times than not. If all elves were as straightforward as you, Shanon, I doubt that the rift between our two kinds would have ever begun."

"Oh, I think most of our folk are just like you and me. It's not the majority of us that favors the separation of our races, just a few fat old fools who think they know what's best for everyone. They're as prevalent in elfdom as they are among you dwarfs. And I've seen them just about everywhere, as well."

A clatter of sturdy dwarf boots rang along the level above their heads.

"You go on to the raft, Brian. Wait there, and if you get into trouble, cast off, and go on toward the meeting place Chinby has arranged. I'll find out what I can, and find you where I'm able."

"Wait!" called Brian, keeping his voice low, but the elf seemed to disappear right before his eyes, and there was nothing left to do but make his way to the rafts, tied securely to a great iron ring bolt on a smooth landing, fashioned by the ancient dwarf clans in the far distant past.

Brian crept along as quietly as he could, marveling at the disappearance of the elf, and trying to make his own plans as to what would be best to do to help his two captured friends.

There could be no mistaking the identity of the one he heard referred to as the blind dwarf, for never in all his days belowground in Den'Lin Fetch had he heard of another blind lore master or dwarf of any calling. It must be Chinby, and the only other one Chinby could be with would be Senja, and these half-dwarf creatures from the dark pages of the dwarfish lore would be only too happy to have as a captive the handsome full dwarf lane and a lore master such as Chinby, who might be able to tell them many things of the defenses and locations of delvings.

Chinby had said at one time these half-dwarfs, the Carbens, as they were called, after the ancient dwarf who had led the original clan overground, had lost almost all contact with the true delvings, and as time went on, they began to fashion their own history and legends, and tried to erase all their ties with their ancestors. That had not been very successful, said the old dwarf, for there were many reminders of the delvings and the old ways, and try as they might, the Carben leaders could not erase the delvings from the minds of their clans.

Chinby told Brian of the Carben lore masters who went from one settlement overground to the next, holding secret meetings and repeating to their enthralled listeners the true dwarfish histories and legends of the old delvings.

The blind dwarf had met and known a few of those lore masters, and he told Brian that he had once visited a Carben settlement deep in the heart of the Fallen Oak Wood, and spoken to a gathering of those who were hungry for knowledge of their own past. Some were disbelieving and hostile, while others had found the tales disturbing, and caused an ache to grow in the heart, and a great desire to return to the old ways underground.

Brian had heard many stories of the half-dwarfs, from many sources, and he wondered at the motives and intentions of these Carben warriors who were out to capture them now, and who, on the surface of it, seemed to have Senja and

91

Chinby prisoner somewhere, either in the higher levels of this ancient delving, or outside, at a nearby Carben settlement.

Brian's mind wouldn't leave speculation alone, and he ran through dozens of possibilities as to the gravity of the situation, and had even gone so far as to think he might be able to reason with these outlanders, for they were, at the bottom of it, half dwarf, which to Brian meant better than not being of dwarfish lines at all.

He was on the verge of leaving his raft to seek out the leader of the Carben dwarfs when he began to notice that the river had grown disturbed, and great ripples began to flow back and forth across the surface.

At one moment, he stood perplexed and terrified, as a gray steely talon crept over the edge of the boat, then withdrew, and there seemed to be grassy green eyes peering up from beneath the depths of the water. After a few more brief scares, the eyes left, and the water around the moored rafts grew quiet again, leaving Brian with his heart pumping, and his knees shaking.

It was one thing to deal with an adversary you could see and feel, but the eerie, wraithlike figures beneath the water were terrifying, and he was glad these watchers were able to discern those who meant harm to the delvings from those who did not. And from the looks of things, they were able to understand more things than he had thought, and knew much more about all who traveled upon the underground river than anyone who did not know of their presence would suspect.

A sharp, chilling scream split the air into a dozen echoes, ringing harshly in the dwarf's ears.

Another piercing cry erupted from around a bend not far from where the keg boats were tied, and Brian strained forward to see what was taking place that would cause anyone to utter such horrible cries of distress.

His first thought had been that it was his friend Shanon, caught by the Carben dwarfs, or worse, injured by an arrow, but there was something in the cry that was not of an elfish nature, and he knew then that it was some unsuspecting victim, caught by the unseen watchers of the river.

Brian hurried back ashore at the smooth stone landing, and ran toward the commotion that was going on around the curve of the fast-flowing stream. Out of the corner of his eye, he caught sight of Shanon, speeding along in the shadows near the wall, but he didn't pause to call out to him, or break stride, and soon he was at the bank of the channel, looking into the roiling white froth of a great struggle taking place in the dark water.

One of the Carben dwarfs' hats was floating on the surface, along with a short dwarfish bow and quiver of arrows, and another of the creatures was flattened against the smooth wall across the way from Brian. Before the crouched figure was a long, lithe shadow, solid gray, with great gray talons extended in front of it, reaching out to grasp and drag its victim into the troubled water.

"Stop!" commanded Brian, surprising even himself.

He recognized the trembling Carben dwarf as the leader, Mathiny, who had spoken to them in the upper levels of the delving and threatened to hold them as slaves.

"Leave them alone," warned Shanon, calling out to Brian. "They know what they're doing."

"They may know what they're doing, but I can't just stand by and see anyone, no matter how misguided, destroyed like this."

The mute evidence of the dwarf cap afloat on the churning water spoke of a quick fate by drowning, beneath the green and black shadows of the river's depths.

Shanon said no more, and detected something in Brian's voice which had not been there before.

"Stop it," called the dwarf again, stamping his foot at the water's edge, and throwing his own hat in his frustration and rage at his helplessness.

The Carben leader stared wide-eyed at the dreadful form that confronted him, then up at Brian.

"Help me!" he squeaked, barely able to control his voice, and his whisper was hardly audible.

"They only hurt those they feel are trying to harm the delvings, or those of the delvings. You only have one chance, and that's to surrender your plans to imprison us, and to release those captives you already hold, the lane and the blind one."

"Anything," whispered Mathiny. "I'll do whatever you say, just call these things off."

Brian, hoping that the Carben was sincere, and not knowing what the dreadful form of the watcher was going to do next, fell back a pace.

93

"O watcher of the river, please spare the dwarf before you. He'll mend his ways, and become one with his ancient kinsmen again, if you'll give him the honor of his continued life."

Mathiny nodded quickly, swallowing hard, for the steely grasp of the watcher had locked in a viselike grip around his ankle, and was dragging him helplessly toward the lapping edge of the river, now quiet once more. Even the dwarf cap and bow were no longer anywhere in sight.

Shanon had come to stand beside Brian, and shook his head.

"I don't know if there's any reasoning with these things," he said. "They seem to know more about what one is thinking than we do, though."

"I can't stand to think of that poor blighter just dragged in and drowned without a chance," argued Brian.

"I don't like it either, but I'm not a dwarf, and don't know the workings of a dwarf's mind. I don't know what it would take to call off the watchers, or what it would take to convince your friend over there to give up his old ways, and become a friend, instead of a foeman."

"I think what it would take is exactly what's happening," said Brian. "If we can just get the riverfolk to leave this fellow alone, we may have made a powerful ally in a camp that has long been closed to most ordinary dwarfs. The Carben clans have been gone a long time, and I know they haven't had anything to do with dwarfdom for many turnings. If we could make a friend of one of them, we might be able to get closer to them all."

Shanon frowned.

"Then all you need is for your watcher to leave this poor bloke alone, and to convince him that you're the one that saved his life."

The elf laughed without humor.

"What happens if he agrees to eternal friendship just long enough for you to try to get the riverfolk to leave him alone, then he calls the rest of his friends, and we're right back where we started? There's nothing that says he has to honor his promise once the danger is over."

"If that's the way this fellow is thinking, I don't know if the watcher will let him go. You said yourself that they seem to be able to understand the secret thoughts of all those who come down here. If this fellow is simply trying to trick us, I'm afraid he's going to join his friend, as well as the bow, **and** my hat."

Mathiny shook his head.

"I swear I won't harm you or your friends. I'll release the others. I'll do anything you say."

Deciding to use the moment to best advantage, and in case the riverfolk were not to be dissuaded from their duty, Brian asked the Carben where the two other prisoners were being held.

"In the outer gatehouse, in this delving," blurted Mathiny, his eyes bulging from fear.

The watcher had slowed his dragging somewhat, but still inched ever backward, closer to the water's edge.

"Are they alive and well?" asked Brian.

"Yes," replied the Carben. "They are not harmed, although there were some in our group who could think of no use for the blind one."

"Is the lane called Senja?" continued Brian.

"I don't know," answered Mathiny. "They were only caught a few hours before we chanced onto you. I don't know how either of them is called."

The riverfolk had stopped, and after a brief pause, began to slip silently away. In another moment, the smooth stone quay was empty of anything except the shaken Mathiny.

Brian had to untie one of the keg boats and paddle over to the other shore, for the two landings were split by the flow of the swift current. Evidently the Carben leader had come down a different shaft to get to the river level, and in doing so, ended up on the other side.

Mathiny, much frightened by the ordeal of losing one of his band to the horrible forms of the watchers, and indebted to this strange dwarf who had interceded on his behalf, clutched at Brian's hand to shake it repeatedly, thanking him over and over for sparing his life.

"I had nothing to do with it," insisted Brian. "Evidently you had a change of heart, or you wouldn't have been let go."

"I'd heard stories all my life that you deep earth dwarfs were cruel, and took pleasure in torturing any victims that you captured aboveground. We have heard those tales all our lives, so I thought there was no harm in capturing some of your kind to do the hard work of moving a settlement. We weren't going to harm you."

"That may be so," said the stocky dwarf. "But your companion seems to have been of another frame of mind. The watchers only take those who are planning evil."

"I don't know," said Mathiny. "Perhaps he was. Abring was always a hard one to understand. He's been my second in command for only a short while. I knew his father and Ianin, and they seemed good enough."

"There's no need worrying about him now," interrupted Shanon. "Whatever he's been, he's beyond it all now. The question is what's going to become of us? We have to move on now, and we have to see to it that this fellow is going to stick to his word, and free his two prisoners."

"If you'll come with me, I'll take you to them," offered Mathiny.

"I'm sure you would," said Shanon, his blue eyes lidded, and his tone cautious. "I'm sure you wouldn't think it amiss if you were to call another of your fellows, and have them bring the two other prisoners down here to us? That way we don't have to worry about you having a change of heart, once you're out of danger here."

Mathiny looked puzzled a moment, then understood.

"Of course. There's no reason you should trust me now, after my behavior."

"I'd just as soon wait on some proof of your good intentions," replied the elf.

"The watcher let him go," broke in Brian. "That tells me that something must have changed, or he wouldn't have been spared."

Shanon nodded in agreement, but still insisted that they should stay below, near the river, to ensure that none of the other Carben group tried to harm or trick them, in spite of the promise of safety made by their leader. The elf reminded Brian that the watchers had already taken one of Mathiny's followers, and that since they were unarmed themselves, it wouldn't be a bad idea to have an ally close at hand that would be capable of protecting them from anyone who wished them harm.

Mathiny finally agreed to sending for the other two prisoners to be brought down to the river, and signaled with a tiny dwarfwrought reed whistle, which filled the lower shafts of the ancient delving with a shrill echo that reverberated long after the Carben dwarf had replaced it into his cloak. And it was sometime afterward that Brian and Shanon realized that

the last echo they were hearing was a different note, in reply
to the first call.

In another moment, they were face to face with a dozen
other Carben dwarfs, all heavily armed, and moving toward
them threateningly.

A Web Is Laid

FEELING certain that they had been betrayed, the elf
prepared to escape by diving into the river, with its watchers,
but Brian held him back.

"We shall see what all this leads to," he whispered to
Shanon under his breath. "And I can't leave Senja and
Chinby."

Shanon was at once angry at the dwarf and grateful to find
one so capable of loyalty to his friends. He reluctantly stood
his ground, and watched as the new band of half-dwarfs
approached them.

Mathiny had raised a hand, and now called out loudly.

"I'm in no danger! These are my friends, who saved me
from the river snake. Abring was taken."

A murmur of surprise rippled through the knot of Carbens.

"We are to arrange a meeting between our friends and the
others. It seems they know one another, and I have promised
their release, in exchange for saving my life."

"Now that it's done, let's carry them all away to work the
wood," snarled an extra-heavyset half-dwarf, all dressed in
deep shades of green.

"Aye," growled another. "There's at least two good workers
here, not to count the lane."

Shanon's brow darkened as he looked at his friend, his
glance accusing and hurt.

"There'll be no such thing go on," broke in Brian, "and if
you continue to displease me with your traitor's talk, I shall

call up the watchers, and you shall all go the way of your friend, Abring, was was devoured without the slightest struggle."

Brian's voice boomed larger because of the echoes of the shaft, and it seemed to the elf that his companion had grown in stature as he spoke.

"Throw down your arms, and rid your minds of those thoughts of harming us, or it will be too late for you. The watchers will allow no violence in their domain."

Brian had not known for certain that the river dwellers were still in the neighboring waters, or if they would rise on cue to carry out his threat. Hoping that they perhaps understood, he risked calling the bluff of the Carben war band, sounding as powerful as he could, and striding forth toward the half-dwarfs, motioning a hand out over the deep, still waters.

A tiny reflection of an elfmoon in the tunnel overhead began to ripple, then the entire surface of the river began to waver, making small splashing noises against the bank.

A look of dismay and horror crossed the half-dwarfs' faces, and they shrank back from the water's edge.

It was Mathiny, the Carben, who spoke next.

"Do as I say, and follow our friend's advice," he warned. "The river snakes are terrible, and there's no escape from them."

And as if to prove his words, a grayish black figure began to emerge from the river, creeping up the stone landing on clawed feet, great head raised. All the Carben party immediately armed and drew their bows, which seemed to anger the thing even more, and with amazing speed and agility, it slithered quickly toward the dozen or so half-dwarfs.

"Don't shoot!" ordered Mathiny. "Throw down your bows, quickly! That thing has a hide a foot thick. Abring's arrow bounced away like a piece of tenderwood."

Caught between the decision to throw away their arms, or to risk being taken by the watcher, the half-dwarfs moaned and gnashed their teeth, but the fear, and their leader's command, won out at last, and they hurled down their weapons and fell back, hoping to be able to outrun the horrible thing, should all else fail.

The watcher halted, the shimmering elfmoons reflected in the cold, dark hide.

"I think they'll behave now," said Mathiny. "It is a hard

98

thing to cool off a deep wood dwarf. They're not used to taking orders from anyone."

"Aren't you their leader?" asked the elf, amazed that there could be a leader whom no one obeyed.

The Carbens had taken their time in following Mathiny's order, and Shanon suspected that had it not been for the presence of the watcher, they would be prisoners now, along with Chinby and Senja.

"I have been elected by the clan to bear that title," replied Mathiny, "although it is little more than a courtesy. The Carben settlements are a loose-knit society, and we have very little to do with anyone outside our own walls, even if it might be another settlement of us."

Brian frowned, keeping an eye on the watcher, which had become as still as a great boulder, and the dozen or more Carben dwarfs that stood frozen before it.

"How is it you can carry on that way?"

Mathiny snorted.

"We carry on that way badly," he answered. "We have lived this way for longer than anyone can remember, and it has grown worse each season. New spanners come along, and if they're tough and agile, they gain a following. Sooner or later they go off to start their own settlement. It has been going on like that now for more seasons than I can count. The capture of the pure dwarf lane was considered a great stroke of luck. It has been many ages since any of our offspring have looked anything like the old stock."

"The blind one you captured can fill you in on all the details of the history you have, Mathiny. He is a high lore master, and knows all the things that you seem in doubt about. We will ask him to give you the story of your kin, and what has happened."

"It's the story of the water elf and wood elf, all over," added Shanon. "It happened a long time ago, just as you say it happened in dwarfdom. Now we live at odds with each other, and have gone our separate ways."

The elf nodded briefly to himself.

"A sad thing, to be divided from your own brothers."

"Or anyone else," put in Brian. "It's no good thing to be apart from anyone, when you get right down to it."

"That's a sentiment I'd never expect to hear from a dwarf," said Shanon, looking more closely at his friend. "That's more

99

what I would expect to hear from one of the high elfin lore masters."

Brian colored slightly.

"I think down inside, we all feel the same things, whether we're elf, or dwarf, or what have you."

As they talked, they began to notice that the shadow which was the watcher was gone.

"I didn't see it leave, did you?" asked Shanon. "And my eyesight is counted as good, as far as quickness and noticing things."

"That must be part of why they are so dreadful if you're an enemy," mused Brian. "They come from nowhere, and disappear just as quickly."

"Not quickly enough to suit my fancy," complained Mathiny. "I won't feel good about it all until I'm topside of this shaft, breathing in some fresh air, and a long way away from this river full of monsters."

"My sentiments," agreed the elf, forgetting for a moment to mistrust the half-dwarf.

"Do you think your friends will follow your word?" asked Brian, under his breath, to Mathiny.

The Carben studied the cluster of his followers, his brows drawn together.

"I think they won't know what to make of you. They don't have to know that these river snakes aren't going along, in some fashion or other. If we can hold a little something over them, I think they'll abide by anything you say."

Brian noticed the half-dwarf's tone.

"I want no command of these folk," he corrected quickly. "They are your followers, and they are yours still. All I require is that my party be allowed to go in peace, for now, and any other time we may be in these parts."

Mathiny's eyes widened, and he was clearly shocked.

"You mean you won't be staying with us, now that you've won the leadership?"

"I think I know what he means," said Shanon. "You've bested him, and now you have earned the role of Elder. Maybe it's a surprise that you have no interest in that."

"I have an interest in your clan's accepting me for a friend, Mathiny, and maybe there will come a day when our two roads will be as one. But for now, all I have need of is safe passage for myself and my friends."

Brian could see the unbelief in the other's eyes.

"You have lived for a long while beyond the bounds of common dwarfdom," he went on. "We are not really so different, you and I, except that I grew up in a more stable delving, and was educated in the old way."

"I would like to hear about that," said Mathiny. "Sometimes there are outlaw lore masters who come to us, and tell us things of the old days. I don't know if they tell it as it truly is or not, but they sound almost like you. Perhaps there has been truth to their fire tales after all."

"Most likely," huffed Brian. "I can see that part of your trouble lies in the fact that you have nothing to fall back on but violence. Chinby has told me stories, and now I begin to understand. It is the division that weakens, and weakens, and in the end causes the complete split."

He fell silent, thinking.

The others had begun gathering their senses, getting ready to go.

Shanon kept a close eye on the Carben band, and breathed a sigh of relief, knowing that at least their arms were gone and they had been badly frightened by the river dweller. And the truth of the matter was, he had been, too, even though Chinby had assured him over and over that the watchers only harmed those who came with violence in their hearts.

"Let's see if we can find our way back to the outer gate," said Mathiny, looking about to get his bearings. "We were in a hurry when we came down here, and I hope we've remembered to mark our tunnels."

Brian was astounded once more.

"You mean you could let yourself get lost in a delving? My elf friend here is more able than that."

Mathiny looked steadily at the dwarf.

"You forget, we Carbens aren't delvers. We're as out of place here as any elf, or anyone who is an overside dweller."

"Well, we have many lessons to impart to you, for sure," exclaimed Brian. "There's no sense in letting you go on the way you are, helpless belowground. I can see Chinby is going to have his hands full with your instruction."

"Oh, that won't be allowed," insisted Mathiny. "Sigman Col won't let anyone do that."

"Sigman Col? Who is he?" asked Brian, growing confused.

"He's our High Elder."

"I thought you said you all followed different leaders," put in Shanon.

"We do, but Sigman Col is the most powerful of all. He has the greatest following, and he taxes all the other settlements every quarter year. He brings all his henchmen with him, so there is never any chance not to pay."

Brian's brow had knitted into a worried frown.

"I can see that you have much to tell me, Mathiny. My good friend Chinby told me some of the tales of the Carbens, but we never got into the details that you speak of."

"Why don't you run, and settle elsewhere, if this Sigman Col is so oppressive?" asked the elf, finding it hard, at times, to understand a dwarf's insistence upon sticking in an unbearable situation long after others of a less hardheaded nature would have already been gone.

One of the half-dwarfs in the other cluster spoke up.

"Come with us to meet Sigman Col, and you'll soon enough get your answer to that."

The Carben dwarf snorted glumly.

"There is no escape from him. He is too strong, and knows all our settlements."

Brian turned to Mathiny.

"How long has this gone on?"

"For as long as I can remember. Sigman Col is said to be over a thousand seasons old. I don't know. He could be. He looks like he's lived forever."

"Chinby might know. Where is our friend? The old blind lore master?"

"We've left them topside, near the outer gate."

"Good! Let's get there quickly, so we can find out what Chinby knows of all this business. He may have some answers that perhaps will free you from the tyranny of this dwarf you speak of."

Another of the Carben clan clucked his tongue loudly.

"You won't want to be saying that out loud as soon as we get overside. Sigman Col has spies everywhere."

Brian looked to Shanon, a half smile across his eyes.

"Shall we bring our friends, the watchers? Perhaps they may be the answer to this Sigman Col."

The elf nodded.

"An excellent idea. I think that rude fellow may have unwanted visitors before too long, to teach him better man-

102

ers, and to show him how his fellow creatures should be
treated."

The group of Carben dwarfs clustered together even more
closely.

"Don't call that thing back! We mean you no harm."

"I know you don't," said Brian. "What I don't know is does
Sigman Col? Am I a fool to travel overside, in the country
ruled by this tyrant? Should I not take along my means of
self-defense?"

A queer, comprehending look began to glow in the depths
of Mathiny's dark brown eyes.

"We could be free once and for all from Sigman Col if you
were to break his hold with your river snakes. His army is no
match for their likes."

"You begin to catch on," said Brian. "If we were to free you
from the grasp of this dwarf, you would be able to go or come
as you please, and to perhaps even learn all the old lore from
the delvings, and of all the old ways. You have been long
gone from your true heritage, Mathiny. Dwarfs were never
meant to live as your clans have been living for all this time."

The Carben dwarf, frightened by the speech of Brian, and
unused to all the happenings that had befallen him, fell into
a sulking silence.

In the beginning the plan that Mathiny had had, when
they had captured the handsome dwarf lane and the old blind
one, was to somehow try to regain the old ways. His followers
had said that the old dwarf might be a lore master, and that
they should claim the reward from their High Elder by
turning him in; but the young half-dwarf harbored the idea of
finding out the secrets of the delvings. He had thought about
that for the entire time they had been camped in the outer
ways, right up until the moment the sentry had spotted
Brian and Shanon, coming up from the depths of the ancient
delving.

After listening to the strangers, he knew that what he had
been looking for was a way to free himself and his clan from
the harsh rule of Sigman Col, and that the way to do that
would be to find out everything he could from the old lore
master and these two strange beings.

Then he remembered that on the night he had left the
secret meeting, the name had been mentioned.

Brian Brandigore!

It was to be a dwarf by that name that was to unite all of dwarfdom again, and to lead the dwarfish folk out of the dark times they had fallen into, and into the light of their former glory. There was something else there, vague as spiderwebs, but he could only remember that it had something to do with powerful beasts, or a Fallen One, or some such.

He had seen enough of beasts to last him the rest of his life, he thought, after the close encounter with the terrible thing that had come out of the river after him, and that had devoured the half-dwarf Abring; far from being Mathiny's friend, he was a spy of Sigman Col's, sent to their settlement to make sure that nothing occurred that his master didn't know about, and to ensure the taxes were not underpaid, or goods hidden that Sigman Col might be interested in.

The band of Carben dwarfs marched on ahead of Brian and Shanon, who walked beside Mathiny, with the elf calling out every so often to bear right at the next turning, or to watch for the shaft that smelled like sunlight.

"How is it this elf knows so much of this delving?" asked Mathiny at last, marveling at the fact that it was an outsider, not a dwarf, that was doing all the underground guiding.

"He's more than an elf," grumbled Brian. "The blind lore master you've captured taught this lightfoot all about these delvings, and the goings-on of dwarfdom."

"Then there may be hope for me," concluded the Carben. "I've always had a secret desire to learn the old ways. I never thought I'd get the chance, after Sigman Col came to our end of the wood and took control of our lives. After that happened, there was no hope of ever being able to do any of the exploring that we wished to do, for his henchmen would keep track of us, and report whatever we were doing, so that we never had a chance to explore any of these old delvings very far."

"It sounds as if he's a pleasant sort," laughed the elf.

Mathiny, unused to laughter, was perplexed by the strange behavior.

"Don't pay any attention to him," explained Brian. "He seems to find a great many things to laugh at that have no real seriousness to them. I suppose it is his own way, being an elf. I have tried to explain to him about the art of serious laughter that we follow in dwarfdom."

"You've explained it to me well," said Shanon. "I know

104

enough to know that for a dwarf to laugh, the matter must be very grave indeed, to warrant so great an effort. I would say that perhaps the only time you'll ever have a chuckle is maybe the day that you surrender up that precious breath of yours, and go over to check out what's happening on the other planes."

"That's very close to what would make a true dwarf laugh," agreed Brian. "That, and floods in the delving, or an avalanche."

The elf threw up his hands.

"Just get me to some fresh air, please. I think I need a long nap under a pleasant tree, and no dwarfs to talk to for a while. I can't make hide nor hair of your clever reasoning."

"That feeling's mutual, I assure you," grumped Brian. "I can't for the life of me see whatever could be enough to set you off laughing, as if you'd lost every bit of sense you might have been born with, or why on earth an elf would ever consent to the ridiculous arrangement of going about underground, messing about in some dusty old delving, hammering and smithing, and chasing along after another fool who's decided he's going to the Sea of Roaring."

After the long, good-humored tirade, the elf clapped his friend heartily on the back.

"One thing I can say without fail, Brian, is that I've certainly found myself a friend who is kind with his praise for those he holds in high esteem, and quick to let everyone know where he stands on an issue."

Mathiny, growing more perplexed by the light banter of the two friends, looked up in time to see the sunlight bathing the dark stones ahead.

"We're here," he muttered, hurrying forward to see where the rest of his clan had gotten to, and to check that the two prisoners were still there, unharmed.

As Brian and the elf joined him, he let out a soft cry of dismay.

There, where he had left the others, all was empty and still, and there was no sign of either the half-dwarf band, or the dwarf lane, or the blind lore master.

"They're gone," he managed at last.

"They took them to Sigman Col," announced one of the other band, who had scouted the area and returned to report to Mathiny.

"Could that be so?" asked Brian. "Is there any chance of overtaking them?"

"It depends. We've been below for over an hour. That means they have a good head start on us."

"Maybe we should let Sigman Col come to us," suggested Shanon, a plan beginning to take shape in his mind. "Perhaps our newfound friend here will send word to Sigman Col that he has important news, and needs to seek an audience with him right away."

"What do you mean?" asked Brian.

"I mean, let Sigman Col come to us! And let's have a warm welcome for him with our good river dogs, who don't like those folk who go about with evil intentions on their minds."

"That's a wonderful plan, Shanon, with one exception. How would we ever get this half-dwarf down into the delving?"

"We tell him it's full of dwarf lore, and that if any of it ever reaches any of his followers, he'll be in for a rough go, once they find out the truth."

Brian turned to Mathiny.

"Do you think Sigman Col is one to fall for such a thinly disguised trap?"

"No," replied the Carben bluntly. "He would simply seal up the shaft. But I could think of something else that might interest him more."

"What would that be?" asked the elf.

"The capture of Brian Brandigore, the delving dwarf who is said to be the one who leads all dwarfs back to their true homelands in the delvings."

Mathiny's broad face glowed with the effort of his thought, and he put a hand on Brian's shoulder.

"I don't mean you any harm, friend. But I think that would interest our Sigman Col enough for him to venture out into our web, if a web is to be spun. Then, perhaps, he might fall prey to your river snakes."

"We don't need him dead," corrected Brian. "But then, I guess the watchers can be the best judge of that. If we can get him close enough so that they might have a chance to rule on the matter."

"Shouldn't we arm ourselves first?" asked Shanon. "We're not far from Erin Frey. And that might be good country to have close at hand, if anything goes awry and we need to make a run for it."

"Good old elf," barked Brian. "Always quick to spot the

106

back doors, and to know a place to get to if the going gets too thick."

Brian almost laughed, which let the elf know that their situation must be indeed serious, and he made a note to explore every avenue of possible escape, for future reference. He was sure that the Carben dwarf Sigman Col would be no easy one to convince that he should free Senja and Chinby, and he began setting out his own plans, should Mathiny's proposal fail.

The Outer Walls of Erin Frey

AFTER a short discussion of what their next move should be, the companions, now joined by the Carben dwarfs and their leader, Mathiny, decided to press on to the elfin dane of Erin Frey, and to find what arms there they could, and to try to formulate the snare that would lure Sigman Col into coming to one of the ancient delvings on the Deep Home Highway, where they would be able to wield their most convincing weapon, the presence of the river dwellers who guarded those ancient halls.

Mathiny had been near Erin Frey, but he and his band had never ventured very close to the beautiful ruins, for it was said in their lore that the ghosts of the elves who had dwelled there still guarded their homes, and it would be death to any who tried to breach the secrets of that dane, or to try to loot the settlement.

Shanon did not try to disturb the Carben dwarf's beliefs, and he knew that stories like that spread about the countryside had probably been the doings of his elfish kin, and one of the reasons that Erin Frey had not been sacked.

A faint glimmer of a plan began to form in Shanon's mind.

"Does Sigman Col know of Erin Frey?" he asked Mathiny, who nodded quickly.

"All the Carbens know of this elf dwelling. Sigman Col has often said that our clan was more closely related to the elves than to the delving dwarfs. He looks down on those kinsmen, and has tried to make all his followers do the same."

Brian could see how a clever mind would have devised that tale, for the Carben dwarfs did bear a faint resemblance to Shanon, being taller than the ordinary dwarf, who was short for practical purposes, since he always needed to go about unhampered by the necessity to be constantly ducking in shafts or tunnels that were close-quartered.

Sigman Col had chosen a scheme whereby he would never be challenged, for the half-dwarf knew that the possibility of any of elfdom ever denying his story was most remote, and if he were able to drive the wedge deeper between the delving dwarfs and the Carben clans, he would be the sole power that would have any sway over the dominion of the deep woods.

Brian began to feel uneasy about this half-dwarf leader, and said as much to Shanon.

"We may be dealing with more than we know about here. I don't think Sigman Col is the closeminded fellow that our friend Mathiny is. There's more than just a Carben dwarf taking control of his fellows, it seems. I keep getting the strange feeling that we're the ones being led into a snare, instead of the other way around."

Shanon spoke without breaking stride.

"How do you come up with that?"

His voice was disinterested, but the elf's quick blue eyes deepened in color, and his mind was quickly at work.

"I wonder that we didn't see Senja or Chinby."

"Mathiny said that there were those in his party who were eager to get into this Sigman Col's good favor. He seemed to have enough trouble controlling those who were with him, so I can understand those who were left behind to guard the prisoners taking off with the booty, so they could be the first to please the Elder."

"There doesn't seem to be much organization to these fellows, does there?" asked Brian, lowering his voice so the others wouldn't hear.

"Oh, they remind me of an elf clutch I once heard of," replied Shanon lightly. "They were all toil and trouble on the surface of things, and you would have thought that complete chaos was just around the corner."

Shanon smiled.

"But it was one of the ways they managed to get on for so long. It threw everyone off their stride, and caused more than enough grief to their enemies, who thought they were going to have easy pickings."

Brian studied his friend from under knitted brows.

"Are you trying to make a point?" he asked at last, after waiting for the end of the story, which seemed not to be forthcoming.

Shanon had begun very carefully picking his way, as if he had been walking on thin ice.

He looked up briefly, and smiled.

"We're getting close to Erin Frey now. I'm beginning to see the old snares they used to set out in these sections of the wood. They had begun to have problems with raiders, it seems, and they devised these things to give them warning, and to dissuade any raiding party from going farther."

Brian halted suddenly.

"Were you just going to let us walk into these traps without warning?"

"Oh, these aren't traps," explained the elf. "These were the alarms, to alert Erin Frey there was someone in the Back Wood. The snares aren't for another while yet."

"Do you think they would still work after all this time?" asked Brian, growing dubious.

"The river dwellers still work, and those delvings have been as long unused as Erin Frey."

Brian thought that over, then nodded.

"It seems our ancestors had a way of building something to stay built, and to design things that worked as they were meant to."

There was a glow of dwarfish pride in Brian's voice.

"It could just as well have been an end of us, if we had had something else on our minds," reminded the elf. "Then we could have wished that all the old things had rusted away, or vanished with their engineers."

"We wouldn't have very many interesting things to look at," protested Brian. "The new delvings are all right, as far as they go, but they don't have near the beauty of the old ones."

"Rubbish," snorted Mathiny, who had joined into their conversation. "It is good the old is gone. Nothing but extra weight to haul about. The old delvings had their place long ago, but these are new times, and things have changed."

"Is this more of Sigman Col's teaching?" asked the elf.

Mathiny blushed.

"I suppose it is. When I look at all the things I've been taught, it's all come from Sigman Col, or his followers."

"You seem a good sort, old fellow," said Brian. "Do you think there are others in your settlements like you? Who would be willing to overthrow this tyrant, and to start out anew? It wouldn't have to be a return to the delvings, or the ways of the dwarfs who follow that life. Even if you wished to carry on as you have been for all this time, it would be better to be free to choose for yourself what you would believe, or not believe, and to be able to look for the truth of a matter, rather than having a truth picked out and given to you, with no other choice but to accept it."

Mathiny squinted his eyes, looking at the other Carben dwarfs who were walking just ahead of them, talking among themselves.

Brian half expected the elf to warn them about the snares that were nearby, but after glancing in his direction, he saw that Shanon was of no mind to warn anyone, so he said nothing.

"I think there are others like me," said Mathiny carefully, seeming to be deep in thought. "I know there are many who have complained to me of Sigman Col and his ways, and who have gone to the secret meetings of the lore masters who have come through our settlements from time to time, and who have told us the old stories."

"Do you know if they could be trusted to overthrow Sigman Col? Could we depend on them if there was a revolt?"

The Carben dwarf's eyes widened.

"Oh, there could be no hope of a revolt! Sigman Col is too powerful, and has too many followers. He would slay anyone who tried to oppose him."

"Has he done so before?"

"Many times. No one has lived to tell any tales of those he has caused to disappear, but we all know that he has had them killed, somewhere out of sight, and disposed of."

"He sounds like a more delightful fellow every minute," said Shanon. "It's a good thing we ran into you first, Mathiny, rather than Sigman Col. He might not have been so willing to spare the life of a delving dwarf from the old ways, or an elf who could dispute his story about the things he had said about being of an elfin background."

Mathiny nodded.

"It is indeed good for you that it happened that way. If it had not been for the river snake, I might even have captured you, and turned you over to Sigman Col, not knowing that you would be in great danger because of what you might say."

"Do you think that will make it more dangerous for Senja and Chinby?" asked Brian.

"Oh, Sigman Col would welcome a dwarf lane as handsome as this one. He would keep her to himself, and have her to wife."

A savage anger welled inside Brian, turning his thoughts to terrible revenges, should anything happen to his captured friend.

Shanon saw the change that had overcome the dwarf, and placed a hand on his arm to restrain him.

"There will be a reckoning," he said softly.

When Brian looked at him, the elf smiled, his eyes dark and shadowed.

Glancing at his friend then, he understood why it was that there were many stories about the secrecy of elves, and not much known about their doings. And he also saw a hardness there, under the surface, that was almost frightening.

"There should well be," Brian said, finally getting his voice under control.

As they went on farther into the wood, the Carben dwarfs that had been marching on ahead of the others began to fall back, and seemed reluctant to go any farther.

"This is getting near to where Sigman Col told us was a dangerous place," said one of the band, stockier than the rest, with a touch of gray running through his long hair.

"We have found that Sigman Col has told us things that are not so," replied Mathiny. "And we have an elf with us, who knows the way to this place we are bound."

"It's a trick," insisted the other, Runion by name.

"It is no trick," broke in Shanon. "I know the way to the dane of Erin Frey as well as I know anything. We can find new weapons there, and settle whatever plans we have without worry from being surprised by any of your other brothers who may be loyal to Sigman Col."

Runion shifted his gaze uneasily.

"That may be so, but we don't have to go to this elf hole to do that. We know of safe spots, and there wouldn't be any danger."

"I go with Runion," agreed another Carben dwarf, stepping forward boldly. "And I think I speak for the rest of us as well."

All of the others nodded, mumbling their consent.

Mathiny, perplexed, looked at his newfound companions.

"What should we do? I know the story Sigman Col has spread about these elf holes. I'm a little frightened about going on myself."

"You have no need to be," reassured Shanon. "Nor do any of these others, unless they're harboring other thoughts about perhaps recapturing us, now that we're out of harm's way of the river dwellers."

Runion's eyes blazed.

"And what would you do to stop us, master elf, if that were our plan? We are a dozen to your three, and with or without arms, more than a match for you."

A sneer crept across the faces of the Carben dwarfs, and they drew closer to Brian and Shanon.

Mathiny, looking from one of his followers to the next, saw that Shanon had hit upon exactly the scheme they had planned, and knew, too, his time for taking sides had arrived.

Outside in the open, he felt that the danger of the river snake had passed, but he couldn't be sure.

And there was a ring of truth to what the odd strangers talked about, of all the happenings of the old days, and Mathiny had heard enough of the lore masters' talk to know that it was more than just lies or unfounded legends.

He also realized that Runion, who had always been a hothead, and an ambitious dwarf, with dreams of becoming a high adviser in Sigman Col's court, was also aware of the fact that perhaps there was no longer any force which the delving dwarf commanded, now that he was out of the deep, confining shafts of the earth, and back into the Carben dwarfs' territory.

His heart beat heavily in his chest as he stood there, torn between the old ways he had known for so long and his old comrades, whom he had been with since he was small.

Brian understood the Carben dwarf's hesitance, and knew the hard choice he was struggling to make.

"There is no need for any of this, Runion," said Shanon, his tone flat. "There is no harm in any elf dane, where it concerns a friend. We have spared your lives, by keeping you away from the river snake, and it would have been easy enough to have stood by and let you be devoured. There was a pledge of our good faith to you. And now you repay that with talk of treachery and false honor. I can see that if this is true, there is no courage in you, or any of your clan. You talk as a coward would, and speak of coward's ways."

Brian thought that they would have to make a stand to defend their very lives after the elf's speech, for a Carben dwarf, no matter how far removed, was a dwarf at heart, and there was nothing more dear to him than his pride.

Mathiny, without realizing it, stepped nearer to Shanon, intending to help the elf, should there be an attack.

The air crackled with the tension of the moment, and Runion, face as red as his cloak, eyes bulging, stood chewing his lip and clenching his fists.

Shanon stood his ground coolly, which Brian noticed with approval beneath his excitement, and prepared to make the best he could of such a lopsided battle.

"There is no way you can know for certain that our river friends have not followed along after us," said Shanon, going on in an even tone, as if he were addressing a friend instead of an enraged Carben dwarf, whose eyes had turned blood-red, starting from his head. "But even that will not save face for you. If it has to be done this way, then it shall. If you leave us no choice, and we cannot allow you to make your own decision to join our camp, then I shall give you the undeserved privilege of a half-hour head start before I release the river snakes. And now you are close enough to my own dane to call up my own elfin watchers, who come from the air, and strike as swiftly as lightning. Sigman Col has given you fair warning about the dangers of Erin Frey. But those dangers only exist for enemies."

Runion, turning a brighter red, doubled his fists, and hissed out his words.

"You shall be made to pay for this, you miserable tree rat. You know we are unarmed, and stand no chance against your river slime. That is all I would expect from your kind, treachery and deceit. We have been forced to disarm, and now our own leader has gone over to the enemy. You will regret this day, Mathiny, you scum, for the rest of your life. I shall myself tell Sigman Col of your betrayal, and we shall find you if it takes all the rest of forever!"

The Carben dwarf had begun jumping up and down in his rage, and the others of his band had to restrain him. Brian saw that they were frightened of Runion, and afraid not to follow his lead, but they also were terrified of the thought of the river dwellers and the new menace that the elf had spoken of.

"You all don't have to go with Runion," spoke up Mathiny. "You are welcome to stay and help us, and you will be safe."

"Safe from all but the wrath of Sigman Col," thundered Runion. "He will hunt down every deserter. Mark me well!"

"All who stay will be safe. Sigman Col's days are numbered. He will fall," predicted the elf. "It will be an elf which delivers the blow to set you free from the tyrant, and from fear. Look at you, shaking in your boots! That should not be. No free elf or dwarf would ever have to go through that."

"You would be able to decide as you like," added Brian. "About who you would follow, or not follow, and be able to explore any area you wished. As long as you abide by the laws of the delving, or danes, or wherever you are, you will be able to do as you wish."

Brian finished his little speech, and saw that he had frightened the Carben dwarfs even more. Their eyes had rolled back in confusion, and they looked about in wild terror.

Runion thumped a fist into his palm, and glowered at the elf.

"We'll take your offer of safe-conduct, elf. Does it still hold?"

Shanon nodded.

"But it's not too late to change your mind."

"The quicker we're out of sight of you, the quicker I'll feel clean again," boomed Runion. "I shall look forward to a meeting under different circumstances, when you don't have your lackeys with you."

"I'll hold them off until you're gone. But I wouldn't tarry, if I were you."

In spite of his bluster, Runion's voice trembled a little as he spoke.

"We have no need to tarry. I have important news to carry to Sigman Col. He must know he has enemies and traitors in his midst."

"Be gone!'" snapped Shanon, in a voice that frightened even Brian.

Terrified, the band of Carben dwarfs hurried back along the way they had come, legs pumping, not taking time to look about for the path, but rushing headlong away from the threatened danger.

Mathiny stood still, watching the retreating forms until the wood had swallowed them up.

"Well, it seems I'm stuck with you," he said, his voice unsure.

"You are indeed," replied Brian. "Stuck with a delving dwarf and a sly trickster of an elf, who is more than half an actor."

"We are known for that ability," said Shanon, smiling thinly. "But then, we are also known for our fierceness."

There was an edge in the elf's voice that cut the air with its coldness, and Brian saw that dark look in Shanon's eyes. It reminded him of watching storms, on the days he had been overside on work parties and seen the sky blacken, but with faint, clear patches of deep blue in between.

"Are the river snakes still with you?" asked Mathiny, more to himself than the elf.

"What do you think?" Shanon asked.

"And these things from the air? Are those really a part of the watchers of Erin Frey?"

The elf smiled at Brian.

"Sigman Col seems to have told his followers they were, from the way those fellows took off."

"You could have fooled me, the way you were talking. I was a little more than half frightened out of my wits myself."

"They will go straight to Sigman Col," said Mathiny, a sour look clouding his dark features.

"They may indeed, once they free themselves from the traps back there," laughed Shanon. "There were snares all over this path, but they were of a nature that would let an intruder in, but not out."

He turned to Brian.

"That's why I didn't seem worried about where we were walking. We won't find the other snares until we're almost into Erin Frey."

"Still, if they are not slain in your elf traps, they will tell Sigman Col our whereabouts, and that I have gone over to the enemy. They may even harm the prisoners!"

Brian's face drained of its color.

"Do you think they might?"

"If that bunch with Runion have anything to say about it. I hope your snares work as well as you seem to think."

"Oh, there's no doubt that they will," assured Shanon. "And there's no need to fear that they'll be slain. These traps

115

aren't of that nature. But they might be detained for a day or so, until they can properly dig their way out again."

"What'll we do now, about the others? Go on, turn back, try to bluff Senja and Chinby free?"

Brian's questions seemed to bother him a great deal, and although some of his old firmness had returned to his voice, he still looked worried.

Shanon, who had taken the lead now, and who showed the two dwarfs where to walk, spoke over his shoulder.

"First, we'll arm ourselves in Erin Frey. There may be more than a few things for us there. Then we'll see if we can't get our good Sigman Col to venture down into the old delvings of his forefathers, to find the traitor Mathiny and the two enemies of his tales, a delving dwarf and an upstart elf."

He paused, laughing in his tinkling, light elfin manner.

"We may have baited our trap more efficiently than if we'd schemed for a year or two, trying to come up with something to tickle Sigman Col into action."

"How is that?" asked Mathiny.

"Don't you see it? Runion will report back that you've gone over to the enemy, a dwarf and an elf. We were caught in the old delvings. That is the very thing that will frighten him the most. When you've built your house with nothing but leaves, the first strong wind that blows will shatter it all. He knows that. We have to be dealt with, or I'll miss my guess about the good Sigman Col."

"But how is all this going to help Senja or Chinby?"

"It's going to help them by your being proclaimed new Elder, and Liberator. Then you'll simply declare that they are set free, and that will be that."

Brian raised his eyebrows and started to protest, but at that very moment, Shanon halted, and pointed into the vast avenue of stately trees, where in spite of the dense overgrowth, there still remained a regal, long archway that led into what looked to Brian to be a huge, high gate, all of thorn and vine, interwoven with hundreds of bright red and yellow and blue flowers. At the very top was a row of white lilies, bending gracefully over the others.

"It's the outer walls of Erin Frey," said Shanon, his eyes shining.

A Long-Vanished Queen

THE elf took a long time to explain the intricate archways
that led to the dane of Erin Frey, and the meanings of all the
elfin runes that were carved into the various stone slates, or
in the living trunks of the great giants that towered upward
toward the sky, until their very tops were almost in the
clouds, or so it seemed to Brian and Mathiny, the Carben
dwarf, who had come along with them.

Although Mathiny had heard Sigman Col's stories about
their clan having elfin forebears, the Carben dwarf, in his
heart, knew it was not so, and did not wish it to be. This dane,
or what he was able to see of it, was very beautiful, and very
old, but it did not set his dreams afire as did the thoughts of a
delving, or of what Deep Home must look like, or any of the
other sacred places of dwarfdom.

He never said as much to anyone else, although he knew
there were many among their clan that felt as he did, and
who believed the lore masters, whenever they were able to
find a place to hold a secret meeting. There were always
many eager faces pressed close around any who professed to
know the old stories or songs, and who could weave a good
tale around a late fire.

Sigman Col had become more severe in his punishment of
these offenders, and recently, Mathiny had heard that one of
the unfortunate fellows who had been caught had been harshly
flogged, and thrown out into the more wild part of the wood,
without even any food or water to see him to the next
settlement. All of which only made the Carben clans more
determined to seek out and find the truth to what these lore
masters were saying of the delvings, and all that went on
there.

Brian, who was not much interested in outside digs, found

117

himself impressed with the sheer grace and beauty of the elfish dane Erin Frey. The outer gardens began just where the arched trees ended in a grand avenue that led up to the green live gates, woven with all the wild forest flowers, and in which some were in bloom almost constantly.

It was an explosion of colors there, but beyond things became somewhat complicated, for Shanon took them through a maze of hedges, all very high, which made it impossible to see where you'd come from, or were going.

"This is very much like our delving shafts," observed Brian. "Only there's no top."

The elf laughed lightly.

"Oh, there's a top. Look at the blue of it, up there."

"I don't call the sky any sort of roof," snorted the dwarf. "It certainly won't keep you dry."

"But look at it this way, my friend; it gives us the rain!"

"That's fine, but don't talk to me about rain, when what I need is a dry spot to sleep, or eat."

"I'll show you those after we get into the inner walls."

They had wound through the hedged paths for another long period of time when Mathiny spoke up, his tone subdued.

"Do you think you could have lost your way, master elf? I've tried to keep track of where we've been, but I've lost all count. If we're lost, I don't know how we'd ever find our way out again."

Brian looked about him, and felt the savage, long, hooked thorns that grew beneath the outer greenery of the hedges.

"These must be most effective, keeping folks out," he agreed. "How would we get out, if we did end up lost?"

"You wouldn't, unless you came across one of the fair citizens who lived here."

"I thought you said Erin Frey was deserted, just like the delvings of my sires?"

"It is."

"Then if one were lost, he'd stay here until he starved?"

"Or worse," went on Shanon, then brightened. "But you don't have to worry about that. You're with a guide who knows his way about well enough."

"How did Chinby ever find his way in here? He surely couldn't have met anyone to have guided him."

"Couldn't he? I wonder? I've thought about our meeting here. It was strange then, to find a total stranger in the inner city, and a dwarf, at that. I couldn't think how he'd gotten there, or who could have brought him. Then after he started talking, it seemed the most natural thing in the world for him to have been there."

"Do you think someone did guide him?" asked Brian, trying to pin the elusive elf down.

Shanon halted, peering around at the dense hedges that rose upward all about them.

"Do you think you could have found your way in here?"

"No," said Brian. "But Chinby isn't your ordinary dwarf."

"He's by no means that," conceded the elf. "Yet I think there was someone who brought him into Erin Frey, and who knew that I was to be there."

"You mean it was set up for you to meet?"

"It seems more and more like that, especially after I think more closely on it."

The elf frowned, as if trying to remember something.

"It was on a day that I was thinking of not returning again to Erin Frey, but I happened to talk to a friend, and told him what I was feeling. He encouraged me to go on and go. And I did, and met Chinby."

"I guess it would be strange, coming on a dwarf in this place."

"A very great surprise, in light of all the bad tales that are passed around on both sides."

Mathiny, enthralled by all the strange topics his two new friends were speaking of, could stand silent no longer.

"Do you mean elf and dwarf clans have differences? You sound as though it were open war."

Shanon laughed.

"It does sound a bit grim, doesn't it? Yet not far from the truth. Our two races haven't had the closest of ties in these later years. I would say without hesitation that Brian and I are probably the only elf and dwarf who are on speaking terms with each other in many miles of here."

"Don't forget Mathiny," chided Brian. "This is a real banner day for all our kinsmen, having not only a dwarf and elf on speaking terms, but a delving dwarf and a Carben dwarf actually in the same spot of ground together."

"I guess that's close enough to the truth," said the elf, growing more serious. "I think that was all Chinby's idea, about the whole thing. He seemed quite concerned about all the division among his cousins, and was full of dire warnings about having to all band together to weather some new threat that's been building up over the Roaring."

"What's the Roaring?" asked Mathiny.

"The Roaring Sea," explained Brian. "It stretches all the way beyond where anyone's ever gone, and then some."

"A sea?"

"Water! Lots of water, until all you can see in all directions is nothing but water."

The Carben dwarf's eyes grew wide in fear.

"That could not be!"

"Even more water than the river below the delvings, where we met you."

"Does it have things in it like the river snakes?"

"Many," replied Brian.

"Then I hope I never have to get near anything so horrible."

"That's where we're bound for, after we get Senja and Chinby back. We were to meet there, before your Sigman Col interrupted our plans."

"Then we may have saved your lives, if you were going to someplace so dangerous."

"Not so dangerous, old fellow. It may sound like that on the surface of it, but there are many others waiting along the coasts of the Roaring who are to join with us."

"That's if we ever get our friends back from Sigman Col," corrected the elf. "Our plans for their rescue aren't exactly completed, and I don't think this fellow is the sort who would just volunteer to give them back."

"Never," said Mathiny. "Sigman Col will be out searching for us now, as soon as Runion has reached him with word of my betrayal."

"Then we'd best go on into Erin Frey. At least we'll be safe from anyone trying to reach us there."

"Are all the entrances like this one?" asked Brian.

"Some of the others are worse," replied the elf gleefully. "I picked the easy way, so you wouldn't find it so tiring. Elves are sometimes prone to use the tops of trees as a path, and it takes a sure foot to get across some of those trails."

Brian grumbled loudly, snorting.

"Then thank you for your kindness. But what I would like to know is what we can hope to accomplish, even if we do find arms in your dane? We are only three, against how many?"

He paused, turning to Mathiny.

The Carben dwarf shrugged his shoulders.

"I don't know how many follow Sigman Col. More than my old settlement, though, which is very large. Our numbers have grown in these last years, and there are many spanners in the settlements."

"No matter, it is hopeless to try to think of attacking this self-styled Elder."

"One need not attack to be on the offensive," said Shanon. "I think our plot to lure Sigman Col into the lower river, where we can count on the watchers to help us convince him to release our friends, is still our best chance."

Brian knitted his brows, and ran a hand over his eyes.

"Sometimes I think it might be best just to confront the fellow. No hoop-lolly, or gimcracking around, just march right into his settlement, and demand the release of his prisoners."

The elf threw his head back and laughed a long note of rippling laughter that echoed softly in the green shadows of the tall hedges.

He had begun moving forward again, and turned to reply over his shoulder.

"I think that plan well suits an impulsive elf, but it hardly sits well on a cautious dwarf."

"There is nothing cautious about me, you tree walker," snapped Brian. "When it comes to my friends being in danger, all I can think about is how to remove them safely."

"And I am glad to count you as a friend," soothed the elf. "Without giving it up completely, I think we should look at some other alternatives first, just to see how desperate our situation really is."

"It's bad enough," grumped Brian. "In fact, I can't think of how it could be worse, unless our good Sigman Col had wings, and could fly over these hedges of yours to find us."

Mathiny, not at all used to the strange talk of his new friends, looked wildly upward, expecting to see that hated figure swooping down from the sky to punish him for his unfaithfulness.

"I don't think we have a need to worry about Sigman Col or anyone else reaching us here," reassured Shanon. "We'll have time to see what we may use from Erin Frey, and to try to plot a scheme that has a hope of working."

"We could always tell him he has the head of all ancient lore masters, and that there's a curse on anyone who stands

121

in his way, or displeases him," suggested Brian, trying to visualize Chinby as an ominous figure.

He could see Senja in that role more easily than he could the old dwarf. Senja, whose flaming eyes could scald a heart, or overcome any argument, might well play out a role of that nature, much more easily than Chinby.

"Do you think there might be any way of sneaking into Sigman Col's settlement, Mathiny? Any hope of being able to see our friends without being detected?"

The Carben dwarf thought carefully before answering.

"It would have been easy, if Runion had not gone back to Sigman Col. I could have guided you, and taken you myself, and no one would have been the wiser. Now they will be on the lookout for me, as well."

"That would have been handy, but it's beyond that now," said Shanon. "But is there any other way we could get into his settlement, and perhaps free our friends?"

"Sigman Col's camp is large, and will be well guarded after the news reaches him of the other two from the delvings having escaped, and that one of those is an elf. He'll have everyone out scouring the wood until we're all caught. I don't think he would waste his time flogging us, either. I think we'll find ourselves in front of a dart if he catches us. We will be too dangerous for him to let us live."

"That's true enough," agreed Brian. "And if one is running away, all it does is to encourage the other to chase along all the harder. I still think we would have our best chance by going straight to Sigman Col, armed, if we can find weapons in your dane, Shanon, and putting on a show of strength. Asking for his surrender, or to risk the fate that the river dwellers have in store for all those who dare cross them."

The three companions had reached a last hedgerow, which thinned quickly into a low-cut, well-bordered lawn, glass-green, and still wet from the morning dew, making that smooth, soft floor sparkle in the gentle sunlight which crept down through the branches of the huge giants that overhung the dane of Erin Frey.

When Brian turned around to see where they had come from, all that met his eyes was the vague face of the tall hedge, rising high above their heads.

"Do you think we could lure him here?" he asked, half aloud, his mind elsewhere, trying to formulate a plan.

122

"Erin Frey?" asked the elf. "I suppose so. Would he come here, Mathiny?"

"After all the stories he's spread about being a part of elfdom, he might. It would be hard to say. And it would depend upon what reasons he had to come."

"We could be the reason," said Brian. "But that still wouldn't force him to free Senja and Chinby. What we need is some bargaining power, or something to convince him we mean business, and intend to have our friends back."

"What we need for that is to have all your old delving of Den'Lin Fetch turned out with full complement of arms," teased Shanon.

"It wouldn't be a bad idea, if it weren't so difficult for them to get here. And I'm not sure they would be so glad to hurry into an elf dane. There are still many among my kindred who might be a bit slow where it comes to dealings with elves."

"They might enjoy a tour of a dane like Erin Frey," went on Shanon. "Give them some idea of how pleasant life can be aboveground."

"It's tolerable," admitted Brian. "But I don't know if any of them would see it as such."

"Wait until you see the main part of the settlement," said Shanon. "We're barely in the outer gardens now. You've seen nothing but the walls and rows of hedges, and all the devices they used to keep themselves safe."

He led the dwarfs farther on into the thinning trees, each a tall giant, with the tops spreading out umbrella-like, shading the ground below.

The lawns grew longer, spreading away into vast reaches of closely cropped small flower beds that surrounded fountains, with white marble statues of elves in various costumes and poses.

In the opposite direction, the bottle green of the grass lawn led onto a thickly wooded stretch, immediately followed by row on row of colored flower beds, forming many blends of design, and making the air heavy with their perfume.

"If the dane has been deserted for all these years, who takes care of all this?" asked Brian, trying to place all he was seeing into the pages of the lore tales that Chinby had told him of various elf danes.

"These are the enchanted gardens," answered the elf. "They were planted by the Queen Corin, in the year Erin Frey was founded. Her magic has remained on all the flowers and

123

lawns ever since. I will show you the North Garden, though, so you may see what has happened there. It was never tended by Queen Corin, and it has fallen into a wild jungle again, and covered all the dwellings that were there. You'd hardly know you were still in Erin Frey."

"It's amazing," said Mathiny, taking it all in, eyes wide, as he studied each new discovery.

There was the start of the buildings now, stately and open, windows full of white curtains that blew gently in the slight breeze from the forest.

"It is that," agreed Brian. "It's almost like a delving, only overground."

As they walked, Shanon pointed out the different places that he had learned of as a small elf at the knee of his teacher, showing them the low-roofed study where many volumes of elf lore were kept, all in neat rows that ran from shining wooden floor to beamed ceiling.

"This is where you would come to find any answers you might seek about the elfin clans. All of the lore books of all the various danes are here. I read many of them, until I grew too sad to go on. It was difficult learning of all those faded great names, knowing that none of them were left."

Brian nodded.

"I felt the same reading or hearing of Deep Home and the other delvings. Yet Chinby kept me interested and wouldn't let me give up on the idea of going back one day."

"It's strange that that same dwarf lore master would be my own teacher," said Shanon. "I had my share of elfish mentors, who taught me all the things I would have need of in order to get along in a trade, or to be able to speak properly, but when it came to the old lore, and the things that had gone before, all that came from Chinby."

"Who is this Chinby?" asked Mathiny, finding his amazement at the two unending.

"Chinby is one of the oldest dwarfs I have ever heard of, for one thing," replied Brian. "He was wounded in his head, and lost his vision, in a great battle with the beasts. He spent most of his time after that teaching, and traveling among the delvings."

"Then Sigman Col will be sure to value him as a hostage," said Mathiny. "I think he has always looked for one who knew enough to give him the tales he would need to help him

124

gain his dreams of a vast web of settlements throughout the wood, where all looked to him as Elder."

"Tell us more of this Sigman Col," encouraged Shanon.

"It's hard to say much of Sigman Col," answered the Carben dwarf. "He's above average height, even for one of us, and his hair is a long gray knot. Sometimes he wears a crown of polished wood and a dark scarlet robe. I've only seen him in his woodland green, and then for only brief times, when he came to our settlement to collect his tithes. He doesn't always go with his henchmen to do that, but he came on a few trips, and I knew that I didn't like him, or any of his ways of doing things."

"Did you ever hear where he hailed from, or anything of his father or lanin?"

"Only of his father. I never heard any mention of his mother, except someone once said it was a shame the way Sigman Col's early life had been marred by so much tragedy, and it wasn't right that a spanner should grow up with only a father to raise him."

"Has he always dwelled in these parts?" asked the elf. "Or does he come from some other neighborhood?"

"He is not from anywhere I have known of. I think I may have heard it said that he was a delving dwarf who left those shafts and became one of the Carben clans."

As Mathiny finished speaking, the companions had reached the first of the petal-shaped pools that were spread throughout the vast expanses of lawns, and other white-walled buildings began to appear, some in the shape of trees, others in the likeness of toadstools or great, smooth boulders. There were red roofs, and green and blue and gold, all blended into the simple forms of the dwelling places.

Brian could detect a grand design, but was unable to put his finger exactly on it.

In explaining the settlement, Shanon had mentioned that his ancestors had at one time perfected a manner in which they could lift themselves bodily into the air and cover great distances in short periods of time. He didn't know what had happened to the secret of it, but the elfish clans no longer were able to perform that wonderful feat, and had to content themselves with mere tree walking, or solid ground beneath their feet, but if one were to have been able to rise above the dane of Erin Frey to a fair altitude, it would have been laid out in the fashion of a great flower in full bloom, with the stem at the bottom of the gardens where the three had entered, and the petals encompassing the four directions of the compass.

Only the North Garden had grown into neglect and disuse, and that, suggested Shanon, was all because of something to do with the Queen Corin, and the secret of the ancient elfin clans' power to rise above the earth.

"If we had that now, I know we wouldn't have to worry about what we'd do about taking care of Sigman Col," said Brian, marveling at the elf's story.

"Maybe it's still out there in the North Garden you spoke of," offered Mathiny. "If that was the place this Queen What's-her-name didn't take care of, maybe it all has something to do with this business about being able to go around in the air."

Mathiny shook his head in disbelief.

"That must be a fair piece of arm beating," he mumbled. "And a fellow would have to be no thicker than a feather."

"It had something to do with other things than arms or wings, old fellow. No one has ever discovered what, though. Some said it was the waters from the old fountain in the Square of Corin, and others said it had to do with the Stone of Elver Tarn. But no one ever was able to describe it, or what it looked like."

"They all sound likely, as tales," snorted Brian. "What I'm after is a way to fool Sigman Col, and to get the release of our friends. And to find our way out of here, back to the delvings, and on to the Sea of Roaring. It has begun to bore me here."

"Would I be allowed to go along with you, if I chose?" asked Mathiny.

"Of course. We couldn't leave you behind now, with all the trouble you've gotten into because of us. You may be able to help us call others of the Carbens to our cause, especially when we get ready to go on to the Roaring."

As they talked, they neared a huge gateway, cut from numbers of square, stacked pieces of marble that formed one giant square.

Passing under the arch, Brian saw the wild tangle of overgrown lawns and avenues, and knew they had come into the portion of Erin Frey that Shanon called the North Garden. There was a sudden chill there, as if the sun had gone out, and the friends huddled closer together against the eerie stillness.

126

The Stone of Elver Tarn

INSIDE the archway Mathiny stopped, too frightened to go any farther. His eyes were rimmed with white, and his knees were trembling so badly he almost fell.

Shanon quickly turned to reassure his friends.

"You have no cause to be afraid here. You are with an heir of the old reign of Corin, Queen of Elver Tarn."

"Why is this place so different from the rest of your settlement?"

The elf's face darkened.

"There is a long story here, of something that happened a very great while ago, when Erin Frey was full of my kindred, and all things were much happier than they are now."

"That must have been a very long time ago," offered Mathiny. "I can't remember any times since I've been about that could be called happy."

Brian checked his tongue.

"That's a sad statement, my friend. As short a while as I've been coming and going, I must admit reluctantly to a little happiness, however fleeting."

"But what of this queen, Shanon? And what happened?"

The elf looked about at the shattered outerwalls of the gardens, and the great trees that had grown weathered and almost bare of leaves, as if preparing for winter.

In the center of the garden as its focal point a great well stood, marked in stone, with finely carved figures that ran around the outer surface. These carvings were moss-grown, and the once white marble was a dingy gray.

"This was the garden of the Queen Corin," explained Shanon. "She would come here to see what she might of the future, and to make any decisions that had to be made for the best interests of Erin Frey. And when there were visitors from the other settlements, or other races, this was where they were entertained."

He walked through the thick weeds and undergrowth to point out an entirely overgrown pavilion with golden posts that supported a circular roof, which had once held many colored canopies of the fine elfin spun cloth. Nothing remained but a few pathetic tatters of the canopy, and the golden posts were a rusted brown.

"Many folk from many places came to see Queen Corin. It was thought she had the powers to see into pasts and futures, and was said to have been a wise adviser, if you could get her to speak."

Shanon laughed to himself quietly.

"Sometimes she wouldn't talk of anything at all but the weather, or how the crops were doing, or ask about distant relatives."

"Elves had been known to be like that," agreed Brian. "Chinby told me many stories of how hard it is to pin down one of your sort."

Speaking of Chinby brought the dwarf up short, and a pang of helplessness and anger flooded through him.

"I wish your Queen Corin were here now," he went on bitterly. "Perhaps she might have been able to put a plan to mind as to how we are to try to get our friends back safely."

"It wouldn't hurt to try the old Fountain of Elver," suggested Shanon. "That was the pool where Corin was said to have looked into the eye of things. No one could ever be sure whether the true power came from the Queen or from that fountain."

"Is this it?" asked Mathiny, stepping closer to the weed-choked and now dry fountain, which was bounded by the low carved wall.

"As far as anyone knows," replied Shanon. "It's the only fountain that I've seen in this garden. No one can be sure, though, for all the old lore books that described it, and told where it lay, and what it looked like, were burned in the great fire. There were many elves lost then, and it was not long after that that Queen Corin was betrayed."

"What caused the fire?" asked the Carben dwarf.

"A beast that came from the wildness of the East," replied Shanon. "It was one of the beasts of the Reckoning, and only by the forces of dwarf and elf joining together was it vanquished. It is said the time has come that they are marching again."

Recognizing his old teacher's lore in the words of his friend, Brian nodded agreement.

"According to the good Chinby, that's the prospect we are faced with. Not a cheery thought, by a long pull."

"Not a very cheery place to be talking about it all, either," grumbled Mathiny.

"Do you think we'll be able to find any arms here?" asked Brian, suddenly impatient to be doing something toward freeing the captives, Senja and Chinby.

"These are the mounds that housed all the storehouses for Erin Frey," explained Shanon, pointing to a low, rounded dome, earth-covered, with wildflowers growing thickly on it. "If there is anything to be had to suit our purposes, we'll find it in one of those."

"Don't you think we should be looking, then? Our good dwarf Sigman Col isn't going to be wasting any time, once he gets the news from his spy about all that's going on."

"You're right. We'll go on until we can find something that will aid us."

"You might start with a war party large enough to hold Sigman Col off," complained Mathiny.

"He'd need more than a host of dwarfs to reach us here," reminded Brian. "I don't think we need worry as long as we're in Erin Frey."

"But we'll have to leave, sooner or later," concluded Mathiny glumly. "They still hold your two friends. All he'd have to do is threaten to harm them, and you'd have to go."

Brian thought about what the slightly taller Carben dwarf said. It was true, he agreed, that if Sigman Col were to come right at this moment, and order them to surrender, they would be forced to submit, lest the others be harmed.

There was something in the tactic so vile and loathsome that Brian felt a knot of nausea clutching his stomach.

These were the sort, he felt, who would stop at nothing in order to gain whatever small power they could, or take advantage of any hold they could find, regardless of its nature.

He tried to recall his meetings with Chinby, when the old dwarf discussed the other beings in the realms of wood and water, who had no such training as Brian.

"They adapt to the life they have," said Chinby softly. "You must not hate them for what they are. You can dislike their behavior, which is fair and logical, but you must always try

129

to remember that they are the way they are because of a good reason."

He tried to be fair in his thinking about Sigman Col, and to understand the Carben tribe that had refused to turn for the better when they had the chance, after they had been spared by the dwellers in the river, who guarded the lower shafts of the ancient delvings. Perhaps, he wondered, he too would have done the same, faced with the circumstances that had been. He couldn't tell, and it would make no difference, at any rate, for he was Brian Brandigore, and was on his own path, and had his own unique part to play, however dim and hazy it seemed, or how gloomy the prospects.

"Do you think Sigman Col has received word yet?"

"That's hard to say," answered the Carben dwarf. "If my old friends have had no trouble in reaching his settlement, then he has probably had news by now. As to what he will do, only he knows."

"I still feel we ought just to march in on him," blustered Brian. "It might take him off guard. He will surely expect us to run and hide, since that is what anyone would do if they were in an enemy camp, and outnumbered."

"Your point is well taken," said Shanon. "I can see the merit to that line of thought. But if our friend doesn't bluff, then we have nothing to back up our threat, and we're all in a pickle, with no hope of rescue, and completely at the mercy of master Sigman Col."

"A place you'd regret being," snorted Mathiny. "He is no easy dwarf to deal with, even if you are of his own clans. An outsider would stand no chance."

Brian looked closely at the Carben dwarf.

"What do you think he intends doing with Senja and Chinby? As you see it?"

Mathiny looked away uncomfortably, clearing his throat.

"I can only speak for myself. And before I ran against you and your river snakes, I would have taken the prisoners and used them to do the hard toil of clearing a place for a new settlement."

"That's all?"

"As I saw it then, yes. I didn't know your friend was a lore master, and dangerous."

"And Sigman Col wouldn't have, if we had let the river snakes finish up their work in the tunnels."

The Carben dwarf colored slightly.

"You asked me for an honest reply."

Brian slapped Mathiny a resounding dwarf thump to reassure him.

"No, no, old fellow, I appreciate your honesty. You've told me what I want to know. It seems things are in a real mess, half in, half out of the fire. And we're in no good shape to do anything at all."

"Yet we must move soon, or Sigman Col will have all the odds in his favor. If we wait too long, he'll assume we're running, and we'll have lost even what small advantage we have."

Shanon pounded a fist into an open palm angrily. The elf took on a more foreboding expression when he was upset.

"Let us go on for the storehouses. We must find what we can, and make our move."

He quickly led the way to the far side of the strange elfin mound, and directly in front of a wild tangle of thorns, he called out softly in high elfish, making the words melodic and soothing.

To the astonishment of Brian and Mathiny, the thorns began to move, then part, and there before them was an oak-hewn door, with a huge brass handle. The wood was finely carved, and even in its decay, looked elegant and mysterious.

"How did you do that?" asked Mathiny.

"An old elf primer used to have the words. My mother read it to me when I was small. Every elf knows the rhyme."

"I couldn't understand a word of it," confessed Mathiny.

"It's my own tongue," explained Shanon, twisting the huge handle with all his strength, and tugging on the ancient door.

"What did you say?"

"Oh, something to the effect of rhyming mountains, and broad meadows, and evening rivers."

"More of that mulhash that Chinby told me of," said Brian grumpily, thinking the elf would have had something sensible to say. "I don't know why I would have expected anything else, though," he mumbled. "Whether it's opening a door in a thorn bush, or giving each other riddles, none of it means anything except gibberish to the likes of me."

"Gibberish to a dwarf is music to an elf's ear," reminded Shanon cheerfully. "You fellows are ever so slow on the uptake, and see no use in anything that doesn't lead to some sort of sense. Which is fine, as far as it goes, but you'll find

131

there are things in life that have no sense to them at all, except that they're perfect in that they make absolutely no sense."

"The absurd elf reasoning," blustered Brian, lending his weight to help open the heavy door.

He turned to Mathiny.

"He told me that the best reason he could think of for going to the Roaring with me was that there was absolutely no reason at all he should go."

"That's odd," agreed the Carben dwarf. "I'd think I'd want to be a little more concerned than that."

"What I added at the end was that I'd love to go to the sea, if it were far enough from a dwarf delving," interrupted Shanon.

"Here! Give us a hand, Mathiny," said Brian, ignoring his friend's humor.

The three companions pulled and tugged at the huge door, feeling it give inch by inch, the ancient hinges creaking and protesting.

"Whew," breathed Brian. "I'm glad we weren't in a hurry to get through here. I'd give a sweet price to have my father's toolbox here now. I daresay we'd be able to grease these skids up nicely. A dwarfwrought door would have been ever so much more sturdy than this, and I'll wager it wouldn't be sticking this way now, either."

"It's coming! Pull on that edge there, can you! We've almost got it."

Brian got a hand through the tiny opening, and pulled with all his strength. The Carben dwarf wedged a small limb from a branch of one of the thorn trees, and with Shanon pulling the handle, they managed to pry the stiff door open wide enough for them to slip inside.

"That's going to be a close fit," warned Brian.

"It'll be big enough for our purposes," replied Shanon. "We only have to have it wide enough to squeak inside."

"Can you see anything in there?"

"Elfmoons," answered the disappearing form. "We've been on to using those too, you know."

Brian peered into the doorway, and was astounded to find that it was as bright as the afternoon sun outside, and that Shanon was nowhere to be seen, even though he had only just entered the opening.

132

Brian called out loudly, and was surprised to hear the elf's voice right in front of him.

"You don't have to yell! I'm right here."

There was nothing before Brian but empty air.

"Where are you?"

"Here! Is your eyesight as bad as all that?"

Mathiny poked his head around Brian's shoulder.

"We can't see you."

Appearing out of nowhere, the elf strode abruptly to a few paces from the dwarfs.

"Now we can see you," cried Brian. "But we couldn't when you went through the door."

The elf looked perplexed, the confusion growing darker in his eyes.

"Let me show you," said Brian, and he ducked past the elf, and into the brightness of the doorway.

To his astonishment, Shanon found that he could see no trace of his friend, although he knew he could be no more than a few paces from him.

"He's disappeared, too," gasped Mathiny, unbelieving.

"There must be an answer to all this," said Shanon, rubbing a hand across his eyes. "I know Queen Corin was said to have had many such places in her own garden. There were things like this spoken of, where you couldn't see things, and there were others where things seemed to be something else."

Mathiny, unable to control himself any longer, moved into the opening, and stepped beyond. As soon as the doorway was crossed, he realized that he could see the elf, who was peering after him, but that the elf could not see him.

He turned to relate his discovery to Brian, but found on turning around that there was not a dwarf before him, but a small hedgehog, carefully dressed in exactly the same clothes his friend had worn, and with the same bold hat on its head.

"Brian?" called Mathiny.

"I'm here. Is that you?"

"Of course it's me."

"Who is it?" asked Shanon, who had followed Mathiny into the opening.

"Who do you think it is?" huffed Brian. "I'm me, but who are you two?"

To Brian, Mathiny was a tall, slender egret, and Shanon appeared as a sleek fox.

133

"I'm me, too!" exploded Mathiny. "I wish you two would stop your silly jokes. They're not funny!"

Shanon calmed his friend's rising fear, but raised a paw.

"This must be one of the spells that Queen Corin put here, to protect the inner rooms. Let's go on, and don't trust your eyes. This is all something that will pass as soon as we go on."

"I hope so. I wouldn't want to be caught out in the forest by Sigman Col with a hedgehog and a fox," complained Mathiny. "He'd soon enough make quick work out of the lot of us."

"Do tell," snapped Brian.

"Come on," urged Shanon. "Let's go on into the next hall. But go carefully. There are some things here that I've never heard of, and can't be sure what they are."

"That's a fine kettle of stew," grumbled Brian. "You knew plenty enough about a stranger's delving, but you don't know the first thing about your own."

"We'll find out soon enough," the elf answered, an irritable edge to his voice.

The truth was that Brian was correct in his opinion, and it seemed a strange paradox to Shanon. He knew the ins and outs of a strange dwarfwrought world, but had few facts to go on when it came to the homeland of his own kindred.

He gritted his teeth, and trying not to allow himself to be disconcerted by what appeared to be an egret and a hedgehog, pushed on ahead into the next room, which was curtained with floor-length royal blue tapestries, all of which depicted odd scenes, of animals with robes and crowns, and strange golden cities, whose towers rose in endless rows, and a whole series of elfin history scenes, each showing a different elfin king and queen, until at the end, he knew he must be looking at the Queen Corin, with all her mysterious powers and frightening beauty.

This queen was so fair it was difficult for the friends to look on her, and it appeared that her eyes moved within the woven cloth, and her long, flowing golden hair seemed to blow in an imaginary breeze.

Softly, so softly that they did not notice it at first, a gentle music began to play, just at the outside edge of their hearing, growing gradually louder. Without knowing how, or why, the three companions were swaying with each note as it filled the air and seemed to blow the tapestries even more, making the room full of softly breathing elfin cloth, and bringing to life the entire story of the elfin kingdoms.

134

"What is it?" whined Mathiny, trying to retreat from the wonderful music.

Shanon grasped the Carben's arm, and held him still.

"Listen!" he said quietly. "Listen! There's nothing for you to be frightened of here."

"Shhhh," scolded Brian, trying to pick up the fragile notes of the song again.

His ears strained, and his eyes were wide, watching the tapestry move slowly to and fro before him.

Without knowing exactly when it happened, or how the change had taken place, he found himself staring into the bottomless blue eyes of a most beautiful elfin lady, dressed all in a pale gold and silver robe that reflected back the gold from her long hair.

The music had grown louder, and all other sounds vanished, and Brian was no longer aware of the others, Shanon and Mathiny. All he was aware of was this beautiful figure of the elf, and the music.

"Welcome, good dwarf. What brings you to Erin Frey?"

Brian could not tell if it were a voice or the music which questioned him.

It took him a moment to find his voice.

"My name is Brian Brandigore. I come with a friend, Shanon, and another dwarf, Mathiny. We have come to Erin Frey to try to find arms, or help, to rescue two others who have been captured by the Carben dwarf Sigman Col."

He was surprised at himself for saying so much, yet he realized that there was no holding back anything from the terrible beauty of the elfin lady.

A slight frown crossed the fair features as Brian spoke.

"Welcome, Brian Brandigore. That is a name that is known to me. I am Corin. Perhaps your good elf has told you who I am."

"But you were here so long ago! How can you still be here now?"

"That is the secret we elves hold, Brian. There is nothing so mystical to it, once you know all that we know. Merely a way of being, just like all the rest."

Shanon's voice drifted into his awareness.

"Queen Corin! My honor is pledged to you!"

"Welcome, my small brother. And welcome to you, Mathiny."

The Carben dwarf choked back his fright, and managed a small bow. He swore to himself that if he ever survived to escape from this horrible place, he would never set foot outside his own wood again. Then, remembering that he had gone over to an enemy, he grew full of a sad bitterness that threatened to take away his small hold on sanity.

"You need not fear me, Mathiny. You are no longer a part of the Carben dwarf clans, as you have told yourself. Now is the time for you to go beyond those small borders you have set for yourself, and the companions you have now are true."

Mathiny gulped aloud.

"Can you help us?" asked Shanon hesitantly.

"I can, and shall," said Corin. "You shall have need of your two friends who are held by Sigman Col, although I fear that you are too late to help them escape."

Brian, a savage anger exploding over him at the pronouncement of the elfin queen, swore a dark vengeance on Sigman Col.

"There's no harm done to your friends, Brian Brandigore, and no need for your vengeance against Sigman Col. I said you are too late to help your friends escape, because they have already done so. They're not dead, as you supposed."

"But how?" shot Brian.

"The dwarf lane and the blind one have used the old shafts to their own advantage."

"What shafts?" asked Shanon.

"The prison where Sigman Col kept them opened onto the old underground paths," replied the elfin queen. "They simply used them. But they will need you now. They aren't safe yet."

"How can we reach them?" asked Brian.

"You will use the North Garden gate, which you know, Shanon. Go straight to the Three Oaks, and from there to the Green Shield. It goes underground at the base of the Elf Cloak Falls."

The figure of the elfin lady began to dim, and at the same moment he heard the others again, Brian noticed that the beautiful queen was merely once again a portrait on the woven cloth.

As they looked closer, Shanon let out a strangled cry.

"The Stone of Elver Tarn!"

And there, at the feet of the elfin figure on the tapestry, was a small, glowing blue stone, perfectly round, and pulsing softly with a brilliant blue-white light. Shanon reached out a hesitant hand and picked it up reverently.

"It will serve you until the time it shall be returned," came the voice of Corin, distant and echoing.

Brian was not sure it was a voice, or music, but his heart lifted wildly as he stared at the smooth, steady, glowing light from the stone the elf Shanon held carefully in his open palm.

Separate Paths

IT was some space of time before the companions' excitement died down enough for them to study carefully the beautiful stone, which had gone from a pale, fierce white light to a steady, humming blue.

And they had the news to discuss, of their friends' escape from Sigman Col, all done without their lifting a hand to help.

"It was Senja's doing," said Brian proudly, confused and astonished at his feelings when he said it.

"Leave it to a thick-necked dwarf lane to rip it every time," laughed Shanon. "Chinby was thinking ahead when he picked out who his travel companion would be. If he'd taken you and me, odds are that we'd be in Sigman Col's basement yet."

"If he'd let you live that long," added Mathiny. "You are too great a threat to him, especially now that the others have escaped. He'll be looking twice as hard for some way to cover his carelessness."

"If your Sigman Col is as one-sided in matters as some other dwarfs I know, then that means trouble for us."

Shanon's face was drawn into a thin frown.

"It means he won't rest until he's captured us all again," concluded the Carben dwarf grimly, his mouth set.

"We can forget any plan we had of surprising him," agreed Brian. "I don't see any use in that now, anyway. It would serve no purpose, except to perhaps give Senja and Chinby a further head start, if we were to draw them off the trail. Yet I

137

can't see that that would do any of us any good. Maybe better for us all to go on with our plans to get to the Roaring as best we're able, and to try to meet there."

"I'd vote for that," said the elf, rising onto tiptoe, and stretching his muscles. "We could be a long time gone before Sigman Col gets organized for a search."

"Remember that he knows about the old delvings, and the paths that lead there," cautioned Mathiny. "He'll know we'll have to make for there if we are to escape."

A cloud crossed Brian's features.

"That's true."

"There are other roads to take," said Shanon. "One often travels best where he's least expected."

"We can't travel above ground," protested Brian.

"You forget that I'm as well at home up here as he is," replied Shanon. "You must remember that this is an elf's domain, and even Sigman Col, for all his claims, is no elf, but a transplanted dwarf. I'm sure he has great knowledge of the immediate areas near his settlements, but he has no way of knowing about Erin Frey, or any of the elfin highways to and from our city. There was a time when all the clans were at peace, both water and wood folk, and traveled much between the settlements."

Mathiny squinted at the elf gloomily.

"Sigman Col has found some of the old roads. That is part of his story of being of an elfish nature, going about telling everyone all his made-up stories about all those places. And if he has the idea that an elf is among us, he'll make sure that there are ambushes on those roads."

Brian clapped Mathiny on his heavily muscled back.

"Good thinking, old fellow, although bad news. I grow more wary of your Sigman Col as time goes on. It seems he is no backwoods dwarf with a big dream of ruling over a large clan."

"He has plans to overrun even the delvings," went on Mathiny.

"With all the haphazard defenses that there are now in my old settlement, I don't doubt but that a well-planned attack and siege would overthrow it. We're ready for the raiders, but they're all beasts, and have no more of a thought about attacking than how much food can be gotten. This Sigman Col evidently has a plan in mind, and enough of the secrets of the delving dwarfs that he might prove dangerous."

"Don't forget the river dwellers," reminded the elf. "Anyone going belowground with the wrong reasons in mind might have their hands full, just getting by the watchers."

"They wouldn't let anyone loot the old delvings, true. Yet they might do nothing if the party there belowground was dwarfish, even though only Carben dwarfs, and just traveling through. Our Sigman Col might also go overground to reach there."

"Do you think that could be?" asked Shanon, his brows raised doubtfully.

Brian shook his head.

"I don't know. But I wonder if we shouldn't go back to warn Den'Lin Fetch, and all the other settlements. I hate to think of my father and lanin back there, unsuspecting."

"Or any of the rest, if it comes to a warning. I don't know. I wish Chinby were here to advise us."

The elf paced restlessly back and forth in the bright fire of the elfmoons.

"Or Corin. I could have asked her."

"Don't forget what she said at the last," broke in Mathiny. "She said you were to leave by the North Gate, and to follow the Green Shield to a place called Elf Cloak Falls."

Brian muttered out loud, and thwacked a palm with his fist.

"You are a cool one, my friend," he said, addressing the Carben. "Sometimes I wonder if there's any more use for my head than a hatrack. Of course, she said exactly what to do."

He repeated the instructions over again to himself, half aloud.

"Follow the Green Shield to the Elf Cloak Falls. The North Gate. Is that near here?" he asked, turning to the elf.

"This is the North Garden, and the North Gate is just beyond where we came into this hall. I don't think it had been used for a long time even before everyone left Erin Frey."

"Where does it lead, then?" asked Mathiny.

Shanon's brow darkened.

"It was said to lead into the Mouth of the Dragon. The lore is vague on the issue. I should have asked our good Queen Corin about it. There were tales that that country was where the ancient dragons of the Elver Tarn came from time to time to dwell."

"Dragons?" asked the Carben dwarf, eyes wide with terror.

"These dragons are not your usual horror story," explained

139

Shanon. "Chinby told me the old stories of the bad luck some of your kin has had with something that might pass for a mock dragon. They even sound to have been described as being similar, but there is a basic difference in the two, and that is that the line of the Elver Tarn were noble beings that guarded all the realms from harm, and kept the Great Darkness at bay for all the first of the Golden Age."

"What happened? Did they lose their powers?"

"No, they never lost their powers, Mathiny, but a time evidently came when they were no longer needed, and they returned to where they came from."

"And then the bad times began," said Brian evenly. "Chinby told me of the end of the Golden Age, and all the things that passed by with it. Seems one thing had ended, and another begun, and the times were all changed."

"For the worse, it seems," grumbled the Carben dwarf.

"Perhaps," agreed Brian. "Yet there has been some good come of it all, when it gets right down to it."

"Whatever might that be?"

"For one thing, here we three are," replied Brian. "A delving dwarf, a Carben, and an elf, standing in one of the old dwelling places of ancient elfdom."

Shanon smiled at his friends.

"You know, I hadn't thought of it exactly like that, but it's true. Now if there were only a wood elf to go along with us, we'd be all set to go forth, with at least a token reunion of all the clans."

"Maybe that's what your Queen Corin had in mind when she lent you the Stone of Elver Tarn."

"That might be. She did say I would one day have to return it, when all was said and done."

"I want to know some more about this dragon business," complained Mathiny. "Especially if we're going to have to be going out where they might be."

"They were an ancient race," comforted Shanon. "You don't have to worry about them any longer. And if they were still around, I'd feel a lot better. I don't think Sigman Col would be anything of a bother to us if that were the case."

"You mean they were something like those river snakes? And what you told Runion was true?"

"Exactly. At one time they had the run of all the lands, and kept an eye on everything, and made sure the woods and seas and mountains were safe."

"Then I wish they were still here," agreed Mathiny.

"Chinby said that in the end, they had to leave because there was no growth, and everything had remained so pleasant and peaceful that everyone began to forget about the High King, and going back Home. That's when the Elver Tarn went back, and that was the start of the downfall. Nothing but trouble from then on."

"I could use a lot less of that," snorted Mathiny. "If it's all the same, I could use a little peace and quiet."

"Is there anything we can arm ourselves with?" asked Brian. "North Gate or not, we need some supplies, and some weapons, if we're to have to travel overground. There's always a chance we won't even see a trace of Sigman Col, but we don't know what else is out there, either."

"Beasts," growled Mathiny. "Flocks and droves of the blasted beasts!"

His dark features grew more troubled.

"The one reason that Sigman Col has grown so popular among the Carben settlements is that he has launched an offensive against these raiders, and has managed to destroy many of them."

"Have the beasts been a problem here?"

"I can remember as a spanner that our settlement lost over a dozen dwarfs in a single raid. We weren't used to having to guard our boundaries, and we were taken by surprise by a great pack of that filth. My own father was slain, and my sister as well."

Mathiny's voice grew tight.

"When Sigman Col came, he organized us all into war bands, and we began to strike back, and to drive that bunch of killers out of our wood, and the surrounding woods as well. There are many that owe their lives to Sigman Col."

Here his voice gave out entirely, and his eyes were rimmed with great tears.

"Here, here, old fellow," soothed Brian. "This will never do."

He clapped the Carben dwarf a resounding whack, and tried to pump up his flagging spirit.

"I think I see your problem, and I can only respect you more for it, Mathiny. You feel as though you've betrayed the one most responsible for helping your settlements, and all the other Carbens, and I can understand that. Then we come along, and upset the entire arrangement, because you're

141

caught now between doing the right thing by us, or being labeled as a deserter from your own kind."

"Exactly what we've all felt," reassured Shanon. "I'm an outcast of my own clan, because here I am, elbow to elbow with a great clutch of dwarfs, acting more as if I were one of them than any self-respecting elf."

"Reverse that, and you'll see I'm in the same boat," huffed Brian.

"And I don't know what to think, or make of it all," complained Mathiny. "I mean, I believe you, and know you're trying to do what's good and proper, but I don't want to go with you to the Roaring."

Having blurted out the truth at last, the Carben dwarf broke into a series of small, choked sobs.

"I had a settlement, and friends, and a job to do this morning, and after running into you all I've got left is the hope that someday I might make my way back to where I had started from, and somehow be accepted again, and prove to my old companions that I haven't been a traitor to them."

Brian leveled an even look at Shanon.

"This sounds serious," he said over the Carben dwarf's trembling shoulders.

"It does, indeed," agreed the elf.

"I don't think that just anyone we chance to meet is going to be of the same mind that we were. It seems there are some who have a more solid sense of home life than we did."

"I should say so. Poor old fellow, he's been on the edge of this ever since his friend Runion left. I could see then he was having a difficult time of it."

"Please forgive me, but I must go back now. I promise I won't tell anyone of your plans, or where you're going."

"You couldn't tell them much, even if you did," laughed Shanon.

"What do you think?" asked Brian.

"I think we should let the poor fellow do whatever suits him best. I wouldn't force anyone to go off with us."

"My feeling, too," said Brian. "And I was thinking, you know, it might not be such a bad idea after all, Mathiny, if you did tell Sigman Col where we're bound. You can always say that you stayed with us to find what our plans were, and where we were off to."

"That might get him off the hook, as far as his friends go," nodded Shanon. "As good a story as any."

"And I'm thinking that if he were to do that, Sigman Col might follow along after us, as well."

The elf's eyes turned a deep sea blue.

"I'm beginning to see your line of thought," he said at last. "If there are as many beast raiders lurking about as our friend leads us to believe, then it wouldn't be too bad an idea to have a large war party crashing along behind us, to sort of stir things up a bit, and keep everyone honest, especially any nasty brutes that might be about, looking for a small snack in the form of two thick-hided fellows that had no better sense than to be strolling about all by themselves."

Mathiny's brow cleared somewhat, and he looked greatly relieved.

"I really mean you no harm, and will do whatever I can to help. But I can't leave like this."

Brian shook his head slowly.

"You may or may not have to do that, my friend, but you won't be faced with it just yet. Not at our hand, at any rate. There may be a time coming when just that will occur, but by then it won't matter, because all things will be on the move. It's hard to sit still in the center of a storm. Some strong tides are running now, from what Chinby has told me, and from what I've seen with my own eyes."

"Can you show me how to get out, Shanon?" asked the Carben dwarf. "I'd like to be on my way as soon as I can."

"I'll show you the way, Mathiny. First I think we'd better find some arms for us all, though. It would be dangerous for you to try to get back to your settlement through the path beyond the North Gate without weapons. I've never gone much beyond the outer boundaries of Erin Frey that way, but the Green Shield and the Elf Cloak Falls are far beyond any safety of the dane. It is a good march to reach the river, and the countryside is wild. Queen Corin left that side of Erin Frey to itself, and not many elves ever journeyed there, except to find the special trees that grow along the river, which make superior bows and shafts."

"Wouldn't it be better to take him back the way we came in?" asked Brian.

"It won't take long for him to find that gate where we entered. I shall guide him toward the outer wall, and all he'll have to do is follow along it until he finds some territory that he's familiar with."

Mathiny started to blubber, and to thank the friends profusely.

"I won't forget this kindness," he wept. "You've been more than good to me, and I shall repay you someday, somehow."

"You can repay us best by telling Sigman Col that we have gone by way of the North Gate of Erin Frey, and are on our way to the Green Shield and the Elf Cloak Falls."

"Come along," said Shanon gently. "Let's get to the armory, and see what we can find in the way of something to deter any of those nasty louts that might be dallying around outside our gates."

"Let's hope there's none near enough to need worrying about," shot Brian, although not very hopefully.

The elf led them on into the inner chambers of the huge rooms, each lit by glowing elfmoons, some red, some golden, and some a fiery white color that made it hard to see without squinting against their brilliance.

The airy, tall dome-shaped passages honeycombed around onto the next, until the two dwarfs had lost count of the turns, which was unusual, especially for a delving dwarf, but not knowing the nature of elfin dwellings, or their love of intricate patchwork designs, or maze-like, weaving hallways that often doubled back on themselves, they were quickly lost in the strange dwelling, and had to depend entirely on the swift-moving elf to get them safely to the other side.

In a chamber at the very center of the domed structure, Shanon turned into a passage that ran off to one side, and the next moment, was crouched before a low doorway that was barred, and double-bolted with what looked to Brian to be good dwarfwrought iron.

"Is that some handiwork of my kindred?" he asked, looking closer at the design of the thick bolt heads.

"Of the very finest order," replied Shanon. "These were done not long before the Elver Tarn went back beyond the Upper River."

"Is this dwarfish?" asked Mathiny, never having seen ores so finely worked.

"It is. And this is the sort of work that you'd find in any delving, although it looks as well placed here in this elfin house as in any halfing I ever saw."

The Carben dwarf turned hesitantly to Brian.

"How is it we got torn apart, our two races? I mean why did we ever split apart?"

Brian shrugged.

"That's for lore masters like Chinby to say. I have no idea."

"For the same reason that the water elf and wood elf split their settlements," put in Shanon. "Ignorance!"

He snorted.

"And look what it has all led to."

At that moment, the locks answered his fiddling, and the thick door swung open slowly, revealing more elfmoons glowing beyond, and a great hall stacked with stores and arms of every description.

Stepping inside, Shanon lifted a hand, and indicated the great heaps of weapons.

"All these were laid in here at the close of the age of the Elver Tarn, just before Queen Corin departed."

"She must not have departed too far, if she can reappear whenever she wants," said Mathiny. "I'm not sure yet I wasn't just dreaming."

"You weren't dreaming, friend. That is part of the spell on Erin Frey. It is watched just as faithfully as the old delvings on the Deep Home Highway."

"For the same reasons, too, I would imagine," said Brian. "According to the version of the tale that Chinby tells, one day all the settlements and delvings everywhere will be filled again with beings, and the great journey back Home will begin."

"That's how the story goes," said the elf. "And I'm not the one to dispute it. Especially after hearing the queen from the olden days speaking out after all this time."

As he talked, the elf began sorting through the tall stacks of various weapons, and began placing some of them into lots that he broke into three divisions.

"Here's one for me, and one for Mathiny, and one for Brian," he repeated, piling gently curved elfin great bows of weathered ash, and woven quivers, colored a deep wood green, full of long shafts, with bright red and blue feathered ends.

There were short swords that had been forged in the deep delvings of dwarfdom, and sheaths woven and spun by the elves.

Near the end were the cloaks that could make the wearer almost invisible to an untrained eye, and the fine-woven mesh shirts that were said to be capable of diverting even the

145

fierce blows of a beast claw, or the teeth of the worst of the brutes.

Separating their new treasures, Brian found, to his surprise, that everything he had gotten fit almost perfectly, and he could not explain the strange sensation he had that he had done the entire thing before.

Looking into one of the shiny mirror flat shields that lined one solid wall of the room, he saw a sight that was slightly disturbing, yet very familiar all at once. There in the reflected light of the elfmoons, Brian saw himself, the light elfinwrought helmet gleaming a pale red, and beside him, Shanon, dressed in the shining mesh shirt, broad sword held before him as he examined it.

And then there was Mathiny, strong face troubled, looking from beneath a forest-green cloak at his new friends.

"I've got the oddest feeling that all this has happened before," said Brian at last, catching the glance of the elf in the reflection from the rows of shields.

Shanon's eyes were a deep blue, and he nodded slowly.

"Yes, I feel that, too. We've done all this, or maybe it's a dream that's yet to come."

"That might be."

"I've got to go," insisted Mathiny. "If I am to be of any service to you, I've got to reach Sigman Col before he leaves on his search."

The Carben held out a hand to each of the two.

"Here's my word that I shall do my best to help you in any way I can. I don't know why I'm feeling this way, but it makes me sad to say farewell; yet I have a feeling our separation won't be a long one."

Shanon, trying to lighten the mood, laughed.

"There'll be no separation at all, if we don't get a move on. We've got some fancy walking to do just to get to the edge of the North Garden gate, and a bit farther on to the path that runs around the outer walls of the boundary of Erin Frey."

"Let's get it over with," said Mathiny. "I must be on my way to find Sigman Col."

They loaded themselves with their new arms, and water bottles, sleeping rolls, elfinwrought cooking ware, cleverly designed to fold neatly into tiny cases, knapsacks filled with a large supply of something Shanon called oat biscuits, which was travel fare among the elves, somewhat akin to

146

a wheat cake baked into a thick round shape that Brian was familiar with.

The three quickly crossed the rest of the spiraled hallway, on beyond, and with a hurried march, reached the outside entrance that was the North Garden gate, weed-tangled and so badly overgrown in thickets and thorn brake that it took the elf a great while to determine exactly where the passage through the outer wall was. Finding it after pricking himself on a particularly bad hedge of thorns, the elf led them carefully, so that they wound their way on beyond the boundaries of the elfin dane, and found themselves in the eerie silence of the wood beyond, shadowed and dim, smelling faintly of ancient, undisturbed forest floors, and new rain.

Shanon led the way to a very faded trace of an old path, which soon disappeared from sight into the thick growth of all sorts of trees, ash and oak and dense pines, with the occasional white-barked aspen adding another color to the deep green and black mood of the wood.

The three shook hands again, and Mathiny, not trusting his voice to speak, hurried away in the direction Shanon gave him.

Watching for a moment longer, the elf and dwarf slumped deeper into their cloaks, and began their own march, which Shanon had said would bring them eventually to the banks of the Green Shield, and from there, beneath the high falls, where they hoped to find their road to the Roaring once more, and with it, Senja and Chinby.

Gram

BEYOND the North Gate of Erin Frey, the wood became so densely overgrown that the two friends had no time to speak, and instead had to pick their way slowly and carefully through the tangled mass of branch and thorn.

147

Brian was suddenly aware of the bird calls, which came from every direction, and there was much scuttling about near them, but just out of sight, which he felt was probably the smaller animals of the forest, coming to check up on the new intruders.

The sounds grew in numbers, until they began to worry the elf somewhat, and he whispered very softly to Brian.

"I'm beginning to not like this! We can't see more than a foot in front of our face, and have no idea of what's going on out there. This is almost as bad as those infernal delvings of yours."

"At least I'm a little more familiar with the things that might be down a dwarf hole," grumbled Brian under his breath.

Choosing that moment to stumble, the dwarf fell forward painfully, tearing his cloak as he did so.

"Blast it all," he fumed, his hands throbbing from thorn wounds. "I've almost had enough of this creeping around in this sticker patch. Maybe we should just go back, and go out another path. Anything has got to be better than this."

His sudden explosion seemed more noisy than ever in the silence that had fallen after his outburst.

"Shhhh," hissed Shanon angrily, turning this way and that to see if he could detect any further sound that would indicate the presence of their visitors.

"I've had enough shushing," ranted Brian. "I'm going to go back now, and you can follow if you want."

The dwarf made a motion toward going back down the thinly marked path, with its dense growth, but was stopped short by an ominous growl from somewhere off in front of him, out of his line of vision.

Carefully stringing an elfin dart to the sturdy bow in his hand, Shanon called out urgently, but in an even, quiet voice.

"Come along back this way, old fellow. I don't think they want us to go back."

"*Who* doesn't want us to? Who is it?" blurted the dwarf. Retracing the few steps he had taken, and moving farther back, he stood beside Shanon.

"I'm not sure. But I suppose they'll let us know soon enough."

"It sounds like beasts. Just because Erin Frey was nearby doesn't mean the forest can't be full of those packs from the Easterlands."

"No," agreed the elf, carefully unstringing the dart, but keeping it handy. "I know that those roaming bands of raiders have taken foothold everywhere, but I don't think these are our friends from over the borders."

"Then who could they be?" insisted Brian, the thick, dusky smell of the wood growing more suffocating, and the feeling of being surrounded making his heart hammer loudly beneath his cloak.

"I wonder?" mused the elf, half to himself; then replacing the arrow in the short quiver at his side, he resumed his march forward, causing Brian to tumble hurriedly after.

The light in the heavy thicket was dim and diffused, sometimes a dark greenish yellow, sometimes barely a trickle of dull gold. It was tricky footing, the path being overgrown with ground vines and exposed tree roots, and Brian stumbled and fell with every other step, but he no longer spoke aloud to the elf of returning to Erin Frey or the garden of the ancient queen, Corin.

Remembering the beautiful lady, and her words, helped him to keep on going slowly forward, stumbling as he did so, and he could not bring himself to believe that the elfin lady would give them directions that would lead them to harm.

He expressed as much to Shanon, who agreed.

"I don't know who it is accompanying us, but I certainly feel that they're not enemies."

"You wouldn't be able to prove that by me," stuttered the dwarf.

"I think we shall see soon enough who our escort is. We'll be reaching a part of the wood soon that opens up a bit. Or at least, it used to. I don't know about now, with everything going wild."

Brian stumbled awkwardly again, and reaching out to grab a nearby branch to stop his fall, felt the wooden limb shudder once and withdraw itself from his hand. Stopping to study whatever it was more closely in the murky light, the dwarf thought he saw, or imagined he saw, a stubby, low tree, moving back from the trail.

Thinking his eyes must be playing him tricks in the poor light, he went on, but the incident troubled him.

"Who used to dwell in these woods?" he asked the elf, needing to hear his voice to reassure him, and not really caring about the answer.

Shanon, engrossed in finding a difficult trace of the path,

149

did not reply right away, but wandered first one way, then another, bent low to the ground, muttering to himself. He pushed aside branches, and turned over rotten trunks of trees, causing small grubs and beetles to scurry in every direction.

Finally, after another few minutes, he turned to the dwarf, who watched him cautiously, not knowing whether Shanon was upset, or lost.

"There's been some strange happenings here," he said, rolling away a small branch with the toe of his boot.

"What sort of things?" asked Brian, trying to detect whatever it was that made the elf make his pronouncement.

"Look!"

Shanon turned over the rotting wooden trunk of a tree, and pointed to the ground where it had been. The dwarf, being unfamiliar with deep wood lore, stared uncomprehendingly.

Glancing at his friend, the elf laughed.

"Don't you see?"

"I see grubs and beetles, and a rotten tree," grumbled Brian. "But what it means is beyond me."

Shanon laughed again, softly.

"This all must have something to do with Corin's instructions."

Brian was looking blankly at the ground, trying to discover what it was that had put his friend into such good humor.

"It is an old wood elf trick," explained Shanon. "I was always fascinated with their lore, and studied it, even though my companions made fun of me for it."

"I know that feeling well enough," agreed Brian.

"Look here. See the mark the tree made when it fell? See the dent in the earth? Now see how it's all moss-grown, and the ground is soft?"

Brian nodded, trying to see the elf's point.

"Over here is where it's been moved. You can see the difference between where it fell originally and where it's been moved to."

Brian saw that there was a shadow of where the tree had been, faintly outlined in the rotting chips and crumbling tangle of the tree, and that it had been moved, as Shanon said.

"So someone moved a dead tree. Why is that important?"

"It's important, because if you look in the direction of the first dent, you'll notice that it's pointing in the way we just came from. But look at where the trunk's pointing now."

"It goes off the path a bit."

"Exactly!" said Shanon. "That's our path now."

"There's no way to go through there," protested Brian, thinking of the frightening noises that had been coming from the surrounding wood, and not wanting to explore them at any closer range.

"This was placed here by the old clans of Corin," said Shanon. "These markers were to show the trail to those who were of an elfin nature. Anyone else would go straight on, and follow what seems to be the path."

"It looks like the path to me."

"I'm going to have to instruct you in the ways of wood elves. We can't have you going around lost, especially not in a wood like this."

"Then I guess I'll let you do the guiding a while longer. I feel rather silly, though. You've done the steering in the delvings, and here, too."

"I've just had more practice," said the elf. "Your time will come."

Shanon looked at his small companion, a sad smile playing across his handsome features.

"Are we going to follow the way this new sign shows?"

"If we want to reach the Green Shield, we will."

"Anywhere will be better than this thorn patch," muttered the dwarf, holding up his cloak to study a torn place on its edge.

The companions settled their loads again, and picking his way carefully into the seemingly solid wall of thorn and undergrowth, Shanon soon had found a way that opened up onto a more defined trail that was wide enough for Brian to walk along beside him. A few hundred feet farther, it broadened into a well-kept alley between tall pines, and the underbrush gave away to neatly trimmed hedges, and soft, thick grass which sank beneath their boots and cushioned their walk.

Brian saw two tall, black staffs planted on either side of the wooded lane, and was about to comment to Shanon when a huge horned head appeared in the eaves of the wood behind the two black pillars.

"What wish ye of the woodland folk?" bellowed the voice, deep and menacing.

151

Brian saw that the great head was attached to a powerful body, four-legged, with a great tail coiled behind. The torso of the creature was something like Brian's own, but the head on the thick neck was that of a great lion, with broad horns grown out above the ears.

"We wish no harm to the woodland folk, or any other," said Shanon, appearing unperturbed by the frightening apparition.

"Then come forward freely," replied the creature, its tone somewhat softer.

Brian was stunned for a moment, but quickly regained his courage.

"Who are you?" he asked. "My name is Brian Brandigore, and this is my good companion, Shanon."

The wide-set eyes of the creature blinked twice.

"You may call me Gram."

"Greetings, Gram," said Shanon, his hands beneath his cloak, out of sight. "We bring you greetings from our two clans."

"And you have mine," echoed Gram, muzzle working into a half smile.

Brian noticed that this huge creature stood very still, but the tail twitched in a series of quick flickers of black and gray.

"Are you familiar with my cousins who dwell here?" asked Shanon. "We have traveled a long way to visit."

"I know the wood elf well," pronounced the creature. "We have had many times together."

"That's very good to hear, O Master Gram. Can you tell me how I might find them? We have urgent need of their assistance, for we have an errand that will take us to the Green Shield, and beyond the Elf Cloak Falls."

"Oh, they're easy enough to find. I think there are probably some about now, not too far from you."

Brian looked around, expecting to see one of the woodland elves, but Shanon never took his eyes off the piercing gaze of Gram.

The giant creature advanced a few paces toward the companions, a deep purr rumbling from the horned lion's head.

"Perhaps we can go to find them together," it said, the voice friendly and reassuring.

In spite of the warm overtones, Brian's every nerve jangled out a warning, and his hand clutched at the hilt of the small elfin short sword, although he did not feel that it would be of

152

much use against an enemy the size of Gram. He saw that at the shoulders of the creature, there were great claws, attached to two long arms, fur-grown, and bulging with muscle.

"Come! Let us go to seek your friends," said Gram, the rumble in his throat growing slightly louder.

"I think we may have discovered the mystery of where they are," replied Shanon, his voice taking on a harder note. "Or at least I think we have met the cause of their parting!"

Gram's smile grew wide and cruel, across the mouth. Brian saw the terrible curved fangs that lurked behind the parted lips.

"You are quick, master tree walker. You see before you the scourge of the pesky elf. I have been sent to rid the forest of such unwanted squatters."

"It may be that you are the unwanted one, Master Gram," answered Shanon. "You were sent by an enemy to my people, and I was sent to rid the wood of the likes of you."

Gram's rumbling laugh echoed grimly across the neatly trimmed grass lawn that separated them. Brian noticed that even as the creature spoke, he edged ever nearer the friends.

"Then these poor bones of mine have nothing too much to fear. If the army that's been sent out to slay me numbers no more than you two, I shall be safe here in these woods for a long while yet to come."

"I come in the name of the Queen Corin," replied Shanon. "And from all the power and glory that was Erin Frey."

"Your queen is no match for the Dark One," snarled Gram, growing visibly tired of his game.

"Then the Dark One was a fool to send one such as you to do her errands," said Shanon.

"I am quite able to do my work nicely," snapped Gram, beginning to circle in yet closer to his victims.

As he talked, Shanon had thrown back the traveling cloak that concealed his hands, and Brian saw that he held the Stone of Elver Tarn clutched tightly to him.

Sensing that the attack of the creature was near, the dwarf threw back his own cloak, and unsheathed the short elfin sword.

Gram, seeing the move, laughed harshly.

"Those will be of no use to you. Why not surrender, and I shall see to it that your death is swift."

Hardly realizing what was happening, Brian watched in horrified fascination as Shanon lifted the hand that held the

153

ancient stone, and as he did so, the air began to ring with the harsh war cry of the woodland elf and the water elf, and a great din beat the hot air into fiery blows against the ear. Looking wildly about, the dwarf watched in amazement as Shanon's form beside him glowed a brilliant blue-white, then began to rise above the clearing where they stood.

Gram's horrified gaze followed the gleaming figure of the elf, eyes wide in fear and hatred.

"Come down and fight fairly, wood scum!" he cried, making a move that carried him close to Brian.

The dwarf bellowed out and lunged forward, the elfin blade held out before him. Partially by luck, and by Gram's attention being taken by Shanon, the dwarf was not killed by the savage stroke that sang through the humid clearing and sent him spinning, badly dazed.

The creature leapt forward then, swatting at the elf, who hung suspended above the terrible claws of Gram, which whistled through the air in harsh whispers, barely missing the elf, who moved higher up and farther away.

Seeing his chance when the creature turned to attack Brian, Shanon, moving swiftly, strung an arrow to his bow, and drew it as far back as he was able to bend it. The shaft sped singing its deadly, whistling call, and buried itself to the feathered tip in the creature's broad back.

A roar such as the two companions had never heard split the air into echoing fragments, followed by the beast's angry attempts to pluck away the thing that had hurt it. Gram squatted and whirled, snarling as he did so, swinging the great forearms with the open claws this way and that, narrowly missing the fallen form of Brian again, and growing maddened at being unable to reach the elf, he began to leap into the air with great lunges, roaring and baring his terrible fangs.

It was one of these attempts to swat the elf down that brushed Shanon just enough to tear his cloak and throw him enough off balance that he stuck out his hand to balance himself, and in doing so, dropped the Stone of Elver Tarn. Crying aloud in dismay and anger at his clumsy mistake, Shanon fell heavily to the ground almost at the creature's feet, stunned momentarily, and breathless. The small, gleaming elfin stone that Queen Corin had given to Shanon rolled across the clearing, exposed and unprotected.

Brian was the first to move, and with strength that surprised even him, he darted beneath the hoofed feet of Gram and snatched the pulsing blue-white stone away from the groping claws of the huge creature. The jolt and shock of the stone almost tore loose Brian's grip, but he gritted his teeth, and held on for dear life.

When he'd grabbed the small object, all Brian had thought of doing was to return it to Shanon, who had been the one who'd received it from the ancient elfin queen, but seeing his friend stretched helplessly before Gram, Brian knew it was up to him to try to save them from the horrible beast that now turned, fangs bared, roaring in a deep, angry voice.

"You are doomed, fool of an earth scum. You are the next tribute to the invincible Gram, the scourge of the wood."

"Think of the air!" cried Shanon. "Think of being up in the air!"

The elf scrambled and crawled his way beyond the reach of Gram, who had turned his full attack on Brian.

Not knowing what else to do, the frightened dwarf thought of a cloud he'd seen as a spanner, on one of his overground trips, floating along in front of a hazy, summer sun. Immediately he felt strange, and clutching the stone tightly, he saw that there was nothing but blue sky around him, and far, far below, so far that it was indistinct and misty, he saw what must be the wood, its green cloak cut through by the wide blue ribbon of the river Green Shield.

His thoughts turned to his friend, and the grave danger he was in, and before he could blink an eye twice he was at the elf's side, with the beast Gram staring at him in disbelief.

"Quickly! Grab my hand," shouted Shanon, struggling forward, toward the dwarf.

Brian held out his hand, while clutching the Elver Tarn Stone in the other.

Gram sprang forward, wide jaws open, and claws grappling the air viciously.

"You fiends!" he screamed. "You shall not escape Gram!"

The hot, foul breath of the creature blew in Brian's face, choking him, and the stench of it almost caused him to lose his grip on Shanon.

"The Green Shield," cried the elf. "The Green Shield, and Elf Cloak Falls!"

Brian, barely able to think of anything at all, except to escape the terrible yellow fangs of Gram, echoed his friend's cry. There was a brief moment when Brian thought the creature must surely have them, and the putrid stench of the thing's foul breath filled his nose with the awful smell of death, but in another brief flash of time, he became aware of his cloak flapping in a strong breeze, and his eyes being tightly shut against the wall of wind that was slowly erasing the heavy smell of Gram, and replacing it with the fresh sweetness of unbroken forest, and the tart, slightly moist smell of clear water.

Breathless, and half stunned from the explosion of events that had occurred, Brian opened his eyes cautiously, fully expecting to see Gram lunging at them again, and his hand left Shanon's, to grasp his sword again.

Looking about in a daze, he saw a tall, misty plume of water flowing over a high cliff beside him and whirling into a deep dark-blue pool before it cascaded on, through late afternoon sunlight that touched the brows of the stately trees that lined the river on both sides.

"The Green Shield," explained Shanon. "And the Elf Cloak Falls."

"Where is that thing?" stammered Brian. "Are we free of him?"

Shanon clapped the dwarf on the back.

"You're learning well, my friend. It has come your turn to pull your load equally. I thank you for my life."

"You're more than welcome, but I didn't do it. The stone did!"

"Good Queen Corin knew well what she was doing when she gave us that gift."

Shanon shuddered slightly.

"I hate to think of the fates of my poor cousins who lived there. Gram has slain them all."

"Couldn't we go back and drive him off?" asked Brian, beginning to think of all the endless possibilities of a gift such as the Stone of Elver Tarn.

He opened his tightly clenched fist, and to his dismay, saw that the object there was a pale dull gray, and it had grown cool to his touch.

"We could go back, but not the way we came, I'm afraid," said Shanon. "That stone only works when one is in great danger, and if the one bearing it is working toward the good of all kinds."

"But removing Gram would be a help to anyone who might ever have to run against him."

"I'm afraid it's too late to help those in the wood where Gram dwells," said the elf sadly. "He has destroyed those who dwelled there, and will move on now. He can't stay there much longer."

"All the more reason we should try to slay him," went on Brian, slightly surprised at the new feelings that had been aroused within him.

"We shall meet Master Gram again," said the elf, his face drawn and grim. "But not yet. We have a few chores we must do beforehand."

"What shall we do now?" asked Brian.

"We must begin to gather the clans," replied Shanon. "Running into Gram answered a question that I had asked myself long ago, even when I first met Chinby, and helped him with his crafting of the tools he gave you. I wondered then what it was all to lead to, and now I begin to see. If things like Gram are on the march, then it is the time that all the clans shall be called together again."

"Who would believe you?" asked Brian, sitting heavily down, looking at the lifeless, small stone he held.

"They will believe."

"Wherever shall we start?"

"Sigman Col," replied Shanon.

"We have to meet Chinby and Senja first," insisted Brian. "They'll be waiting for us."

"With any luck at all, and if they didn't meet up with our friend Gram, we'll all arrive together, I'd wager."

The elf laughed, and without further word, vanished into the roaring mists of the falls.

THE GREEN SHIELD

Drub Fearing and Falón

BRIAN stood before the roaring wall of water a moment longer before he plunged in after his friend, and his eyes traveled upward, toward the top of the falls, which Shanon called the Elf Cloak, and there lingering just along the edge of where the rim of the horizon was, he thought he saw the grotesque figure of Gram. He couldn't be sure, but it was frightening enough to hurry him along through the tumbling curtain of water.

Although he had gritted his teeth, and had expected to be thoroughly drenched by the icy spray, Brian stepped into a small grotto on the other side as dry as before. All about him, elfmoons gleamed, some blue, some golden white, and there were red and green ones as well, leading on around the far corner, where the cave became a shaft that led downward toward the Deep Home Highway.

The elf was nowhere to be seen, but Brian was not worried about where his friend had gotten to, so much as he had horrible visions of being trapped in this small space by the awful Gram. It was a mystery to Brian how the beast could have come along behind them so rapidly, and although he had no idea how far they had traveled, he knew it was a long way, and no normal animal would have been able to cover such distance in so short a time.

He became aware of the music that was playing, growing louder now, of reed pipe and lute, and the beautiful sounds of the elfin instruments that were held beneath the chin and stroked with a long, graceful bow. Chinby called them the elf souls, for the plaintive, sorrowful sounds they made described well the sad state of affairs of the elfin nations.

There was the tinkle of laughter, which shocked Brian, for it was not merely his friend's laugh, but many voices joined as one, chanting now in time to the roaring music. The dwarf's fear exploded into a torrent of anger, and he called out as loudly as he could for silence.

"Stop it, you ninnies! Stop that racket right this minute! There's a beast outside, and you've given us all away!"

He stamped his foot as hard as he was able, but the music went on unabated, and the noise of the laughter grew yet louder.

The bend in the shaft which led out of the grotto prevented Brian from seeing who the merrymakers were, although he knew one of them had to be his friend Shanon.

"Shanon, get your friends quiet! Gram isn't far away!"

At the mention of the word Gram, the instruments began to cease playing one by one, first the elf soul, then the reed pipes, and lastly, the laughter slowly died away.

Shanon called out from beyond the shaft turning.

"Did you say Gram?"

"I did, you lump-brained tree strider. He's at the top of the falls, although I imagine he's on his way here now, right enough, after all this fal-tra-blab."

Shanon's head appeared around the corner, the laugh lines still wrinkled in his face.

"We have more company than Gram," he said, jerking a thumb toward the tunnel behind him.

"Gram is quite enough for me. Is there a back door to this hole?"

"The Highway. We're on our way there now."

"Who's we?"

"Friends of mine."

"Then I suggest we get at it. I don't want to have to meet Gram in this cramped dungeon."

A voice behind Brian sounded, its tone semi-scolding.

"You've certainly learned the tone of voice to give orders in," it said.

There was something very familiar about the voice, and Brian hurried past Shanon, who moved quickly aside, still smiling. As the dwarf turned the corner of the shaft, the music sprang up again, as loud as before, but he hadn't time to mind the noise, because there facing him stood Chinby, with Senja by his side, holding tightly to his hand.

"Chinby! Senja!" shouted Brian, totally forgetting the dreadful form he had seen at the top of the waterfall, and he rushed forward to greet the long-absent friends.

161

He was embarrassed and painfully shy in his greeting of Senja, but he clasped the old blind dwarf roughly, and gave him a strong hug.

"We thought we'd seen the last of you, after we heard Sigman Col had captured you."

"He's no match for Senja," laughed the old dwarf.

Brian blushed crimson, and blurted out something that caused him to turn even redder.

"No one is a match for Senja. I'd be a poor dwarf to ever hope to ask for her hand."

Why he'd said that particular thing, he never knew, except that it had often been on his mind, and in the confusion and chaos of being face to face with her again, it somehow tumbled out.

All about the larger cavern, there stood the forms of the sturdy wood elves that Chinby had spoken of, dressed all in green and pale gray, with long ash bows, and quivers of brightly feathered arrows. Brian could not count their number, and he saw, too, the more familiar elves that were of Shanon's clans, the water elves, somewhat taller, and lighter of skin and hair. And in the very back, he was startled to see a dozen or more Carben dwarfs, clad in their earthen shades of dark browns and blacks.

He called out to the one nearest him.

"You there, good Carben, do you come from the settlements of Sigman Col?"

"We do," replied the fellow, his voice deep and booming. "But we have come to join the one who will bring all our clans together again, as is spoken of by the old blind sayer."

Brian looked quickly to Chinby, who was smiling his most disarming smile, hand entwined in Senja's.

"And who might that be?"

"Brian Brandigore," replied the Carben, who went by the name of Drub Fearing. "We shall all be one in the delvings again."

A torrent of strong feelings flooded through Brian, one after another. His face was the color of his best vest, which he had left behind when he went to the kellers to go away with Shanon, yet there was something else that made him feel wonderfully strong.

Senja caught his eye once more, and bowed slightly to him.

"Welcome, Brian. We had thought perhaps we would have a long wait for you to arrive, but I see you are no slow shoe."

The lane's tone was light and teasing, and Brian could think of no reply, so he turned quickly to Shanon, and said in a voice that was just a fraction too loud, "What are we to do with the problem upstairs? Gram, if it is Gram, won't have any good feelings when he knows we are not only just the two of us, but wood elves, and Carben dwarfs, as well. It would be a dandy feast for him to find us all cooped up in this dig, with nowhere to turn."

"We have plenty of places to turn," corrected Shanon. "And we have a good host here to see to it that Gram doesn't get himself too close to our parts for comfort."

"The beast you met is an old one in the wood, Brian," said Chinby, drawing the dwarf nearer to him.

His heart pounded loudly in his ears at being so close to Senja, but she seemed not to notice him, and went to speak to the Carben, Drub Fearing.

"Gram is one of the ancient beasts who come down out of the ice fields at times. He has been at large here and there for all the time I have lived. I've heard of him first one place, then another. But there are larger, more dangerous beasts than he, now. They have begun to gather across the Roaring, and a time of reckoning is upon us."

"What could be worse than Gram?" asked Brian, glad to be distracted by Chinby and the talk of the invaders from the Wilderness.

"A hundred Grams, or a thousand," replied Chinby. "The dangerous ones are those that are the descendants of the Elver Tarn which have gone wrong. They are the flying beasts, which are the most dreadful of all, and who come at the ends of the ages, to burn and destroy all life."

"Is this an end of an age?" asked Brian, wide-eyed, and always fascinated with the tales of the old dwarf.

He had listened to him for so long now that it seemed only natural to be talking of flying beasts, and strange times that would come, when all the living beings there were would be faced with destruction.

"It has been so for some time, Brian, although you have not seen it, safe as you were below the world outside."

"But that still doesn't answer what we are to do with Gram."

"This isn't the same beast you saw, Brian, but another. He has lived here near the falls for some time, ambushing

163

whoever he can, and biding his time. There have been others, but many of them have been slain by the Carben Sigman Col."

"I thought you were held captive by him? Isn't he one of the enemy?"

Chinby stroked his long beard absently, thinking deeply before he answered.

"If it were only that easy to draw sides, things would be a lot simpler to understand, and to explain."

The Carben dwarf Drub Fearing came to stand at Chinby's side.

"The old one has visited us in many past winters, and always at great risk. Sigman Col has tried to pull the Carben settlements together to keep them from being slain off by the beasts like Gram, and the others. They find easy pickings where settlements are separated and have not much defense."

"Do you know Mathiny?" asked Brian suddenly, remembering his new friend.

"Mathiny? Of course. He is an Elder under Sigman Col. He commands a large settlement near my old home."

Shanon dug his hands deep into his cloak as he spoke.

"He may have been a highly trusted Elder at one time, but you couldn't have heard the news of what's happened of late."

"What news might that be?" asked Drub Fearing.

"I'm afraid that Mathiny has been named traitor, and may even now be in grave danger, unless the plan he told us of has worked."

"Mathiny is one of the most respected Carbens of all. Sigman Col would never hear a word against him."

"He may now," said Brian. "Mathiny tried to capture Shanon and me in one of the old delvings on the Deep Home, and the watchers there frightened him into listening to us, and finally, he agreed that he would try to help us get Chinby and Senja free. They got loose on their own, so we found out, and then Mathiny felt he must return to his settlement, even at the risk of being branded a traitor. There was a band with him that was led by an ugly fellow named Runion, who promised to tell Sigman Col everything about Mathiny helping us and the other two they had captured."

Drub Fearing glowered as he listened to the delving dwarf, his fists clenching tightly.

"Runion has been at the bottom of many a good dwarf's

164

fall," he muttered gruffly. "Yet no one can ever quite catch him at his tricks. He has Sigman Col's commander at arms in his camp, and is only dangerous because of that. Sigman Col would never listen to Runion, or his odorous tales."

"Then it sounds worse for our friend than I had allowed myself to believe. I only wish there was some way we could aid him."

The leader of the Carbens laughed a short, curt bark.

"If you need someone to spring him, you've got your dwarf in Drub Fearing. We could find our way there and back, and meet you again within two days."

"This Mathiny sounds as if he could be of great service to our cause," said Chinby. "It might be a good plan to gather all that we may, for the next step of the way could well be the most difficult and dangerous. We could use all the allies we can find, whether dwarf or elf."

Shanon, who had been talking intently with one of the wood elves, turned to Brian.

"Falon says there are many wood elf danes spread about in these parts. He thinks he could gather more than half the number of them to go with us to the sea. They don't care much for larger bodies of water than a river, but they've found that the time has come for them to make a stand against these beasts who have taken over much of the wood."

"It's more than just that," said Chinby. "Although the beasts are bad enough in themselves."

"It's plenty enough worry, if you have one for a neighbor," snorted Falon. "And our woods have been overrun with first one, then another, and we've been forced farther and farther toward the heart of the wood, but there's no safety even there. That seems to be where the biggest beasts of all are drawn to."

"These are bad times for all of us," said Chinby, nodding in agreement with the wood elf. "I have been studying these things for all my life, and I would be leading you astray if I told you that things have not been growing a turn for the worse. It has been coming now for ever so long, and it only seems that in the past few turnings has it gotten really bad, but that's because most folks choose to ignore problems when they arise, and go on for a long time pretending that there is no cause for any concern."

"Con Den Fetch," blurted Senja. "Exactly! Where I spent

165

my time, with everyone assuring me that everything was fine, unless you went to Brian's delving, on those wild borders. Then you had trouble."

Brian blushed heavily again, yet strangely moved by hearing the handsome dwarf lane speak his name.

"You should have listened to them," replied Shanon. "Then you'd be there safe in your delving, and not out on a wild-boar chase in the middle of a strange wood, with such traveling companions as these rogues you see around you."

Senja threw her head back, shaking the dark curls from beneath the yellow forage cap she wore.

"I'd much prefer this company to those that were with me in my old delving."

"And we thought that we would have a terrible time of it, trying to rescue you and Chinby," said Shanon, clicking his tongue disapprovingly.

"That probably would have been the end of us all," scolded the lane. "Chinby told me when we were captured that there was nothing to be afraid of, and that we would be freed before the day was out."

"How could you be so sure, Chinby?" asked Brian. "With all the things you know, I guess one small item like the hour of your freedom is no large guess, but I'd still like to know how you could have been so sure of your escape from Sigman Col."

"He almost forced us to leave," said the old dwarf sourly. "I knew that we would be free before the day was out, because I overheard one of our guards say where we were to be locked up. It terrified them to think of a prison so deep and stifling, yet it's nothing to a delving dwarf. They thought it would be a terrible experience for us, to lock us there, and we didn't tell them any different, by a long throw."

"I don't think any of those Carben dwarfs have any idea about life underground," Senja said, adding her feelings to what Chinby was saying. "They had never heard of any of the lore that Chinby mentioned to them, and they treated him as if he were a criminal."

"Well they might," broke in Drub Fearing. "Sigman Col has long spread the word that all lore masters who come into the realms of the Carbens are to be brought to him. But I think he has spread that in order that he may himself have news of the goings-on of the delving dwarfs, and the elfin nations. Someone else has taken the order to mean that the

166

lore masters are criminal, to be caught and punished. Our friend Runion has taken it on himself on more than one occasion to fit Sigman Col's instructions to his own purpose."

"Should we send Drub Fearing to fetch Mathiny?"

Brian's question was directed at Chinby.

The old dwarf seemed to ponder a moment, his clear, unseeing eyes fixed on empty space.

"It might be wise to do so," he said at last, coming to a decision he was trying to make. "Drub Fearing has expressed the opinion that he may go and come quickly. If that is possible, I'd give my vote to that. Mathiny might prove to be a valuable friend to have."

"What of Sigman Col, Chinby?" asked Brian, his thoughts confused by all the conflicting reports of the Carben leader.

"I think he is behind us, although he doesn't know it yet. He is a strange one."

Shanon and Falon moved nearer to the blind dwarf, and sat beside him.

"He has caused some grief to my settlement, and my neighbors in other settlements," said Falon. "But I can understand that, seeing as how he has put out the story that the Carbens are half elf. It wouldn't do to have an elf dane next door as living proof that dwarfs are in no way tied to the elfin clans."

Drub Fearing puffed his chest out testily.

"I wouldn't go so far as to say that, good elf. You can see for yourself that we aren't so much different than the wood elves."

"No bickering, please!" snapped Shanon. "It's of no importance to us here whether or not who's who, or goes where. That can be left for a dozen seasons from now, when we're bored of sitting on our front porch, with nothing new or interesting to do. Now what we need is all speed to gather those who will follow us, and to set our course for the sea."

The elf paused, then turned to Chinby.

"Am I right, old one?"

"Your orders are valid, my quickwit. A dwarf would take days getting down to the point, but you've said it exactly. Falon, you and your band should return to your settlements, and gather all who will follow. We'll look forward to meeting with you again this time three days from now. That should give you time to visit each of the danes, and to seek those out who will follow you."

167

"Where will we meet?" asked the wood elf.

"Where shall it be? You're most familiar with these parts."

"I don't think it should be here," offered Shanon. "If what Brian says is true about Gram, or one of his brothers, then they will be watching the Elf Cloak, and waiting for their chance to strike."

He paused, thinking, then turned to Drub Fearing.

"What say you, good Carben? Is there a place you know that would be safe, yet easily found by the likes of us?"

The stocky Carben dwarf met Shanon's even gaze.

"I'll come with your group myself. I have a good second-in-command who can run the chores easily enough, and wherever we decide to meet, I can lead you."

"That's a well-made reply," agreed Chinby. "I think it rings true. Outside of the Deep Home Highway, none of us are familiar with the countryside, and it isn't a place I'd like to end up lost in."

Falon gathered his group, and stood waiting at the grotto entrance.

"I say we meet next at the old elf dane of Three Stones. That isn't so far, yet it is handy enough to find, and I don't recall seeing any other signs of anyone having found it of late."

"I know Three Stones," said Drub Fearing. "That sits well with me. My good band should have no trouble finding it."

The dour-faced second-in-command of the Carbens nodded curtly.

"Now our only problem is this bothersome thing outside," said Brian. "Getting out and not being seen is going to be something sticky."

"Perhaps not," said Chinby softly, a thin smile playing across his old features. "Maybe we'll invite him in for a game of riddles."

Brian was aghast at the idea, remembering well his encounter with the grotesque creature.

"That might not be wise," began the elf Falon, but Chinby cut him off.

"I have no intention of being here when he comes," he snapped. "No, what I had in mind is to go on a bit deeper into the shafts here, and use the second doorway that should still be there. It leads aboveground just beyond the next bend of the Green Shield. That's where Senja and I discovered our good Drub Fearing and his band, and Falon, having a good talk about the general state of things."

Senja offered her hand to Falon.

"Well met, too, my friend. I am glad we have run across such as you."

The wood elf bowed politely.

"It is my great honor to count you as an ally. And a very great thing indeed, to know the Chinby."

"All this fancy talk won't get our work done any quicker," grumbled the old dwarf. "And buttering me up won't do a bit of good toward making me change my mind about anything."

"That would be a first, if it were to happen," said Senja cheerfully.

"Whenever I hear of a dwarf changing his mind, I'll know times are dark indeed," added Shanon.

"Out, out, get on with you," blustered Chinby. "I won't have any more treason talked in front of me. Let's go on to the bottom door, and see if we can't stir up enough ruckus there to attract the attention of whoever or whatever is outside there. That will give everyone who's bound for the wood a chance to slip by undetected."

"We'll give you enough time to reach the lower door," said Falon. "Meanwhile, I'll send along a scout to see if he can tell when the way is clear."

Brian was staring at Senja again, recalling all his old feelings about the striking, outspoken lane when he had visited her in Con Den Fetch. That seemed another lifetime away from where he stood, in the shafts of the Elf Cloak Falls, on the Green Shield, far beyond the borders of his old delving, and far removed from anything he held familiar, except for the old dwarf Chinby and Senja.

She crossed the damp, cool floor, and smiled at him.

"It's good we've found each other again, Brian. Chinby said there was no way we would be able to get rid of you, but I was frightened for a while, after we were captured by Sigman Col. I thought that was an end of all the grand plans of the sea, and all the rest."

Brian's throat constricted, but he managed to find a part of his voice, although he spoke very softly.

"I'm glad, too. It was awful, knowing you and Chinby were held by the Carbens, and there was no one but Shanon and me to try to save you."

"He was going to huff up, and just march in, and demand

your release," teased the elf. "I had a terrible time talking him out of that."

"I knew I had made no mistake in judging my dwarfs," grumbled Chinby. "Had I not been with Senja, I guess I'd be there in Sigman Col's kellers yet, waiting for my stout Brian to come to demand me."

Hating all the attention, Brian tried to turn the topic away from himself.

"We have a long march ahead, and plenty of tasks to keep us busy enough without baiting me. I would suggest we get to it."

And saying, he bent quickly, and began to adjust his gear, rearranging his pack and bow, and strapping on his short sword in a more comfortable position beneath the long cloak.

"Enough," agreed Chinby. "Let's call a truce, and be off. You, Falon, and you, good Carben, wait until you hear our decoy. You can't miss it. Then make all haste to finish your errands, and to meet us at Three Stones."

Falon and the Carben nodded, and began to prepare for their departure.

Turning to the others, Brian asked if Drub Fearing would lead them on into the shafts beneath the falls, and settling into their own thoughts, the friends prepared to follow the stout figure, Brian and Shanon bringing up the rear, with Senja walking beside Chinby, to guide him.

The shaft split into a lower tunnel within another few yards, and the elfmoons there were a pale green. Within a dozen more steps, the path turned sharply downward, and the companions heard the indistinct rumble of the Deep Home Highway, somewhere farther on below them.

The Varads

FARTHER down the tunnels, Brian found an excuse to walk beside Senja, who was telling Chinby of the color of the elfmoons, and describing how the shaft walls were constructed.

"You have learned well," he replied, listening to her list the various ways the stone was split and joined, or the way a crack had been repaired, or a corner blocked and squared.

"I think she'll be more of a dwarf than any of the spanners I've seen in a long while," he went on.

"You've got no such notion," scolded the lane. "You say that to make Brian feel ashamed."

"Why should I do that?" asked Chinby, reaching out to seek the younger dwarf's arm. "He is the best of all spanners, and the next hope of the delvings. Just because he's a bit slow-footed, and not too quick to think on his own, doesn't mean that I don't admire him immensely."

Brian had grown more disturbed by the minute, listening to Chinby, and walking so near Senja.

"Well, if it's all the same to you two, I think I'd like to hear a little less of what Brian Brandigore is, or isn't. What I'm more interested in is how you came to be taken by that band of Carbens, and how you escaped."

"Oh, that," said Chinby. "I had almost forgotten it."

"Chinby!" nagged Senja. "You have done no such thing. When we were put in that keller, you were explaining to me the last rites, and that if we were lucky, the end would come swiftly."

Chinby huffed up, face red behind the white whiskers, and his face standing out in bold relief.

"Was it that bad?" asked Brian.

"Bad enough," replied the lane. "We had been going down

the Deep Home, on those keg boats that were there, and decided to stop off in one of the old delvings to go overground for a short while, to rest a bit, and to see what sort of condition this part of the country was in."

"If I'd known about the Carben band being so close, and that they had begun to try to go into the old delvings, I never would have suggested we stop," said Chinby, rising to his own defense.

"But the fact is, you didn't know everything for once, and we went up from the river, and were near the gate to the outside, when we were confronted by a band of Carbens. I only had Chinby's description of what they looked like, and knew that these strangers must have been of the half-dwarf clans, because they were slightly taller than our own delving folk, and seemed to be a bit wild."

"This Mathiny that you spoke of," said Chinby, "was the leader. I heard him called by name several times when we first met the group."

"They told us that we were trespassing in the realms of Sigman Col, and that we would have to answer to him."

"I had heard that name before, when I had traveled in those parts some time ago. He is a hard one to put into a niche, this Sigman Col. Some say he's evil, and some argue for him, but I knew he couldn't be very kindly disposed to see us, a lane from the delvings, or me, the blind lore master that had stirred up some trouble for him from year to year."

"They didn't know who we were at first, though, and said we would be taken to their camp, and would be put to work helping to move their settlement, which they said they were relocating. They didn't know what to do with Chinby when they found he was blind and would not be of much use to them."

"Why didn't you try to lure them down so the watchers could help you?" asked Brian.

"There was no chance to do so," explained the old dwarf. "I had thought of any number of plans to do that very thing, but they tied us up and placed us in the old gatehouse, where they were waiting for the others in their party to return from scouting farther on in the wood."

"And then we heard another fuss, and that must have been when they started chasing you."

"There was a fuss there, all right," agreed Brian.

"Maybe we should try to lure this beast outside down to the tunnels, and block him in. I'm sure the watchers would be able to destroy him."

"There are too many shafts he could escape through, before he could be lured to the river," said Chinby. "I can smell many tunnels somewhere ahead, and not far away. There's one that comes from outside."

At that moment, Drub Fearing halted the group, and came back to discuss their plan with Chinby and Brian. Shanon, standing nearest Senja, suggested that he might go on ahead and scout around the mouth of the outside entrance, to try to discover the whereabouts of the creatures, if there were any, and to see if there was anything else they needed to know.

"That's a most excellent idea, friend," said Drub Fearing, and went forward with the elf, to show him the layout of the entrance shafts, and to wait there, should he be needed.

"What sort of ruse do we want?" asked Senja. "Loud? Noisy?"

"One that will draw our friend's attention away from Falon and the Carbens," agreed Chinby.

"We could start a fire, and see if the smoke wouldn't attract him," offered Brian, trying to think of ways to draw the hideous beast, and remembering well his own close call with Gram.

"That might just do the trick," agreed Chinby.

"Let's see if Drub Fearing has any better plan."

Brian brought the Carben dwarf back to the old lore master, and the two conferred on what was to be done to lure the beast away from their friends, and how they would escape, once the plan had succeeded.

"These tunnels are wide open until you reach the lower levels," said Drub Fearing. "There wouldn't be any advantage to trying to get away into the shafts, for it's all too exposed."

"What shall we have to do then?" asked the lane.

"We may have to slay the thing," replied the Carben evenly.

Senja saw that the stocky, thick-muscled Carben would be well equipped to do such a deed, were it to come down to hand combat. The Carben was slightly bigger than Brian, she noticed, but also that he wasn't quite so handsome.

"Then wouldn't it have been better just to fall on it back at

173

the falls, when we had all our strength?" asked Brian, not relishing the thought of any more fights with the powerful beast, unless the odds were slightly more evened out.

He and Shanon had been no match for Gram, and if it had not been for the Stone of Elver Tarn that the elf carried, he did not doubt that the reunion of Senja and Chinby and himself would never have taken place, and that he and Shanon would have ended up nothing more than supper for a horrible creature that ranged about on the outskirts of the Carben dwarf settlements that dotted the deep wood.

"A fight's not what we want," said Chinby. "If that were the case, you were right in saying we should have attacked when we had the strength. But what I propose doing is nothing more than luring that thing in this direction, and going on before it arrives to find us."

"Then let's set a fire in the upper shaft here, and use it so it will block off anyone from following along after."

"That's near what I have in mind, Brian. I have a few old tricks left in my bag from the days when I had my sight and was something more than a blind lore master."

Chinby reached into his cloak and withdrew a small leather sack that rode on his shoulder, torn and ancient, and smelling slightly of mildew. He produced some odd-colored dust and placed it in Senja's hand.

"This is what we would have fallen back on if we had not found the doors out of the kellers of Sigman Col," said the old dwarf.

"What is it, Chinby?"

"Ground powder from the Deep Home mines," he replied. "It can be used for many things, and has been a well-kept secret for a long while. They used it in those days to delve into the deepest parts of the earth that dwarfs had ever gone. I have used it on occasion to dress wounds, and to scare spanners by throwing it into a fire, and it's said to have excellent qualities in clearing up a poisoned stream."

Senja held the strange powder carefully.

Out of thin air, Shanon appeared, suddenly next to Brian, and the startled lane cried out, almost spilling the precious secret of Chinby's.

"There's much activity over toward the falls," he said, ignoring the frightened Senja. "I could see two or three of those things there, Brian. They look like Gram. Must be

174

some horrible pack of them in these parts. Not a very attractive wood to settle in."

"Not with neighbors like that," agreed the dwarf.

Drub Fearing came back to the small group, and placed his hands on his hips, feet wide apart.

"What is it to be?" he asked. "A fight of it, or shall we draw them here and disappear?"

He took the thick-handled dwarf bow from his back, and settled the quiver of ugly green darts within reach of his hand.

"We'll need wood, and kindling," said Chinby. "And then we'll see what next."

The Carben dwarf, along with Shanon, went out the concealed opening to the outside to gather the firewood, while Senja and Brian helped their old teacher to get all the things from his bag laid out so that he could easily reach them.

"If this doesn't surprise our friends, I don't know what will," he chuckled. "I was on the verge of getting all this out when the Carbens held us, but our fair Senja found the back door first."

"And a good thing, too," agreed the lane. "I don't see how this smelly old dirt is going to be of any use to us in dealing with any beasts, much less how it would have helped us out of that hole the half-dwarfs had us in."

Brian was on the point of scolding the harsh-tongued lane for her disrespect of Chinby, but he detected the note of concern and worry underneath, and saw that the old lore master enjoyed the teasing.

"They're coming this way!" hissed Shanon, following the Carben into the shaft and placing the armload of wood on the smooth floor.

"I don't know what's aroused them," said Drub Fearing, "but they act as though there's something of interest down this way."

Brian's heart fell.

"Did they catch sight of you when you were out?" he asked the elf.

"Never!" replied Shanon indignantly. "An elf is not seen unless he wishes to be."

"There must be something else out in our wood," said the Carben, stroking his thick red beard. "We'll have to take a look."

175

"Why don't we go on, and leave whatever's there on its own?" asked Senja. "We've gotten the falls clear so Falon and the others can slip away. That's what we were after, and now it looks as though that's done, so we may as well go on ourselves."

"I don't like not knowing all the things that are in the wood with me," said Drub Fearing. "Nasty surprises, sometimes, when you're looking too close to your own nose."

"Agreed," said Chinby. "We don't have any idea as to who, or what may be going on, and it won't hurt to find out. Maybe Shanon would take a quick look?"

The elf bowed.

"Sometimes it is of a great disadvantage to be known to be sly of foot," he laughed. "I shall find out what I can, and be back as quickly as I'm able."

As always, the elf seemed to vanish into thin air.

"This companion of yours is even more handy at scouting than myself," said Drub Fearing. "And we Carbens have long considered ourselves masters at that art."

"Shanon is a unique friend, indeed," agreed Brian. "Sometimes I think he's more dwarfish than some I have known."

"What do you think has happened out there, Chinby?" asked Senja.

"It could be anything," said the blind lore master. "And it may be nothing. The beasts may have just tired of waiting near the falls, and have decided to try their luck elsewhere."

From somewhere far behind them, a faint note rang out twice, then three times. It sounded as if a small bell had been chimed, softly, and the notes carried through the solid stone walls to where the companions stood, waiting for the return of Shanon.

"That sounds like a signal from the others," said Senja, trying to concentrate on the soft, bell-like notes.

"They must be moving," agreed Drub Fearing. "They've seen the beasts leave, and probably think we've drawn their attention this way."

"We said we'd signal," said Chinby.

"It's no matter now, for I think they've gone. I just hope our friends out there don't change their minds, and decide to return to the falls before the others are away clear."

"They won't, if we make sure they have something to explore here."

Brian's voice was tight when he spoke.

"If we can, we'll wait for Shanon to come back, but if not, we'll have to go ahead with Chinby's plan."

"That might be dangerous, if the elf is caught outside," grumbled the Carben.

"It'll be dangerous for us all," went on Brian. "And he has a cousin that's depending on him. There would be more trouble if the beasts turn back and fall on Falon and your kin, Drub Fearing."

"They would at least stand a fighting chance, with their numbers."

"Who says a beast is any match for the likes of an elf like me?" chimed in Shanon, startling the group with his uncanny arrival.

"Shanon!" cried Senja. "We'd almost given you up, from all our talk."

"That's never a thing to do, especially when you're dealing with our clan."

He laughed lightly, but his voice was serious when he spoke again.

"There seem to be big doings in the wood. It has attracted the beasts, and probably everyone else that may be in this neck of the world."

"What is it?" asked Brian.

"From the sound of it, I think it must be a clan hearing, although I'm not sure who lives in this wood, or why they would pick here to have their shinny."

"Elves?" asked Chinby, stroking his long white beard.

"And many of them, by all the noise."

"Wood elves?"

"It sounds so, Brian. Although there were a few reed pipes there that speak of waterfolk, as well."

"Now there's something worth thinking on," mused Chinby.

"The two clans mingling again, after all this time? I'd like to see what's going on that made both halves of elfdom decide to sit down together."

"Shall we try to join them, Chinby?" asked Senja.

"It will mean getting by these nasty louts outside," reminded Shanon. "Unless we could find some other way through the tunnels."

"Or unless we draw them off, as we were planning."

"It may not even be necessary, Brian," argued the elf. "It doesn't look as though the beasts are going back toward the

177

falls, and I think we could be in the camp long before they spotted us."

"Should we risk this? We told the others we'd meet them at Three Stones."

"I think we should warn these folk," said Brian. "And we could use their added strength, as well."

"Then let's be at it," grumbled the Carben. "All this jabbering is getting us nowhere. We're either going, or we're not."

"Let's take a vote," suggested Senja.

"An excellent idea, my dear. You call for a show of hands." Chinby nodded his approval of the lane's plan.

"All for going on," she said, and noted aloud for the blind dwarf's benefit that no one voted that way.

"And for joining this new band of wood elves?"

Having decided by unanimous vote to try to reach the elfin band and warn them, the friends now set about trying to decide on a plan for reaching their destination safely.

"There's plenty of deep wood between us and any beast," said Drub Fearing. "And the quarters are tight enough through most of this patch of forest that no one can gang up in numbers. Too much undergrowth. What trails there are are narrow and hard to follow, but the forest beyond is so thick that you wouldn't have to worry about anyone lying in ambush."

"But we might bump into someone coming from the other direction," offered Brian.

Drub Fearing smiled a gnarled smile.

"If that comes to pass, then you throw your manners over your shoulder, and look to your bows."

"Come on, then," snapped the elf. "We're losing time. We must make every minute count."

Collecting their gear, and arranging for Chinby to travel close behind Brian, holding to him by a strap passed through the younger dwarf's belt, they carefully filed through the tunnel that led to the wood, and set off after the elf, who picked his way carefully through the dense thicket.

Wildflowers bloomed on the thorn trees, covering long, barbed thorns that were painful if touched, and the ground was covered with a lush, thick carpet of grass so green it was almost black. The smell in the forest was green and damp, and tickled the nose.

Brian was grateful that their passing was almost totally silent, and no one spoke as they made their way on, but Senja would catch his eye every few steps, and wave briefly to him. His heart was a turmoil of opposing feelings, and he could not seem to find out exactly what he was doing, and grew confused when she smiled.

He supposed that this was what his father felt for his lanin, all those years ago, but they never spoke of it to him, so he could not relate to the oddly uncomfortable emotions, although they were not all unpleasant. He thought perhaps if he asked Senja to become his mate, then the feelings would calm down, and they could go on in a more regular manner.

A firm tug on his belt brought his wandering thoughts back to watching where he was going, and he sped up, hoping Chinby could not read his last thoughts.

His face was brilliant crimson, although no one had time to notice, except Senja, who turned and caught him staring balefully at her, and waved, which threw him into worse confusion. She seemed to enjoy teasing him, and he tried to become angry at her, but could not.

In a small glade, amid a stand of really ancient elders, moss-grown and covered with creeping vines, Shanon called a halt.

"This is where I first heard them," he explained. "Not too far ahead, but I don't hear anything now."

His brow was knitted into a puzzled frown.

"Perhaps they spotted the beasts," suggested Drub Fearing.

"I hope that's not the reason," said Shanon. "Because if the beasts were that close, then we may be in for a fight of it ourselves."

They looked around them, their every sense alert to any movement, but there was only silence.

"How much farther were the sounds?" asked Chinby.

"Not far. We'll have to go on to see."

Their voices were low and muffled in the stillness of the clearing, but it sounded to Brian that they must be able to be heard for miles around.

Shanon had set his direction for the small, indistinct opening at the end of the clearing, where the trail resumed, and taken a few steps toward it, when a fine web of a net dropped, whistling softly over him, and he fell clumsily to the damp earth. The others had hardly time to cry out, or realize what had happened, before more of the gauze-like nets spun out of the air above them and imprisoned them all in the sticky, suffocating strands.

"Use your short swords!" bellowed Drub Fearing angrily. "It's the Varads!"

As he struggled to reach his sword, Brian's hand became entangled in his cloak, and then the belt that Chinby was holding onto to keep up. He got the blade free at last, and began hacking at the web of strands that weighed him down, but soon saw that it was a hopeless task, for the nets were too thick, and it took much too long to cut through even a small portion of them.

His anger boiled to a rage, and he fumed helplessly as he watched the strange beings who were now dropping out of the thick foliage of the trees, to see what treasure spoils they had gathered in their webs.

A swart, dark-skinned figure knelt beside Brian, pushing his face close to inspect his catch.

"It's dwarf," the stranger reported.

"I have an elf," called another, his voice crackling with excitement.

"Get the nets off. We have a good haul, lads, no doubt. More than we've seen this way since we lost that batch of elves we were tracking."

"Ho ho," gloated a third voice, which belonged to a figure taller than the rest, although he wasn't more than a hand taller than Brian. "We have more than a treasure here. We have Drub Fearing!"

This last disclosure caused many clackings of large teeth, which protruded out of bony faces, and much hubbub and jabber.

"He's mine, he's mine," chanted one, dancing near the vainly struggling Carben dwarf, but he was pushed away by the one who appeared to be the leader.

"He is Stran Bor's," exclaimed Stran Bor, flashing a thin, two-edged sword at his followers.

"He is Stran Bor's," conceded the others in unison, whining.

"Now get them to camp. We must see what we have."

Grumbling and complaining, the Varad band trussed up their captives, and slung them between poles, and two by two, carried them away, opposite the opening that Shanon had been making for, and going directly into a part of the forest that looked to be impassable.

A few paces into the thick brush, Brian felt the ground tilt up toward him, and he realized they were going down an incline, and from the bumps, he assumed they were descending steps of some sort. There was a short interval of darkness, as they passed through an earthen-smelling tunnel, rudely scooped out by someone who obviously knew nothing about digging, he concluded, and then they were up on the other side of the shaft, in a cleared portion of the wood, where Brian saw shelters of mud and thatch, and smelled cooking fires.

He twisted about until he could see the others of his party, all wound in the sticky nets, and was relieved to see Senja put down next to him, where he could speak to her without their captors overhearing.

Drub Fearing was placed in a heap at the feet of an even larger Varad than Stran Bor, who snarled, and chattered his teeth wildly together.

"So this is our terrible enemy, is it?" shouted the Varad chieftain. "Now we shall see to it that we need never fear him or his awful tribe again."

There was more chattering of teeth, and some swords hammering on shields.

Senja, although shaken and frightened, held herself in check.

"It sounds as though they have had dealings with our friend before."

"I'm afraid they don't seem to hold him in too much esteem," replied Brian. "And it doesn't look as if there's going to be much we can do about it."

"There will be," said Chinby gravely from behind Brian, where he was mashed against him, "if we can wiggle our way near enough to that bonfire for me to work a little of my old lore magic."

Brian thought he heard a muffled laugh from his blind friend, but couldn't be sure in all the uproar that had broken out all around them.

A Fight in the Dark

WHILE the Varad band was busy celebrating its great fortune in capturing Drub Fearing, whose name seemed to be known to all of them, and the mere mention of which seemed to put all the ugly creatures into a frenzy of anger, Brian had a chance to loosen his bonds to the point of being able to wriggle free of Chinby, and loosen his hands from the netting enough to reach across to where Shanon lay, and to help him free the stifling webbing from his shoulders and face.

As he worked, he carefully took in his surroundings, and tried counting the number of their captors, but kept getting confused and losing track, for many of the Varads seemed almost identical to him, and he could not tell them apart in the deceiving light of the crackling fire.

The giant Varad, who went by the name of Golin Ling, chattered his protruding yellow teeth loudly, and raised a hand for silence.

Brian noticed that the Varad clan had hands much like his own, but they were covered with a thick gray-colored skin, and the feet were bare, being very large, and so tough that they didn't worry with footwear at all. He remembered seeing a few indistinct prints made in the soft earth along the trail, but they had not registered as any danger.

Drub Fearing, who was obviously aware of the Varad bands, and who knew the signs, should have been more wary of a trap, but for some reason had not, and as a result, they all stood a very good chance of being slain, or made slaves, by the savage creatures.

"Where do these things come from, Chinby?" asked Brian, just loudly enough for the old dwarf to hear, but not loud enough to call the attention of their guard back to them.

He was most disturbed and upset by what Golin Ling was

182

saying about Drub Fearing and the Carbens, and Brian began to worry that in the fever pitch he was reaching, he might turn his violence onto his prisoners, who were helpless before him.

"I don't know, Brian. My lore studies have very seldom led me across beings of this nature. I have studied mankind, and animalkind, and elfdom, but I can't remember too many references to these fellows. Drub Fearing would be the one to tell us more, if we all survive."

"He knew we were going into a trap," snapped Brian angrily. "I saw some tracks that I know belong to these things. I can see from their feet that it could have only been their trail. I paid no attention, and thought it must be a random beast, who would give us no trouble because of our numbers. Drub Fearing had to have seen the marks, yet he never once mentioned anything about these creatures, or that we might be in danger."

"We have been in danger since leaving Den'Lin Fetch," said Chinby. "He has his own reasons, I'm sure, for remaining silent about the Varads. It may be he didn't want to worry us."

"I think I'd rather have known. We might have been able to avoid being trapped like this."

"It's no matter now," said Chinby sternly. "What we have to do is see what unfolds, and try to do what we can to remove ourselves from the hands of these fellows."

Senja, silent while they talked, spoke in a very low voice, which was almost inaudible, and the lane had to repeat herself twice to be heard.

"Have you forgotten the stone you were telling me of? The one that saved you from the beast you called Gram?"

"I haven't forgotten it," mumbled the elf, still struggling with the bonds that smothered him. "I don't even know for sure if I still have it. After the way we were handled being brought here, I'm not sure that it didn't slip out of my cloak."

"You couldn't have lost it," wailed Brian, his disappointment galling and bitter. "It would give us a chance, at any rate."

His distrust of elves came back full force for a moment, until he remembered that it was not Shanon's fault, and there was nothing to be done about it, if the Stone of Elver Tarn were lost forever and they would see it no more.

"No, I think I feel it," called Shanon softly. "Yes, it's

punching my ribs through my cloak. But it will take some time for me to reach it."

"Scoot over closer here," ordered the dwarf. "I have my hands free, at least. If you can get close enough, I might be able to get it."

"Be careful," hissed Senja. "The Varad is watching you!"

The lanky, dark face of their guard clouded, and he eyed the captives suspiciously, and came to stand next to Brian. After a moment, he gave him a painful kick in the ribs that took the dwarf's breath and caused him to moan aloud in pain.

"Here! You stop that this minute!" blurted Senja. "You rude oaf, you don't have the courage of a flea, kicking a helpless dwarf that way."

The Varad's thick lips parted in a rough smile.

"Kicking is good fun," he crooned, and kicked Brian once more.

When he tired of that sport, he started on Senja. Brian's rage was so great he had split apart the last of the netting that held him, and was on the verge of leaping on the Varad guard, but Chinby restrained him.

"Quiet, my friend. This is a great thing to bear without striking back, but we must not waste ourselves uselessly. Wait!"

The old dwarf's grip was an iron vise, and Brian was surprised by the terrible strength Chinby had in his hands.

"Our time of reckoning is coming," he whispered. "I hear some others in the outskirt of the wood."

Falling back against Chinby, Brian looked about the Varad camp, a crude affair of grass-roofed mud hovels. Beyond the perimeter of the cleared space, the forest began again, and he tried to see anyone that might be there, just out of sight of the dim light of the fires, but there was nothing to be seen.

"I don't see anything," he whispered to his friend.

"Of course you don't!" snapped the old dwarf. "I said I heard something. There are some of the Carben clan out there."

"How can you be so sure?"

"I heard one."

"What?"

"He gave a signal. Nothing the Varads would suspect as a signal, but a sign, all the same."

Brian's thoughts flashed to Drub Fearing, who was a well-seasoned Carben woodsman, who would not likely be trapped in so simple a fashion, unless he had a plan of action in mind.

"There are elves there, too," added Shanon.

This last statement by the elf was drowned out by a thundering roar of voices upraised in a savage war chant, and many swords crashing on shields.

"Death to Drub Fearing!" cried the crowd, in a dull chant, and the Varad leader, Golin Ling, paraded about through the members of the group that surrounded him, waving a short, ugly stabbing knife in the air before him.

"Who shall it be? Who shall plunge the first blade into this hideous mouse?"

Cries from all sides shook the camp.

"Me, Golin Ling, me, me, me, me."

In every direction there was a multitude of volunteers to slay the Carben dwarf.

And Drub Fearing, bound and gagged on a rough stone slab in front of the group, lay without moving, eyes closed. Brian could not see well enough in the faulty light to try to see if the Carben was badly injured or not, but he thought he caught the regular rise and fall of the stocky chest, and an eye opening for a brief moment before closing again.

The elf had managed to scoot himself painfully along, until he was near enough for his friend to reach into the tangled mesh of webbing, to try to grasp the precious stone Queen Corin had given him to help him in his quest to reach the Roaring Sea, and he felt that being captured by the fierce Varad band was a time when the true strength of the stone would enable them to free themselves at least, and perhaps throw their captors into a state of fear that would keep them from pursuing along after them, if they were able to make good their escape.

Brian rolled this way and that, and had Shanon doing the same, but all to no avail.

"I can't find it," he complained. "I thought you said you had it!"

"I did, when I started crawling over here. It must have slipped out of my cloak."

"Oh no," moaned Brian, but his voice froze in his throat as he watched the Varad who had kicked him come swaggering back toward him, his huge, thick feet looming ever closer.

At the very spot where the elf had been, the Varad suddenly stopped short, and bent down to look at something he

185

had stepped on. Straightening up, the Varad warrior held small, dark stone in his rough hand.

"He's found it," lamented Shanon. "He's got the stone."

"Shush!" snapped Chinby. "He won't have it long."

The old dwarf had wormed and twisted himself free of th web that held him, and he was now lying quietly besid Brian, breathing evenly.

"There have been more signals. It sounds as if it is ver near time for them to attack. I'll give this to you, Brian," h said, pressing a cloth bag into the younger dwarf's hanc "When it seems right to do so, throw that into the fire."

"But the stone!" protested Brian.

"I have an idea it will probably take care of itself," assure Chinby. "Just you be sure to throw the powder in the fir when everything starts."

"Give me something to do," said Senja, her voice tight fror fear, but her gaze was steady, and her hands did not shake

"You be ready to grab the stone. Our friend will be sur prised enough, if I don't miss my guess, and he'll forget hi new plaything for a moment when the action starts."

And as if on cue, the Varad soldier who stood looking at th Stone of Elver Tarn he had stepped on and found droppe silently to his knees, a startled expression on the cruel, dar] features. In another moment, he had toppled forward, with out ever uttering a single sound or cry, and the stone fell ou of the lifeless hand and rolled, looking to Brian as if it wer alive, directly to the elf Shanon. It was another split secon before Brian saw the dark green shaft buried to the hilt ii the Varad guard's back.

Eyes wide, Brian looked to his left, where the giant figur of Golin Ling was, and to his dismay, saw that his hand wa high above Drub Fearing, the ugly stabbing knife poised.

"You are a coward and traitor, Golin Ling," shouted Brian kicking free of the last of the webbing which held him, an standing, feet wide apart, confronting the huge Varad chieftain

Another of the swarthy warriors had noticed the slai] guard, and began to alert the others.

"Who is this rodent that speaks as though he were some one? A dwarf of the cursed tribe of Drub Fearing, th murderer?"

"I am Brian Brandigore, delving dwarf of Den'Lin Fetch and I stand beside Shanon, an elf of Erin Frey!"

"Then they shall be the ones you die beside, earth scum

186

Golin Ling has long hunted and destroyed all your filthy kin, in cave or forest."

Two burly guards moved menacingly toward Brian, to rebind him, but he threw a hand up to halt them.

"No closer, if you value your lives," he said, his voice low and dangerous.

At that precise moment, the Varad who had discovered his slain companion called out.

"Someone has stuck Togin! Quickly, search the wood!"

Cries and shouts went up from all about, and Brian chose that moment to throw the sack Chinby had given him into the roaring fire that burned in the center of the camp, and Senja followed his lead, hurling her sack as well.

"Brian Brandigore," bellowed the dwarf, leaping for the slain guard's sword.

"Erin Frey!" shrieked Shanon, and held aloft a wildly flashing pillar of fire that erupted from the Stone of Elver Tarn.

Golin Ling, a veteran of many battles, was startled, but quickly recovered, and settled down for a fight, drawing his own heavy sword and stalking the dwarf that leapt toward him.

From the perimeters of the camp, the whistle and rush of arrows sang through the tumult of the confusion, and a dozen or more Varad warriors fell, pierced by Carben dwarf and wood elf arrows. The high, clear call of the elfin war horns and the lower, urgent notes of the dwarfs filled the enemy camp, and a great number of the Varad warriors fled, trying to escape the deadly arrows that came from everywhere.

Golin Ling rallied a troop of his regular soldiers, and began a counterattack against the onrushing elves and dwarfs, and soon the battle was joined in earnest.

The Varads had been stunned, and their number greatly reduced by the initial barrage of darts, yet they quickly regrouped, and Brian saw that it was settling into a steady, bloody fight that would take a huge toll of lives on both sides, if it were not cut short in some fashion. He had been sadly disappointed when the sack he had thrown into the fire had failed to do anything at all, but he had no time to think on that now, being faced with a wild-eyed Varad warrior who slashed the air viciously with a thick, two-edged sword.

He was trying to parry the thrusts of the husky attacker when a strange change began to settle over the clearing, obstructing the light, and dampening the harsh sound of the fierce combat.

A faint, tingly music began, softly, then louder, and a breath of wind swept through the gathering, kicking up dust and smoke, and causing the flames of the bonfire to dance wildly, casting long shadows on the ground and on the thicker eave of the forest behind. There was a dim rumble in the air, jarring the ear and making the stomach feel tight, and a great, dark mass of deep-blue clouds appeared directly overhead, and a rain of blood-red drops began to spatter the Varad tribe, turning their dark skin a fiery orange.

As Brian looked on, amazed, a thunder of hooves beat savagely at his brain, and overhead, a tall, armored form astride a huge white steed appeared, armed with a long sword that gleamed in a deadly white-hot glow.

"Surrender, Golin Ling, and let these friends go in peace. I shall destroy all your camps, and your lands, if you do not obey."

The voice of the figure was deep and resonant, but Brian was frantically searching his memory for where he had heard it before. It suddenly struck him as he turned to ask Chinby. It was the voice of his blind friend, but somehow magnified many times into the terrifying, booming bass that appeared to come from the mounted horseman.

"Give up, Golin Ling. Your Varad tribe will perish if you do not leave these strangers be. You are not to harm the Carben, Drub Fearing. I will see to it that he is punished, if he has done anything that requires it."

Golin Ling, an able and stout warrior, was a frightening enemy to have, but the Varad chieftain was not in the habit of dealing with such dreadful phantoms who spoke and threatened him with doom for his entire clan. Shuddering a shiver of resignation, he held up a hand to signal his warriors to halt the attack.

Chinby went on.

"All you elves and dwarfs in the wood, cease your attack! Return to the Green Shield at once. And take these strangers with you!"

Shanon, who stood next to Brian, turned to help Senja to her feet.

"We'll soon see how long all this lasts," he muttered to himself. "I hope we have a good head start on them, at least."

"You must stop your raiding, Golin Ling," burst the fearful

188

voice of the hovering, spectral form. "You will come to a hard end if you continue on with your cruel ways."

"Let's not go too far," whispered Brian to his blind friend. "There's no need to try to get Golin Ling to become an upstanding citizen of the wood."

The Varad leader stood, eyes half lidded, great dark face turned to the wavering white form of the horseman.

"I shall let these strangers go, O white one. But the Carben has butchered many of my tribe. He must be punished."

"If that is so, he shall be," boomed the voice.

Golin Ling's eyes narrowed into bare slits.

"You are strong, and may slay me, but I will not let the Carben go while I yet remain alive."

"You try my patience, Golin Ling. Beware! But what do you wish me to do?"

"Slay him!" snarled the Varad leader. "Slay him, and I shall release the rest."

A tense silence fell on the clearing and over the elf and dwarf companies that waited for the next developments.

"No!" shouted the group of Carben dwarfs who had forced their way forward to be near Drub Fearing. "He shall not die!"

The Varad band moved in the direction of the dwarfs, but Golin Ling halted them.

"We shall turn all the rest loose, but the Carben must die!"

His face set in stubborn defiance, Golin Ling's hands wrapped about the heavy hilt of the iron sword.

A tiny muscle at the base of his hard jaw twitched and jumped, and he stared, a flat, cold look, at the figure of the mounted rider on the blazing white steed.

"It shall be done," replied the booming voice, almost immediately drowned out by the uproar of the Carben soldiers.

"Hush, you Carbens! Back to the Green Shield, and take these captives with you. You shall bear back the body of Drub Fearing for burial at the Elf Cloak Falls."

The Carben dwarf who was held by the Varad chief nodded his approval, his face drawn and white beneath the bright red beard.

"It is best this way, my brothers. There shall be no more useless bloodshed. My life is nothing, if you all get away safely. Do as you are told, if you don't wish to hurt me."

"No, Drub Fearing," protested one of the Carben company, coming forward. "We cannot let you do this!"

"I wish it," replied the stout dwarf, his deep blue-gray eyes flashing. "You have never questioned my orders before, Holin. I ask you, as a good companion, not to now."

Holin clenched his teeth in a vain attempt to hold back his tears.

"Then slay him," called Golin Ling, gloating.

He felt he had won the greatest victory of all, if he had tricked this fearsome enemy into destroying the hateful Carben, Drub Fearing, who had hunted and stalked his band for many seasons, and who had slain many of his warriors.

The mounted, shimmering figure seemed to loom larger, and the white-hot flames grew brighter still, until those gathered there had to shield their eyes from the blazing form.

"Move away, Golin Ling, or you shall die, too. You will get your sacrifice. I am going to slay the Carben, Drub Fearing, in the name of justice, and to guarantee the lives of all the others here. The bloodshed between your tribe and the Carben camps shall end here. And it shall be so with the wood elves, as well."

The voice fell silent for a moment, then went on.

"Pick out one of your followers who may serve as the offering from your tribe."

Golin Ling's face darkened, and the yellow teeth flashed in a short, chattering spasm.

"What are you saying, O white one?"

"I am saying that this shall mark an end to the feuds between the elves and dwarfs and Varads. I shall take as sacrifice one each from all the tribes, as the Law demands, if it is to be perfect justice."

An outburst of angry voices broke over the clearing, as all sides protested the decision of the flaming white figure astride his tall mount.

"It will be so!" boomed the voice, and the crowd fell silent, involuntarily stepping back a pace or two from the dreadful form.

The fire grew hotter, and the shimmering form dimmed somewhat, until Brian could see through the wavering shadow of the figure, and so quickly that he hardly had time to follow it, the form moved across the clearing, covered Drub Fearing like a cloud blanketing a mountain peak, and when it was over, and the form back again where it had been, the Carben dwarf Drub Fearing was vanished from sight, as well as Golin Ling's second-in-command, Stran Bor.

In another flash, an elf was vanished, and then the form of the mounted horseman rose until the clearing shuddered, and the wind howled, stirring up the fire and scattering flames and ashes in all directions.

"Let this be an end of the turmoil between your tribes. There is a new force coming, and you would be wise to join ranks when the time comes for you to stand up and be counted. Let this mark an end to your isolation and hostilities."

Another flash of the white fire, and then the clearing was cloaked in darkness, which set every voice there clamoring for torches to see by, and cries from all directions.

Brian knelt next to Chinby, and placed his mouth next to the old dwarf's ear.

"What did you do with them?"

"They didn't go anywhere," assured Chinby. "Nobody went anyplace other than right where they were."

"I saw them disappear," argued Brian.

"You did see them disappear, but that doesn't mean they're gone," replied the lore master, chuckling a bit at his good performance.

At that moment, Brian felt a tug on his elbow, and was startled badly as he spun around, and was gazing directly into the untroubled eyes of the Carben dwarf Drub Fearing.

"We had best gather our clans and remove ourselves from here while everything is still confused," he said, picking up his knapsack from the heap of equipment the Varads had taken from him while he had been held prisoner.

"Get your elves out of here," ordered Chinby, directing himself to Shanon. "And you, my good Carben, kindly take your fellows on away from this camp. They will be undeceived soon enough as to my little hoax. I hope you tapped that lout a good clout, Drub Fearing, so he'll stay peacefully asleep until we're away from here."

"A dwarf cudgel is no thing to underestimate," said the Carben.

"Good. Let's talk on the trail. I don't want to still be here when Golin Ling figures out that he has been tricked into letting us go."

"Are we going back to the tunnels?" asked Shanon.

"No, my shaft rat, you won't have to go underground again so soon. We'll strike on toward Three Stones overside. I have remembered that this part of the world was once called something other than what it is now, and I recall that there is

191

a way to our destination that will get us there quicker than going by Deep Home."

"It won't be as safe," protested Drub Fearing. "Golin Ling won't be far behind, if he thinks he has nothing to fear."

"We now have two armed companies with us," said Chinby calmly. "Not that I would relish a fight, but we'll be ready for one, should it arise. Golin Ling is not one to like the odds we have on our side."

A high-pitched Varad voice wailed aloud from across the clearing of the camp and the smothered bonfire.

"Quickly, it sounds as if they're catching on. Let's move on."

"You heard Chinby," echoed Brian. "Shanon, you head the elves, and Drub Fearing, you bring along the Carben clan."

"And I'll tell Senja what to look for, so we can find the old trail that should be just beyond this camp," said the lore master.

"There is a story about how the blind can lead one only into darkness," scolded Drub Fearing. "But as I see it, that might be a marked improvement."

Hurrying to hold tightly to Chinby's hand to guide him, Senja brushed against Brian.

"We are to look for the split oak," she said. "Chinby says it is the road sign we are to follow now."

"A split oak?"

"They were planted in the old times," she explained. "A sort of code."

"It was at the beginning of these troubles," said the blind dwarf. "Long before they knew it would be needed by the likes of us."

"I'd prefer a lot more than a split oak now," complained Shanon. "Another few dozen archers wouldn't set so very badly, and a long mile or two between us and Golin Ling."

"First Sigman Col, now this Varad leader," grumbled Brian. "If we keep on, we'll have the whole wood up in arms and pursuing us."

"That's exactly the point, my thickheaded friend," said Chinby. "Exactly the point."

Brian thought he heard the old dwarf chuckle, but had to concentrate on his footing in the dark, and the conversation was closed.

The Split Oak

LONG, sharp thorns tore at the friends on every side, and the march had hardly begun when a steady, hard rain began to fall.

Brian could smell the wet smoke of the Varad bonfires and the thick green mist of the deep wood, and heard the others, slipping and hanging their cloaks on the painful underbrush or falling in the pitch-black night.

"Can you light our way with an elfmoon?" asked Brian at last, seeing the hopelessness of their situation, and knowing, too, that the forest would soon be full of Varad soldiers searching for them.

Almost at that very instant, Brian heard the curt, short barking of the Varad horns sounding the alarm.

Drub Fearing dropped back to where Brian was bringing up the rear of their group.

"We can go faster if we can find one of the old elf roads," he said, his voice low. "We have discovered them to prove most handy at times, when we're in need of getting someplace in a hurry, or when we don't want anyone to see us come or go."

"The elf roads?" questioned Brian. "What are they?"

"They are the trails from the old days I have told you of," answered Shanon. "Erin Frey had many of those trails in the sky. Some of them were for only the surefooted, though."

"The split oak," chuckled Chinby, who was being led by Senja, a few paces in front of the others. "The split oak is the stairway to those roads that kiss the treetops from the Dark Hills, all the way until you reach the Balsen Marshes, which border on the Plain of Reeds."

They could not see the old dwarf's face, but his voice sounded cheerful and confident, which was more than anyone else could claim.

"How came you to know of these old elf trails, Chinby? I'm not even sure my kindred in these parts know of their existence."

"Lore talk, my fine tree walker, mere lore talk. I have exchanged views with many in my time, and you come across certain things that lead you to look for certain other things, and then you keep looking until you find what you know should be there."

"That's a dense way of putting us off the track," complained Senja. "Why can't you just say it right out?"

Her voice was petulant in her anxiousness.

"How did you come to suspect the old roads, Chinby?"

"As I said, Shanon, by talking to others. I couldn't see with my eyes any longer, but I could certainly reason with my head. I knew that the Deep Home Highway was built to allow the dwarfish clans to travel unhindered, after the Troubles began, and figured that our elfish brothers were just as farsighted in that way, and would devise a plan that would allow them access to the other danes, where they could travel safely and secretly."

"The fountain I found you sitting by, Chinby, had a carving on it that gave the date and year of the first part of the elfin roads. Was that what you found out?"

"I'm surprised at your memory, Shanon. Yes, I had traced it with my fingers, quite by accident, at first. I was merely out that day on a study tour, although it had been told to me that you might be there. But after I found out that piece of the puzzle, I kept on, and added bits of information here and there. Not long after I left you, I ran across a most interesting sort of fellow, who had taken to bees and honey gathering, and he spun me hours of tales over his fire about the ancient clans of Roundhat, and of the doings at the danes of elfdom. He said he had seen Queen Corin once, in an old garden, and he seemed quite the authority on many events other than bees."

"Who was this?" asked Drub Fearing.

The friends were interrupted by a solid wall of coarse thorns, and in the end, they had to go far out of their way to reach a spot that was passable.

Leading the group were the wood elves and Carben clan, who knew the countryside the best, and even they were discouraged by the slow going they had encountered.

194

"I've never seen anything to beat this, Drub Fearing," complained one of the Carben dwarfs, hacking his way through a solid bramble patch, which seemed to grow thicker as he struck out at it.

"I know. It makes me uneasy. This is too thick and too ordered to be natural growth."

"What else could it be?" asked Senja. "Things like this don't get here without growing."

"Sometimes," explained the Carben, "old woodfolk will use tricks to deceive someone. Thorn brake like this can be planted to keep things in or out. I don't remember anything like this being here, though, on our last trip through this end of the wood."

"Could it be the Varads?" asked Shanon. "Do you remember the steps we went down, Brian? And that tunnel we went through? All that seemed out of place, too."

"I remember thinking they didn't know very much about delving."

"Exactly. So these might be traps they've planted to try to keep their prisoners from escaping, or enemies from getting in."

"The Varads are smart and crafty," interrupted Drub Fearing, "yet I don't think they would go to all this trouble. Too much work! They prefer to rob easy settlements, and to catch lone strangers traveling through the wood."

"Who are these Varads, anyhow?" asked Brian. "Chinby said you would have to be the one to explain them."

"They are not a tribe I am very familiar with," confessed the old dwarf. "And I have become acquainted with a good many kind. I would find it most interesting to discover more about them, and where they come from, and who their ancestors were."

Shanon had brought forth a small sack of elfmoons, and passed them out to the others, both elf and dwarf, and the party moved along slowly, the thin light dancing in mysterious black and green shadows on the wet leaves and thorns of the underbrush.

Drub Fearing helped two of his clan clear away a great fall of recently cut-trees, which blocked the dim outline of the trail, then turned to answer Brian's question.

"I first began to see traces of them as a spanner, just as I see these marks that they have been about not too long ago.

Yet no one knew much about them, or their doings. Strange fires in the forest, or an occasional sighting, and once in a while, we'd come across a rude camp, just like we were in tonight, only they were much smaller then. Mud huts, with a crude thatch roof, and not much else. Whoever lived there always seemed to be away when we'd find the shelters, so we left them alone for a time. If they wanted nothing to do with us, then we felt safe in assuming we didn't need to fear them."

"They all knew your name," said Senja. "And they most certainly wanted you slain. How did that come about? And how do they know you?"

Drub Fearing frowned, and his voice took on a deeper note.

"I'll have to finish out my story before you'll know the answers you seek, my good lane. There is a lot of water by the bridge between the time I'm talking of and now."

"Go on with the first," instructed Chinby. "We may as well get to know those chasing us well enough to find how to escape them. Go on."

"They began by stealing small things we forged," went on the Carben. "They seemed to like our blades, and arrowtips, and the ways we worked metal in shields. We didn't foresee any danger in a few small robberies, and it was a well-known fact that there were many beasts crossing from the ice fields, and everyone needed to be armed to merely survive."

"They didn't look too small or harmless to me," snapped Shanon.

"Golin Ling is one of the oldest of the Varad tribe, or so it seems, from all we've learned since. He has been around for as long as I've known of them. But they weren't as many in the old days, and hadn't banded together. We thought at first they might be a cross between wood elves and mankind, or our cousins, the old delving dwarfs, who perhaps had mingled with the settlements of mankind. We soon changed our minds on that count."

"Indeed!" snorted Brian.

Shanon flushed, but said nothing, and the Carben went on without glancing at either of the friends, wrapped up in his tale.

"That was a fair assumption," agreed Chinby. "In those places where mankind abound, they have a way of mingling and intermingling, until it's hard to tell about anything in its proper light."

"I first noticed an omen of danger when we began to see the traps in the inner wood," went on Drub Fearing. "They weren't of a dwarfish nature, and had no mark of mankind upon them. We felt they might be traps set for the beasts, for there had begun to be many packs of them plundering our settlements by then. I let myself be lulled by this reasoning, telling myself that it was probably a deep wood clan of our brothers who had set the snares, and there was no more to it than that."

"Had the beasts been abroad long?" asked Chinby, still guided by Senja.

"Not for so long a time. They had never been much of a problem before. I think they feared our numbers, and they never seemed to be in groups large enough to attack a settlement in force."

Drub Fearing picked his way cautiously through more bramble and thorn before going on.

"I think I can see it thinning out now," he reported hopefully. "At least it looks that way."

"That would be a piece of news I'd welcome," blustered Brian. "I'm beginning to feel like my lanin's pincushion, from all these thorn bites."

"Go on with your story, Drub Fearing. When did you begin to suspect the Varads were something other than a lost branch of your own kindred?"

"When we missed one of our wood party on a midwinter trip," replied the Carben.

"You mean one of your band was slain by the Varads?"

"Not in battle, no. We found him trapped and starved in one of the snares. He'd been unable to escape."

"But you didn't know for sure then who was setting the traps?"

"No, Brian. We'd seen the huts, and knew the owners were about somewhere, but we were never able to catch sight of anyone. After the death of our clansman, we set out to scour the wood in earnest."

The companions found that talking relieved them of the misery of being wet, and welcomed the excuse of taking their minds off their discomfort. What had started out as a tale now turned into a brief history course on the Varad tribes.

Pausing to catch his breath, Drub Fearing sat down heavily on a great gnarled tree trunk, which spread its long fingers across their path.

197

"We spent more and more time in the deep wood, both here and in the Lower Flume. More signs, and many more settlements of the strange creatures, but no proof positive that they really existed. And then one of our scouting parties took a prisoner."

"You captured one of them?"

"If capture is the word. I think this fellow had seen us all along, and decided to see who we were, and what we wanted. He gave himself up, and it was from him that we began to learn what sort of neighbors we had."

"They weren't my idea of someone to have in the next-door yard," said Shanon, shuddering.

"Mine either," confirmed Brian.

"The prisoner told us little about backgrounds, but we did find out that all the rest of his tribe looked similar to him, so we had found a model to study."

"What made him decide to surrender?" asked Brian.

"I don't know. At first, I thought he was fearful that we were going to hunt them all down and slay them, and that it would be best to fall on our mercy. Then we began to see that the Varads didn't know the word fear, and that they were able soldiers."

"Then what happened?" asked the elf, impatient to get to the end of the tale.

"This fellow stayed with us for quite a time, and traveled among our camps, and even made some friends among the Carben clans."

Drub Fearing's brow clouded.

"And then he disappeared. We looked high and low for him, but all to no avail. There wasn't a piece of wood in a day's march in any direction that we didn't search, but he had vanished without a trace."

At this point, the friends called a halt to wait for the rest of the Carben dwarfs and wood elves to catch up and regroup. While they were halted, they listened carefully for any sign that would tell them if the Varads were anywhere near them, but the horns had gotten farther and farther away, and could only barely be heard.

"We may have lost them," said Senja. "They certainly don't sound as close as they were."

"Don't count on losing a Varad in his own wood. He has ways of getting places that other woodcrafty folk might never catch on to. Stran Bor is a most excellent teacher, and has a nose that could sniff a fish in the water."

"At least we have a head start," comforted Shanon.

"And that's not much, my good elf, when it comes to these fellows. They're ugly, and don't have many manners, but they're excellent trackers, and have great staying power."

"I was hoping for that," chuckled Chinby. "If they are to reach the sea, it is necessary that they have great powers of tenacity."

"Maybe more than we bargain for," growled Brian. "And I have no desire to see any further into the camp life of those fellows. They didn't make me feel a welcome guest at all."

"They'll have time to do all the fighting and tracking they'll want, if they continue on after us."

"Bad luck for anyone they come across in the process," muttered Shanon.

"Not so much," corrected Chinby. "Maybe an occurrence to shake up one's ordinary routine of living, but I wouldn't say bad luck. It might be the very thing that might wake them up to save their lives."

"I'd like to know what else but bad luck you could call it. First, there was you, old one, perched in Erin Frey, which I should have known was going to mean trouble in the long run."

"And then there was this business of another delving dwarf, at Den'Lin Fetch," added Brian.

"There is that."

"You were telling a story, Drub Fearing," chided Senja, who was eager to hear the rest of the strange lore of the savage Varads.

"This fellow had vanished, as I said, and we had no clue as to where to find him, but he obviously knew where to find us, for a few weeks later, a large war party set on our settlement, and I barely escaped with my life. I wasn't more than a mere cub of a spanner then, and I've been keeping myself at war with these things all these years hence. They've come to know and fear Drub Fearing, and have taken to leaving parts alone where my settlements lie. Or at least until now they have."

"Did you ever find out what happened to your prisoner?" asked Brian.

"Golin Ling. You saw him tonight," said the Carben.

"The Varad chieftain?" cried Shanon. "You had one of the Varad chieftains as prisoner, and let him escape?"

"None of us knew about the tribe he now commands, or the danger they would one day be, not only to our clans, but to every living thing in the forest."

His voice hardened, and he went on.

"It's been said, and I have begun to believe it, that the Varads are an ancient tribe that comes from the ice fields. They are too crafty and cruel to be merely descendants of the beast clans, yet they are closer to those lines."

"Are there many of them in the woods around here?" asked Shanon.

"Here, and beyond as well," replied Drub Fearing. "We've found traces of them all the way to the end of our borders, and I doubt not that they have spread abroad farther."

Chinby pulled Senja to a halt.

"Now that I think back on my history, I remember mention of a tribe from the Easterlands who might be the first sires of these Varads. There were stories of the Fallen One, and how the armies of the Darkness were built upon the likes of these fellows."

"The Fallen One?" asked the Carben. "Who is he?"

"Not so much who, as what," said the old lore master. "There are tales, and then there are tales, yet none know what features fit, or any other name. I have talked with lore masters from all the delvings of known dwarfdom, and quite a few of those from the other races, yet none have spoken of this trouble other than as the Fallen One."

"Was that from the old Troubles?" asked Shanon.

"It was, good elf. The flaw that was with us from the very beginning, the crack in the bowl, the best as well as the worst."

Another sudden downpour drenched the friends and made further talk impossible, and they had to hasten on through the confining thickets, which tore at their faces and cloaks and caused them to cry out in pain from time to time.

Drub Fearing went ahead with another Carben dwarf, to inspect a portion of the wood that seemed to be totally impassable, and spent some time looking to the left and right of the trail for a break that would allow them through the dense green wall.

"Hush!" warned Chinby, suddenly turning his old head first one way, then another. "Listen!"

Brian strained his ears to detect any sound other than the rain and the muffled noise from Drub Fearing and his scout, but could tell nothing more from the thick, scented darkness that cloaked them.

"I hear nothing," whispered Senja. "What is it?"

"Shhh," rebuked Chinby, raising a gnarled, bony old hand to his ear, cupping it.

For a full minute or more, he stood frozen, as if suddenly transfixed into a piece of stone.

The Carben leader was returning with his report before the lore master had moved again.

"There seems to be a small break in these thickets not far ahead. It's a little close going, but I think this will be the end of the worst of it."

"Chinby has heard something," said Brian. "What has bothered you?"

He turned to the old dwarf.

"There are some others with us," replied the lore master. "And not so far away."

"How can you be so sure? Would it be the Varads?"

"It may be that there are some Varads about, but this isn't the case. There's someone else out there. I've heard signs for quite some time now, but they've grown louder."

Drub Fearing stood listening for a long moment.

"I can hear nothing but the rain, old one, and the others in our group, on the trail behind us."

"It's when those sounds stop that you hear what I'm speaking of."

Brian's face darkened in heavy thought.

"I wonder what other misfortune could be in store for us? It seems that all the very worst has already happened."

"Expect the worst, and never be disappointed," chanted Shanon. "Or that's the way the old line was always read to me. If there is anything worse that can happen, it will."

"There's a cheery piece of news," admonished the lane. "All we need now is a good way to look at things to really become discouraged."

"Oh, don't mistake me, Senja, I'm not in the least upset. Those are the most cheery of thoughts for an elf. The contrast of a thing is what lends it the flavor."

"He is fond of saying things like 'The best reason in the world is no reason at all,'" interrupted Brian. "Elf logic!"

201

"You two hush," cautioned Chinby. "I need to hear something more, before I can be sure."

"Sure of what?" asked the Carben.

"Of what we are dealing with here."

The old lore master knelt and put an ear close to the ground, and remained there for quite a space of time, hardly breathing, and knotting his brow up into a deep frown. He then asked that the elfmoons be shaded or put away, in case there was any danger of being discovered by being given away by their light.

"We won't be able to move a foot without light," complained Shanon.

"And with light, we might draw down something on us that would be worse than a stubbed toe in the dark," scolded Chinby, losing patience because of the great strain he was under.

He had been hearing the noises all along, ever since they left the Varad camp, but had not told the others, seeing no reason to paint their picture any darker than it already was, with the savage Varads now after them, and the dense thicket that formed a solid thorn wall to hold them back. And then there was the rain, and the miserable wetness that began to prevail over everything after a while, so that one's thoughts turned to the wonder of what a miracle it would be simply to have dry boots and a cloak that didn't cling to your back.

The sounds Chinby had been detecting, in the intervals between Carben band and wood elves, had come from both sides of their trail, and had confused him at first, for he could not determine what made the strange noise, or how many might be in the party that seemed to be following along on a parallel with them. After thinking it over, he could come to only one conclusion, and it seemed to be the only one that fit the facts.

They were bordered on both sides by a large pack of the hoofed beasts Brian and Shanon had chanced across in the old wood elf dane, and which had been spotted again at the entrance to the Elf Cloak Falls.

The brothers of Gram were close at hand, and Chinby had turned to whisper the unwelcome news to Brian when a terrible crashing noise announced the arrival of one of their unseen pursuers, and there on the cramped trail, in the hazy light of a half-covered elfmoon, stood a huge giant, which resembled Gram in every way except the eyes.

Carben dwarfs and elf clan alike froze before the dark shadow of the monster that confronted them.

Oranbar

DRUB Fearing was the first to recover from the astonishing appearance of the lion-headed creature that paced ever closer to the companions. He unslung his bow and touched an arrow to its string, but the deep, resonant voice of the strange newcomer halted him before he had let the shaft fly.

"Hold, Carben! You have no need of challenging me to battle, for I come in peace, and bear a message from many others of my kind of the same nature."

Stammering out the words, Brian's voice yet was clear and determined.

"We have met one of your kind already, not far from the fastness of Erin Frey. He called himself Gram, and he is responsible for the deaths of many from the wood elf clans in those parts. If we hold you in suspicion, you can surely understand why."

The grotesque creature bowed low.

"You may call me Oranbar. I know well the cousin you speak of. He has plagued those woods now for a long span, and has brought much grief to many who have crossed his path."

Drub Fearing had eased his bow, but kept it at the ready.

"There were others of your clan at the Elf Cloak Falls. They were certainly of a mind to have us in a stew, I'd wager, yet none of us had a mind to wait about to see."

"That would be Oral Ben and his two allies."

"You know them, then?" asked Shanon, one hand creeping

close around the short sword beneath his cloak, and the other tightly clutching the Stone of Elver Tarn.

"Of course, I know them well. We came from the same settlement in the ice fields, long ago."

"What good reason do we have for not slaying you now and ridding these terrible woods of a dangerous peril?"

"In the first place, it would take more of a shaft than you've drawn, good Carben, to do me much harm. And the best reason I can give you is that one doesn't slay one's friends."

"Friends, aye," growled Drub Fearing, taking to heart the remark about his inability as a bowman. "But what cause have I to dub you friend?"

"Cause enough to hear me out, and to listen to my warning about the snare they have laid out for you if you continue on as you are. There is a large band of enemies not far ahead of you now."

"Why should we trust you?" asked Brian, his memory still vivid and fresh of his encounter with the dreadful Gram.

"Send your water elf there to confirm my report. He should be able to tell you fairly if I speak the truth or lie."

"It may be a trick to separate us," warned Drub Fearing. "Don't go! We don't know how many others of these things are in the bush, out of sight."

"There are myself and three others," replied Oranbar. "They allowed that I should carry the message, since I am the least frightening of all our small band."

"The least? The others must be handsome fellows, indeed, if you are the beauty among them. And no offense, for none is meant, if it is as you say, and you're a friend come to warn us of a danger."

Surprisingly, the terrible face split into a wide smile, and Oranbar's great teeth showed as he laughed.

"I am counted most handsome by our standards, but then I can see that I must be disturbing to someone who is not used to seeing the Bolinge."

The old lore master's eager voice drowned out the others.

"Are you truly of that most ancient, noble line?"

"I am counted such, good dwarf."

"May I be permitted to run my hands over you, that I may judge for myself? I have no sight in these old eyes, and must form my impressions through my fingertips."

"I see no harm in your request," replied Oranbar.

"You mustn't go near him," cautioned Shanon. "It may be a trick. Let me scout ahead, to see if what he says is true. Then you may have your curiosity satisfied, Chinby. I can tell you for a straight truth, our good Oranbar will win no beauty prizes in our realms."

"The Bolinge are an old and honorable race," began Chinby, in his best teacher's voice. "They were close companions of the even more ancient race of the Syrin Brae."

"Better known to you as dragons," said Oranbar. "It seems the dwarf had his own reason to dislike those times."

"As well as many others."

"The Elver Tarn were dragons, and they were the friends of all," added Shanon.

"Not all, my good elf. There were those who hated the Elver Tarn, and the clans who protected the world."

The great being, his tawny coat shimmering in the light of the elfmoon, advanced closer, and before anyone could prevent him, Chinby had reached Oranbar's side, and stood, silent and in deep concentration, running his old, gnarled hands over the stranger's form.

"You see, it is as I say," said the great creature.

"And so it is," agreed Chinby. "I had never really hoped to meet one of the old line. I thought at best to perhaps one day study one of the slain cousins, who went the darker road. But that would not have answered all the questions I have about great gaps in my knowledge about the Syrin Brae and the Bolinge."

Senja, gathering her courage, went to join Chinby by the side of Oranbar. Soon the others were laying aside their fears and joining their friends.

Shanon, slipping away in the general confusion of the moment, went on ahead to see what he might of the report the great being had given, but had gotten no farther than a few stones' throw from the rest of the group when he detected a movement to his right, barely perceptible, and invisible to any but those of his keen vision. He knew it was the Varad band, just as Oranbar had said, and hurried quickly back to tell the others, and to see what else this strange creature might have in the way of information about their enemies, who had them surrounded on all sides.

Reappearing beside Brian, Shanon told of his findings.

"The Varads have an ambush, just as Oranbar said. I think

205

these must be from a different band than Golin Ling's, though. Somehow, they've gotten the word to their other cousins."

"The ones you speak of as Varads we have battled long in these woods. They have overrun many peaceful settlements, and slain many from all clans. They have outgrown our efforts, it seems. There are not enough of us left to keep them from raging out of control, and beyond these woods where they've first come to appear."

"Do you know any more about them?" asked Drub Fearing. "My clans have battled them as well, but we've never known for certain where they came from, or that they were such a great danger."

"They are a great danger, Carben, and they are almost new, compared to our kinds. The Fallen One has moved from the ice fields and has started across all the lands, and with that invasion came these you call Varads. They have been started as an inferior race by the Trouble, to fill out a great army. We have seen a time when there were none of them about, and then now, not only this wood, but every wood we have traveled has been full of these, or worse."

"Worse? You'd have to go a long way to find worse," grumbled Brian.

"Yet there are the ones who are even more powerful, and more dreadful enemies," said Oranbar. "My own cousins, who have fallen under the spell of the Trouble, as you know, are not enemies to be taken lightly."

The dwarf shuddered, remembering the horrible fear when confronting Gram, and the hypnotic eyes that made the victim want to surrender.

"What are we to do now?" asked Drub Fearing, indicating the direction where the Varad ambush lay. "Do we make a fight of it, or go back, or try to find another way around?"

"If we could make the split oak, we'd be able to take the elf road," suggested Shanon. "But I don't know how much farther we'd have to go, or even if we'd have any luck, if we did."

"The old elfin roads are yet open," nodded Oranbar, his great, horned head turned a burnished gold by the light of the elfmoons. "They have been used of late, by others of your kind, escaping to the sea."

Brian's heart hammered beneath his cloak, and he felt light-headed and giddy, hearing the sea mentioned, and the

206

fact that others were going, too. For a long while, he had felt alienated and alone, living in the safe confines of Den'Lin Fetch, and the butt of many unkind remarks, and constantly troubled by the gnawing doubts and fears that he had, and the terrific pressure he had been under to be a good, simple dwarf, following along in the footsteps of his father, as his sire had done before him.

The old lore master's voice was soft when he spoke, as if he were speaking aloud only to himself.

"So it has finally begun, has it? After all these turnings, and the warnings, and all the times I've wondered if what I was doing was simply a lot of hot air, puffed about by an old blind dolt who had seen his better days long before."

"Who have you seen on the elf roads?" asked Shanon. "I would hear news of the clans in these parts."

"More than elfs have been upon that highway," replied Oranbar. "There are those of the dwarfish clans, as well, and I have heard from others that even a band of mankind has been on the march, and not too long before you arrived in these parts."

"There has been no recent sighting of man, since the last Crossings," argued Drub Fearing. "How could it be that now they are suddenly tracking through a part of my old wood without me having a word of it?"

"These things I don't know," replied Oranbar. "I know I have seen many clans of man come and go, in first one place, then another. I watch them grow in number, and go from peaceful, useful beings into worse than beasts. Yet these I have heard of, who are moving on the elfin roads, are of the descendants of the Fair One, and are supposed to bring aid and comfort to their brothers here."

"Humph," grumbled Drub Fearing. "I've never heard anything but trouble to come of anything to do with our larger cousins who come from mankind. They are a strange lot, and most difficult to understand."

"That they are," agreed Oranbar. "Yet I think the time has come that we shall have to take them as comrades, if we are to overthrow the new threat from the Fallen One, and the Troubles."

"That would lead us nowhere," protested Brian. "What we have a need of is to protect our own, and seal off our own borders. Let each kind look to his own."

207

Chinby, taking his hands away from his exploring of the huge Bolinger, turned to Brian, clucking his tongue in disapproval.

"That is the sort of talk that began all this, my young hothead. First one thing, then another, and it has ended with the High Court broken into two camps, and the Fallen One taking that band of followers, and going to war down here against all the others of the Kingdom. It is for that reason that we have to unite under a single banner if we are to meet the challenge."

"Uniting with a tribe of men isn't my idea of trying to save anyone or anything," grumbled Drub Fearing.

"There are others on the elf road," continued Oranbar, ignoring the debate he had sparked with his information. "There are the elfin kind, as well as dwarf, and not long before, there were other delving dwarfs from the old border lands."

Brian's heart stopped, and he asked his question quietly, his voice unsteady.

"Do you know which of the delvings, or which borders?"

Oranbar looked evenly at the stocky dwarf before replying.

"There has been an invasion of the borders by a great number of beasts, and these half-ones you call the Varads. They have been gathering strength in the upper wastes beyond the Felin Dare for a long time."

"But no one ever listened," snapped Chinby. "I've been saying that we should have to watch our borders all along, but it was laughed off as a tale for spanners, and everyone went right on, ignoring the beast packs that had started raiding the delvings, and simply trying to ignore the fact that it was harder and harder all the time to defend the settlements by trying to overlook the problem."

"Do you know the names of any of the delvings?" cried Senja, fearing in her heart to hear the creature's answer.

"All the delvings on the border have been taken, or forced to flee," said Oranbar gently, looking steadily at Brian. "There was the delving called Den'Lin Fetch, and others, farther up the river, but some of the settlements are still battling on, according to the news from those who are passing through here."

Brian's heart was leaden, and he could not find his voice for a moment.

208

"Then we'd best make on for Three Stones as fast as we're able to find a way," he said at last. "Is there any way around these traps, Oranbar?"

"We shall see if we can't outflank our good Varads. I know a few tricks to this wood that they haven't caught on to yet, and with any luck, we'll have you on the old elfin road before they've found out the hare is out of the trap."

Oranbar left the friends to give out their instructions to the elf and dwarf bands that were with them, and went to tell his comrades what the new plan of action was to be.

He returned a short while later, his wide muzzle set in a slight smile.

"We shall have some fine music to set off to," he laughed. "My friends have chosen to see if they can't stir up this nest of Varads in front of us, and give us a chance to make our departure."

"Won't they be captured?" asked Senja, suddenly hating the idea of the tall, powerful creatures imprisoned, or killed.

This brought another deep purr of laughter from the Bolinger.

"It would take a bit more than these half-ones have to threaten us. Yet we shall scatter their ranks enough to allow us to get all those with you safely beyond their reach."

"We could hold our own, if it came to it," growled the Carben Drub Fearing, and he was joined by others of the sturdy band, who shook their short swords in front of them. "The Varads are no match for a Carben, given even odds."

"But the odds aren't even, good Drub Fearing. Your band has merely brushed against the outer surface of the camps these half-ones have. You would have been swept away, sooner or later, and not because you're not brave fighters, and good woodfolk, but simply because you are outnumbered. We have lost count of these Varad camps that have begun growing up here, and in other woods as well. They come in groups of two and three, from the ice fields beyond Felin Dare, and then there are two and three more, and they pour over the borders now, hundreds strong."

"We never had any idea," said Senja. "I knew there were beast packs that would make a raid here or there, but even those were mostly down toward the borders. I was beginning to half believe that what my family said was true, that the worst of the problem was the delvings like Den'Lin Fetch,

209

and those others, settled right in the way of the packs that came across."

Senja looked sheepishly at Brian.

"I hope my family has escaped," said Brian. "And my friends, Jeral and Jaran."

Oranbar looked away into the darkness, and the great ears shot forward, and his body tensed.

"Come! We have our diversion. They will be thinking of other things over there, and we'll be able to slip through the thorn brake in a spot I know, not far from here. We helped the others who used to dwell in these parts to plant the green fences, to thwart the Varads, but it hasn't done much to really stem them, or keep them from spilling out on the other side."

"It must have done some good," said Shanon, "because they haven't reached Erin Frey yet, or the woods around."

"Then our effort shall not go as wasted," purred Oranbar. "We each do but what we can, and hope for the best. But quickly, we must make the most of the moment! The Varads won't be kept away from a prize long, once they've gathered themselves up in numbers. Even the presence of two of the Bolinge won't keep them at bay all night."

Oranbar, moving in quick, smooth motions, leapt forward, and surprising the others, swept straight into the terrible fastness of a high hedge of the dangerously crooked thorns, wicked and gleaming in the light of the elfmoons.

"Come along with you!" commanded Oranbar. "I'll clear the way."

Stepping gingerly up to the hole in the underbrush where the great creature had disappeared, Brian hesitated, then crept forward, holding his breath.

"You'll have to do better at waging war on the Trouble than you do at stepping into a briar patch, Brian Brandigore," boomed Oranbar. "You must take heart, and leap to the fray!"

"The only thing frayed here is me, if I were to go hopping into nests of these crooked darts. Give me a battle anytime."

"See, there aren't any here," cried Senja. "On both sides, but here the way is clear."

Upon looking more closely, the others saw that the space where Oranbar disappeared was indeed clear of thorns, although on first glance, it looked the same as the impassable brambles that grew on both sides.

"It helps to remember where you've put the doors," laughed Oranbar, out of sight and somewhere ahead, crashing noisily along through the thinner tunnel of thorn-free brush.

"I don't see how anyone could help hearing all this mulhash," grumped Drub Fearing, tugging his hat firmly down on his head, and arranging his cloak to cover his shoulders and arms, before following the giant Bolinger.

"I guess they have enough to keep them busy where they are," said Shanon. "It certainly seems so, from all the ruckus from that direction."

Away toward where he had gone to scout out the Varads, a great turmoil had erupted, with the blowing of a dozen or more Varad war horns, and screams of terror and pain, and the loud, rumbling roars of the ancient creatures, intermingled with all the rest.

The dirty orange color of flames burst into the dense cover of the wood, and the urgent calls of Oranbar were unnecessary to hurry them on, for the Varads had torched the wood, and even though the rains came in sudden downpours, the smoke that came from the wet wood was thick and stifling, and made the eyes water and the nose run.

There was no more talking for a while, as each of the groups of wood elf and Carben dwarf hurried into the dark hole behind the others, and Brian was hard put to keep up with Oranbar, for he held Chinby again by the belt to his waist, and Senja clung to his hand, as they fled toward the hopeful safety of a distance between themselves and the savage bands of their pursuers.

Much was going through Brian's mind as he huffed along, pushing aside the dense foliage, trying to keep up with the strange creature ahead, and trying at the same time not to go too fast for the old dwarf and the lane. Shanon was beside him, then Drub Fearing, then all was lost in darkness again, and except for the noise Oranbar made, the dwarf would have missed his way.

They went on at this grueling pace for what seemed forever, and Brian welcomed the relief of not having to think about Den'Lin Fetch, or the news he had had of it, or to worry about the fate of his father and Ianin, or his friends. They had teased him at every chance, and taunted him about his dreams, and beliefs, and his adoration of Chinby, yet he held them as loyal, staunch friends, and felt a deep pang of sorrow

211

when he thought of the possibility of anything having happened to them.

Brian realized, as he panted and groaned after his guide, that deep down inside, he had been secretly counting on returning to Den'Lin Fetch, justified and accepted. With the news of the fall of his delving, all that had fallen away, and he didn't even know for certain whether or not he had a family, or friends, left.

The disturbing facts that Oranbar had given were new to the stocky dwarf, and he knew that although he had been drawn to the tales of Chinby, there was a part of him that had never accepted the tales of the old lore master as anything but romantic fancies, some love of life as it had been in the long-ago past, where everything took on a rosy glow, and seemed right, and fine.

Dwarfs, it was well known, had a love for anything to do with history and dwarfdom, but seldom did they go so far as had Brian, overstepping the bounds of good dwarfness, by being swept away with a passion for the fireside tales of a blind lore master, who obviously muddled his histories, and made up distressing reports to upset a delving, and keep a good, hardworking fellow from pursuing the important business of life, of delving, or smithing, or sewing, or mending, or any number of other things that kept one occupied, and from having to think about the consequences that were to be faced.

Senja's hand was firm and warm in his own, and he blushed in the darkness, hoping she couldn't tell what he was thinking by his grip, and he was painfully aware that his plam was sweaty.

Thinking of that, he almost lost his footing on a piece of tree root, causing the lane to hold to him even tighter.

"Be careful!" scolded Chinby. "I think I might be able to do as well about keeping my feet if I were alone. Mind your business, and stop your pipe dreams."

Blushing even more, he turned his eyes forward, to try to concentrate on following Oranbar, and it was a second or two before he realized that the dense wall of thicket about them had thinned, then disappeared entirely, and he was standing on a large lawn, up to his ankles in thick green grass, all bordered by rows of brilliant yellow flowers.

And there, too, was the Bolinger Oranbar, crouched at a small stone fountain near the opposite side of the broad area,

212

drinking his fill from the bubbling stream that shot out of the ground, through the figure of what was easily recognizable as a water elf, holding a bow aloft, and streaming a thin ribbon of water out of his mouth.

And at the same time, Brian, and the others as well, became aware of an early morning gray slate of a sky, beginning to lighten and turn a burnt gold, as the sun started his long climb out of the night's darkness.

Falen Rin

"HOW long have you lived here?" blurted Shanon, running his hand over the finely carved bowl of the fountain.

Oranbar paused, as if in thought, his pale gray eyes studying the companions.

"I have known those who dwelled here in the old days," he said. "We have had long discussions of all the roots of things, and the whys, and why nots, and the reasons for the end of summer and the arrival of spring. Your great-grandsires were solid thinkers on matters of weighty subjects. They never let a single topic go by, that it wasn't turned about once or twice around an evening fire."

"You mean you knew the water elves that lived here?"

"The dane is called Falen Rin, and I have known it and its dwellers well over the years."

"Are there any of those still upon the world?"

"Oh, many of them," laughed Oranbar. "If you are worried that you will not meet them, you may set your mind at ease. They will be sending help along shortly."

Shanon's jaw dropped open in his surprise, and he stammered out a mumbled reply.

"You mean they still live?"

"Very much so, good elf. They have been whiling away their time, preparing for the Great Crossing."

"What crossing would that be?" asked Drub Fearing, becoming a bit apprehensive about being in an unknown dane, now said to be still full of the strange clan of elves that were friends with the Bolinge.

He was familiar with their woodland brothers, and did not mind so much traveling with them, but the waterfolk were alien to him, unless he counted Shanon, the canny comrade of Brian Brandigore. That fellow, he thought, was all right, because he was in the company of the delving dwarf who was to lead the revolt that would bring all the clans of dwarfdom together again, and unite them in the delvings, and present a solid front to all enemies.

Oranbar had laid his huge frame down beside the fountain, great forefeet stretched before him, and massive head grown still.

"The Great Crossing of the Roaring. There is much to be done yet, and many to gather, but the time grows near."

As he spoke, the companions watched in awe and wonder as the tawny body began to pale, then turn ash-gray, then was nothing but solid stone, just as the form of the elf in the fountain. The gray eyes were no longer alive, and now stared blankly out at the friends, as the eyes of all statues do, cold and sad.

"What has happened?" called Chinby, hearing the loud groans of the others.

"Feel him," answered Brian. "Not a moment ago, he was talking and answering questions, and now he's solid stone."

"Do you think the elves he was speaking of are stone, as well? Are they like this fellow here, who is spouting this stream of water in the fountain?"

"I don't know, but I hope not. It will be difficult to lug about any of their sort, and he said they were gathering for the Crossing."

"This is most interesting," said Chinby, running his old hand over the smoothness of the cold stone that but a short while before had been the Bolinger Oranbar.

"Interesting, indeed," said Shanon. "And most distressing. The Varads aren't that far from us, and now if the others he sent to draw them off turn themselves into stone as well, that means we're right back where we started from."

"Not quite," said Brian. "We are now in an elf dane, Falen Rin, and Oranbar says there is help to be had here. He didn't lie about anything else, or I don't see any reason for doubting the truth of this."

"He said nothing about turning into this piece of rock, either," protested Shanon.

"I think he had his work to do, and did it, just like your Queen Corin, in Erin Frey. Perhaps his errand was to get us safely here, so that we could find aid."

"Then where is it is what I'd like to know. And where are the Varads? We've heard nothing now for an hour or more, and I don't like it when things get too quiet, especially when there's an enemy in the wood with you."

"I'll send out a scout party on this side," said Drub Fearing. "We'd better do the same all around. We might be able to scare up the help Oranbar was speaking of. I have a thought, though, that we're going to need more than the likes of those two."

He jerked his thumb at the unmoving stone forms in front of them.

"They would be wonderful fellows to have on your side if all you were doing was trying to blunt an attacker's darts, but give me a lad with a little more lightness of foot, for my taste."

"You'll have plenty of fellows with light feet, Drub Fearing, if all the Varads and Sigman Col collide and we're caught between them. That may be one dance I'd like to be out of, and I say that truthfully."

The groups split up, each exploring in a different direction, leaving Senja and Chinby to go with Brian, who kept running his hand over the statue of Oranbar.

"I could have sworn I saw him wink an eye! It doesn't make any sense that he should lead us all this way, and then just desert us."

"I don't think he has deserted us, Brian," said Chinby softly. "And it could be you saw him wink. I have read of these beings who are able to change forms as it is helpful to them, or who have the ability to live long periods of time by slowing everything down until they're merely stone. Oranbar speaks of living a great long time, and it seems he has the power to do this. That would explain how it came to be that he knew that this dane was called Falen Rin, and knew the dwellers, as well."

"Do you think all the elves here are like him?" asked Senja. "I mean, can they change themselves, if they want to?"

215

"We'll have an answer to that soon enough," answered Chinby. "Oranbar spoke of the Great Crossing, and that the clans would all be gathered together, and the delvings united once more. It is said in the old books that the dwarfs won't be united again until the day comes that the van of the dwarfish army is led by an elf."

"Shanon!" breathed Brian. "My old friend Shanon, who spends his time down a shaft as well as any dwarf."

"I would suspect that it is Shanon, when it comes to speaking of those things. Yet there are the others, and I don't think it was intended that we are to be carrying on a war to drive out the beasts, and Varads, and the Trouble, with an army of stone warriors."

"I certainly hope not," agreed Senja. "And I wish Oranbar would come back. I was beginning to like him."

They turned their eyes to the silent statue.

"He is amazing," agreed Chinby. "I never thought I'd have an opportunity to actually speak to one of the Bolinge. As it seems now, I'm not entirely sure I have. And you have done what few dwarfs have ever dreamed of, Brian. You've spoken to one of the most ancient of orders, our friend Oranbar. His kind are the companions of even the most ancient of the Syrin Brae. You have spoken to a being who counts dragons among his friends."

"Shanon was speaking of the Elver Tarn, and that they were of the light, and tried to protect all that was good."

"The Elver Tarn and Oranbar must be companions," agreed Chinby. "My lore is sparse in some areas, because the subject is so old, and there are not many who have written of those ancient subjects. But I have spoken with a Bolinger face to face, and have heard from his own accounting of how it was. That is the greatest privilege of all for a lore master, to speak with living history."

"Can you imagine what the Great Crossing must be?" asked Senja. "It sounds like a great adventure."

"If you don't get sick on the water," muttered Brian. "And have a proper scow to go on. I don't imagine a dwarf keg boat will be anything near up to the task of that little chore."

"I wouldn't be so quick to belittle the keg boats, Brian," said Chinby. "They have done many other things in the past, and they may yet have another part to play."

"What's more pressing to me at the moment is where is Three Stones, and how are we to meet our friends there?

216

Falon and the other Carbens will be there with whoever they were able to call together, and there will be an end to it."

"That's true, Chinby," conceded Senja. "That's what we agreed on when we split up at the Elf Cloak. And now we've lost our best allies, just when we need our numbers. Oranbar frightened me with his talk of the Varads, and the great bands of them that are loose."

The old dwarf's brow knitted into wrinkled parchment.

"Sometimes they are called one thing by one, and another by the next. That's what leads to a lot of misunderstanding about things. I've known that there were beasts coming over the borders for a long span of years, but I was never aware of these others. I had heard rumors now and again, and vague tales as to the half-ones, as Oranbar called them, but I hadn't put the facts together properly. Now I understand that many folk lump the beasts all together as one, and a four-legged beast is the same as a Varad."

"So you would have never known one from another," said Senja. "Yet I can see how it happens. Not many folk have lived through a meeting with these Varads, as we have. I can see how there are not a great number of reports of them."

The lane was interrupted by Drub Fearing, who had come racing across the lawn toward them.

"Chinby!" he called. "We've found something that might be of interest."

"What is it that excites you so?"

"We've found Three Stones!"

"Then it couldn't be far. You haven't been gone long enough for much of a march."

"We're standing in it. This is Three Stones!"

"Falen Rin is Three Stones?"

"That is the ancient name."

"How did you come by this welcome bit of news?" asked Brian.

"From reading the note that was left by some of our other party. They say they will be back tomorrow. They left the message, in case we missed them."

"Well, I'll be," muttered Brian. "Here we've been led by this lump of cold stone directly to the spot that we were making for to begin with."

"It seems that fortune has indeed smiled on our venture," said Drub Fearing.

"Good fortune, and a powerful hand from the Great Lan Himself."

"There are those who would doubt all that we have seen today, yet I think we are indeed most fortunate in our encounters. Not everyone has conversed with one of the Bolinge, or watched living things return to stone."

"Nor seen the Varads and escaped to tell of it," added Senja.

"Shanon should be returning soon," said Brian. "He'll be relieved to know that the others are to meet us here before another morning passes."

"Our band has grown into a tidy-sized war party," said Drub Fearing. "I won't feel quite so lonesome, with all the company. And it'll cause our ugly friends in the bush to consider carefully before joining a skirmish with such a number. They prefer to deal with the helpless and lame."

"They are in the wrong neck of the wood, then."

"Not if you count dealing with an old, blind dwarf," grumbled Chinby.

"They wouldn't dare risk scratching you, old one, if the lane is with you."

"A fine lot you know, Drub Fearing," snapped Senja hotly.

"We'll all know a fine lot if that wayward elf ever comes with his report," complained Brian. "We've got plans to lay, and a course to set, and he lingers at his walk, as if nothing were afoot."

"Which way did he venture?" asked Drub Fearing.

"Toward the opposite end of the clearing there, just beyond the fountain."

"Let us see where our good elf has gotten to. We may as well gather our party and set out our plan, and the direction we are to set our course."

As he spoke, the Carben took a long reed pipe from his cloak and blew a series of short blasts on it, which brought his entire band to his side, faces eager and questioning.

"We are going in search of our good tree walkers now," instructed Drub Fearing. "It seems we are in the right place to meet the others. This is Three Stones, where we are to congregate, and go on toward the Roaring."

The Carben paused to let that information sink in, then went on.

"Now we need to explore the rest of our layout, and to see

what needs tending to, and what needs to be patched, or mended, and what supplies we shall be wanting on a march."

He turned aside to Brian.

"Do you know if there are any stores to be had here?"

"Shanon might perhaps know," replied the dwarf. "Or Falon. He seems to be more familiar with these parts than any of the rest. We may have to wait on his arrival to see what we shall find."

"I'd rather have a full pack now, and stores laid up for marching," grumbled Drub Fearing. "It seems we're forever waiting on an elf for this or that, but then so be it. We've waited upon worse."

"By a long throw," said Chinby. "And I think we may go ahead and explore the dane without either Falon or Shanon. I have been in my share of elfin settlements, and all of the classic ones, as are Three Stones and Falen Rin, are very much like our own delvings. There should be a commons, where the trade and feasts were held, and the area where the dwellings lie. Then there will be the areas of more interest to us, when we reach the storehouses."

"Do you know the layout well enough to tell us, old one?"

"With Senja guiding me, I can make do," replied Chinby. "Unless our good elf, Shanon, returns before."

Drub Fearing broke his band up into four parties, and each was assigned a task to fill, food to find, or weapons to sharpen, and he left one group to stand guard around the perimeter of the dane, on the off chance that a wandering band of Varads might find the concealed entrance that Oranbar had led them through.

It was a slim chance, having it discovered by accident, yet the Carben wanted to take no more risks than necessary, and although he had said nothing to his friends, the narrow escape from Golin Ling had bothered him more than he had let on. He had known of the trap the Varads had set, for he had laid his own snare well in advance, before the meeting of Brian and Shanon and the others, and had staked his army about the camp of the Varad band, planning to destroy their leader and to drive the rest from their hold in the wood.

All that had been planned would have to be changed, now that he had the information that Oranbar had given, and had found the threat much greater than any of the Carben dwarfs had ever dared imagine. By good luck, and the timing of Brian in halting the Varad chieftain's hand in striking, his soldiers had time to lay on an attack, and cause the confusion that had enabled them to escape.

And of course, there had been the wood elves, and all the flapdoodle of the white rider, and the smoke, and frightening lights. That had been as good a trick as Drub Fearing had ever seen worked, but he firmly believed in the old lore master, and had been raised as a spanner to respect those of the old ways.

His father had been one of the outlaws of Sigman Col's realm, and always attended any gathering where the forbidden teachers were to speak, even after the grim Carben leader made the punishment for being caught at those meetings more and more severe. Chinby's name had long been on his father's lips, as one of the oldest of living teachers who came from the ancient delvings, who were of the true race of dwarfdom, their delving cousins, and who knew the history of all things on back until the dawn of the Beginning.

Chinby, of course, never made any such claim, although he did not discourage it, but thought of himself as merely a student of living, and the old ways, and of the more distinguished of the famed dwarfish leaders. He knew he was not on a par with the more powerful of the lore masters, the last of which, to his knowledge, had gone to the Tombs after the passing of the Syrin Brae and the Elver Tarn had returned to their secret lands, beyond the knowledge and lore of any living being.

The meeting with Oranbar had been a highlight of Chinby's life, for it was a rare event, indeed, to be able to talk with one of the lion-headed beasts that had been the sentries of the Syrin Brae and the stewards of the Lower Realms after their noble masters had departed.

As simple a life as Drub Fearing had led, and even though he was one of the Carben clan, he still had found the tales of the lore masters his father had brought home to feed, or hide, full of the values and ideas that glimmered vaguely inside his spanner's heart. There was something that made him feel excited inside when he thought of perhaps one day returning to the delvings of old, to start a new life there, or better yet, and a dream he had long held, to start a new settlement beyond the realms of Sigman Col and the confining rules and regulations that slowly choked the life out of every Carben citizen.

It was a strange day, when he thought of it, to be following a delving dwarf toward the distant sea, which he had heard of at times from the lore masters, but which he had never expected actually to look upon. That sea was spoken of in awed tones by those who spoke of it at all, and there were many horrible tales of disaster and doom, from one end of it to the other.

The Carben dwarf was looked upon by all his band as one of great courage, and much wisdom, for he had lived many turnings, and his beard was already full of gray, but he did not know if he would be truly glad to reach the shores of the Roaring, or if he would be able to go on beyond it. Yet something deep inside him stirred, some inner strength that he was becoming aware of, and he felt that the reserves of courage that he had counted on in so many times past would not fail him.

Chinby broke in on the Carben's thoughts, his old voice lowered in conversation with Brian.

"He's been gone much too long for a quick look around. Shanon is not one to misspend his time in overlong studies of the sunrise. I think we had best follow along in the direction he went, and see what's happened."

"Hadn't we best set out our troops?" asked Senja, looking to Drub Fearing for support.

"You have learned quickly, my little one," replied the Carben. "I was beginning to think of suggesting that myself."

"I wish Oranbar hadn't left us," said Brian. "Right at a time when we could use his help the most, he's taken to decorating the lawn with a lump of stone that won't be of much help to us."

"He got us here, don't forget," reminded Drub Fearing. "And through the worst of the Varads."

"I'm grateful for that, right enough. But I wish I knew what we have left to face before we're beyond these woods and these nasty fellows."

"From what the Bolinger said, the bands we have met under Golin Ling are but a small part of a vast army," said Chinby.

"And there are others, even beyond here," added Senja.

"I wonder if they are at the sea?" asked Brian, beginning to think how incomplete his plans were, and wondering what he was to do, if and when they reached their destination.

The old lore master turned to his student.

"They are at the sea, I'm sure," he said. "But so will the

221

others be. We have powerful allies who are to meet us at the Roaring."

"I'd settle for Oranbar, for now," admitted Brian. "He seems to be familiar enough with the woods, and doesn't fear the Varads."

"Who knows what we shall meet with next? There may be some reason for him to return to stone. Perhaps the danger is past."

"A likely story, Senja, but one that I'm not holding with, until we're beyond Three Stones and safely out of this wood."

A slight movement out of the corner of his eye caught Brian's attention, and when he looked more closely in the direction of the small stirring of branches beyond a carefully trimmed flower bed, he detected an elfin cap, forage green, with a blue feather stuck jauntily into it. And then there were the others, appearing all through the hedgerow, until at last a tall, agile elf, with light blond beard and hair, dressed all in pale gray, stepped out into the open, and without seeming to walk at all, came toward the friends at a rapid pace.

"Well met, old one. Our service is yours."

Brian stammered a hasty greeting, stuttering and fuming, and turning to Chinby for help.

"Is that you, Crown? Have you mended your ways enough to come offering your help?"

"Crown it is, Chinby, but not with mended ways, or much more sense."

The tall elf laughed quickly, although there was a note of hardness beneath the mirth, and the soft features had the slightest edge of grimness.

One by one, the elfin faces in the hedge appeared, and soon there were a hundred or more of the members of Crown's band gathered before them.

"We ran into your good Falon yesterday, down by the Two League meadow. He said there was to be a gathering of the clans up here at Three Stones soon, and invited us, as polite as you please, and said we'd be most welcome to join in."

He laughed again, eyes twinkling.

"And he said you were leading the whole fracas, Chinby, and I had to throw in my lot to that thought. What guide would a true elf ever follow any quicker than a sightless old dog like yourself? It was too good to forgo."

"It seems Shanon isn't the only one that takes leave of his senses when he begins to use his elf reason," snapped Brian.

"It sounds as if we shall have another waterfolk among us," chuckled Crown. "Shanon? The name is not one that is known to me."

"It will be," assured Chinby. "Given time enough."

And at the moment, as if appearing on call, the missing elf appeared at Brian's side, startling him, as always.

"The Split Oak is open and waiting," he announced gravely. "We have taken the Varad guards there, and opened the old road."

"This is Shanon?" asked Crown, advancing and offering his hand.

"At your service," replied Shanon, bowing.

"Crown, also of the fair clans of waterdom, lately up the Salt Marsh, but now marching with Chinby to the Roaring, also at your service."

"Welcome, Crown. We have a need for all who would go with us."

"Is it true we go to fight under a dwarf?" asked Crown.

"Of the most stubborn order," replied Shanon. "Stiff-necked, through and through, yet a good companion, when one gets down to it."

"We have heard rumors of this march for a long few seasons past. There were tales of it spread throughout the upper reaches of the Salt Marsh, and even in the new danes out beyond the Ash River. No one knew what to make of them, except that the beast packs were getting worse, and these clumsy-footed gnomes that have been lurking about all this time started getting bigger numbers. Things have not been so good here since before the last leaf fall."

"And will be worse still, before all is said and done," muttered Chinby sourly.

His voice had barely died away when there came the faint call of a Varad war horn, and the answering note was blown almost at the hedgerow behind Brian. In the next instant, the air was full of hissing arrows, and the companions were flying for the cover of the inner buildings of the ancient dane of Falen Rin.

The Stone Warriors

FROM all sides of the old elfin dwelling, there poured forth scores of Varad soldiers, grim in their dark-brown battle garb, and armed with bows, and great black iron shields, and ugly, curved swords.

The companions, Shanon and Brian at the lead, sheltered Chinby and Senja between them, and put up the best defense they were able, hoping to find a spot they might hold, and rally their surprised and outnumbered forces. Crown, with his newly arrived waterfolk, made up the rear guard, and every few feet they would halt, turn, and loose a volley of long, yellow-tipped arrows into the advancing hordes of the enemy.

Great Varad chieftains, some much larger than Golin Ling, headed the attackers, and the fleeting looks they caught of their pursuers made their hearts fall, and Brian knew they could not hope to stand against so great a force as the dark wave that flowed endlessly out of the surrounding wood. His thoughts turned to the idea that perhaps Oranbar might come to their rescue, for their danger was greater than at any time before, but the hope slowly began to dim, for they were running away from the statue of the Bolinger, and even at the moment, a great war band of Varads surged past the sleeping stone form, and no change took place.

"We're on our own this time," he said grimly, loud enough to cause Shanon to turn quickly to look at him.

Brian burst out laughing, a deep, mellow sound that chilled the elf, but he saw that some strange change had occurred in his stalwart friend, and even as he ran, he could see the battle fire igniting in Brian's eyes.

"Brian Brandigore!" called the elf, as loudly as he could and still keep his breath for running.

They were nearing the inner wall of Falen Rin, and as all elfin danes were copied from the ancient ways of building, Shanon knew that their place to make a stand was here, where they might turn and drive their enemies away.

"To the wall!" he roared, pointing ahead to the dark gray finger of rock that cut the clearing in half.

Someone in the rear had taken up the battle cry.

"Brian Brandigore!" called the deep bray of a Carben, and it was followed by a dozen others, somewhat higher-pitched, but in rich, clear tones.

"Brian Brandigore!"

"Erin Frey!" boomed a water elf, followed by more deep brays of the Carbens.

Shanon watched his friend, stumping along, clasping the short sword in his hand. It seemed somehow out of place as a weapon for the stocky dwarf, but he could think of no other at the moment, and was glad that they had anything to defend themselves with at all. Looking behind, he saw the Varads continue to grow in number, and he saw, too, with crestfallen heart, that the elfin warriors of Crown had lost more than a few to the long black darts of the enemy bowmen.

There were Varad bodies to be seen amid the sea of reinforcements that kept spilling out of the wood, but the small injury suffered by them appeared to make no difference, and they charged on, washing over all before them like a raging storm tide, driven by the howling wind of the dull war horns.

The elf pipes and dwarf calls were drowned out by the din of the Varad hordes, and even the small lift he had gotten a moment before, bravely calling out the rallying cry, was lost amid the terrible fury of the dreadful chaos unfolding behind.

There was a brief moment of time when Brian thought they wouldn't make the wall that now loomed before them, and his hopes were dashed almost completely, when he realized there was no gate to be seen, and that instead of saving them, it was to be their downfall, for it was blocking all further escape. A dead end, with only death awaiting them!

A terrible rage tore through Brian, and he held the elfin sword aloft and slashed the air, eyes turning blood-red and an icy vengeance surging through his veins.

"Put Senja and Chinby over!" he bellowed. "They shall at least escape to tell Falon what has befallen us here. Over the top with them, if you value your hides!"

He had the Carben dwarfs nearest to him pick up the two struggling figures, and was about to have them thrown to the top of the gray stone wall.

"Wait, Brian. Let me!" cried Shanon, amid a clatter of arrows that hailed down upon them.

One of the shafts struck the elf, but fell harmlessly to the ground at his feet, much to the amazement and relief of Senja.

"Good dwarfwrought shirts, to avoid those pinpricks," he laughed, his tone low, and grim.

"Have you no protection?" cried Brian, and realizing the lane had none, he tore off his cloak and shirt, and handed her the thin, fine-linked metal shirt that turned both blade and shaft, and that had been handed down to the delvings and danes ever since the first Troubles began.

Shanon touched a piece of solid wall that showed no sign or mark of any portal, and very low down, so low that they had to stoop to get under, a wide gate suddenly appeared out of nowhere. Beneath the opening they all shot, scrambling for their very lives, and no one had a chance to study their new surroundings until Shanon had touched another spot on the other side, and the howling throng of Varads were shut off from them, except for a few, which were quickly dispatched by the waterfolk of Crown, or crushed beneath the archway which clamped solidly down at the elf's touch.

Breathing heavily, Shanon gave a quick briefing of the place they had safely reached.

"These walls were built in the Ancient Troubles, and served as an outdoor meeting place in summer, and a commons, where oldsters could gather to exchange their talk, and merchants could come to display their wares. You can see that we're safe here for the moment, under these overhangs, and if we stay under the eaves of this path that runs to the other gateway, there under the oak tree."

"They'll be coming over the top as soon as they get the idea!" cried Crown. "This wall is tall, but not enough to stop a Varad!"

"It may be," laughed Shanon. "I saw Brian when he was going to heave these two husky dwarfs over, and he was right in thinking that way, and brave in doing so. Yet I'm afraid it all would have come to naught."

"Look to it!" commanded Crown, setting his band out in a

kneeling position, bows drawn taut, ready to repel any intruder who might show his head over the fence.

He turned to Shanon.

"This has given us a breather, cousin, but I think we'd best look to a safer spot yet. This isn't going to hold them long."

Shanon smiled slightly, pointing to the top of the wall.

"I think our friends might find it somewhat difficult getting over."

"They shot their arrows across," said Crown. "So why shouldn't they follow?"

"For the simple reason that they built these old walls to be gone through, not over."

A harsh, angry growl of rage surged over the enemy beyond the walls, and Shanon laughed again.

"They weren't so ignorant to the danger of a wall being scaled in the old days, so they had a variety of traps to build in to discourage anyone from going over the top. They thought, and rightly so, that anyone who didn't know the secret of opening the door had no business inside."

"Then let's be on our way, before they run out of traps. Where does the other gate lead? Don't you think they've cut us off?"

"Perhaps, perhaps not. But that doorway will stand us in good stead. It leads onto the old road, and is marked by the Split Oak."

Chinby seemed pleased, and raised his voice to be heard over the excited Crown.

"If we are indeed at the Split Oak, then we may have the best of them yet. They have a greater number than any of us has suspected before now, but I have hopes that our own allies will be up to the test. All we need do now is reach them."

Drub Fearing, who had lost a number of his band, was white with rage, and his voice came out a mere whisper.

"I have had the worst of it this day. My band is less five hardy souls who set out with me from the Elf Cloak, and I'll see that a fair exchange is had with that rabble beyond the wall before I leave here."

"Your day will arrive, Drub Fearing. It is useless to stand against the numbers they have mustered now."

Another hail of arrows rained down all around the companions, clattering harmlessly off the covered archway they crouched under.

This was followed by another assault on the wall, accompanied by a din of Varad war horns, blaring and calling harshly against the soft side of morning.

Shanon's eyes narrowed, and he looked to Crown.

"I think we may need think of our own departure, but first let's see if we can't give those louts a little taste of the elfin idea of warfare."

He gathered all the elves of the party together, and along with Drub Fearing's crowd, they marshaled all their bows, and sent one last volley of arrows flying over the gray stone wall.

Cries and groans of stricken Varads rose up from the far side, and they fired another quick flurry of the long elfin shafts and sturdy dwarf darts into the raging hordes, which they could only hear, clamoring about beyond the old wall built by the elves' ancient kinsmen long before.

"We'd best look to our exit now," said Brian, turning to his friends. "If indeed there is an exit that you know of, in this Split Oak, or old road."

"Stay under the cover of the walkway," cautioned Shanon. "We must keep ourselves away from their reply!"

And as his words died away, a huge clatter of arrows rained down on the companions, and they were only saved by the stone overhead that ran the inner length of the wall, and by the protected walkway, which covered the open ground of the enclosure from one side to the other.

"I hope Falon has heard all this commotion, and steered clear," said Crown, his fair features clouded with worry.

"Falon has been at this business far longer than many of us," replied Shanon. "I don't think he'd let himself fall into a nest of these ugly fellows."

"Falon is a swift thinker on his feet, and as good a soldier in these matters as any," agreed Drub Fearing. "If I were to have to stand beside someone outside dwarfdom, he'd be the elf."

"Thank you for the compliment to our cousin," said Shanon, bowing. "I'm sure we'll all have enough opportunities for that soon enough. Look about us, here! There's waterfolk, and Carben, and delving dwarf, and woodfolk out there, somewhere. Brian Brandigore has already united more of the warring clans in a single blow than most others have done in a long history of warfare on the borders, and during the Troubles."

"I've not done any uniting," grumbled the dwarf, fidgeting, and unable to find what to do with his hands.

At last, he replaced his sword in its sheath beneath his cloak, and strode toward the gateway beyond, which stood framed below the old, worn oak.

"I would think we'd all best look to our feet! Those rabble outside sound as if there's more come to help!"

"It's something more than that," warned Chinby, listening hard.

"All I hear are a lot of Varads," shot Drub Fearing. "And where there is a lot of them, I'd like to lessen the ranks, when possible."

He raised his hand, and signaled his following to loose another round of arrows over the fence at their unseen attackers.

At that moment, a dozen Varads appeared over a portion of the high elfin wall, not more than a stone's throw from the friends, but were quickly cut down by Crown's bowmen.

"Well done, lads," he cried, "We'll have no need of worrying here! There's enough Varad arrows stuck all over for us to shoot back, if we run short. I guess it'll come down to who gets tired of shooting first."

"Who would want to get into an arrow match with that lot?" asked Drub Fearing, glowering. "Shoot when you're able, and draw back to strike again when they're not looking for it."

"Exactly," agreed Chinby. "That's the way we shall have to deal with these fellows for the time being. It is not yet that we shall face the full force of the Varads, or any of the others that have been slowly building their numbers. That shall have to wait for the proper blow to fall."

"There won't be any blow struck, anywhere, if we don't look to our back door," snapped Crown. "I've had my share of run-ins with these lads, and they don't take kindly to being stuck from behind walled elfin forts. That's a thing that will make them mad enough to learn to fly, if they have to, to get to us."

"Drub Fearing, loose another shaft or two, to try and keep them busy, then we shall loose a volley, to give you a chance to come along after us. I think once we hit the old road, things should fare much tamer, but should we still have a fight of it, let's break ourselves up into small squads, so that we'll always have a shaft in the air, no matter how pressed we are."

"A good thought, Shanon. We'll divide up into five or so archers, each with his own, so that we can cover ourselves at all times."

Drub Fearing gave the order, and it was followed shortly thereafter by Crown.

"At least we shall have more of a chance if we don't lose our heads, and keep organized," he agreed. "These odds aren't the sort I'd wager on, but I don't see any other way to play out this hand we've been dealt."

"Hush," called Senja, dangerously near the wall, her head pressed near the crumbling gray stone that separated the companions from the raging hordes outside. "There's something else going on out there."

At first, all the companions could hear was the war horns and the strident cries of the Varads, urging each other on. Then, as they accustomed their ears to the furious din, there came another sound, softer than the Varad bugle, but as deadly-sounding, and somehow heartening to the hard-pressed companions.

"Who could it be?" asked Shanon. "There are no others but the Carben clans and the woodfolk of Falon, and these horns are not theirs."

"They're not the horns of either," nodded Chinby. "It sounds as if it might have to do with Oranbar."

"Then he came back!" shouted Brian.

"Perhaps," said Chinby, his tone guarded. "Or it may be someone else."

"Let's go and see," urged Brian. "It sounds as if we could join the fight in earnest now. With enough reinforcements, we might drive these Varads out of the wood, and free this part of the world of their likes. That would be a worthy thing to do."

"True enough, Brian, but we have to reach the sea before you find the means to do what you plan. We shall need many more allies than those we hold now. The Varads are but scarcely drawing together. We see but a small part of their number out there now." Chinby shook his head slowly. "No, we'd best save our valor for a time when it might count for more."

"There is never a better time than the moment," argued the younger dwarf.

"At most intervals, I wouldn't haggle about that," said Chinby. "Yet now, I say we bide our time, and strike with a heavy blow when we do make our move. They would scarcely feel our sting today. But give us our time and place, and the allies we shall find at the Roaring, and we shall rid this wood, and all the woods wherever, of the likes of the Varads, or the other beasts that have kept the decent folk of field or forest, plain or sea, at bay, and trembling in fear at their coming."

"That's well spoken," said Crown. "I hope we shall all be alive when that moment comes."

"There shall be enough time for that, don't fear, my glad-headed elf. I have long known of the exploits of good Crown of Salt Marsh and Reed Hollow. There has ever been a bane on any beast who might be so unfortunate as to end up in your territory."

Another long wail of anguish drifted over the wall, and the companions turned their heads once more toward the Varad hordes.

"What can it be?" cried Shanon. "I know of no large force of elves or Carben dwarfs that would cause all the furor out there."

"It doesn't sound like they're attacked," said Senja. "It sounds more like they're frightened of something."

The cries and shouts of dismay and terror grew louder, and the flights of arrows that had been clattering about the friends slackened, then ceased altogether.

One great Varad war horn sounded, bleating above the clamor and din of the confused cries and shouts, then another, which was answered by a dozen more, all high and strident and wavering, as if the blower himself had been badly frightened.

"They're signaling retreat," muttered Drub Fearing, disbelief heavy in his voice. "I've not heard that call often, but I know it when I hear it."

Brian studied the Carben before speaking.

"They don't seem the sort to back away from a skirmish."

"They are good soldiers, whatever else they may be," agreed Crown. "Not the sort I'd want to lift a mug with, but they have been trained well."

"Too well," grumbled the Carben. "They have no code, and no common sense of fear."

"Any soldier is afraid, at times. It keeps him alive. But these fellows are reckless, and have no fear, most of the time. They can be ruined because of that very thing."

231

"Too much fear is equally bad," offered Shanon. "For then one freezes, and can do nothing at all."

"It is the in between that we search for," laughed Crown. "Give me the lad with just enough, and not too much."

Beyond the elfin wall, the sounds of the Varad horns grew fainter, and farther away.

"Let us go and have a look at what army has caused a panic in the Varads' ranks," said Brian. "If they are so fierce, then surely there must be something terrible there, if it has frightened them."

Shanon knitted his brow, then shook his head.

"I think only one of us should go. It may be a trick to lure us out from behind our wall. I know these fellows are fierce fighters, but I saw that they are also dangerous enemies in their cunning, as well."

"You will do well, little brother," called Crown, thumping Shanon a resounding slap on the back. "It is one thing to be a good fighter, but you must needs be a fast thinker as well. One without the other is useless."

The waterfolk elf shrugged his shoulders and smiled slightly, crossing to the wall as he did so, and listening carefully before he touched the hidden spot that opened the low, broad-necked gateway in the solid gray mass of the wall.

A strange silence greeted the companions as they flocked to see what they could of the mysterious disappearance of the savage Varads. Armed, and with the bows of the archers drawn and ready, the small company advanced to the opening, and peered out on the green lawn that bordered the barrier.

Chinby, led by Senja, asked in a tense, hushed whisper, "What is it, child? What's happened here?"

The lane, wide-eyed, did not respond to the blind lore master's questions until he tugged urgently on the sleeve of her long cloak.

"What is it, blast you? Have you lost your tongue, after all this time? There's not many occasions I can recall that Senja, the outspoken lane of Con Den Fetch, had not a word or two on almost any subject."

"It's strange, Chinby," she muttered at last. "I don't know what's happened."

"Brian? Shanon? Crown? You, Drub Fearing?"

The others were all held spellbound by the same sight that had bewildered Senja, and it was another few moments before anyone could recover long enough to relate the scene to Chinby.

All across the broad, deep-green lawn, there sprawled many slate-gray forms in many positions. Some were in the act of falling, others in the motion of running, unseeing faces turned toward some terrible form that enlarged their eyes and bulged their tongues in stark fear. There were Varads fallen on their backs, some in the process of hurling their curved throwing knives, some trying to defend themselves, and others merely flinging down their arms. All were turned into the same hard, gray stone that the figure of the Bolinger Oranbar was, standing still by the statue of the elf, bow uplifted, in the fountain.

"There's something beyond me gone on here," whispered Crown. "What sort of black tricks are played in these parts?"

Chinby's scolding set Senja to describing the scene to him, while Shanon and Brian and the others carefully marched out to inspect the silent Varad army, which now camped at the very gates of the inner city of the ancient Falen Rin.

The friends counted over a hundred enemy soldiers, struck into solid stone where they stood, some fighting, some too stunned to move or fight, and others, realizing the danger, in full flight from whatever foe had beset them.

Shanon reluctantly reached out a hand and tapped one of the ugly Varads upon his crooked, misshapen face, the great fangs protruding in fear and anger.

"They are ugly enough fellows," concluded Crown, sitting atop a crouched figure next to Brian and Drub Fearing, who was studying the form of another Varad very closely.

"Here is Tolith Bor himself! I have pursued him through many a night, and by all that's fair, he's chased me a time or two. Now we've seen an end of all that sport."

"But who's to say these stone things won't revert back, just as Oranbar did? We may be out here in the middle of all these nasty lads, and just poof, they'll be on us, as quick as you please."

Shanon laughed as he watched the effect of his speech on the others, but a tiny tremor of fear passed over his heart at the thought.

"They'll be here a good long winter or two," assured Drub Fearing. "I don't know who we owe our thanks to, but I'm offering mine up now, whoever it was."

"Or whatever," corrected Brian.

"Or whatever," conceded the Carben.

Shanon had gone to stand beneath the upright statue of the elf, bow raised heavenward and a solid stream of water shooting out of his laughing mouth.

"All this business has given me a thirst," he said, and was on the verge of dipping his hands into the fountain when a booming voice, right at his ear, startled him badly.

"Do not touch the water of Falen Rin," echoed the voice, and Shanon, hand poised over the fountain, fell back aghast.

"It was Oranbar!" cried Crown. "Or the statue! It spoke!"

"So it did," said Chinby, pulling and tugging at his long beard. "I believe I know what's happened here, after all you've told me, and after the Bolinger has warned Shanon away from the fountain."

"What is it, Chinby? Why can't I have a drink?"

"Oh, you'll have your drink, as all of us will," went on the old dwarf. "But not from the fountain of Falen Rin. It is the weapon which has turned our enemies into these obliging rocks."

Chinby stepped nearer the elf, and held out a hand to him.

"Give me a cup, one of you. I'll show you what I mean."

Drub Fearing was the first to place the needed object in the old lore master's hand.

"You should be up on this, Shanon! I'm surprised that you overlooked so much of your lore in those early years. You remember that you found me beside the fountain in Erin Frey?"

"I remember very well, Chinby."

"I had had a chance to go over the figures that were carved there, and I knew enough of the elfin tongue to discover that I had been lucky indeed, for that well was dry. Had it not been, I would have been one of these lumps of rock that you say are all about us now. And even as Oranbar, although I think that somehow the Bolinger has mastered the secret of the fountain, and may use it as he wishes."

"The water is what's done this?" asked Crown. "I'm an elf, old one, and I don't recall any of our lore ever mentioning water that would turn you into stone."

"You are too young to have had it from any of the old lore masters," replied Chinby. "And you have grown up in a dane that is far from the old settlements."

As he spoke, Chinby handed the cup he held to Shanon.

234

"You may fill this, but be most careful not to touch the water at all. Then hand it back to me."

Shanon did as he was told, and carefully passed the cup back to the blind dwarf.

"Is it full?" he asked, sniffing at the contents of the small drinking cup that had been carefully crafted in the settlement of Drub Fearing.

"It is."

"Then take it, and cast it on some tree or bush, and observe what happens. Be very careful not to spill it on yourself or anyone else. I know not the secret of undoing the spell, and we'd leave a sad marker behind us, I'll warrant, if someone touches this water."

Shanon had taken the cup, and very gingerly walked with it to the nearest hedgerow, and threw the contents of the cup onto the living green shrub. At first, no one could see that anything was happening, but very slowly, in shades of green to gray, the portion of the hedge that the elf had thrown the water from the fountain on began to harden, then set into a perfect image, down to the last fine detail, of a coarse hedge, perfectly carved in stone.

Between Two Camps

AT the very moment that Brian stepped forward to examine the stone hedge more closely, a long sigh of an elfin reed pipe was heard, from both sides of the dane's boundaries.

"It's Falon!" cried Shanon, and was joined by Crown, in placing his pipe to his lips, and keening a long, low call in answer to their comrades.

Brian turned from the handiwork of the waters of the fountain in time to see Falon, the wood elf, come striding toward them from the shadows of the outer wood. His band was wet, and much bloodstained, and it was not hard to see that they had had to make a fight of it to regain the safety of Falen Rin.

Behind the elves came the remainder of the Carben dwarf clan, sadly depleted.

And directly behind Drub Fearing's followers was the beginning of another group, which although cloaked and hooded, and dirtied by battle, still somehow seemed familiar to Brian. As the newcomers drew closer, he let out a strangled cry of joy and pain, and fell on the leader of the band, a dwarf of husky build and large, powerful shoulders, from long hours of working ore, and bending the hot metal into usable shapes.

"Jeral!" he cried, clasping the figure of his old friend to him. "What of Jaran? Do you know how my lanin and father have fared? How have you found us?"

The questions came so fast that Jeral, for Jeral it was, could only weep, and shake his head, and hug the stout young Brandigore with his powerful arms.

"Easy here," cautioned Chinby, releasing his young friend from the grip of Jeral. "You'll squash each other before we get the news."

Senja had come to stand beside Brian, and much to his discomfort, had taken his hand. He was on the verge of blustering, and removing it, until he saw the frightened look on her pale face, and he was overwhelmed with compassion, for the news led them to believe that Con Den Fetch had been overrun as well, and he could see the worry there, and the deep lines of grief that formed about her eyes. She was not openly crying, but she was not far from it.

He was becoming aware of the fact that he was not much removed from it himself. Biting his tongue for control, he questioned Jeral again, in a tight voice, which was very near the edge of breaking.

"How fares it, my friend? I can see you have had a fight of it. Where have you come from? And how have you reached us?"

Falon, turning away from the question he was answering for Shanon, replied for the still stricken dwarf, who had yet to find his voice.

"We had been here, and gone, and came upon a Varad war party attacking these fellows. It was nip and tuck, as well as I could see, and they were giving as good as they got, but the

236

Varads had a greater number. We threw our weight into the fight, and were able to escape, but they followed us through the better part of yesterday, and we had a go of it, all the way to the outer forest. We came on these good Carbens there, and between our three bands, we got clear."

Over the last of Falon's speech, there was the distant, ugly bleating of Varad war horns, and the sounds of a great crowd coming noisily through the wood.

"They see no reason for stealth anymore," said Drub Fearing, a tight smile across his features. "They see that they have us outnumbered now. It is their kind of battle."

"They may have us outnumbered, but that doesn't mean we're done," snorted Shanon defiantly. "We have come upon a good secret in this fountain of Falen Rin, and one that may yet see us in good stead, before all is said and done."

Jeral recovered his voice, and spoke in a low whisper to Brian.

"They have taken Den'Lin Fetch, my friend, and slain all but a few of us who were able to escape. There were others, from Con Den Fetch and the other delvings, and we have brought what strength we could."

He looked wearily into Brian's eyes.

"I have been a fool, my friend. All of us have."

His features clouded, and tears began to stream down his face.

"Jaran was lost at the first attack. We had no warning. We were ready for the beast packs overside, but we had never reckoned with these others. They seemed to come from nowhere, and their numbers were too great."

"We are getting a hard lesson, Jeral," replied Brian softly. "We have all been fools, it seems, for none of us ever suspected the true threat to our delvings. The Varads have been very crafty, and they have managed to gather a great force with none of us ever the wiser."

"I must take a great part of the blame for that," said Chinby. "I am the one who should have known, yet I never began to put the parts of the puzzle together as they were given to me. I made the old mistake of assuming that beasts were beasts, and that they would all be alike. And I never looked for the mind behind the scheme of things."

"No one can be blamed for this, old one," comforted Drub Fearing. "Even those of us who were living in the same wood as these rodents didn't see the true danger of them until it had become too late to do anything about them."

He removed his forage cap, and twirled it about his hand once, studying it intently.

"At least we have a right cheerful band to make our stand. I can't think of any better companions."

"We'll talk of that business sometime later, over a good supper table, my friend," laughed Crown. "I know your clans well enough to not start despairing yet, if it is to come to a fight."

"And there is the fountain of Falen Rin, and the mysterious water that seems to bring things to a hard end," added Shanon.

"Now I want more news of Den'Lin Fetch," protested Brian. "We have our work cut out for us here, so that matter is closed. But tell me, Jeral, of what fell out after the attack."

"It was more than one attack, Brian. It came as two blows, one from each end of the delving, where the overside gates are. Both sentries were taken by surprise, and slain, and the rest was a sheer matter of numbers. We put up the best defense we could, but there was no time to arm in any efficient manner, and some of our best soldiers were on a wood party, and away when the attack fell. They were trapped, we learned later, outside."

The spanner's heart turned to lead within him as he listened to the heartbreaking, enraging news of his old home, overrun now, and despoiled by the savage tribes of Varad warriors. A burning rage filled him, and a sorrow so deep he did not know if he would ever touch the end of it.

All the pictures of his old halfing passed before him now, with his lanin at her baking or sewing, and his father, bent with the labor of many years, talking of small matters of the delving, over a cup of late night tea.

Then there was his friend Jaran, cut down in his youth, by the very enemies that howled nearby, the strange, savage beings that seemed to have sprung full-blown into a dangerous threat overnight.

He was full of flooding emotions, and had to turn his face away from the others, so they would not see him with such helpless tears streaming down his broad face.

Senja was beside him, and held his hand between her own.

"I'm sorry, Senja. I know you have had enough of your own

grief. From what Jeral says, all the delvings have been destroyed and taken. You have my sorrow, and my vow that I shall one day retake our homes, and drive these ugly louts all the way back to the ice fields, or go to the Tombs in the effort."

The lane's chin quivered, but she held her head high, and struggled to control her voice.

"I shall be at your side when you do it, Brian. I owe my family that. And Con Den Fetch, even though there is no pleasure in knowing I was right and they were wrong."

"There is no pleasure in failure," muttered Chinby. "It was I who should have known of these creatures, yet did not."

"No one could have saved the delvings, old one," said Jeral, his voice flat, as one spent from too many feelings.

"I could have made the warnings more open," argued the blind lore master. "Everyone took my words as mere tales of amusement, and looked at me with pity."

"Don't go on, Chinby. I was one of those who told Brian he should look to himself, and forget your glory yarns, and find a craft to learn. But I am also not a dwarf that is beyond reason, and who won't admit a mistake when he makes it, and sees it."

Jeral grasped the old dwarf by the shoulder.

"If there is anything I can do by my hand to make up for the damage I have done, I swear it is in your service, until it can be of no more use."

"You can put it to use right away, then," shot Brian. "We have a need for blades, and shafts, and not much time to prepare, from the sound of it. You are the best smith that handled a hammer at Den'Lin Fetch. Now Den'Lin Fetch shall forge its revenge in your arm's work."

"Show me a forge, and give me the ore, Brian. I am your dwarf in that line of labor."

"Are there any smith shops in this elf dane?" asked Brian, turning to Shanon.

"There should be. Not the heavy-forged shops of the delvings, but still a forge, where the elfin smith worked his metal."

"Lead on, and quickly. We have no time to lose."

Brian's tone had hardened, and he found action easier to bear than being alone and still with his thoughts.

"You, Crown, and Falon, and the rest of you! Fill every-

239

thing you can with the water from the fountain, but keep in mind what it means to touch it! Save that fate for those of our enemies who would close with us."

The sound of the war horns was more urgent, and the din was growing closer on all sides, as if a great party of the Varads was converging on the dane of Falen Rin.

"Do you still have the Stone of Elver Tarn?" asked Brian, turning to his friend.

"Here, in my cloak," replied Shanon.

"I wish we knew how to wake Master Oranbar. He has a certain way about him that seems to displease the Varads."

"He, and his brothers as well."

Brian shook his head.

"But we must work with what we have, and that will have to do."

While the others raced madly about the smooth lawn of the elfin dane, Brian and Shanon took Chinby aside for a conference.

"We shall have our say first, then let the others know what we have decided," said Brian. "Since we have been in on this misadventure from the beginning, it is only fair."

"Where is Senja?" asked the old lore master. "She must be here, as well."

"I already am," replied the lane. "There is no way you could keep me from this."

"Good. Take your place, and let's cast lots to see who does what."

"I'll take charge of the elves, Chinby. We can handle the stone water from the trees. We'll be able to cover greater areas that way, and can do the most good from there."

"Excellent, Shanon. That is proof there is more use for your head than hair growing."

"We'll place Crown and Drub Fearing at the head of the other parties. That should cover that. And Jeral will handle the forge work, and the arms, and the mending of whatever is broken."

Senja had remained quiet as the others spoke, but she came forward again, her voice aloof and cool.

"Is it necessary to make our fight here?" she asked, pacing to and fro in the intervals. "What would keep us from going on to the Split Oak that marks the elf road? And from there on to the sea?"

240

"A point well taken," said Chinby. "But it sounds as if we shall have to either make a stand here or run the danger of having the Varads at our backs, pecking away at us."

"And what of the others who have escaped from the delvings? And all the other Carben settlements? Or wood elf danes?"

"They will probably be faced with doing just what we are doing," replied Brian. "With the numbers they have now, the Varads will probably be attacking any settlement at all, no matter what clan they are from, whether dwarf, or elf, or Carben."

"We should try to gather all we can under our banner, Brian," persisted Senja. "Otherwise, all the stragglers will be slain, and we will have been separated, and divided even more."

Chinby, who had been tugging at his chin whiskers as he listened to the lane, suddenly clapped his hands loudly together.

"Well spoken, my hothead! Well spoken, indeed, for Brian Brandigore is to be the name that draws all allies together, that we may face this problem once and for all, and get on with the business of dealing with other matters."

"What other allies could we hope to find here?" asked Shanon. "Everyone has been accounted for now."

Brian's brow darkened.

"In all the excitement, I forgot to ask Falon about Mathiny and Sigman Col. He had gone to fetch our friend."

The elf's face grew troubled in his own turn.

"Falon spoke of that. The settlement of Sigman Col was in flames, and there had already been an attack there. Falon said his party saw many Carben warriors slain, but it looked as though they had held their own, and escaped."

"Then they must still be about, looking for others to join, or to join them."

"Send for Falon, that we might question him further on this," ordered Chinby. "It could be that he might find our camp not so bad, after all, when compared to these other foul things that are loose in the wood."

The companions agreed on that account, and they quickly called Falon, who was at the head of a group of his wood elves, stringing the trees above the broad lawns with hundreds of stone bottles of the powerful water from the fountain.

241

"We are making good progress, old one," he reported. "But we have to be careful not to douse our own side, as well."

"There might be a proper end for it all," laughed Shanon. "Friend and foe alike turned to stone in the very act of making war on each other."

"Not likely, if we handle the affair right," scolded Brian. "When the Varads attack, it will have to be through the way they have come before, and that's over the lawn."

"But they may see all their friends who've already been that way," reminded Senja. "The lawn is full of those lumps now."

"This new band won't have a mind for that. It sounds as if they're worked into a fever pitch."

Brian's words were almost drowned out by the growing clamor of the Varad horns.

Above the rest, they could hear the chilling cries and shouts of the half-ones, calling out encouragement to each other, and cursing the heads of their foes.

"Listen!" shouted Drub Fearing, forgetting his tasks of readying his band for the battle. "They have added a new name to their lists of those they hate."

The voices were garbled, and the tongue difficult to follow, but after another moment, Brian heard a deep chant, repeating his own name, over and over, followed by a loud shout of "Death to Brandigore!" and the clashing of many swords and stabbing spears on iron shields.

"It is indeed a time," said Chinby softly. "You have become a watchword in the enemy camps."

He reached out and touched Brian gently on his sleeve.

"You will forgive me for all this, I hope?"

Brian, a strange inner fire burning fiercely in his eyes, gave his old teacher a strong hug.

"It is well that they carry my name on their lips as enemy, for I shall endeavor to give them good cause."

"There will be more than these who will one day come to fear that name, Brian. We are but the setting of the stage."

"Then let it be said that we have done well whatever it is we shall put our hand to."

Senja whispered something under her breath into Chinby's ear that set the old dwarf to smiling and nodding, patting her hand as he did so.

"You're quite right in that, my dear. I can think of no better place, nor of no more fitting a time."

The handsome lane came forward to Brian, her brow clear, her step proud.

"We are now homeless, and without families. It is our duty to join together in the bonds, Brian. You have a great task before you, and you shall need a strong mate to carry it to its end. Chinby has agreed to read the rites of the halfing vow, and we have enough friends to witness."

The sturdy frame of the dwarf was racked with a series of tremors, and he gaped, openmouthed, at first at the bold lane, and then at each of his friends, who were all smiling and nodding their approval.

"You needn't be so quick with your flattery," chided Senja. "At least you could give me the respect of your voice, and what sits on your mind as to my plan."

After a few stammering starts, Brian finally managed a reply.

"I am most greatly honored, Senja, and think, even as you, that the old delvings are gone, along with our families and friends, and we need to think of taking steps to ensure that the proud names of our sires don't disappear from the lore books. But I can hardly agree to this foolhardy plan of saying the halfing vows on the edge of a battle that is yet to be fought, and the outcome of which no one knows."

"All the more reason to say the vows now," insisted the lane, coming closer to him. "Chinby has said he'll repeat the vows, and we have witnesses. Why wait?"

"Why wait, indeed?" called Jeral. "It is the fate we often spoke to you of."

The dwarf's voice was light, but his features were drawn. Brian recalled the teasing he had undergone each day at the forge of his friend, and the banter he had had from Jaran, the gentle brother who was lost to them now.

"Let me think on it," he said at last, thrusting his hands deep into his cloak, and pacing away from his friends, his thoughts tumbling over each other, and his heart pounding in his throat.

The thought of the Varad armies did not frighten him nearly as badly as did the thought of being vowed to the outspoken lane of Con Den Fetch, and he had never given it much thought before, but had assumed that sometime in the great haze of future days, there would have come a time that he would have entered into the halfing rite with her, after all

243

the adventures were over, and his errand completed. To think that right at the moment, on the very spot he stood, he would be made one with Senja both terrified and elated the dwarf, and his mind was in such turmoil, he did not even hear the warning skirl of the elfin pipes.

"Stand to it, me leaf benders, stand to it!" called a dozen elfin sergeants at arms, mustering their troops.

There came the usual ugly swish and whir of arrows through the air, and the loud clatter of the shafts as they struck all about them.

Most of the small army they had rounded up had sought cover, and the attack had gained little for the Varads, except to announce their arrival.

"Hop to your business quickly! Hand out these!" ordered Shanon, passing out the small vials of the stone water from the fountain of Falen Rin.

"Well?" asked Jeral, ignoring the ominous skree of the pipes on all sides, which told them the Varad attack was but a split second away.

"If we survive this battle, then we shall see to it that our illustrious families will not be forgotten," blustered Brian. "Now, we have some affairs that need tending to."

He removed his cloak in a single motion, and drew the elfin blade from its sheath.

"I still have a need for something more of a dwarfish nature than this, but it shall have to do for now."

Senja, looking frightened, but unperturbed by his behavior, took Chinby's belt from his cape, and buckled it to her own.

"Now we won't get separated, old one. And we are going to have need of that belt to hold us, for I am staying next to this stiff-headed dwarf, no matter what he has it in his mind to do."

"You stay with Chinby," ordered Brian, turning away, to answer a tug on his sleeve.

"You said you had a need of something of a more dwarfish nature as a weapon, my friend. Here! I would that you had this, and I shall take your short sword for the nonce. I shall forge new arms for all who wish, the first chance I have, without being breathed upon by these Varads."

Jeral took the elfin blade from him and put in his hand a stout, fierce-looking ax, broad at both tips, and honed to a razor's edge. There was also a finely worked mail coat, gleaming a dull bronze.

The ax was the weapon that Brian was most familiar with, next to his bow, although he had only used it before as a tool, to hew the thick oak or ash or elm trees into small enough pieces to transport back to the delvings.

Remembering the news that had been first carried by Oranbar, then confirmed by Jeral, Brian clutched the dreadful ax with both hands, and took time to swear an oath to the Great Lan, that if he did nothing else with his life, he would avenge the death of his father and lanin, and the passing of Den'Lin Fetch.

"Give me the sword, Jeral," said Senja, her voice hard, and her hand outstretched.

He looked at her steadily, then surrendered the blade.

"I have other arms in my kit," he said. "And I have taken it in my mind that I might make best use of a bow, from all the darts those louts are shooting. I'll have no end of shafts to pluck back at them."

The air had grown thick with Varad war horns and arrows, and the companions and all their numbers found that they had to be careful of where they walked, for the green lawn, broken by the figures of the stone forms of the Varads who had been touched with the water from the fountain, was bristling with the black-feathered shafts, and more flew at them, loosed from behind the blinding underbrush and bramble thickets.

There was no need for the elf Crown, or any of the others, to give the order to loose their own shafts, nor to retrieve the arrows shot by the Varads. In the interims of volleys, nimble elves and Carben dwarfs flashed into the open long enough to pluck up armfuls of the arrows, then scamper back to the safety of their shelter.

Many of the band of Crown were directing their arrows back in the direction they had come from first, and adding a few of their own into the bargain.

Drub Fearing had drawn his company into a square, and the sturdy dwarf warriors were prepared to repel any attack that might fall upon them, no matter what the direction.

The terrible din in the woods around them grew louder, and as the attack began in earnest, the flying arrows became fewer, then stopped altogether.

"Watch for them now, lads," called Drub Fearing, in his own element of battle and command.

It was the closest thing to security he had ever known, and it was a familiar role to fall into. All the fear of the unknown, and the waiting, dropped away, and he was left with the calm, steady hand, and the coolness which had made him into a respected leader among his companions, and in all the clans.

Brian, hefting the thick handle of the broad-bladed ax, turned briefly to Senja.

"If you insist on standing beside us, at least give Chinby room to defend himself. Cut that belt loose from him, and hand him a sword. I don't worry that he's never held one in those old paws before."

"I can hear well enough to know when to strike a blow, even without sight. One can smell these brutes well enough to know where to make a thrust or dent a head."

"You'll have plenty of chances," whistled Shanon. "Look at that!"

At the end of the lawn, where it had begun to blend in with the thorn brake that formed a living fence, there appeared a hole, growing larger by the second, as line after line of Varad soldiers flung themselves into the breach, and spilled shrieking onto the lawn of the outer gardens of Falen Rin.

"Be ready to fall back to the wall!" cried Brian, and Shanon raced back to the stone barrier to open it ahead of time, so that their next line of defense would be open and ready.

At that moment, the leading troops of the Varads came within range of the first of the strung bottles of the stone water, and thin, elfin lines were tugged, which spilled out the strange, transforming liquid onto the surging, burly mass of the savage creatures that came shrieking and foaming at the mouth, great yellow teeth clacking in rage. In a single heartbeat, what had been a terrifying attack was reduced to nothing more than a pile of heartless stone, strewn about a smooth green lawn.

Yet the wave of Varads swept on, sending new assailants to fill in the place of those who had been transformed, and soon it was time for the companions to gather their forces, and to retreat into the fastness behind the elfin wall.

"Straight on across!" shouted Shanon over the noise. "To the Split Oak! We shall have to trust this wall to keep them off our back until we can make good our escape."

Crown, aided by Falon, fell back step by step, his line of archers, and the lines of the dwarfish bowmen, keeping a constant hail of deadly arrows raining in on the Varads, and at last, all the remaining party of rear guard were under the wall and on the other side.

As they fled across the space that led to the gate that opened onto the Split Oak, a new war horn joined in the fray, from the very direction in which they had hoped to be able to find a clear road on the old elfin highway.

The call came again, high and long, and it wasn't until Drub Fearing spoke that they knew it wasn't another band of Varads that had outflanked them and been able to seal off their only hope of flight.

"Sigman Col," he shouted over the roar of the noise behind them.

Brian clinched his teeth, and grasped the great ax more tightly. He had begun to wish that he had taken the halfing vows with the bold young lane at his side if they were caught between the Varads on one hand, and Sigman Col on the other.

THE GREAT WATERS
BECKON

A Closing Door

THE wood beyond the gate that was called Split Oak, and that led onto the ancient highway of elfdom, which spread like an intricate web to connect all the danes with the others, was a nightmare of noise, and the air full of arrows, turning the dim shadows of the wood even darker as the shafts blocked out the sun.

At every turn there had been scores of the Varad warriors, misshapen figures looming out of the undergrowth, wielding ugly, curved swords, or short stabbing spears, yellow fangs drooling and snapping.

At every step Brian had swung the terrible dwarf ax, hewing his way through the broiling mass of tormented bodies locked in deadly combat.

Senja and Chinby began the trip next to him, but once the Split Oak was passed, there was such chaos that they were separated, and in the confusion, pushed far away from his side.

At one instant, Brian could see only the dark, foul-smelling bodies of the Varads all around him, completely cutting him off from his companions, but after what seemed an eternity of arm-weary effort, he managed to win through the line of enemy soldiers and regain the safety of the Carben dwarf wall, led by Drub Fearing.

Upon another instant, he was amid a group of Carbens he had not seen before, and it took a moment or two to realize that this band was headed by one that he vaguely remembered from the outer gate of the Deep Home Highway, when they were confronted by Mathiny and forced to flee back into the tunnels. It dawned slowly on Brian that these Carben dwarfs were of the camp of Sigman Col, and that the war horns that he had been hearing were those he had heard just as they had left the dane of Falen Rin.

Rising higher than the Varad bugles, the Carben horns were calling from all around Brian, and for a fleeting moment, he felt hope deadened inside him, thinking he must be taken by the harsh leader of the Carben clans, but that passed, as a grim-faced warrior next to him turned and nodded briefly, raising his hand in a shallow salute as he did so.

Brian fought onward, his weary senses reeling, his arms growing more numb with every blow he struck.

There seemed to be no end of the Varad tribes, who poured forth unabated from the shadows of the wood, and for the first time since the struggle had begun, he found himself face to face with the realization that it might indeed be impossible to escape from the overwhelming numbers of the Varads, who now pressed their siege on all sides of the embattled companions.

Chinby and Senja came back into view for a moment in a lull of the fighting, and he could see the old lore master was limping badly, and had a portion of Senja's cloak wrapped as a bandage about his head. The lane seemed to be uninjured, although her arms hung wearily at her side, the sword that Jeral had given her dented and bloodied.

Their eyes met and locked for a moment, but he was swept away in another swirl of fighting, and lost sight of his friends, and was soon engaged in a fierce combat with a huge Varad, who took the blows of the dwarf ax on the face of a great iron shield, and dealt Brian a stunning blow across his shoulder in return.

Had it not been for the mail shirt that Jeral had given him, he felt sure it would have meant the end of him on the spot, so vicious was the stroke.

His arm numbed, and the great ax dropped uselessly to the ground at his feet, which now ran red with the blood of the slain, making the grass slippery, and hard to keep footing.

The dull yellow eyes of the Varad blazed brighter as he lifted the wicked curved sword to deliver the death blow, but the young dwarf's hand had seized the dagger at his belt, and he lunged forward at the Varad, going in under the blow of his sword, and striking with all his might in an upward stroke that slipped between the edge of the huge shield and the bottom of the leather battle shirt the enemy wore. At the same instant, a yellow-feathered dart from the bow of Crown buried itself to the socket in the Varad's back, which sent him tumbling forward, crushing Brian beneath the heavy, lifeless hulk.

That event proved to be fortunate, for two Varad soldiers, great teeth bared and clacking angrily together, fell upon the corpse that covered Brian, and began to rain heavy blows of their swords onto the unyielding body, which saved him from being instantly killed.

His shoulder was entirely numb now, and he could sense he was on the verge of passing out, but struggled dizzily against it, trying all the while to regain his feet.

A sudden buzz of excitement near his left side caused him to pause to gather his breath for his next effort, and in that time, he saw a lithe, fleet form swoop from out of the corner of his line of vision, hover directly overhead a moment, then flash away.

When he regained his senses, and started again to move from beneath the heavy body of the slain Varad, he caught sight of the stone figures all around him, touched with the water from the fountain of Falen Rin.

"Shanon," he muttered to himself. "And the Stone of Elver Tarn!"

Brian saw that he had been completely surrounded by a pocket of Varad soldiers, cut off from his companions on all sides, and that the water elf had used the Stone of Elver Tarn to lift him over the enemy troops that kept him from his friend's aid, and doused the Varads below with the water from the fountain of the ancient dane that he carried in a small elfin vial.

Brian struggled to his feet, and retrieving the ax, made his way to the side of Drub Fearing, where he was joined by Crown, and Senja, leading the wounded Chinby.

As they regrouped their forces, a new figure appeared, striding quickly to Brian and taking his hand.

"Mathiny!" he cried, ignoring the pain from the movement of his injured shoulder as his long-absent ally pumped his hand.

"It seems we come in time, Brian Brandigore. From the noise the Varads were making, we were afraid we would be too late."

"Hello, old fellow," said Shanon, spying the Carben. "We thought your lot was lost for certain when we had the news

252

from Falon that Sigman Col's settlement had been attacked and burned."

"They came on us by surprise," shouted Mathiny, over a renewed attack that was being mounted by the Varads. "I don't know what's happened to Sigman Col, but I've heard his own horn in the skirmish, so it seems we're all pulling together this day."

"I heard his signal," confirmed Drub Fearing. "But I haven't caught sight of his banner yet."

"Look to it!" shouted Shanon, stringing an arrow to his bow. "They're coming again."

"Try to break free toward the beginning of the upper trail," yelled Crown over the confusion. "If we can get to there, we'll have the advantage of them, and they can't come on us all at once."

The order was repeated whenever the noise was lessened enough for those farther away to hear, and very slowly, so slowly it seemed that they would never make any progress at all, the bitterly embattled tiny army made its way inch by inch toward the point of the elfin road that rose above the ground and wound beneath the roof of the wood, high above.

That craftywork had been done in the golden age of elfdom, and was a marvel of engineering and design, and built so cleverly that one who did not know it was there would never have suspected that high above them was a path wide enough to carry three elves abreast, winding to and fro among the trees, sturdy enough to support whole colonies on the move, and built to serve out the entire time that there might be an elf left to tread its course.

Some said the old road meandered far and wide, from dane to dane, with no purpose, and was laid out as it suited the elfin craftsmen who fashioned it, and finally reaching the broad plains that swept from the rolling hills onward down to the seacoast, left the hidden corners of the forest, and bent straight on, straight as an arrow shaft, without varying to right or left, for the entire distance that lay between the last of the great forests and the beginning of the Roaring.

There were others, Shanon among them, that knew of the Elver Tarn, and the strange and wonderful powers of those beings, and that the danes were all designs of one sort or another, directed from above, and that the old road was laid so true because of the ability of its builders to see how it should run, and how was the best way to accomplish that feat.

Yet those thoughts were far from Shanon's mind, embroiled as he was with mere survival, and faced with the sticky problem of how best to escape the terrible onslaught of the Varad warriors, whose numbers continued to grow by the minute.

Crown and Drub Fearing had mustered their bands together, and showed a solid front to the crushing weight of the invaders, and for a moment, the assault wavered, then fell back upon itself.

In the narrowing confines of the entrance to the elf road, the superior numbers of the enemy were lost as an advantage, and the simple weight of their attack encumbered them, and slowed them down somewhat, long enough for the rest of the companions to fight their way clear, and forward onto the trail that led up through the huge trees, upward toward the beginning of the old highway.

Brian's shoulder throbbed in a steady, aching pain, but he managed to sling his ax in its sheath over his back, and drew forth his bow, which he found he could use, although not as strongly.

Senja carried his arrow quiver, and guided Chinby, who was complaining bitterly of an arrow which had pierced his boot and forced him to limp along, bent double, until Mathiny, coming from the rear defense, stooped and plucked it out.

"You'd best look to that, old one," he said. "They sometimes poison their darts."

He handed the old lore master a pouch of sweet-smelling herbs, and instructed him to put them on the wounds.

"We have found these to be good to fix the hurts these louts give."

"I'll do it," snapped Senja. "Just as soon as we're away from here, and safely on our way."

Mathiny laughed, shaking his head.

"He may well have rotted if we wait to get to a place of safety."

Ignoring the Carben's advice, she dragged her old teacher onward, toward the gradually rising trail that ended a few hundred feet farther on, in a stairway, all inlaid in elfin work, of bright metals, of gold and silver and mithra and elaborately carved hardwoods, all in the forms of the ancient manners of animals and plants, bees and queens, and the shape of the wind on a winter night.

"We'll stop to patch you up once we get on the upper trail," she said, her voice strict, although she was worried about what Mathiny had told her about the darts being poisoned.

Had there been time, she would have stopped and dressed his wounds with the herbs, but the fight, although slackened somewhat, yet raged at the Split Oak Gate, and the only reason the Varads were not close upon their heels was the efforts of those who had remained behind as rear guard, and who stemmed the onrushing tide of the dark soldiers long enough for their friends to make the upper trail.

Foot by foot, Crown and Drub Fearing began withdrawing, never showing their backs to the howling mobs of Varads, and exchanging volley after volley of arrows, shooting back the Varad darts when their quivers were empty, and realizing with every exchange that they would not be able to hold back the enemy hordes much longer.

Many of their number were slain, or wounded, and many of those were left behind, which enraged the Carben, and the elf as well, but there was no way to save their hurt comrades, and they watched in horror and helpless fury as the Varad soldiers jabbed them with the short stabbing spears, and lifted their severed heads atop their swords.

"Death to the elves! Death to the Carbens! Death to Brian Brandigore!" they boomed, chanting in their dark voices, and advancing in a solid line, filling in their losses from the still flowing reserves of fresh warriors come to fill the ranks.

"Death to Brandigore!" rang the chanting Varads, firing another volley of black arrows, then another, and the elf realized that they would have to make their way quickly now, risking turning their backs, to reach the more sheltered area that lay in front of the beginning of the actual elfin road.

Where they stood, their numbers crumbling slowly under the crush of the Varad onslaught, was a broad, open space immediately behind the gate to the Split Oak, and it allowed the Varads to muster their great strength, and to send a broad line of attackers against them.

The two friends knew that in order to survive, even for the moment, they would have to fall back to the narrow opening of the trail, bordered on both sides by great giants of ancient trees, which would protect their flanks, and keep their assailants to the front.

255

"Make a dash for it!" shouted Crown. "Then have your lads stop to give us cover. Hop to it! Now or never!"

The elf's face was composed, although he was pale, and bled from a dozen wounds.

"I'll give the cover, and you hop to it," corrected Drub Fearing. "My lads have more arrows, anyhow."

Glowering, each remained immobile, neither of them willing to turn away from the fight first.

A blast of a Carben war horn broke the impasse, and from behind the Varad lines it came, high and deadly, sounding out the advance.

A wedge of Carbens, tightly bunched in a square, appeared amid the very scores of the Varads, creeping forward in their formation, repelling all attack, until they were very near the front of the Varad line. With a loud cry, they beat upon the remaining Varad defense, and were through, although their number had been vastly reduced by the terrible fury of the battle to reach the companions.

"It's Sigman Col and his private guard," called Drub Fearing, and his heart raced to see the small, tattered company slip through the deadly talons of the enemy army.

"Buck up, lads, help them in," he shouted, mustering his own band to help the straggling group into their ranks.

Whirling on Crown, he shouted his order again.

"Quick, blast you, now!"

The Varads were just off balance enough that the small knot of elves had disengaged and reached the narrow entrance to the upper trail before they pressed their attack forward again. Raging onward, they threatened to sweep away the stalwart defenders, until a clutch of wood elves, led by Senja, burst out from the narrow entranceway and leapt into the fray, brandishing small vials of the stone water from Falen Rin.

Drub Fearing kept his party loosing arrows, and just as they quit, the lane and her small group dashed out between arrow flights and hurled the contents of their containers at the closing flanks of the Varads.

An almost solid wall of the enemy soldiers slowed down the advance, causing those behind to half climb over their transformed comrades, which gave the archers of the Carben easy targets, and allowed them to retreat quickly into the opening of the upper trail.

The Carben leader Sigman Col, an older version of Drub

Fearing, waited with his group at the head of the stairs, his cloak torn and bloodied, and his face drawn in pain.

"Holla, Drub Fearing. I see you have stood me in good stead this day."

"I've stood no one in good stead, Sigman Col. You are with friends, is all. We serve our new leader, Brian Brandigore. The old one spoke of his coming, and now he's here."

The older Carben knitted his brow, and wiped a smudge of dirt and blood off his sleeve, almost absentmindedly.

"It seems your Brandigore does not set too well with our fine Varads."

Drub Fearing nodded, determined not to argue with his old chieftain.

"It seems that no one sets too well with them," broke in Mathiny, who had joined the group. "Not elves, not delving dwarfs, nor woodfolk, nor waterfolk, nor Carbens."

Sigman Col turned abruptly.

"We have not played out our final scene as yet, my good Mathiny. Runion told me of your betrayal, before the attack on our camp."

"Runion is dead," replied Mathiny. "He had his own ends to serve. We are all beyond what we have known before. There is no more wood, no more delving, nor dane. We shall have to look to a new order if we are to outdo our enemies. They have great numbers, and a single purpose, and that is to slay all living things outside their own, and to overpower all settlements, no matter who has built them."

Mathiny paused for a breath, then went on.

"We shall have to band together as one if we are to overcome them. The old one has spun many yarns in his time, yet I see now that he was but telling the truth. You had all his kind punished and outlawed, and had that not been so, our settlements might have had warning, early enough to have avoided this last blow."

Sigman Col's eyes blazed, and he met the young Carben's glance with an iron gaze.

"You speak as a spanner might, my young friend, and I cannot fault you for feeling as you do. But you know not the true state of affairs."

"We shall have to have our debates later," shot Crown, organizing his archers into smaller teams, and helping the others to gather arrows from the ground, which was covered by the black-feathered Varad shafts.

"Come on," bellowed Brian, from the top of the elfin stairs. "To your work! They're coming again!"

Mathiny rounded up his small troop and began the ascent of the steps, but stopped beside Sigman Col when he noticed that the older Carben was having trouble holding his balance, and seemed unable to lift his foot.

"Let me help," offered Mathiny, suddenly feeling great sorrow at seeing the once proud, iron-hard Sigman Col old and feeble, and wounded.

"Get on with you," he ordered, brushing away Mathiny's hand, but the effort cost him dearly, for he slipped forward, and stumbling, fell to the edge of the stairway.

Gathering quickly around him, his band lifted him gently up, brushing Mathiny aside, and carried him up the stairway toward the path above.

As he passed, Sigman Col's torn cloak flapped loosely about him, and Mathiny could see the blood-soaked mail beneath, and the numerous wounds the tough old Carben had sustained in the fight to reach the companions.

Senja, hurrying up the steps behind the others, stopped beside Mathiny.

"Is he sorely wounded?"

"I fear so, good lane. He is a hard dwarf, is Sigman Col. But no one can fault his bravery."

"Get on with you," roared Drub Fearing, at the rear of his group. "Don't clog up the stairway. Hurry!"

Carben and delving dwarf, along with the wood elves, under the command of Falon, all leapt forward up the stair, racing for the upper trail, where they would be able to keep the Varads at bay, and where they might be able to think of making good their escape.

Running lightly beside his friend, Shanon turned to Brian, a crease of worry lingering about his eyes.

"I don't like the idea of you going without having your wound treated. There is no knowing what tricks these Varads will use."

"I'm all right," insisted Brian, although he felt far from it, and was beginning to have frightening spells of dizziness, and a creeping, leaden sensation at the pit of his stomach.

"I think we should give you the herbs that Drub Fearing has said will help, and put you on our shoulders, to let you rest."

258

"There is need enough to look to your own feet, you leaf bender. I'll look to my own!"

His voice sounded loud in his ears, but to his amazement, Shanon was looking at him with real concern.

Brian tried to ask what was wrong, and was vaguely disturbed to see that a hand was reaching out to him across a great void, and a slight roaring noise filled his ears. He thought it was a new Varad attack for a moment, but then Senja's face loomed over him, dirty and smeared with blood, and he tried to reach up to her, to wipe her tears away, but he could not find his arm, which he thought was odd.

He began a sentence for Chinby, but before it was finished, he had lapsed into a long blue tunnel, lighted by dazzling, flashing yellow lights, and strange-smelling visions that wafted to him in that thick darkness, and he slowly eased into the easy rhythm of the roaring that he heard, and then there was nothing more.

Senja, in tears, turned helplessly to Chinby.

"Oh, I hate all this. I wish we'd never started this stupid trip. I'll never forgive you, Chinby, if Brian dies."

"Here, here, little one," soothed the old lore master. "No one is dying yet. It's not in the way of things. Not unless we are all to die, which I hardly think is the case."

He patted her shoulder gently, and went on.

"I think you should give him the herbs that our good Carben suggested. That will probably do for now, since we won't have time to tend him properly before we get to a spot that's relatively safe from the half-ones."

The lane was fumbling with the small pouch that the Carben had given her, but Drub Fearing appeared at her shoulder and took it from her hands.

"Let me, good lane. Your hand is too gentle for the treatment of such wounds. You must be forceful if you are to be of any use."

And saying, he pried Brian's mouth apart, and pressed a handful of the fragrant herbs past his bruised lips. The dwarf struggled feebly, and his eyes rolled, but Drub Fearing never let go his hold, and kept on forcing the small leaves into Brian's open mouth.

"Give me a water bottle," he ordered, leaving one arm under Brian's head. "And none of the flasks with the stone fountain brew!"

A hand shot out, and the Carben took the offered water,

and after pouring a small amount of it on the ground at his foot to see that there was no confusion, he dribbled a few drops at a time over Brian's parched mouth.

Gasping and choking, the dwarf coughed up a good part of what Drub Fearing had forced down him, but some remained, and after a few swallows, the Carben laid his head gently down, and looked at Senja.

"There. He should be coming around in a little while. In the meantime, you must apologize to Chinby for your words, and we must make a litter to bear our wounded comrades. We have no time to lose."

"Sigman Col needs the herbs, too," said Mathiny.

"Then give them, if you wish."

"I have none left, except that pouch I gave Senja."

Drub Fearing tossed him the small sack.

"This has been a fine day indeed," he muttered. "We're beset by a Varad army that is big enough to wipe out the wood, and then our good Sigman Col comes calling, and after a hard fight of it, we have him cozy in our camp, worried about his recovery."

Drub Fearing snorted.

"He has never been anything but trouble and sorrow to me and mine, Mathiny, but my heart won't stand to see a Carben, no matter who he is, killed by the likes of that foul stench of a Varad's poison."

"Chinby needs it, too," said Shanon softly.

Senja broke into heaving sobs, and threw her arms around the blind dwarf.

"Chinby, please forgive me! I'm so worried about that stiff-necked student of yours. And I'm tired, and hungry, and scared!"

The old lore master patted his ward gently as she cried into his bloody cloak.

"It's all right, little one. We all feel that way. But I can promise you that this will turn out for the best. We just need to go on a bit farther, and then we can rest."

She put her head deeper into his shoulder, and tried to believe him, but they were interrupted by a wood elf, who came racing breathlessly up to Shanon and Drub Fearing to report that the way ahead was blocked by a wall, and that there were noises all about in the wood and they were unable to tell whether these noises were Varad troops or something else.

As the elf finished his report, a short, high reed pipe keened a long note, and it was answered by others all about them.

Drub Fearing, looking back in the direction in which they had climbed, was slightly startled to see that elves, and small ones at that, were scrambling all about the lower entrance, and with a silent, sudden motion, there fell into place at the foot of the stairwell a great body of a tree, blocking the entranceway completely, and shutting off his vision of where the Varad troops had gone.

The Sorodun

THERE was no going back, so the companions lifted their wounded on the litters they had fashioned together of long tree branches, with cloaks tied between, and went on toward whatever awaited them next on the ancient elfin road.

Drub Fearing, prepared for the worst, sent out a forward party of bowmen, followed by the best of his infighters, although the space was cramped, and there was not much room to deploy, and the eaves of the great trees bent close upon both sides of the path, blocking off all vision with a thick green wall.

There were noises all about, yet none of it sounded like a Varad war party, so they hurried on, hearing the blaring horns behind them growing fainter and fainter.

Crown and Shanon walked together beside Brian's litter, along with Senja, whose face was pinched with anxiety.

"I hope the herbs you gave them work, Drub Fearing," she whispered, not trusting her voice to speak aloud.

"They'll be fine in a few hours, if we don't run into worse yet."

His head turned from side to side, and his arrowbright eyes darted from one section of the underbrush to the next. After another few paces, he asked Crown, or Shanon, to go forward, to see if they could detect who or what was in the wood around them.

"I'm sure it's elves, but I've never seen any so small. I know the wood elf is much less in stature than the waterfolk, yet I've never seen any so wee as the ones I spotted back there. They were hardly more than knee-high, even to me."

Shanon scratched his head, trying to think of any of his kindred that would be anywhere near the size of those the Carben described.

His companion, Crown, turned to Drub Fearing.

"Could you tell how they were dressed? What color were their vests and caps?"

"It was too dim to make out anything much, but it seems that they were dressed in bright colors. The shadows there were thick, and I couldn't swear on it, but I think it was red, both vest and cap."

"It may be the Fens, or perhaps some of their cousins. I haven't had word from their clans in a long season or two, but the last word I received was that they had come this way, and were taking up new danes in the woods beyond the Outer Seeking. I wouldn't be surprised to find some stray bands of them here. They're very prolific, and seem to grow in leaps and bounds. I can't recall ever being in danes where there were so many fry."

"Fry? Is that like dwarf spanners?" asked Senja.

"It is. And the Fens are very good and young, and hard working. They plant all sorts of crops. They also take a hand in forestry, too, when they're in woods. I've known them to live in absolute treelessness, though, and be just as happy."

"They sound as if they are an odd clan, for elves, if they spend time beyond woods or water," said Shanon, unable to see how it would be possible to exist without either of his two favorite elements, woods and water.

He wasn't sure he was going to do so well with the amount of it that a sea might prove to be, but that remained to be seen, and he was more concerned with what they were to do in the next half hour, more than a debate of what to do in the next month or year.

There was Brian, wounded and unconscious, and Chinby, weakened from hurts as well.

Even the iron ruler, Sigman Col, who was a frightening

warrior, and a good soldier to have on your side, was slung alongside the others in the litters.

The small band of Carbens were taking turns at bearing the injured, for they were by far the most powerful of the companions, and Shanon marveled that the staunch fellows carried the extra weight without complaints, and without slowing the others off their pace.

Speed, at the moment, seemed to make no difference, for the road behind them was sealed, and the report was that the road ahead was blocked by another wall of some sort, and guarded by these small beings who Crown thought might be a group of Fens.

Shanon had heard the name in passing hundreds of times in his life, in the old danes, and from the elfin teachers he had had in his early years as a fry, but nothing more specific than vague remarks as to the rareness of them, and that it was a long time in between since any of the Fen clans had moved about in the mainstream of elfdom.

Shanon smiled to himself, thinking of that statement, and he wondered what would be thought of him, one of the elite of waterkind, mingled not only with woodfolk and Carbens, but delving dwarfs as well. And next, it looked likely that they would add the mysterious Fens to their small following, as well.

Crown had gone ahead with the archers, and studied the dim eaves of the wood on both sides of the path, but there wasn't a clue of their pursuers, or any other sign that any life at all existed behind the dense greenery.

The small band crept on, edging forward, until around a faint bend and rise in the treetop path the wall the wood elf had reported was spotted.

"It looks new," said Shanon, turning to Drub Fearing. "I don't think it was anything the old elves put up."

"Chinby might be able to tell us, if he weren't so hurt," offered Senja.

"He's blind, little one. And I don't think that he'd be able to tell us anything without feeling it, to see how the stones were cut and laid. That's the way Chinby tells. They don't do stone work, or wood work, either, like they did in the old days."

"We might not be interested by then, if it is a band of Varads, or any of the other beasts," snorted Drub Fearing, always the cautious one.

"I don't think we shall be kept in the dark long," said

263

Crown, squinting his eyes and staring at the wall. "There appears to be a welcoming party coming out now."

He quickly called for his archers to lower their bows, which they did reluctantly, for they still had the battle fire burning inside them, and the pain among them of lost comrades. Almost everyone among the little band had lost at least one friend in the fierce fighting with the cunning Varads, and no one wished to lose any more to some new enemy.

Very cautiously, the archers halted their advance, their bows lowered, but arrows ready to string.

Crown and Shanon went on at the head of the procession, weapons slung to their back, or beneath their cloaks.

Little by little, all sound gradually faded away, and a deep silence fell over the forest around them, and over the wall that blocked their way forward. Faintly they heard the hum of the distant Varad horns, as they struggled to get past the giant tree that sealed the entrance to the upper elfin highway, but of the newcomers, nothing could be detected.

A fly buzzing near his ear distracted Shanon for a moment, and when he looked back at the empty face of the wall, he saw an archway that stood open, and six small figures approaching them.

The leader of the group was a fine-boned elf, of very great age, and he walked supported on each arm by a younger version of himself. All were dressed in deep green, save for the brilliant red vests and red forage caps.

The old elf spoke, in a clear, high voice, but it was a strange tongue that Shanon had never heard spoken, and he raised a hand in salute, but turned quickly to Crown.

"Can you understand him?"

"I've never heard this dialect before. It's almost like something I could understand, yet I can't make out a word."

One of the younger elves beside the old leader tipped his hat and bowed deeply.

"We bring you greetings, cousins, from the ancient line of the Fenhorn clans. Our elder, Pin Dray, speaks only the old tongue. My name is Baten, and this is our worthy group, Bly, Torin, Wessle, and Athon."

Crown and Shanon bowed low in their turn, fulfilling the elaborate elfin procedure of greeting.

"My name is Shanon, and this is my friend Crown, of Erin Frey, and the Salt Marsh danes. Behind us are our compan-

264

ions of the journey, which is to take us to the Sea of Roaring, where we are to meet other friends. We are the comrades of the delving dwarf Brian Brandigore, and the wood elves of Falon, and the Carbens of Drub Fearing."

"We heard you knocking at our back door," laughed Baten. "We built these walls when it was clear that those nasty louts out there had discovered the high road, and were threatening to cut it off from friends."

"How long ago has that been?" asked Crown.

"Oh, many turnings now. But the dark ones have grown in number and boldness, and continue to attack us whenever they have a chance."

"The tree you cut should take them some doing to get around," said Drub Fearing, who had joined the group. "It will take them a while to hack their way through that."

"It was a shame that the Sorodun destroyed itself. It was an old, old being, from the first planting."

"The tree?"

"The Sorodun are the green ones, and have lived here longer than any of us. We have come to know them as neighbors."

"Baten speaks for all of us when he says we are sad to see the loss of such as the green one. Yet the choice was its own. It sacrificed itself to help save the rest of us," said Bly.

Pin Dray spoke in his clear, old voice, and Baten quickly looked to the rear of the friends' column, and pointed to the injured lying on the crude stretchers.

"You have wounded! Quickly, bring them in. We have no time to lose. We must close the way again. Pin Dray says he can hear the yellowfangs coming."

"Hop to it, lads!" shouted Crown to his followers, and the elves began the march again, and Shanon returned to Brian's side.

His litter lay next to Chinby's, but both of them were pale and silent, hardly breathing.

"There is something wrong," said Senja, clasping her hand tightly over Brian's. "He has a fever, and the herbs don't seem to be helping."

Shanon knelt beside his friend, and took the hot, motionless hand.

"It does seem hot," he agreed. "But that is a wound fever, as always."

He pulled up Brian's shirt and vest, and whistled loudly as he did so.

"Here may be the problem," he said, pointing to a broken arrow shaft, the tip of which had barely penetrated the folds of mail, and which just allowed the point of the barbed dart to touch Brian's side.

"If we had not laid him down on his back, this probably wouldn't have worked its way in. Here, hand me your handles, Jeral, so I can slip this out."

The dwarf joined him, and after removing the shattered arrow, Jeral reclosed the mail with the small tools from his kit, which he carried in a leather holster, just as he did his weapons.

"That was a lucky thing for Brian, to be wearing my brother's shirt. I built it extra strong, from the purest ore."

He shook his head sadly, his voice softer.

"And it did Jaran no good, for he never had a chance to get it on before they took the delving."

Senja patted him reassuringly.

"But if you had not brought it, we would be without Brian, too. He gave me his shirt just before the battle. His cloak wouldn't have stopped that arrow."

"It was shot by a powerful arm, to have penetrated at all," said Jeral. "That mail is good enough to turn a dragon bite, and would, I'd wager."

" Did you see the size of those Varads at the very last?" asked Shanon. "One of them could drive a dart in that way if he set his mind to it."

"They're not like the rest," agreed Crown. "Must be from a different tribe."

"Hurry!" cried Baten, urging them to hasten their march. "Pin Dray says they have broken down the better part of the Sorodun barricade. They will be on us soon. We must be ready!"

"Here, take him on," said Shanon, lifting the unconscious dwarf and putting the mail shirt back in place, and he turned to help the others lift Chinby.

Behind his litter was Sigman Col, borne by his own clan.

"How is he?" asked Drub Fearing.

"Alive," growled one of the Carben guard. "No thanks to any of you."

"You'd best take the hot coals from beneath your anger,

friend, at least until we can settle the matter more to our own designs. You are with us now, whether you want it that way or not, and we shall be elbow to elbow yet awhile, so it would be best if we keep our yammers shut."

"You don't see mine flapping," growled the guard, and turned away.

"That's the spirit we need in a war camp," grumbled Drub Fearing. "But may the Great One skin me if I'd like it when we're at peace."

"No need to worry about that, my friend, not for a good while yet. I don't think those lads behind us have any idea of giving up their pleasure so easily."

"They do take an unholy sort of liking to this business, I'll admit," said Mathiny. "I think it must be something to do with their housekeeping, and having to go barefoot all the time."

"That would keep me out of sorts," muttered Crown. "Especially in those sticker patches that we came through to get here."

The small band had moved their injured into the confines of the arched gateway, and all the rest of their battered army followed.

As Crown watched the column move, he shook his head.

"I've lost a third of my lads," he said. "And no one else has fared any better. I don't see how we can last if we keep tangling with the half-ones. They wear us down with every attack, and we can't seem to hurt them at all."

Baten, the Fenhorn, stood beside him on the battlement, looking back down the elfin road.

"There shouldn't be any more need of your soldiers to battle them, further than a skirmish or two. The yellowfangs will be in an entirely different wood if they try to break into our fastness here."

The small elf laughed, a fleck of sadness touching his eyes.

"We are a small clan, in size and in numbers, and wouldn't have lasted against any adversaries the size of the half-ones. We have lived by our wits, and by making friends among the more helpless, and the weak. We have also discovered a friendship with the Sorodun."

"Are you saying the trees are an ally?" asked Drub Fearing, his eyebrows curved in disbelief.

"I am, good Carben. That has been the reaction of most travelers through our portion of the old road. If one was an enemy, it was an end of that, for the Sorodun have their ways of dealing with those. For someone who wasn't, but disbelieved, it was only a matter of never meeting a living, breathing Sorodun, who can recite the numbers of rivers since the first planting, and the names of every shrub there is. Other things, too, if you have the time to wait upon the reply."

"I wish Chinby were well enough to hear this," said Senja. "It sounds as though he would find himself with a new subject to study. I've never heard him mention either the Fenhorn or the Sorodun. I had no idea that anyone could be so small and still survive the wood."

"A dwarf lane is ever tactful," chided Baten, turning to his friend Bly. "We have known of the delvings, and of the Carbens, and our more familiar cousins, such as Falon there, for as long as we have been going about our work here in the Shrane Fal Wood."

"Is that the name?" asked Shanon. "I thought it was all the same. The old charts I have seen name some portions, but leave others blank, or with notations such as 'This is a deep wood, and dangerous. It should be avoided when possible.' I've never really thought much about all the woods or plains that lie between Erin Frey and the sea."

"You're trying to reach the sea?" asked Baten.

"That's where we have set out to find. Now we must wait upon the recovery of our good Brandigore, and Chinby, and to find out if we shall escape that nest of Varads that are bent on our destruction."

Bly broke in before his friend could reply.

"We've taken your friends to Pin Dray's quarters. He is the best there is at healing of wounds. He was a pupil of the Old Ones, when the danes were first upon the world."

"And Sigman Col, too," added Drub Fearing. "I don't want him on my conscience. It's one thing to quarrel with him, but I don't want to lose him to a Varad's arrow. Mend him, if you can, so I can go on with my sport."

"Your speech is odd, Carben," said Baten. "I thought these were of your party?"

"No party of mine. I've been at odds with the thick-headed scoundrel ever since he showed up, and I can rightly say that he bears me no good will, which is at least to his credit. If you must have an opponent, it is only fitting that it should be an honorable one."

"Pay him no mind," said Crown. "He is an outlaw in his own wood, and an outcast among the Carbens, but there are none who wouldn't fight under his leadership. And the Varads hate him with a passion, for he has long been the silent death that has stalked them in the woods."

"It is only a shame I wasn't able to do it better," grumbled the Carben. "Then maybe it wouldn't be so heavy against us now."

Baten shook his head.

"These half-ones have begun coming over the outland borders in greater numbers than we've ever seen. Our scouts report that the old man roads are all full of them on the march, and that they have begun banding together. There is a mind behind it all, it seems, some powerful, evil mind that is bent on destruction of the order of things."

"Chinby has spoken of that," said Senja. "He said it is the Fallen One, gathering all the beasts, and any who will follow, together under one banner."

"It was nothing but mere beast attacks to begin," agreed Crown. "But now it has reached this!"

He waved a hand behind him, to indicate the Varad army they had barely managed to elude.

"The Sorodun will help us to reach the other end of Shrane Fal. That's as far as the old road leads, which can be traveled safely. It runs farther, but we have not traveled on it in some time, because of the half-ones. We have held our section of the road, but I don't know if any of the other settlements have been as lucky, or as well armed."

"Then we will take your kind offer, once we have our leader back, Baten. He is the one who is to unite the delvings once more, and to destroy the threat of the Fallen One."

Baten, trying hard not to be impolite, stifled his grin.

"The dwarf, there?"

"Brian Brandigore, from Den'Lin Fetch, which has fallen."

The Fenhorn's brow darkened, and he studied the silently struggling figure of Brian as Pin Dray tried to pour a liquid from a small vial between his lips.

"Is this the home of Pin Dray?" asked Shanon as they walked, never breaking stride as they talked.

"This is one of his quarters. He has many between here and the Bent Willow."

The friends gathered around the tiny elf as he poured and mixed his herbs and washed the dwarf's forehead with a rag dipped in cool water from the river that ran through the Shrane Fal Wood, the Bent Willow.

Pin Dray muttered to himself in the confusing, lilting tongue, and turned this way and that, his quick, deft hands, although gnarled and twisted with extreme age, still sure as they measured portions and lifted the dwarf's unyielding head up to take some new mixture.

Baten questioned the old elf, and turned to the companions.

"He says it was a bad thing, the arrow, but that it can be dealt with. The poison that the Varads use is a slow and painful one, and it can be counteracted before it is fatal."

"And Chinby?" asked Senja.

"The old dwarf has a head wound that shall give him a headache for a day or so, but he should recover. He has no business out on these errands, at his age."

"That's what we've always tried to tell him," said the lane. "And I begin to wonder at our own good sense, because here we all are, out here with him."

"That's a point," said Drub Fearing.

"But not for an elf," corrected Shanon. "The very fact that there is no rhyme to it at all is the thing that makes it the most attractive."

"I'll never get used to that line of thought," grumbled the Carben. "You hold a good sword, and you're passing fair as an archer, Shanon, but I've yet to see you make any sort of common sense. And that can go all the way back to how an elf ever got tangled up with all this dwarfish business to begin with."

"I must admit, my friend, that it does not speak well for me, seeing as how I have spent a great deal of time wandering around in delvings. Sometimes I begin to think it has rubbed off, and that I shall soon even begin to look like a dwarf."

A low moan caught the elf's attention, and he turned, finding Brian struggling to sit up on the cot where he'd been placed.

"I don't know which is more bothersome, this lump I've got from a Varad, or your chatter. I was having a fairly nice nap until you all started yammering in my ear."

"If he laughs now, I'll know it goes badly with him," said Shanon, and seeing that the huffy dwarf had no intention of laughing, he felt better about the chances of his friend's recovery.

"Where are we?" questioned Brian, trying to rise, and falling back in pain and surprise as his gaze fell on the ancient Fenhorn Pin Dray.

The old elf spoke, and turned, waiting for Baten to translate for him.

"He says your comrade is out of danger now. He is going to tend the other, and the old one."

Brian weakly pulled himself into a sitting position, supported by Senja.

"What's happened here? Where are the Varads?"

His head still rang from the fury of the fight and the pain of his wounds.

"We won through to the old road. The Fenhorns here helped us, and the lower trail is blocked off by a tree that is of the Sorodun."

Crown's information rolled off Brian's mind, and he could grasp none of it.

"Slow down a bit, Crown," scolded Drub Fearing. "He must have time to digest it all."

"We'll all be better off to slow down and try to reorganize," said Falon. "I've got a lot to do with getting my band back in order, so I think I shall leave the other chores of catching Brian up to you."

The wood elf turned to Shanon.

"I'll see to it that we've distributed the rest of the arrows, and try to put the stores back in shape. Maybe Baten can tell me where I can restock our supplies, if they have any to spare."

"We do indeed," replied the Fenhorn. "There is more than enough. And it looks as if we shall be going with you."

This brought a small stir from Bly and Torin, who were standing next to him, but he raised his hand and went on.

"Pin Dray has told us all along that a time would come when we would have to leave the Shrane Fal Wood. It has been our home for a long while, but the hour has struck that we shall have to go onward if we are ever to be able to be truly at peace again."

"The Sorodun will protect us," protested Athon, and Wessle and Bly nodded their heads in ready agreement.

"The Sorodun can only do so much, my good cousins. They have been here forever, and will still be here once we have all gone to the Tombs. Theirs is not to struggle with the lot we face, nor to be concerned about what sort of beings are on the

271

move across the lands. They have no interest in danes or delvings, or elfin roads, or any of the rest. They have been kind and decent enough to keep us safe while we are among them, simply because it would not suit them to have such noise and uproar as has happened today. One of their number let himself fall, which we all know, from talking to them, is a slow death, since if they ever topple, they can never rise again. That loss will make them quite angry, even though it was freely done."

Brian's head was spinning and he asked Baten to explain again who it was he was speaking of.

"The Sorodun," he said patiently. "They might look like common oak or elm, but they are the seedlings from the Old Ones, of long ago, the Shrane Fal."

"We need Chinby to sort all this history out," muttered Brian. "But I gather that these things that look like trees, but aren't, are the Sorodun?"

"Exactly," explained Baten. "And I'm afraid we've upset them, this time. There have never been so many Varads before, and they have never attacked in such force. And I don't like to think of what they might do if they get angry enough."

"The Sorodun?" asked Senja.

"They are not quick to anger, but I have heard them tell stories among themselves of what they have done in the past."

"What was it they did?" asked Brian, rubbing his head and trying to work some feeling back into his arm.

"There have been walled man camps in the Shrane Fal, and they made the mistake of slaying one of the Sorodun when they tried to clear away a spot to dwell. The others heard, and came, and there was the end of the man camp, stone walls and all. It was said that no one lived to escape, and the Sorodun still stand, rooted to the spot, all this time after."

"Are you certain they're friendly?"

The Fenhorn studied the surrounding wood a moment before he replied.

"I wouldn't exactly call them friendly, nor would I say not. It's just that they're different. We have gotten along well with them, and understand them."

"I can see how that would help, from what you tell me of them."

"But here, you'll get to meet one of them for yourself," said Baten, facing away into the heavy gloom, where a slight stir of leaf and branch had caught his eye.

Brian followed the small elf's glance, and there, where there had only been the wide space of the old elfin road, was a huge form, blocking his vision of the forest behind.

Before he could ask Baten how you addressed the formidable figure, the very air trembled, and a deep, resonant tone, like a great bell, rang out.

Once More Toward the Sea

THE companions stood transfixed as the sound deepened and rolled over the forest, making the earth tremble and the high elfin road jump and sway. There was no way to tell if it were one sound, or many, and it droned on and on, until the senses dulled, and it became difficult to concentrate.

Brian noticed a great desire to sleep, and almost succumbed, but fought with every ounce of strength he had left to overcome the desire. In a dreamlike trance, he saw the others around him, their eyes wide, then drooping, all standing in various poses upon the road itself, or on the battlement of the wall the Fenhorns had constructed to prevent attack by the Varads.

After a few moments, the dwarf noticed Bly and Baten, their eyes closed, swaying to and fro, as if blown by some invisible wind, murmuring an odd-sounding reply to the bell-note voice of the indistinguishable new presence in the stifling air.

Crown and Shanon stood beside him, along with Senja, who had left Chinby's unconscious form momentarily, and Drub Fearing had fallen back a few paces to guide his small band of warriors, should they be attacked. Falon, the wood elf, was on his knees, chanting in time to the snoring of the deep, rumbling voice.

As suddenly as it had begun, all was silence again in the wood, and it took the companions a moment or two to realize that they were hearing the gentle sound of the wood again, from the soft hum of a hive of honeybees, to a small bird's song, somewhere beyond the thick eaves of the trees that bordered the road.

"You haven't really had a chance to see him," said Baten, apologizing to the friends. "It is most difficult to form any idea about a Sorodun unless you are able to talk to him properly, at the right level."

Having no idea what the Fenhorn elf was talking about, Brian merely nodded weakly, but could not find his voice.

"I have often heard these voices," interrupted Falon. "In our old homes, long ago. When I was a fry, my grandsire would tell me stories about the great woodhearts who dwelled in the hidden parts of the forest, and that they guarded all the good souls who went about. But the voices went away, somewhere between the death of my grandsire and my own coming of age. It has been a long time since I have heard them."

Shanon looked at his woodfolk cousin.

"I, too, have heard these voices, but from far away. They were always mysterious, and you could almost understand them, but then they were gone, and you never knew if it were only your ears that had played you false, or some avalanche or earth change someplace almost out of hearing."

"The Sorodun have been on the march since the first planting," explained Baten. "They have been in first one wood, then another, from the first beginning. It was said that they were the friends of the Old Ones, and gave them shelter when the Fallen One sent the Garoyle Brag to slay them."

"We need Chinby to fill us in on some of these names," complained Senja. "Who were they?"

"The Garoyle Brag were the enemies of the Syrin Brae. They are in the armies of the Fallen One."

"And the Sorodun were here even then?" asked Crown.

"And before. They have moved from one part of the world to another in their migrations, trying to find their way back to their home of old."

"Where was that?"

"It was more than a place, good elf. It was a plot of ground

274

that was special to them, and where their roots could tap the mystical water of the Secret Source. It is to be the only way they will be able to be free of this ungainly form and these long lifetimes."

"What has happened to them, then? Why are they forced to go on for so long here? Can't they just go to the Tombs?" asked Senja.

"Not even the Sorodun who volunteered his life," replied Bly. "He will be born a seedling again, as soon as the old tree body is rotted away. They had asked the Old Ones for the secret of long life here on this plane, and the Old Ones gave it. They didn't begin as mere trees, in the very beginning, but after all this time, that's what they most closely resemble, to an eye that sees only appearances."

Pin Dray, who had finished his tending of Chinby and Sigman Col, came to stand beside Baten. His old voice took up the story, as the young elf translated.

"He says he knows you must be startled by the Sorodun, and he understands. It took him a long, long span of time to understand them, and he has spent many seasons in conversation. They seek the old spot where they were born, for that spot is where they can tap the sacred water that will let them die and go home. Nothing is ever changed until then, and they have given him the power to have long life also, but he does not share their fate of being unable to die eventually."

The old elf droned on, and his translator had to work hard to keep up.

"They are near where they are going now, and have only a small journey left. That may take them three lifetimes, by our standards, or even more. What the Sorodun asked, when he spoke a moment ago, was for one of us to go for the sacred water from the hidden well, that they may be spared another long torment of waiting. It is very unusual for a Sorodun to ask any for boons, for they have never felt their lives were involved with any others."

Brian struggled to comprehend the elf's words.

"You mean these trees are asking that someone go and find this secret well they are talking about, and bring back some of the water, so that they may die?"

Pin Dray listened to Baten explain Brian's question, then replied. After listening carefully, his translator went on.

"He says the leaders of the Sorodun have been struck by a dreaded tree blight that they picked up in another wood. It has rotted their core, and makes it difficult for them to travel at all. They wish to be spared the last agony of being stranded so near their salvation, yet unable to save themselves."

"What an awful thing," murmured Senja.

"Yes, it is," agreed Baten. "These were once great leaders in the old High Court, who had much pride, and many designs on the next successor to the Throne. They came down originally to help the Syrin Brae, and the other Old Ones, in hopes of good rewards and advancements. What happened was that they received their reward of the secret of long life on one plane without death, but you may see for yourself what form of long life it took. And now they have been reduced, according to what this Sorodun said, to asking for help in being freed."

"I thought you said they were interested only in their own affairs," said Crown.

"And so I thought," replied Baten. "This is the first time that Pin Dray has ever said any different. Things must have been changing over all this time."

"All things do, it seems," agreed Shanon. "Even these strange fellows that have lived all this time seem to have their problems, as well."

"They are willing to help us," went on Baten. "In exchange for the aid we may give them."

"How would they help?" asked Brian. "If they are too weak to move to the place where they can find freedom, how would they be able to aid us?"

"By not moving at all," said Baten, again translating for Pin Dray. "They have shown how helpful they can be when they do nothing more than fall where they are. And there are other ways too horrible to speak of that they have in dealing with their enemies."

"We don't seem to have a choice then, do we?" asked Shanon.

Baten shook his head.

"I don't know that they would harm us if we didn't help them. I don't believe that they would do that. Yet I do think they might try to convince us to help them become free of all these turnings they have lived in these lower wilds."

As the elf quit speaking, a new and deeper rumbling erupted over the gathering, causing the battlements to tremble and begin to topple on the stone walls that blocked the

276

high road, and the very surface itself began to sway, knocking all, elf and dwarf alike, off their feet. First one rumble came from one side, then another from farther away, and then a chorus of them joined together.

Brian's ears began to numb, and the one clear thing he could think of to do was to stop the terrible noise that threatened to tear the elfin road from its high perch in the old treetops and send them all crashing to their doom.

"Blow a call on your pipe!" he called out desperately. "Quickly, lad, or it'll be the end of us all!"

Shanon did as he was ordered, and Brian cried out as loudly as he was able that he would go himself to seek the fountain that would save the Sorodun, if they would only stop their noise.

After he had repeated himself once more, Baten called out in a strange-sounding monotone, but the rumbling ceased, and the path beneath their feet stopped its sickening sway.

"What was it?" cried Senja.

"The Sorodun," replied Baten, looking all about the surrounding wood. "I have not heard so many of them speak at one time in my life. They are in a hard place, it seems."

"What do they want us to do? We'll help them, if we can! It's better than being deafened, or having the road beneath us crumbled."

Baten raised a hand.

"It's not so simple, my friend. I think we shall have to go down below to talk to the Sorodun who is there."

"Do they have names?" asked Shanon. "I mean, like us?"

"They are known only as the Sorodun," replied Baten. "You will see why. To us, they all look the same, and it was explained that they do have names for each other, but it would take them too long to say them."

"Let's go and see this Sorodun, then," insisted Brian. "I have no desire to anger them or upset them, seeing the way they carry on. I'd almost as soon go back to the Varads."

His wounded shoulder had begun to regain some feeling, and the arrow cut still made him slightly sick to his stomach, but he felt that as long as he was able to walk, he should be doing what he could to try to get them all safely beyond harm's way. Pin Dray's treatment seemed to have helped immensely, and Brian was hoping that it would have the same effect on Chinby, for he realized more than ever that he needed the advice of his old teacher and friend.

Events were continuing to turn even stranger, and with the old dwarf injured and unconscious, Brian was brought face to face with the fact that without Chinby, he had no idea what the journey was about, or what they were to do if and when they reached the Sea of Roaring.

"Come along. We'll go down to see the Sorodun," said Baten. "It has been a long while since we've opened the bottom doors. I hope they still work."

Wessle and Torin stood beside a runged doorway that was built flush into the floor of the stone fortress that spanned the elfin road, and on a signal from Pin Dray, they began struggling to open it. After a fruitless series of attempts, Drub Fearing offered to help, and he and Mathiny, along with two other Carbens, put their combined strength to the trapdoor and heaved with all their might.

At first, it looked as if the huge, rusty metal rung would simply pull away from the wood, but at last, creaking and groaning, it gave way, revealing a dark hole that led downward into the thick darkness below.

Brian looked down the trapdoor, and could see that a ladder ran all the way into the shadows beneath, but he could not tell where it ended.

"Check to see if the ladder will still stand weight," ordered Baten. "What may hold a Fenhorn might not hold another."

Wessle descended rapidly downward, and after a moment was completely vanished from view.

The lane cried out sharply, but the small elf was soon back among them, safe and sound, and excited.

"The ladder is in good repair. You'll have to watch out for the branches, though. They've grown wild down there, and it's like a thorn brake."

"Is the Sorodun there?" asked Baten.

"I think he is at the very lower part of the ladder. We'll have to get through the undergrowth to reach where he is."

"Let's go, then. Are you up to it, Brian?" asked Baten. "We can take another, if you are still too weak from your scrapes with the yellowfangs."

"Let's go on. I shall have something to tell Chinby when he gets his wits back."

"Be careful!" warned Senja. "Don't be foolish and go, if you don't feel like it."

"I'll see that he doesn't do anything silly," soothed Shanon. "He won't dare try anything while I'm around."

There was another faint tremor that passed through the elfin highway, and the beginnings of another distant roll of thunder threatened, sending the dwarf, and two Fenhorns, hurrying as fast as they were able down the trapdoor to speak with the Sorodun.

As they left the upper road, the darkness grew closer around them, and deep green hues turned more muted brownish black as they descended, until at the very bottom rung of the ladder it was difficult to see more than a few feet in any direction, so deep the shadows, and so thick the growth there.

Brian's heart raced, and he felt very weak, his knees shaking and his arm numb. He was used to well-ordered shafts with their regular width and height to them, but the wilderness of the green wood beneath the old elfin highway was stifling and frightening, and he found it very hard to breathe.

"This way," said Baten, although his voice was absorbed by the dense thicket all around them, so that it sounded almost a whisper.

"I see him, Baten. He's beyond the stand of elders, there."

Baten pointed, but the dwarf was unable to make anything out of the thick shadows except more limbs and branches, some sharp and long, while others were fuller and smelled of old leaves and rain. He tried to imagine what these creatures, or whatever they truly were, could want of a fountain that supposedly held water that would allow them to go to the Tombs, but if that's what they wanted, and he or any of his party might be able to help, he was going to do his best, for otherwise, there was no safe gamble on them being able to get to the end of the highway before it all crashed down, if these odd beings all decided to go into their rumbling way of speech that seemed to shake everything else to pieces.

"It's him, all right," confirmed Baten, who turned to Brian and pointed out a vast shadow that seemed to be broader than the surrounding gloom.

"The Sorodun!"

Baten broke into a low, singsong voice, and went on for quite some time.

Brian, who could see no difference, other than size, between the tree Baten was addressing and its neighbors, tried to study the strange being carefully.

Aside from a tremor that passed through its lower boughs

279

occasionally, he was able to detect no movement at all. And even that, he suspected, might be some wild thing, journeying through the upper branches on its way to some unknown destination.

Baten went on a few more seconds, then fell silent.

"What did you say?"

"That we are here from the clans of Fenhorn, delving dwarf, wood and water elf, and Carben, to pay our respects to the most ancient Sorodun."

"That took all that time?"

Baten nodded.

"It may take until sundown for him to think about it and reply."

Sitting heavily down, Brian rubbed his sore, aching shoulder, and wished he were far from the sweltering, airless hole he found himself in. He had hardly finished his thought before he was aware of a lightness in the bottom half of the huge tree, not exactly a brilliant light like a torch or elfmoon, but a greener sort of brilliance that glowed from all around the bottom of the trunk of the Sorodun. The air began to quiver, and a sound, much like the distant rumble of a faraway storm in summer, began.

The dwarf was fearful at first, but then realized that Baten was listening intently, and making short replies in the same singsong voice he had used before.

"He asks that you come nearer, Brian. For what you will do for him, he is willing to grant you a thing of great value in your errand."

"What?" quizzed the dwarf, but was urged forward by his two companions.

Suddenly he found himself directly in front of the Sorodun, and he felt a faint tremor beneath his feet, and the air all around him seemed to crackle to life.

Brian was afraid to move at first, lest he not be able to find his feet, but a warm feeling of security and peace began to pervade his being, and a gentle flow of soft breathing from the great form seemed to soothe away the last of his fears, and from a great long way away from himself, he began to see a golden light, pouring forth from the earth all around the Sorodun, until the very wood was a bright, honey color, and the sound of a deep, humming bell, combined with pipes, skirled away, until he lost all sense of time or space. How long it went on Brian could not tell, but it seemed as though it was forever, and yet only a passing breath.

An odd thing began to happen then, and he felt a strange sensation start at the bottom of his feet, creeping slowly upward, a numbing sort of feeling that at first, he felt, must be death. That passed shortly, however, and the tingle went on, slowly inching upward, until he felt it reach his thoughts.

There was a long period of time when there was merely blackness, and silence, until very slowly, he felt the steady throb of a heart that surged powerfully, but was more than a heart, reaching through his very being, beating slowly and surely, over and over. He was tempted to call out for help, but could not find his voice, and as before, the fear soon went away, to be replaced by the warm feeling of peace and well-being.

Through the mist of confusion, and the strange, strong throb of the alien heart, a thought took form in his mind, although he seemed to have no conscious will of his own to create it.

There was the very hazy outline in his thought of an old, old graybeard, not exactly a form that he could readily identify, but it was a form, and very old. He thought of Chinby, and somehow the thought fit, and did not vanish.

Then there was the sensation that he had felt earlier, leaving him, and somewhere deep inside, he knew he had been healed of his wounds, swiftly and surely, by the strange heart that had throbbed in his presence.

And then there was the thought of water, of a strange sort of water, which flowed from the deepest wells yet known in the lower worlds, which had the power to free one from the tedious existence of living forever.

The thought that Brian had made him feel a bit uncomfortable at first, but he overcame that, and tried to see what it was that upset him. There were Varads concerned, and an elf dane, and he knew it would be of no use to try to fight the huge army of the half-ones beyond the elfin highway, no matter how much he wished to help these Sorodun or repay them for healing him of his wounds.

And it was more, for he was to find out much later that the feeling he had had of the strange heart throbbing strongly in him was a process he would be able to repeat at will, to heal his mind of confusion, or his body of fatigue or wounds.

And then the thought came clearer of an elfin dane, and

281

the water that the Sorodun needed to be able to free themselves from their long earthly journey, which had kept them far from their true home for many turnings beyond when they would have returned.

Another thought occurred to Brian, and that was that he was communing with the huge, glowing being just as surely as if he were speaking aloud.

There were a dozen pictures at once then, all jumbled and confused, of Varad hordes, and elfin danes overrun, and the dangers that lurked beyond the safety of the stone walls and fastness of the old highway.

Another long, blank space startled him, then there was a definite picture of a fountain, distinct in outline, of a carved, round wall, with a statue in the center, of an elf, one hand held high above him, clutching a bow, and a thin stream of water spewing forth from his mouth, ending in a bubbling froth in the cool blueness below.

Overcome with understanding, Brian called out aloud.

"Quickly, get me some vials of the stone water! I don't think we have to go far to help out our friends. The water they want is the stone water from the fountain of Falen Rin!"

He had whirled, and jostling aside Baten and Wessle, climbed rapidly up the ladder to the trapdoor, where all the others were gathered anxiously around. They had heard him cry out, and couldn't tell if it had been a call of warning or surprise.

"I've found that we can help the tree folk," he blurted, climbing quickly up, explaining as he went.

"The stone water is what they need. The Sorodun told me."

He stopped, shaking his head.

"Not exactly told me, but he thought it, and somehow I saw it. Anyway, it's the stone water they want."

"Do we have any left?" asked Drub Fearing, his voice doubtful.

"I have," replied Senja, and a few others of both Carben and elf bands.

"Good! Get it all together, and I shall see what they want done with it next."

"Do you think they'll just turn themselves to stone, like Oranbar?" asked Shanon. "That's a strange thing to want to do."

"There is more to the stone water than we know," said Crown. "It may be some secret we know only the half of."

"I'm sure that's true. Oranbar could have explained it, had he chosen to, but it doesn't seem our lot to have much explanation of things."

Shanon clucked his tongue.

"It's been that way ever since I got involved with this venture."

"Doesn't seem likely to improve, either," concluded Crown glumly.

Pin Dray touched Brian's injured shoulder, and spoke in his soft, strange tongue. Even without a translator, Brian knew that he was marveling at his rather sudden, unexplainable recovery from the sword thrust and the arrow wound.

"I know, old one. The Sorodun did it. I was aware of becoming one with him, then there were a lot of odd feelings, and when I came out of it all, I was as good as new. Baten said they would give me something in exchange for the thing I was to do for them, and that was to get the water from the fountain of Falen Rin."

"Quickly, give it to them, then, and let's see if we can't make our way out the back door before the Varads find their way onto the old road."

Drub Fearing's voice was urgent, but calm.

"I think that's exactly the thing," agreed Crown. "I can hear them piping up again back there."

The friends gathered all the vials of the water from the fountain they had left, and bundled them together into a knapsack handed to them by Athon, and without further delay, Brian, followed by Shanon and Crown, descended the ladder to the forest floor once more.

Baten and Bly waited by the foot of the great oak that raised its head into the gloom above and supported a part of the ancient elfin highway.

"Did you find what you were looking for, Brian? You left in such a terrible hurry, we didn't know what had happened."

"I found it. And it was here among us all the time. The water they need is some water we took already, from the fountain in Falen Rin. It has a strange quality to it, which turns any who touch it to solid stone."

"That's the water they have spoken of. Only none of us dared to set out to find it, for fear of the yellowfangs. We have been trapped here for some time, and with no real way to help. And none of us knew of the fountain being so close.

283

Somehow, we all thought it must be a place that was far away, and no one knew of any powers that the water of Falen Rin had."

"Let's give it to him," said Brian, returning to stand in front of the huge form, bowing low.

He placed the sack in front of them, then stopped, wondering how the green one was going to open the vials. His doubts were soon put to rest when he noticed the earth split across a band of roots from the Sorodun, and a thick, black armlike form curled from the ground and grasped the sack securely, dragging it to the base of the thick body.

Brian was beginning to form a thought in his mind when he was interrupted by a great wail of warning horns, blown all about, and pipes from the Fenhorns above. The air bristled with arrow flights, rustling through the dense wood, and a smell of smoke wafted over the green gloom in the stifling air below.

Without realizing it, Brian was hot on the heels of Shanon, who was behind the two Fenhorns and Crown. As he fled with his friends, he received one last, clear picture, and that was of his entire party moving along the ancient road of elfdom, toward the hazy outline of a great body of water. And behind were the insurmountable mountains of huge trees, in a walled line across the entire border of the wood.

The Sorodun would be holding back, for a short while, at least, the tides of darkness from beyond the ice fields of the Wilderness, and in doing so, they themselves would be freed.

Brian turned for one last quick glimpse of the golden light about the greenheart, raised his hand once in silent salute, and scrambled on after the others.

Without waiting longer, and within moments, the companions, with their new allies, the Fenhorns, were marching as rapidly as they could muster their bands along the old highway, toward the sea, and away from the clamor of the Varad troops behind.

The moment of reckoning was not yet struck.

The Wait

IN the time that passed after their escape from the Shrane Fal Wood, where their flight had been made possible by the Sorodun, the companions reached the Sea of Roaring, after crossing the great Flats of Ollen Wor and the nameless coastal swamps that bordered the sea.

The armies of Brian Brandigore grew, joined by both wood and water elf, and the survivors of the old delvings, and Carben folk, as well as Fenhorn.

There had been Varad bands and great beasts from below the borders, but not in the numbers they had seen in the woods behind them, and the battles had been mainly skirmishes of little consequence, although Sigman Col and the Carben Mathiny had been slain, along with Baten the Fenhorn and a few others who had grown close in the companions' hearts.

During those battles, Brian learned of the truly remarkable gift the Sorodun had given him. He had only to remember the meeting with the great being and feel again the strong surge of that heart within him.

The ability it gave him to lead his followers tirelessly, without rest, and even injured, gave him the well-deserved reputation of a fearless and fierce leader, strong when need be, yet merciful when justice was to be done. Over the turning round of days by the Sea of Roaring, his legend grew, along with Shanon's, who was never far from his side, and who was second-in-command of all the growing numbers who flocked to the dwarf, who by word of mouth, and other means, they had learned was to reunite the delvings and drive out the Darkness from their lands.

In that place where Brian set up the great war camp that readied itself to cross the Roaring, two major things occurred, the first of which was the full recovery of Chinby, the lore master, who helped supervise their settlements, and spun more yarns, and wove their own exploits into the lore that would be handed down to future spanners and fry.

The second grand occurrence was the halfing rites repeated by Brian and Senja.

There was more to come, he knew, and Brian prepared against that time, for they awaited the ships that were to come to them from across the sea, to bear them away to their distant allies, both animalkind, and a strain of half-man, half-Elder, who came from a direct line of descendants from the Old Ones themselves.

Chinby said they were to look for signs of Borim Bruinthor, and Trianion Starseeker, and the young King of Olthlinden, who was already doing many amazing things in his own lands, and who was said to be of many forms.

In this lull, the Fallen One crept away into the ice fields, to bring more horrible soldiers into the fray for the destruction of all who yet lived and breathed in goodness and peace.

Brian Brandigore walked by the sea each day, his eyes far-seeing and misty, awaiting the hour they would join their forces to strike their blow at the Darkness, and to fulfill their destinies upon the vast Wilderness of Four.

That day, he knew, was not long in its coming.

To Everyone Who Loved
The Lord Of The Rings —
Welcome to Atlanton Earth!
THE CIRCLE OF LIGHT SERIES
by Niel Hancock

Enter the magical twilight world of Atlanton Earth, where the titanic struggle between two warring sisters, the Queens of Darkness and of Light, creates deadly enmities as well as deep loyalties, and evokes unexpected heroism among the beings who fight together against the evil that threatens to overrun them all. You will meet the mighty magician Greyfax Grimwald and his allies: Bear, Otter, and Broco the Dwarf, whose devotion to a common cause overcomes their individual differences and welds them into heroic fellowship.

MORE GREAT BOOKS
from WARNER